Dedicated to Lou
The first (and only) Mrs Lovegrove

FOREWORD

My great friend Mr Sherlock Holmes is fond of chiding me about these published narratives of mine. Apart from their "meretricious" qualities and the way in which I sacrifice forensic methodicality in favour of literary effect, however, there is one aspect of them that exercises him less frequently but with no less passion.

"You tell your readers practically everything about me," he has said to me on more than one occasion, "and practically nothing about yourself. You reveal to them my moods, methods and motivations at considerable length, my many idiosyncrasies and peccadillos, but about Dr John Watson you disclose precious little by comparison. You are a cipher in your own stories, forever eclipsed by me and at risk of disappearing altogether in my shadow."

"That may be true," I reply, "but it is how it should be. They are your adventures, Holmes. My task is to recount them as objectively as I can, and to that end I must perforce step into the wings and cede the limelight."

"Nonetheless I imagine the public might care to learn some further personal detail about you, beyond your profession, your love of gambling, your rugby playing, your brother's sad fate, and your experiences in Afghanistan. There surely must be a case of mine that allows you to share with them a hitherto unilluminated facet of your life history."

Although these words were spoken in jest – the kind of chaffing Holmes is wont to indulge in – they harbour a grain of truth. Hence I am setting down in these pages a series of events that I have chosen to call *The Labyrinth of Death*, and which will, I trust, colour in a corner of the public picture of myself that has previously lain barely touched.

John H. Watson, MD, 1902

PART I

CHAPTER ONE

THE EVENING CALLER

"A judge, Watson, if I am not much mistaken," said Sherlock Holmes.

We had just driven back to 221B Baker Street after a very pleasant afternoon spent at a Crystal Palace Saturday Concert, where the highlight of the programme was Rivarde premiering Lalo's *Symphonie Espagnole*. The American violin virtuoso had handled the concerto's Spanish flourishes admirably, and as we travelled homeward by hansom, Holmes alternately rhapsodised about the performance and hummed various portions of the melody, with accompanied fingering and bowing as though playing the piece on an invisible instrument.

Upon our arrival at our lodgings, Mrs Hudson informed us that we had had a visitor. "Nicely spoken gent he was," she said. "Very cultured and polite, although very agitated too. I told him you were not due back until the early evening, Mr Holmes, but he insisted on waiting. He was upstairs for all of two hours."

"Your use of the past tense indicates that he is not there now."

"He must have got bored, because eventually he gave it up

and went out, with an assurance to me that he would return by-and-by."

"The fellow was a prospective client, I take it."

"I should imagine so."

"But he left no card."

"I invited him to but he declined."

"Hum! Someone who desires anonymity, or at least privacy. Come, Watson, let us go up to our apartment and see what we can observe. Perhaps we can learn something about this mysterious caller in advance of his return."

My companion set to work in his usual inimitable fashion, studying carefully the sitting room and in particular the chair in which our visitor had taken up temporary residence. The man had smoked a number of cigars during the course of his stay, the stubs of which occupied an ashtray perched on the chair's arm. Holmes held up one for close scrutiny, sniffing it with the eyes-closed attentiveness of a connoisseur.

"Cuban," he declared. "Flor Del Rey. Far from the cheapest brand on the tobacconists' shelves. So it is safe to infer that our guest is reasonably well-to-do. He is also a man who is not in the habit of ostentatiously flaunting his wealth. Note that he has removed the bands before smoking the cigars, and since the bands are not in the ashtray he must have pocketed them. Not only is that a courtesy, so that others looking on will not have cause to envy his material fortune, but it is a sign of good breeding. None of which contradicts Mrs Hudson's enchanting thumbnail sketch. I would go further, however, and aver that this stranger is a member of the legal profession. Indeed, of the judiciary."

"In other words…"

"A judge, Watson, if I am not much mistaken."

"And you know that how, precisely?" Holmes's deductions were hardly a novel phenomenon to me, yet seldom failed to entertain.

"The smallest details often generate the largest quantity of data, old friend. In this case, I point you to a single hair that has attached itself to the fabric of the chair in our absence."

The strand in question was short, white and wiry.

"Many a judge has white hair, I grant you, Holmes," I said. "The profession is largely reserved for those who have attained a venerable age. But not all judges are men with white hair, and the reverse statement is even truer."

"You make the mistake of identifying the hair as human."

"It is not?"

"The thickness and composition suggest otherwise. As you may or may not recall, I have written a monograph on the differences between human hair and that of animals, the latter of which we should, of course, properly refer to as pelt or fur. A principal variance between the two is that the hollow core of an animal hair, the medulla, is broader in diameter than that of a human hair. Were I to place this strand under a microscope alongside one of my own, I could demonstrate that to you beyond argument. The texture is quite different, too. The keratin of animal hair is almost invariably coarser."

"And somehow you know that this one came from a horse?"

"As a violinist intimately familiar with the feel of the horsehair on a bow, I consider myself well qualified to recognise the substance when I see it. You will note, though, how this one is tightly curled."

"No horse has naturally curly hair."

"Just so. Artificially curled horsehair has only one practical application – in the manufacture of wigs for the legal profession."

"Very well. And this hair has become detached from our visitor's wig and transferred itself to his day clothing and thence to the chair upholstery."

"Exactly."

"But judges are not the only ones to wear horsehair wigs as part of their formal attire. Barristers do too."

"Yet this man is a judge. I assert that with some conviction by virtue of the fact that the wig traditionally worn in court by both judge and barrister is short and stops above the collar. By contrast the full-bottomed wig of a judge, which he wears on ceremonial occasions, hangs down over the front of his robes, and its flaps are liable to come into contact with the lapels of the jacket he is wearing beneath. The statistical probability is therefore far higher that our visitor is no mere member of the Bar but is in Chancery."

"Well, we shall find out for certain in due course, shall we not?"

Holmes fixed me with a stare, as if to say, *Oh ye of little faith*. "I can confirm one other element of Mrs Hudson's description of the man, proving that good lady's great feminine perspicacity. Our visitor is indeed in a state of agitation."

"Such a thing would not be uncommon amongst your clients. Few come to engage your services who are not in dire emotional straits."

"Yet observe, Watson, how the ends of the cigars are mashed. The smoker has chewed hard on them. It is hardly the mark of a relaxed mind. Then there is the condition of the chair's other arm, the one that would have been positioned beneath his free hand."

"It appears to be just as it always has. A trifle worn, showing its age."

"A trifle *more* worn than we left it," Holmes declared. "The damask on the top seam of the front panel has been picked at. Several already loose threads have been pulled further out, and some fresh ones added to their number. Our unknown caller has, no doubt unconsciously, worked at the fabric with his fingernails. A sure sign of nervous tension."

My companion sat down in his usual armchair, opposite that in which the client had been ensconced, drew his knees up and steepled his fingers. His grey eyes were lit with a joyous anticipation that bordered on glee. At that time, the summer of 1895, Holmes was truly at the height of his powers, having lately solved a succession of his most celebrated and intriguing cases, among them those I have chronicled as "The Adventure of Wisteria Lodge", "The Adventure of the Solitary Cyclist" and "The Adventure of Black Peter". These were in addition to many that I have not committed to print either because they were relatively minor or because they involved affairs of state or prominent individuals and thus require that a veil of discretion be drawn over them. There are a number of further cases from this period that I may well yet write up, not least the singular affair of the oculist and the ormolu mirror, the enigma surrounding the disappearance of the King of Diamonds from every pack of playing cards in a single consignment from the makers' printworks, and the perturbing matter of the suet pudding, the paring knife and the scullery maid whose tongue turned a deep shade of indigo. There are also the circumstances that, the spring just past, had brought us to one of our great university towns and into the orbit of a mathematician, a certain Professor Malcolm Quantock, whose remarkable invention seemed poised to end Holmes's career and his life as well. Someday I shall perhaps make these episodes public, but until then they must remain nothing more than scribblings in my notebooks.

At any rate, Holmes was in fine fettle and keen to discover what had brought a high-ranking member of the legal fraternity to our door. I for my part was not much less curious.

We were not kept in suspense long, for within ten minutes a ring on the doorbell heralded the appearance of a distinguished-looking personage in our rooms. He was tall, if a little stooped, with a leonine mane of whitish-grey hair and a nose of imposing size and bulbosity. His eyebrows were substantial and even somewhat intimidating. Were he genuinely a judge – and I had no reason to doubt Holmes's supposition – I could well imagine them knitting together above his penetrating eyes as he delivered a stern verdict from the bench or briskly curtailed some piece of time-wasting legal tomfoolery.

Yet, for all that, there were patches of hectic pink in his cheeks, and his movements and gestures were rapid and disjointed, fraught with anxiety.

"Mr Holmes," said he. "Thank God. I had to step out and get some fresh air. I could not sit still a moment longer, cooped up in this room. But you are back now. I hope to heaven that you can be of assistance."

"Pray, take a seat. Watson, would you kindly pour our guest a brandy? Good man. Drink, sir, if you will. That is better. Even a blind man could tell that you are in need of a calmative."

"I am half out of my mind with worry."

"Then I trust I shall be able to allay your fears. I have already determined that you are a judge, but I now divine that you are a Freemason and also have lately been widowed."

The fellow looked startled, but then regained some composure. "I have been told on many occasions that your powers of perception are second to none, Mr Holmes. Around the Inns of Court and the Old Bailey you have garnered a formidable reputation, one that goes beyond the acclaim your exploits have accrued from publication in *The Strand*, courtesy of your colleague here. Scotland Yard inspectors speak about you in tones that contain awe, although sometimes also a hint of spiteful envy. Lawyers, too, have been known to utter your name with admiration. Plenty of them have pocketed handsome fees prosecuting or defending a miscreant whom you have been instrumental in bringing to trial."

He finished off his brandy and held the glass out to me for a refill.

"It is one thing to hear how you can sum up a man's circumstances at a glance," he continued, "quite another to have the feat practised upon oneself. I suppose you have identified my vocation from a certain bearing I exhibit – a judicial demeanour."

"The process is more scientific than that." Briefly Holmes explained about the single horsehair that had formed the kernel of his deduction.

"Well, as for my being a Freemason, it is hardly a wonder. There are few in my profession who are not 'on the square'. The odds are weighted heavily in your favour."

"Your cufflinks rather give the game away. The compass-and-set-square motif is distinctive."

"Oh. Ah yes. But as to your guess that I am a widower…"

"I do not guess," Holmes said sharply. "The evidence is plain. You have a gold wedding band on the ring finger of your right hand, and a mark on the ring finger of the left that indicates the selfsame band resided thereon until recently. You have switched the band from one to the other, showing that you have accustomed yourself to the loss of your wife but that she will never fade from your memory or your heart."

Our visitor bent his head and thumbed the corner of one eye.

"In addition," Holmes went on, "a strip of the upper left sleeve of your jacket is marginally cleaner than the rest. It accords with wearing the black armband of mourning, a habit you have only newly abandoned. I would hazard that it is but six months since your wife passed away."

The man was now tangibly upset, his shoulders heaving, and I motioned to Holmes, indicating that he should, for the time being at least, refrain from further comment on the subject. I laid a hand on the judge's arm and offered a comforting word or two. I myself had suffered a similar bereavement in the not-too-distant past. My own wife had left this world some three years earlier, during that period when I was under the impression that Holmes likewise was dead after his fateful clash in Switzerland with Professor Moriarty. The blow of Mary's demise, coming on the heels of the apparent demise of my closest friend, had sent me reeling, and I still had yet to recover fully from it. A part of me continued to nurture the hope that my late wife would, as Holmes had, make a miraculous return from the grave, for all that I knew this was impossible. In Holmes's case there had been no body, and therefore always a lingering element of doubt, whereas with Mary I had been there, holding her hand, as she slipped slowly away from me.

Eventually our visitor mastered his feelings and, drawing a sharp breath, said, "You are correct, Mr Holmes. My beloved Margaret is no longer with us. But I have worse to contend with, for now my daughter, my only child, has gone missing!"

CHAPTER TWO

THE DISAPPEARED DAUGHTER

"My name, Mr Holmes, is Sir Osbert Woolfson," the judge said. "I have served the Law loyally all my adult life, from studying jurisprudence at Cambridge to becoming a pupil, an advocate, a QC, then eleven years ago being appointed a Justice of the High Court by Her Majesty. You would be hard pressed to find someone who has faith in the British legal system to the extent that I do. You will appreciate, therefore, that it goes hard for me to throw myself on the mercies of one such as yourself, who operates outside that system."

"I am no less ardent an upholder of the law than you, Sir Osbert," Holmes replied. "My methods may be my own, but my goal is never anything other than the apprehension of criminals and the application of due justice."

"Given that so many in the constabulary approve of you, I cannot believe it to be otherwise. Nor would I have come here if I had not been failed by the same processes to which I have dedicated myself for so long. Put simply: Hannah, my daughter, vanished a week ago. She went out for a stroll in the morning and did not return home. I have not seen hide or hair of her since, and the police have shown themselves signally incapable of finding her."

Holmes rolled his eyes. "That is, alas, all too typical. Scotland Yard has plenty of triers in its ranks but precious few achievers. Even the best of policemen, however well-intentioned, are apt to make a situation worse rather than better through their involvement."

"You take a dimmer view of their capabilities than I, yet on present showing I cannot entirely gainsay your assertion. As soon as I became aware of Hannah's absence I alerted the appropriate authorities. I cannot fault the alacrity and diligence with which they responded. There were officials thronging my house within the hour, and I received all manner of assurances that no stone would go unturned, no avenue unexplored, no lead unpursued, and so forth."

"For a man of your rank and standing, that is hardly surprising."

"Indeed," Sir Osbert Woolfson allowed, "but the promises have come to naught. The Yard has dedicated a great deal of manpower to the search for Hannah, but so far not the slightest trace of my girl has been discovered. There have been no reported sightings of her. No witnesses have been unearthed who may attest to her movements or whereabouts. She has, it would seem, been whisked off the face of the Earth."

"I am sure that is not the case," I said. "She is somewhere, safe and sound. She must be." The words sounded banal even to my ears, but I felt that some consolation must be tendered to the judge and it undoubtedly was not going to come from Holmes.

"When I went to the Yard today to vent my frustration at the lack of progress," Sir Osbert said, "one inspector drew me aside and confided that Sherlock Holmes might be the answer to my prayers. Lester, I think his name was. Pale, rodent-like chap."

"Lestrade," said Holmes.

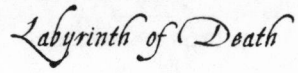

"That is he. He told me that he could personally vouch for you. You had, he said, been useful to him on a few occasions."

"'Useful'. How generous of friend Lestrade. Perhaps, Sir Osbert, you would be so good as to give me some information about your daughter and the circumstances of her unexplained disappearance."

"I shall endeavour to do so. What do you need to know?"

"First of all, how old is your daughter?"

"Twenty-nine, nearly thirty."

"A spinster?"

"She is, yes. That is not for a lack of suitors, nor a lack of accomplishment and physical attractiveness. Far from it. Though I say so myself, Hannah is a charming, lively, beautiful creature – the very spit of her mother in those respects. She plays the piano with expertise and finesse. She has a gracious air. She is well-educated, highly articulate, not to mention well-read. She is, in short, a catch for any man, a pearl of great prize. There have been numerous offers for her hand, the majority from candidates I would have no hesitation in welcoming as a son-in-law. And yet…"

"She turns them down."

"Hannah is deucedly headstrong." Woolfson gave a heartfelt sigh. "I would not go so far as to say she is the sort who would join the campaign for women's suffrage, but she has definite leanings in that direction. She reckons herself the equal of any male and goes out of her way to prove it. Those who would have her as a wife are not deterred by this. I suspect they believe that marriage would reform her, making her more compliant and biddable. All the same, no man cares to be made to feel that he is a woman's inferior. For instance, when one of these aspirants plays Hannah at tennis, invariably she wins, and by some margin. She does not, as a wiser woman might, feign incompetence and allow her opponent to be the victor. Far from it. She trounces him with merciless aplomb."

"That is something masculine pride will not easily support."

"And she insists on indulging in high-flown conversation, relishing the cut-and-thrust of a good intellectual argument. Petty small-talk and a pretence of dull-wittedness – not for my Hannah. Often, at a dinner party, she will refuse to withdraw with the rest of the women and will insist on remaining at the table with the men, to join in their discourse. My friends tolerate the habit but privately one or two of them have had words with me to complain. It is exasperating. She is a tremendous girl and I am inordinately fond of her, but I do wish she had more in the way of feminine wiles, as her mother did."

"All the same, it is not beyond the bounds of reason that she may have eloped. Can it be that some beau has come her way and swept her off her feet?"

"Inconceivable. She would not do that to me. During these past months, and before, when my wife Margaret was gravely ill, Hannah has been my rock. She has coped with the tragedy far better than I have."

"Perhaps this eligible bachelor I am hypothesising about is an unsuitable match. Knowing he would not gain your approval, your daughter has absconded with him, and the two of them will traipse home in the near future as husband and wife, presenting you with a *fait accompli*."

"Again, inconceivable. She would never betray me like that. Each of us is all the other has. Hannah would never do anything that she knows might cause me pain, especially not at present."

"Is she employed?"

"She lives with me but works part-time as a private tutor for various respectable families in the locality, helping those of their children who have fallen behind in their studies. By all accounts she excels at it. She also performs the duties of personal secretary to me, managing my correspondence and my diary and suchlike."

"You have checked, I presume, with these families? They have been unable to supply you with any clues regarding her disappearance?"

"They are all as baffled as I."

"And her behaviour immediately prior to this event – there was nothing untoward about it?"

"I must confess," said Woolfson, "I have not been the most attentive of parents in recent weeks. I have been distracted, you understand. Not in my right mind. My work has not suffered. Indeed, I have thrown myself into it wholeheartedly, finding a refuge there from grief. But domestically, I regret to say, I have rather let things go. The solace of alcohol has beckoned to me and I have regularly answered its call. Many an evening I have lapsed into an inebriated stupor, necessitating that Hannah conduct me up to my bedroom. It shames me to tell you this, but I must, for it means that if she has been acting in any way unusually, out of character, I will not have been in the best position to notice."

"So any secretiveness on her part, any divergence from her normal pattern of life, will have escaped you?"

"Most likely. Oh, Mr Holmes, Dr Watson, I cannot help but feel that I am responsible for all this. I have driven Hannah away by being an intolerable burden on her at an already difficult time."

"Come, come, let us have none of that," I said. "Self-recrimination will get you nowhere."

"There is another explanation, of course," said Holmes. "I am loath to raise the idea, but it is not beyond the bounds of possibility that your daughter's disappearance was not of her own volition."

"She was kidnapped, you mean? Abducted?" said Woolfson. "That did occur to me too, though I have tried my damnedest to discount it."

"A man like you must have enemies: a wrongdoer whom you

consigned to jail and who has since been paroled might well nurse a grudge. Likewise a relative of someone whom you ordered to be transported or even sentenced to death. How better to strike back at you than through your closest kin?"

I shuddered. "The very notion chills me to the bone."

"Militating against the probability," Holmes said, "is the fact that you have received no notification from any abductor. You would have mentioned it if you had."

The judge nodded. "There has been no ransom demand, nor any crowing message from a captor."

"There would surely have been by now. A week is a long time for someone bent on revenge to stay silent. If the aim of taking your daughter were to hurt you, the miscreant would want you to know that she is in his power. It would feed his sense of superiority over you and satisfy his feelings of grievance. No, we may regard the dearth of activity on that front as a positive sign."

"Is Hannah even alive, though?" said Woolfson. "That is the thought which torments me the most. Has she met with some accident? Or has she, God forbid, fallen foul of some savage lunatic like that Ripper fellow of recent memory? Is her body even now lying… lying somewhere—"

He broke off. One could only imagine the nights he had spent wide-awake wondering, the unspoken terrors that assailed him every hour of the day. It was chastening to see so illustrious and upright a man humbled and broken.

"Sir Osbert," I said, "listen to me. I feel I can speak for Holmes as well as myself when I say that we will do everything in our power to locate your daughter and reunite you with her. Is that not so, Holmes?"

My friend waved a hand abstractedly, which I could only take to signify assent.

"In the meantime," I went on, "I advise that you go home and try to get some rest. I have a soporific draught in my medical bag that I will give to you and insist you must administer to yourself. A good night's sleep will have a remarkable restorative effect."

"You are too kind, Dr Watson. I – I suppose it can do no harm. As a matter of fact I feel a little less frantic already, knowing that Sherlock Holmes has agreed to take the case."

"We shall pay a call on you first thing tomorrow. Your address?"

Woolfson fumbled out a card. He lived, it transpired, on one of the smartest streets in Mayfair.

"I thank you both, gentlemen," said he. "I shall see myself out. Good evening."

No sooner had he left the premises than Holmes said, "Watson, you should not have been so quick to give Sir Osbert false hope."

"False hope? You saw the man, Holmes. I had to do something to alleviate his distress."

"Still, it was far from prudent to make him a pledge we may not be able to keep. What if we fail to find this Hannah?"

"Then he will know that we have tried our best and will surely find it in his heart to forgive our lack of success."

"You vaunt my abilities higher than perhaps they warrant. There seems precious little to go on here."

"So far, yes, but doubtless an inspection of his home tomorrow will scour up clues."

"That is as maybe," said Holmes. "Nonetheless I fear the worst. For a daughter so loyal and devoted to go missing without warning or explanation is a matter of the utmost gravity. I pray I am up to the task for which I have been volunteered."

I let out a huff of exasperation. "As if you would not have volunteered yourself!" I ejaculated. "I was merely confirming the inevitable."

Holmes reached for his clay pipe and the Persian slipper where he kept his tobacco. "Well, what's done is done. We shall learn tomorrow, shan't we, whether or not I can shed some light on this very dark prospect."

CHAPTER THREE

A PRACTITIONER OF THE EPISTOLARY ART

Accordingly, we turned up the next morning at the door of a large Regency townhouse on one corner of a garden square in Mayfair. A butler ushered us within, and we presented ourselves in Sir Osbert Woolfson's study, where the man himself greeted us warmly. He looked markedly improved from the previous day. His face had a more even colour and was less haggard. Yet his eyes remained haunted and there was something desperate in the profuse gratitude he expressed to us, in particular to my companion.

"Anything you need to ask, Mr Holmes," he said, "any question at all, do not hesitate. I am at your beck and call, as are my household staff. If you wish to interrogate them, go ahead. I have instructed them to cooperate fully."

"Before anything else, I should like to see Hannah's quarters."

"Naturally. Right this way."

Woolfson led us upstairs to the second floor, where Hannah had a suite of rooms to herself, consisting of a bedroom, a bathroom and a modest drawing room. The last of these was so bedecked with books that one might legitimately have dubbed it a library. Upon the shelves I spied titles by Mary Wollstonecraft and George Sand, which added weight to her father's depiction of her as an independent-minded and free-thinking woman. Yet I was also pleased to note that her tastes in contemporary fiction reflected mine, with the works of Dickens, Scott and Mrs Gaskell prominent in her collection. Moreover, my own writings were well represented, and I would not be human if I were not flattered to see this. An author, above all else, craves confirmation that he is read.

Holmes, for his part, embarked on a lengthy perusal of all three rooms in the suite. He subjected the furnishings to close analysis and, with Woolfson's permission, went through the contents of Hannah's wardrobe and chest of drawers. These, judging by his shrugs of dissatisfaction, yielded nothing of significant value to him.

More fruitful, however, was her writing desk. It was a bow-legged escritoire fashioned from walnut and fitted with a plethora of drawers and cubbyholes. Ink stains on the veneer suggested that it had received plenty of use over the course of its lifetime. Holmes studied it for several minutes, running a hand over its contours and now and then rapping on its surfaces with a knuckle.

"May I?" he said, gesturing at packets of letters tied up with string and lodged neatly in the cubbyholes.

"By all means," said Woolfson. "Hannah is a prodigious letter writer. She produces three or four at a sitting, sometimes more, and receives at least one a day."

"I am reluctant to intrude on personal correspondence, but I believe it could prove worthwhile."

"Anything that will help."

The letters were from friends, relatives and acquaintances, and Holmes scanned them one by one with an appraising eye, lingering longer over some than others.

"Amongst the contents of the more recent specimens there is a lot about your wife, Sir Osbert, and her illness and eventual passing. Expressions of sympathy, regret and condolence. Going further back we find copious amounts of gossip. An aunt who did this, a neighbour who did that. All very trivial and unrevealing. Of course I am getting only one side of the story. Hannah's own letters would, I am sure, have more meat to them. Indeed, to illustrate, here is one correspondent – a Winifred Forshaw – who upbraids your daughter for being so intense and serious."

"Winifred is a cousin of Hannah's on my wife's side of the family."

"'There are times, dearest Hannah, when your earnestness ill becomes you,'" Holmes read aloud. "'I say this lovingly and with respect. I realise you are infinitely cleverer than I shall ever be, but you perhaps do not always have an appreciation of the lighter side of things. Nor do you hold in high enough esteem the role that I and many other women have chosen for ourselves – that of dutiful wife and caring mother – when it is, I would submit, the highest calling any of our sex can answer.'"

He flicked through several further letters, muttering to himself as he assessed the intrinsic merit of each. "Irrelevant. Uninteresting. Boring. Less boring. Noteworthy."

I began to grow uncomfortable. I felt that simply by being in this room we were already prying pruriently into Hannah Woolfson's life. By reading her letters so extensively, however, Holmes was going further than that.

"Holmes," I said, "is this really necessary?"

"It is more than necessary, Watson. It is vital. The Scotland Yarders did not think to examine these letters. Am I not right, Sir Osbert?"

"They were thorough but not, to my recollection, *that* thorough."

"Of course they were not. And if they *had* elected to examine the letters, they would certainly not have returned them to the cubbyholes in the orderly and methodical arrangement in which I found them. Hannah has been scrupulous in her filing. The letters are all alphabetised from left to right by name of correspondent and, within each category, organised by date. Policemen, who when it comes to combing a premises for evidence behave not unlike chimpanzees, would never have been so punctilious about replacing them."

I was still uneasy about violating Hannah's privacy. In order to stave off my embarrassment I went outside and took a turn around the streets for an hour or so, leaving Holmes to his business, under Woolfson's watchful eye. By the time I returned, my friend had completed his perusal.

"Well," I said, "what have you gleaned from the correspondence?"

"Much that is useless but some that is not. Again and again I have come across references to a friend of Hannah's, a certain Sophia Tompkins."

"A girl she first met at boarding school," said Woolfson. "The two were close, very close when young. 'Thick as thieves', Margaret used to say about them. They have remained on cordial terms since, although they see each other seldom. Sophia lives in Dorset, where she works as a governess for the children of a prosperous importer."

"Yes, that jibes with what I have been able to gather from my reading. The mentions of Miss Tompkins crop up exclusively in the letters from others who were at the same school, Cheltenham Ladies' College. Little can be deduced about her from context other than that a solid bond exists between her and Hannah. Which raises a question."

"Namely?" I said.

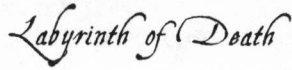

"Well, Watson, if the two young women were – are – such bosom companions, why are there no letters to Hannah from Sophia herself present in this assemblage?" He swept a hand across the various sheaves of writing paper. "I have been through them all and found not one. It is a singular and surprising lacuna. Here is somebody who excels as a practitioner of the epistolary art and is in regular contact with numerous intimates and not-so-intimates, but of this one particular friend, allegedly so dear to her, there is no sign."

"Maybe Hannah and Sophia had a falling-out."

"That is not even hinted at in any of the letters. On the contrary, in one of them the writer makes it clear that Sophia attended the funeral of Lady Margaret and was seen giving Hannah support."

"It is true," said Woolfson. "Sophia came up from Dorset for the ceremony and stayed overnight afterwards. It was the last time the two of them were together, to my knowledge. But, now that I think about it, Dr Watson may be correct – there was some sort of disagreement between them."

Holmes cocked an eyebrow. "Tell me more."

"I don't remember much about it. That day – the entire period – remains something of a blur. But there were words between Sophia and my daughter on the morning after the funeral; that I do recall. A spat of some kind. I was not privy to it. It happened while they were breakfasting. Having awoken early, I had already eaten by then and was alone in my study. If they raised their voices, I did not hear, but I do know that Hannah was in high dudgeon afterwards, while Sophia left the house precipitately, without a goodbye. I did not think much of it at the time. I should perhaps have asked Hannah to explain what had upset her, why she and Sophia had so clearly argued, but…" He spread out his hands. "I had my own preoccupations. I simply took it for a passing squall – emotions run high at times of tragedy – and assumed the two of them would make amends sooner or later. Thereafter, the incident slipped altogether from my mind, until now."

"Could it have been a more serious contretemps than it appeared?" I hazarded. "Could it even have prompted Hannah to burn every letter Sophia had written to her, out of pique?"

"That would account for their absence," Holmes said. "But there is a curious feature about escritoires such as this one. They are often more than they seem. The example here dates back to the early eighteen-hundreds, I believe."

"It is an old family heirloom," said Woolfson. "It first belonged to my great-great-great-grandmother."

"Back then it was not uncommon for the lady of the house – and the desk's smaller dimensions and ornate marquetry signal it as the property of a lady – to wish to keep certain correspondence hidden from her husband, love letters and the like. Not, I hasten to add, that I am attributing any impropriety to your thrice-great-grandmother, Sir Osbert. The practice among joiners was, nonetheless, always to include a secret compartment where such letters might be stowed safely, without risk of discovery."

"It would be news to me if there were one in this desk," Woolfson averred.

Holmes bent to the escritoire. "Observe the panel just below the cubbyholes and above the writing surface. Seems innocuous enough, does it not? A solid, immoveable part of the construction. Along its upper edge, however, are some tiny scrape marks. And if we tap it – like so – it sounds hollower and looser than it ought to be. Now all one has to do is press carefully here, or perhaps here, or here, until…"

His probing fingers triggered an unseen spring-catch, and the panel dropped outward on a pair of hinged arms.

"Well, blow me down," Woolfson exclaimed.

In the small cavity thus exposed was a stack of more letters, several dozen all told.

"*Voilà*," said Holmes, extracting these and rifling through them. "The hand is feminine. The letterheads bear a Dorset address. The sender is none other than Sophia Tompkins. Let us see what the young lady has to say for herself."

CHAPTER FOUR

A KIND OF PURDAH

Initially the letters from Sophia were much like the rest, in so far as they were chatty, superficial and, for our present purposes, unrewarding. Holmes perused them one after another, with mounting impatience. I began to wonder if this would all be a fruitless exercise. Could it be that Hannah had tucked the letters away inside the secret compartment for no other reason than resentment of Sophia? Her friend had slighted her and she wanted the letters out of sight so that she would not be reminded of the offence, a symbolic banishment?

Then the scowl that was deepening on Holmes's brow smoothed out and a small smile touched his lips.

"This is more like it. The letter is dated the fourteenth of August, a little under a year ago. It seems that your wife, Sir Osbert, was taken ill around then."

"That is when she received the diagnosis. It was a cancer of the stomach. The doctor predicted she had mere weeks to live. Margaret was made of stern stuff, though. She lasted until Christmas."

"Sophia writes with tenderness and sensitivity. 'How awful

this must be for you, dear Hannah. Know that you and both your parents are in my thoughts and prayers.' She goes on to say, 'The ways of the world are strange and sometimes appear inimical to happiness. I am beginning to learn, however, that the cruelties of existence may be overcome and even surpassed. I cannot expand on that statement at the moment, but I feel that I am on the cusp of a great discovery – an adventure such as we used to talk about in the dormitory at school. Remember that, Hannah? How you and I would huddle beneath the bedcovers together after lights out and talk about the future and the remarkable things we might do with our lives? Just such an opportunity is in prospect for me, and I am inclined to grasp it and embrace it, however much it scares me to do so.'"

Holmes thumbed through to the next letter.

"Hannah evidently requested clarification," he said, "because here we have some development of the hints Sophia dropped in her last communication. 'There is, nearby, a place. Such a wonderful place. I have visited it as the guest of a young man who attended the Duprees' summer ball.'"

"Dupree," said Woolfson. "That's the chap Sophia is governess for. Humbert Dupree. Sugar merchant with interests in the West Indies."

"'You would approve of him, Hannah, this young man. His name is Edwin and he is very handsome but, more to the point, he is progressive. He holds views about the world that are not dissimilar to yours. He seems wise beyond his years; I would even go so far as to call him enlightened. He came to pick me up in a liveried brougham the day before yesterday, and our exchanges on the journey to our destination were not only lively but uplifting and inspiring. And oh, when we got there! Words alone can hardly do justice to what I saw. I really should not go into it in any further depth. Edwin has insisted I keep it under my hat. But I am convinced I have found paradise, Hannah. Heaven on Earth!'"

"Paradise?" I echoed. "Heaven on Earth? What is all this?"

"Questions Hannah herself must have asked," said Holmes, rifling through more papers and scanning through the words with his quick eye, "but perhaps with some asperity, for Sophia, in her subsequent missive, adopts a defensive posture. 'You would have me betray a confidence, and that is something I am not prepared to do. I will say that I have gone with Edwin a second time to the place I mentioned and am no less enraptured with it than I was before. You advise me to be wary of him. "He sounds too good to be true" – your exact words, Hannah. Well, just because you have no great regard for men does not mean all men are bad. Could it be that I discern a note of jealousy there? You would not have me liking, and being liked by, Edwin when you yourself have such high standards for a mate that you will probably never find one who can meet them. Rest assured that Edwin and his associates and what they have to offer are everything I could hope for, and more.'"

"Sophia sounds smitten," I averred.

"Yes, Watson. This Edwin is obviously a paragon. The next letter is dated November the twenty-first. Some time has passed. Sophia says she has been slow to reply to Hannah's last letter: 'such was the censorious tone you took. It is not until today that I have been able to compose myself and clear my thoughts. You were always the clever one at school, I just a bumbling old duffer by comparison. There were times when I felt you looked down on me, and I feel that again now, most keenly. Anyway, I am dismayed to hear that your dear mama is fading and that she is so enfeebled and listless. It raises in my mind the spectre of my own poor late mother, and my late father too. At least you have the good fortune of being able to make your peace with her and being there with her in her final days, a privilege I was denied with my own parents and their abrupt, unexpected passing. Please do keep me abreast of the situation. I remain a true friend, I hope you know that, and I harbour you no ill will. I myself feel blessed these days and wish I could somehow share that blessedness with you.'"

Holmes closed the letter.

"'Edwin and his associates,'" I quoted. "Clearly he is part of some larger entity, some league or club."

"So it would appear," said Holmes, glancing momentarily up from the pages. "Now we hop forward to January. Your wife died when, Sir Osbert?"

"Mid-December."

"This comes after the funeral, then, and the breakfast-time argument. Yes. Sophia is not contrite. 'Your words stung me, Hannah, but perhaps not as much as the contempt in your eyes. I was merely attempting to explain myself, to justify my decision, and you bit me like a viper. My mind is made up and I will not be dissuaded. I came to your mother's funeral not only to pay my respects to the departed and offer you my shoulder to cry on, but in the hope that you and I might set aside our differences, to share with you my growing strength and demonstrate how much better a person I already am than I once was. (I anticipate becoming even more improved in the weeks and months ahead.) I came, in short, to lay all my cards on the table. Yet, shrewishly, you rounded on me. I opened up to you – about Edwin, about Sir Philip, about the Elysians – and I can see in hindsight that I was foolish to have done so. I expected more from you. More compassion, more understanding. Instead all I got was blind, wilful spite. What has become of the open-minded, far-sighted Hannah Woolfson I once knew? She has turned priggish and myopic. You said you fear for my wellbeing. What you actually fear for, if you want my opinion, is yourself. You see me broadening my horizons and embarking on a journey that will surely lead to greater self-knowledge and the unlocking of my full potential, and you wish you had the same courage. The truth is you are hidebound. You have painted yourself into a corner and know your chances of escaping it are diminishing daily. Trapped as you are, it galls you to see someone like me who is taking a daring step into the unknown and, if everything goes well, towards freedom.'"

"What step?" I said. "A 'decision'. What is she talking about?"

"It is all somewhat nebulous," Holmes allowed. "Had we but been there when Hannah and Sophia argued, we would be able to fill in the blanks. But words like 'Sir Philip' and 'the Elysians' at least give us some handholds to cling on to. I don't suppose they ring any bells with you, Sir Osbert?"

Woolfson shook his head. "Regrettably, no."

"You are not familiar with any Sir Philip?"

"None is known to me socially."

"There remain two further letters," Holmes said. "The hand on both is not Sophia's. The signatory instead is Mrs Humbert Dupree. The first is short and to the point. 'My dear Miss Woolfson. Sophia Tompkins is no longer in our employ. She left our service in April, having given notice in March. It was all perfectly amicable, Sophia doing us the courtesy of remaining in her position until we had interviewed candidates to take over from her and selected the best of them for the role. However, she left no forwarding address, and I am afraid it was not until yesterday that your last three letters to her were discovered by her replacement, buried at the back of a drawer in her bureau. I would be surprised that Sophia did not see fit to inform you of her change in circumstance, were it not for the fact that the letters were unopened. Yours faithfully, Mrs Humbert Dupree.'"

Holmes held up the final letter.

"The second from Mrs Dupree. This one is even more curt. 'I cannot help you any further on the subject of Sophia Tompkins.

Her status and whereabouts are no longer any business of mine.'"

"This is all very cryptic, Holmes," I said, "and rather sad, but what bearing can it possibly have on Hannah's disappearance?"

"The date, Watson. Consider the date of this last letter from Mrs Dupree."

"It is ten days ago."

"Ten days. And Hannah has been missing for eight. Do you not think that there may be some connection? That the one thing may have had a direct influence upon the other?"

"My goodness," said Woolfson. He sank into a chair as though he no longer had the strength to hold himself erect. "Are you saying what I think you are saying, Mr Holmes?"

"It remains conjecture, but conjecture built on a firm foundation. Your daughter has not been abducted or murdered. She has not been the victim of some sinister conspiracy or dire misfortune. Rather, she was the active agent in her departure. She has gone looking for Sophia Tompkins."

CHAPTER FIVE

WOOLFSON'S STILETTO

Sir Osbert Woolfson, for the first time since we had made his acquaintance, became sanguine.

"You mean she has acted out of concern for her friend?" said he. "Out of fear for Sophia's wellbeing? That is what has happened?"

"It is far from the only logical interpretation of the facts, but it is the likeliest," replied Holmes. "One may infer from Sophia's letters that Hannah was uncomfortable about this Edwin person and felt that his intentions towards Sophia might not be wholly honourable. Equally, these Elysians – whoever or whatever they are – did not meet with Hannah's approval. Once she learned that Sophia had quit her position with the Duprees, her apprehension deepened. Her assumption must have been, as mine is, that Sophia had made a rash and unwise move and that it related somehow to the Elysians and Edwin. Her entreaties to Mrs Humbert Dupree for further information met with no success. Therefore she took it upon herself to become personally involved in the matter."

"But, if so, why did she leave so abruptly?" I said. "Why go without first telling her father, or anyone else in the household, what she was doing?"

"As to that, I cannot say. Only Hannah herself can provide the answer."

"You must have some inkling."

"You are asking me to speculate, Watson, and that is anathema to me. Sir Osbert, I strongly suspect your daughter is currently in Dorset, having embarked on a mission to rescue her friend from a situation she deems undesirable. Would you not concur?"

"It is feasible," said Woolfson. "What should I do? Instruct the police to focus their search efforts in that part of the country?"

"I would submit that a greater lightness of touch is required. Sending in the police force is like letting loose a herd of stampeding buffalo. Reputations could get trampled. In delicate situations like these, the stiletto is often more effective than the blunderbuss."

"Ah. Yes. I see. You propose that the affair be handled on the quiet."

"By a specialist with years of experience in the discreet management of problems."

"The case is all yours, Mr Holmes," Woolfson said with finality. His legal brain had clearly calculated his options and alighted upon the one least liable to make headlines. "You be my stiletto. I will pay whatever fee you levy. Please retrieve my daughter and restore her to me."

There followed a half-hour during which Holmes quizzed Woolfson's staff, which comprised the butler, a cook, a housemaid and a coachman. The housemaid was the sole eyewitness to Hannah's departure. She had been polishing the front-door brass on the morning of the Saturday before last when Hannah had passed her on her way out, with the stated goal of taking some exercise. The weather had been clement and the housemaid said it was not unusual for the mistress to go for a walk, sometimes for up to two hours, when the sun shone. Hannah had taken with her a "largish handbag" and had last been seen heading in the direction of Hyde Park.

"The maid's testimony supports the theory that Hannah has travelled to Dorset," said Holmes.

"Does not contradict it, at any rate," I said. "What if her goal was only the park after all, no further than that?"

"And what if it was Paddington Station, which lies a short walk north of the park and is the gateway to the west of England?"

"But if Hannah knew she was setting forth on a lengthy expedition," said Woolfson, "would she not have packed accordingly?"

"It depends," said Holmes. "One wonders how long she expected to be away. If she thought it was merely to be a daytrip, at most an overnight stay, a largish handbag might suffice. I noted a Gladstone bag in her wardrobe. She would surely have taken that, along with several changes of clothing, had she foreseen that her task would detain her for over a week."

Woolfson looked pained. "Then it is still possible that something untoward has happened to her in Dorset."

"I would like to think not, Sir Osbert, but I cannot offer you complete reassurance on that front. Much hinges on the nature of these so-called Elysians. Hannah clearly was of the view that their influence over Sophia was not in the latter's best interests. Whether or not her opinion was coloured by spite or jealousy, as Sophia claims, is open to debate. From the picture I am forming of your daughter, though, I would say that she is a fairly astute judge of character. Furthermore, she would not allow personal feelings to stand in the way of doing the right thing."

"I would not disagree with you, Mr Holmes. I only wish Hannah had confided in me and not just hared off in pursuit of Sophia. I would have endeavoured to talk her out of it, or at least striven to convince her to take a less forthright approach, perhaps going through an intermediary instead."

"Would she have heeded that counsel?"

"Probably not," a rueful Woolfson admitted.

"The situation is as it is. My job now – and I trust that faithful Watson will assist me in discharging it – is to extricate Hannah from whatever predicament she has got herself into, if any. And with your permission, Sir Osbert, we shall take our leave in order to go about doing just that. There is one last item, however. It would be of benefit to us to know what your daughter looks like. Do you have a picture to hand?"

From his desk Woolfson fetched a small photographic portrait in a tortoiseshell frame. "This was taken a couple of years ago."

The woman in the picture, her head angled in three-quarter profile, was of breathtaking comeliness. Her eyes shone with wistful intelligence, her face was entrancingly heart-shaped, and her lips were full, with a tiny, impish smile creasing their corners. Her hair, which she wore in the pompadour style with a clasp atop her crown and ringlets falling over her forehead, had a rich lustre that the sepia-tint reproduction could not diminish. In all, she was the very model of feminine beauty, and I wished I could have gazed at her image for longer than the few seconds I was allowed to over Holmes's shoulder before he passed the photograph back to the subject's father.

"Thank you," said he.

"You will keep me posted on your progress?" Woolfson asked.

"At every turn, I promise."

As we strode away from the house, Holmes said, "I hope I was not being presumptuous, Watson, in hoping that you will join me in unearthing the errant girl."

"My caseload is relatively light at present. My neighbour Jackson can take over my practice for me or, failing that, Anstruther. I am more than a touch curious to know what has become of the girl." I thought of the photograph of Hannah and wondered if my curiosity did not bear a shade of self-interest. I was not averse to the notion of meeting the picture's subject in the flesh. "I am, of course, concerned about the fate of Miss Tompkins, too," I added, "and intrigued to discover what these Elysians are."

"You seem invigorated, Watson, as you always do when an adventure is in prospect."

"I cannot deny it."

"You also, if I may say so, seem less careworn. The melancholy that has become a constant shadow in your life recedes whenever something comes along to pull you out of the rut of routine."

"The same might be said of you, Holmes."

"Touché. This case undoubtedly has many singular and absorbing aspects. However, before we set off to Dorset to pursue it there is some preliminary research I must perform."

No sooner were we back at Baker Street than Holmes delved into his extensive array of commonplace books, index books and scrapbooks, keen to dredge up references to "Elysians" amongst the thousands of newspaper clippings he so industriously collected and collated. He was disappointed, if unsurprised, to find none. Similarly, study of *Debrett's* and *Burke's Peerage* was not helpful. The "Sir Philip" mentioned in one of Sophia's letters could have been any one of several knights of the realm. Three of them had specific ties to Dorset, but that did not mean that the remainder could be disregarded.

"After all," Holmes said, "it is not axiomatically true, based on the evidence we have, that Sophia's Sir Philip is a Dorset resident. Nor, for that matter, is it by any means certain that this 'Heaven on Earth' of hers, a brougham ride away, lies within that county rather than in one of its bordering neighbours – Hampshire, Devon, Somerset, Wiltshire. Our first port of call, all said and done, must be the Duprees'. The letterhead used by Sophia tells us they reside near Poole. So if you would, Watson, look up the train timetables. I, in turn, shall wire Humbert Dupree to warn him that we are coming."

I fetched down *Bradshaw's* from the shelf, while Holmes summoned Billy the pageboy and scribbled a note for him to take to the telegraph office.

Shortly we were aboard a Great Western train outbound from Paddington. A change at Winchester and another at Southampton got us onto a branch line to Bournemouth and thence to Poole, where eventually we alighted, some four hours after setting off.

"You seem relieved, Watson," my companion observed, "to be watching that train pull away. Can it be that, at the ripe old age of forty-three, you are beginning to find rail travel arduous?"

"No. If I must be honest, the Brunswick green of a Great Western locomotive stirs up bad memories."

"Bad…? Ah yes. Six years ago. The last occasion when we were in the West Country. Dartmoor. Baskerville Hall. Of all of our escapades, that is the one which appears to have affected you the most deeply, has it not, old friend?"

"I would rather face a blizzard of jezail bullets at Maiwand again than that enormous devil dog. The beast has left me with an abiding aversion to all canines, even the smallest and most harmless-seeming. Only the other day I was making a house call and the patient's Yorkshire terrier started yapping at me. The thing was no bigger than a cat and its attentions were clearly playful, but it was all I could do not to take to my heels and flee. Likewise I have developed something akin to ophidiophobia ever since our midnight vigil at the home of Dr Grimesby Roylott in Stoke Moran, and whatever the rodent equivalent of ophidiophobia is ever since the *Matilda Briggs* affair and our far too close encounter with the giant rat of Sumatra."

Holmes chuckled. "Fairly soon, if you're not careful, there will be no animal species left that you do like, Watson. At least on this particular errand the odds of us running afoul of any dangerous fauna are remote. Now look lively! We must secure a cab to take us to the Duprees.'"

CHAPTER SIX

A MAN TOO CHARMING BY HALF

Humbert Dupree was a corpulent, genial sort, whose girth and decaying teeth suggested that, as a sugar importer, he was over-fond of consuming the product he traded in. Mrs Dupree, in stark contrast, was a pinched, rake-thin woman who seemed a stranger to smiles and immune to humour – the sourness to her husband's sweetness. Their home, Apsley Grange, was a rambling manor a few miles outside Poole, populated by servants and a quartet of loud, rumbustious offspring, all under the age of ten.

One of these children, a boy of some seven years with a dirt-smudged face and tousled hair, confronted us as we stepped out of our cab.

"Who goes there?" the urchin declared, leaping into our path from a clump of shrubbery by the front door. He carried a cardboard shield and was brandishing a wooden sword. "Halt and identify yourselves, in the name of King Arthur."

"My name is Sherlock Holmes," said my friend, evincing a glimmer of amusement. "And which knight of the Round Table might you be?"

"I am Sir Isidore of Apsley."

"Not one I am familiar with. Tell me, Sir Isidore, does your mother know you have filched jam from the pantry?"

The lad's eyes widened in astonishment and horror. "How did…?"

"Your fingers tell the tale." Holmes leaned closer to the boy, lowering his voice to a conspiratorial whisper. "My advice? Lick them thoroughly before you next see her. Then your crime shall remain your secret and mine."

"You will not snitch on me?"

"I promise."

"Nor you?" said Isidore to me.

With a chuckle, I shook my head. "I shall not breathe a word."

The young knight scampered off back into the shrubbery, hand in mouth.

"A tricky situation," Holmes said as we climbed the front steps. "Thank the Lord I was able to defuse it before one or both of us were impaled."

As we entered, a further three children, two girls and another boy, were rampaging up and down the main staircase, blithe to the protests of a harried-looking woman whom I took to be their governess. Mrs Dupree was likewise unable to curb them, while Humbert Dupree merely looked on and chortled. I quickly gathered the impression that the junior Duprees exasperated their mother to the same degree that they amused their father. She found their noisy antics a tribulation, he nothing but a source of great merriment.

We were ushered to the library, the one corner of the manor where, it seemed, peace reigned. Over tea, Holmes enquired about Sophia Tompkins. Mrs Dupree, however, revealed little we did not already know. Sophia had parted company with the family on decent enough terms. She had been an efficient governess, if slightly too ready to indulge the children's whims, and Mrs Dupree would gladly have written her a letter of recommendation had she requested one.

Her husband was more forthcoming. "Lovely lass. Shame to have lost her. Children still miss her. 'When is Miss Sophia coming back?' is the constant refrain. Breaks my heart to have to keep telling the little tykes she is not going to. The new girl is sterner and they care for her company less. Play tricks on her all the time. Hide from her, cheek her, deliberately lose their slates and textbooks…"

"They did that with Sophia," his wife pointed out.

"Only she never minded, whereas what's-her-name, the new one, does. That makes it funnier for them and spurs them to do it more."

"Might I ask," said Holmes, "if Miss Tompkins changed at all in the weeks prior to her terminating her contract with you?"

Dupree shrugged his shoulders. "Not so as one would notice."

"She did not strike you as happier? Or unhappier?"

"No. Hence her decision to quit came as something of a shock. I thought everything was going swimmingly, no complaints, and then all at once, out of the blue, she upped and said she was off."

Mrs Dupree's pursed lips suggested she did not agree. "There was a man," she said with patent distaste.

"Name of Edwin, by any chance?" said Holmes.

"That is he."

"What can you tell us about him?"

"Not a lot. I believe his surname is Fairbrother. He visited a few times."

"Took Sophia out for drives on her days off," said Dupree. "Handsome lad. It was obvious he'd taken a shine to her, and she to him. What is the harm in that? Way of the world. Young man, young woman – nothing more natural."

"I did not like him."

"My dear, you do not like many people." Dupree's tone was affectionate. "Not on an individual basis. Sometimes it is a wonder you even tolerate me."

"You act the buffoon, husband, but you have redeeming qualities."

"This Edwin Fairbrother was a guest at your summer ball," Holmes said. "How is that possible if you do not know him well?"

"Oh, the summer ball carries an open invitation to all in the vicinity," said Dupree.

"All within a certain social bracket," his wife amended. "Of a certain cachet."

"They come, we entertain. We throw open the doors, lay on an orchestra, food, drink, dancing, jugglers, conjurors, fireworks at midnight. Quite the occasion. Costs a bob or two but worth it. Been doing it annually for a while now. People say they look forward to it all year. All Bess's handiwork – my wife's. She conceived and organises the whole thing. We have been blessed with material good fortune. Bess likes to share it around, and so do I."

"I do recall Fairbrother occupying Sophia's attention for most of the evening," said Mrs Dupree. "Other men asked her to dance and she obliged, but he monopolised her. Not against her will, either," she added.

"There was more than one kind of fireworks that night," her husband said, wagging his eyebrows.

Mrs Dupree sighed, the epitome of longsuffering wifely forbearance. "Mr Holmes, I must ask: is Sophia in trouble? Your telegram informed us only that you wished to discuss a matter of urgency with us, and since the sender was the great London consulting detective of international repute, what else could we do but welcome you and your colleague across the threshold?

However, I am beginning to experience feelings of disquiet. Was Fairbrother instrumental in Sophia's leaving our employ? Has he exercised some sort of malign hold over the girl?"

"Did he seem to you the type of man who might?"

"Yes, to be frank. He was charming, Mr Holmes. Too charming by half, if you catch my drift. I could easily see him leading a girl astray, especially a girl like Sophia who, for all her outward sophistication and poise, has a certain naïve streak, a certain impressionability."

Holmes nodded gravely. "Very well. One or two further queries, if I may, and then Watson and I shall incommode you no more."

Mrs Dupree made an acquiescent gesture. I was forming the opinion that the woman was kinder and more compassionate than she liked to let on. Her icy surface belied warmer depths. There was not such a disparity between her and her husband as one might at first assume.

"Mr Fairbrother must be local, if he were an attendee at the ball," Holmes said.

"I believe he hails from somewhere not far away."

"You do not know where precisely?"

"No. Humbert?"

"Can't say I do either."

"It is of no great matter," said Holmes. "Now that I have a surname to go with the forename, he will be infinitely easier to track down. On a related topic, does the name Sir Philip hold any meaning for you?"

Mrs Dupree pondered. "There is a Sir Philip who has a place to the west of here, Dorchester way. That is the only person of that name I can think of. Sir Philip… Buchanan. Yes. That is the surname. Buchanan."

"You have not met him?"

"No. I believe he is an architect and was knighted for his services to that industry. Beyond that, I have no intelligence about him."

"I likewise," said her husband.

"Finally, I do not suppose either of you has ever heard of 'the Elysians'?"

"Elysium?" said Mrs Dupree. "As in the paradise of the Ancient Greeks? The place where heroes went after death?"

"Elys*ians*," said Holmes, emphasising the final syllable.

She shook her head, as did Mr Dupree. "It is a queer coinage," she said. "It implies a race of people inhabiting a perfect eternal realm."

"It does indeed," said Holmes.

"Well," said Humbert Dupree with a laugh, "Poole is nice enough, but if it is a perfect realm you are after, I think you will need to look a little further afield!"

Just as Holmes and I were climbing into our cab, which we had ordered to remain parked outside the house until we were done, the sugar importer emerged at haste from the front entrance.

"Dr Watson. A moment of your time."

"Yes?"

"It has occurred to me – you may well be turning this visit into an episode in one of your stories, may you not?"

"Not necessarily, but I would not discount it."

"Well, should you happen to, might I beg that you present a fair image of Bess? She makes a severe impression but her heart is in the right place. Her philanthropic and charitable efforts around the county are second to none."

"My goal is always to be objective and accurate in my narratives. In that regard, Mr Dupree, you and your wife need have absolutely no cause for concern."

Relieved, Dupree headed back indoors, where it sounded as though war had broken out, although it could just have been four children thundering through the hallway, whooping like a tribe of demented Red Indians. Their father gave vent to a monstrous roar, which elicited squeals of delighted terror, and some sort of mad, hilarious chase ensued, which vociferous remonstrations from both Mrs Dupree and the new governess did nothing to hinder.

"Objective and accurate," Holmes echoed as the cab rattled off along the drive and Apsley Grange receded behind us. "I suppose there is a first time for everything."

I bristled. "I know that you would prefer me to represent your investigations as though they were treatises, Holmes, with a premise, an explication and a conclusion. But what would be the point in that? Who would read them bar a handful of academics and intellectual snobs?"

"They would at least have the virtue of serious and lasting scientific value. Thanks to you, I strongly doubt that my achievements will be heralded in the future. Whereas a more sober, factual record of my deeds would live on indefinitely in scholarly libraries, adding to the sum total of mankind's wisdom and benefiting the student of crime for generations to come."

He was being ironic. At least, I like to think that he was.

"Holmes," I said, "it is not up to me, or to you, what of us lives on past our deaths and what does not. A higher power determines that."

"God?"

"Posterity."

My companion grinned. "Then let us hope that posterity is kind to me and you. Perhaps you are right. Perhaps, a century from now or more, my renown will persist through your jottings. Who knows? Other authors might even pick up where you leave off and invent chronicles of their own about me. Since you fictionalise my doings, Watson, who is to say I will not in the end come to be considered completely fictitious, a figment of the imagination, and therefore fair game for pasticheurs and homageurs and similar such mountebanks bereft of originality?"

He seemed tickled by the prospect.

"An afterlife as the hero of literary works by diverse hands," he mused. "A very specific Valhalla. My own private Elysium. Ha!"

CHAPTER SEVEN

WATERTON PARVA

After dinner at the seafront hotel we had booked into, Holmes and I took a turn along nearby Branksome Chine, the strip of sand-and-shingle beach that lay to the east of Poole Harbour. It was a delightful evening, the sun still radiating warmth as it sank, a light breeze wafting onshore across the turquoise waves. Low, sloping sandstone cliffs overlooked the strand, which petered out to a narrow spit connecting the mainland to the Sandbanks peninsula, a small hump in the harbour mouth that was barely inhabited and seemed an isolated, undesirable spot to live.

Holmes was in a ruminative mood. I could see his brain churning behind his sharp grey eyes. The sunset and Channel views were of no consequence to him just then. His mind was on the case, to the exclusion of all else.

The next morning, he was up, dressed and out before I even awoke, and was gone until lunchtime. I enjoyed a few leisurely hours reading the papers and supping tea in the hotel lobby, but the moment Holmes reappeared I knew my period of respite was over and it was back to business. My friend was a veritable whirlwind of manic energy.

"Watson, there you are. Good. Good. A bite to eat for both of us, and then we must gather up our belongings, gird our loins and go."

"Go where?"

"To a village called Waterton Parva, halfway between here and Dorchester."

"And what lies in Waterton Parva?"

"Questions, questions. You, boy!" Holmes seized the sleeve of a passing waiter. "Sandwiches, and plenty of them. Beef, ham, cheese, cucumber – do not stint."

Within the hour, a dog-cart was ferrying us out of Poole, driven by a ruddy-cheeked rustic who insisted on chatting with us over his shoulder even though his thick Dorset burr was more or less indecipherable to our London ears. I understood roughly one word in three he uttered, but I nodded and smiled nonetheless and supplied what I hoped was the appropriate response whenever it seemed that input was being solicited.

After a while the fellow realised that he was making scant conversational headway with us and lapsed into a disgruntled silence. The dog-cart jounced inland, passing through a landscape of graceful, rounded hills and soft, shallow valleys. Summer was approaching its height, and the fields burgeoned with arable crops while the meadows were richly verdant. The sun shone over all like a benign smile, and I caught a reflection of that benignity in the face of Sherlock Holmes, who sat opposite me in the dog-cart's sideways-aligned rear seats, close enough that our knees knocked. He had spoken more than once of his intention to retire to the countryside when age and the vicissitudes of life caught up with him to the extent that he could no longer pursue his calling with sufficient vigour. He had mentioned the Sussex coast, but I wondered whether Dorset was exerting a Siren-like allure over him and inviting him to alter course.

For myself, much though I am an admirer of the novels of Thomas Hardy, which are set in the region, Dorset's charms were lost on me. The scenery around us had a raw splendour – that, I could not deny – but I found its wide open spaces intimidating, in the same way that I had found the desert vistas and rugged mountainsides of Afghanistan intimidating. I am, I would avow, a city dweller through and through. I like streets, trammelled horizons, the bustle of my fellow men, the relentless activity of the urban hive. Nature, whether tamed or untamed, hides too many potential threats.

After the second hour of travel along paved roads and rutted bridleways I fell into a kind of stupor. The afternoon heat bore down heavily upon me. The dog-cart's motion was lulling. My eyelids drooped.

A sharp tap on my thigh roused me.

"Watson, if you can bear to drag yourself back from the Land of Nod, you will see that we are nearing journey's end."

We were rolling into thickly forested terrain. A signpost planted on the verge advertised WATERTON PARVA – ½ MILE, and as the road wound deeper into woodland a few lonely, meagre cottages could be glimpsed, set back on either side. The tree foliage closed overhead, casting us in shade and bringing a chill to the sunlight. Then, having crossed a humpback bridge over a trickling stream, we entered the village proper.

"Village" is possibly too grand a descriptor. "Hamlet" might suit better. There was a parish church with a crooked spire, an inn, a post office, a tiny schoolhouse and a green the size of a tennis court, around which a handful of houses clustered. That was the sum total of Waterton Parva. I noticed a sign pointing toward a Waterton Magna some three miles further on. I could only hope that this other settlement, the suffix of whose name proclaimed it the larger sibling, had more to offer, for Waterton

Parva was a place of paltry blessings.

We stepped down from the dog-cart and Holmes paid the driver, who took the money with a mumbled volley of words that could as easily have been insult as gratitude. He turned the vehicle about and clattered away, and watching him go I felt a sudden pang. It was as though we were relinquishing hold of a lifeline. A sense of isolation fell upon me, a feeling of having been marooned. The forest encircling the village seemed an impenetrable stockade, and the village itself, over which the trees cast long shadows, was like some small, fragile outpost of civilisation in a remote wilderness. An eerie hush hung in the air. Birds sang, distant unseen sheep bleated, but within the confines of Waterton Parva nothing stirred. There was no one about save Holmes and me. Just stone walls, mossy slate roofs, empty windows, the dusty roadway, and the odd drooping wildflower.

"Well, this is a cheery spot," I said.

The church bell abruptly chimed, loud, startling me. Four o'clock tolled.

"Come, Watson." Holmes picked up his bag and made for the inn. "Let us secure accommodation before we do anything else."

We took adjoining rooms, and the landlord could not disguise how pleased he was to be able to let them, for his establishment, it was easy to tell, was not overburdened with paying guests. The inn rejoiced in the name "The Fatted Calf", about which Holmes wryly observed that it promised both culinary abundance and ritual slaughter. "I trust we shall be the subjects of the former and not the objects of the latter," said he. "Speaking of food, I recommend that we rest for an hour or so, then go downstairs and partake of a meal. We shall need the energy."

"I envisage a sleepless night ahead."

"You know me so well, Watson."

"I should hope I do, after all this time. A reconnaissance mission?"

"Your powers of deduction do you credit. My influence must be rubbing off on you."

"I suppose I shall be needing my service revolver."

"You have brought it, of course."

"It is in my suitcase. From experience I have learned never to leave home without it when I am engaged on business with you, Holmes."

"Capital."

"Perhaps, before I retire to my room, you might share your reasons for taking us here to this... rural idyll." I had planned to say "benighted nowhere" but amended it as I did not wish to sound churlish or querulous.

"It is fairly elementary," Holmes said. "A quick search at the Land Registry office in Poole this morning turned up a residential address for Sir Philip Buchanan. He owns a sizeable plot of land in the environs of this village. He purchased a stately home, Charfrome Old Place, back in 'eighty-seven and swiftly bought up as much of the contiguous land as he could over the following two years, paying over the odds for each parcel and combining it all into a single sprawling estate that now comprises a good three hundred acres."

"How nice for him."

"Also this morning I availed myself of the reference section of Poole's town library and the records morgue of a local daily, *The Dorsetshire Echo*, sifting through both in order to amass what further nuggets of data I could about Buchanan. He is not a native of the area but has chosen to domicile himself here, having taken retirement at the age of fifty-five after a much-lauded career as an architect. For thirty years he contributed significantly to the infrastructure of this nation. His public works include museums, railway termini, hospitals, banks and university buildings, all favouring the Palladian and Neoclassical styles. Bazalgette consulted him on the construction of the London sewer network. In short, Buchanan is one of the great technologists of our era, and a preeminent Briton."

"It is a wonder that I have not heard of him before now."

"I too, but by all accounts he is a modest and very private individual and eschews publicity. He almost refused his knighthood, before being persuaded to think again by none other than the Queen herself. He has maintained a low profile all his life, preferring to let his work speak for him." Holmes smiled teasingly. "How different all that might be, had he a Watson constantly by his side."

"Holmes, one of these days I shall set aside my pen permanently, and when I do you will realise how much you relish being its primary subject matter and you will miss it."

"Promises, promises. As for the Elysians, there I regret to say my researches drew a blank. Nocturnal surveillance of Charfrome Old Place, however, may well add to the sum total of our knowledge. It will certainly be a useful first step, in advance of taking a more frontal approach."

The anticipation of a furtive expedition after dark set me on edge somewhat, but not so much that I failed to doze off within minutes of stretching out on my bed. When I awoke, the light outside the windows had grown hazy and mellow. It was past seven. I put on my boots and went downstairs, where I found Holmes at a table in the inn's small dining room. There was an empty plate before him and he was deep in conversation with the landlord.

"You let me sleep longer than planned," I said reprovingly.

"You looked as though you could do with it. Besides, I have not been idle in the interim. I have filled the time productively with Mr Scadden here." He gestured at our host. "He has told me a number of things about Charfrome Old Place and its inhabitants. Perhaps, sir, you would care to enlighten my friend too."

"Well, there bain't much as any of uz knows 'bout they as lives up at the Old Place," Scadden said. "Keep theirselves to theirselves, them does, an' uz bain't the types to go pokin' uz noses into others' affairs. But you hears 'em sometimes on nights when there be no wind an' sounds carry. Chantin' outdoors in zum unknown lingo. Holdin' torch-lit ceremonies o' zum kind. Wearin' robes and other zuch flummery." His eyes narrowed slyly. "There be rumours, too."

"What kind of rumours?"

"Nothin' specific, but there's zum as say them holds sacrifices, zur. Animal sacrifices."

I suppressed a shudder. "You can't be serious. Animal sacrifices? In England? In this day and age?"

"Several head o' sheep wuz stoled from a field not two combes over from the 'ouse. This were just last lambin' season. Bain't too difficult to put two an' two together." Scadden set his broad, homely features into a sagely grimace. "An' it don't stop at just animals, either."

"I'm not sure I follow."

"Wurz than animals."

"Worse? As in… *human* sacrifice?"

"I bain't be sayin' as them does, but I bain't be sayin' as them doesn't either. I grant you, it zounds like a parcel of ol' crams" – I took this phrase to mean *rubbish* – "but I knows a couple o' labourers from this 'ere village what works on the estate, casual-like, gardenin' an' mowin' an' coppicin' an' zuch. Them has told of visitors to the Old Place arrivin' an' then not bein' seen to leave. These folks come, month or two later there be a ceremony o' zum zort, an' dreckly after that no more sign of 'em. Now, it could o' course just be coincidence…"

Scadden let the sentence hang darkly in the air.

"Anyway, I reckon as you be gurt hungry, zur," he said.

I hesitantly acknowledged it.

"I can recommend the lettuce soup as a starter," Holmes said, "and the lamb crumble I had to follow is also very good."

"My wife be a dab hand at lamb crumble," said Scadden. "You'll never taste the like."

Soon I was tucking into my meal, and while Scadden was busy serving ale to a handful of locals in the bar, I said to Holmes, "Human sacrifice? Surely not. Surely that is just speculation. Tittle-tattle."

"Whatever the truth, it seems inarguable that Charfrome Old Place is a locus for unorthodox behaviour."

"The Elysians are some kind of secret society?"

"If even half of what Scadden has told us is true, I would go further and dub them a cult."

"You mean a religious sect? Like the Shakers and the Jumpers and that lot in the New Forest a few years back, what were they called?"

"The Girlingites."

"Yes. Them. The group who believed the Second Coming of Christ was imminent and lived communally in various camps and borrowed houses and did nothing but till the land and worship. They caused quite a stir for a while, before falling into disarray and dispersing."

"The Elysians may be of that ilk," said Holmes, "but the name itself hints at older, pre-Christian roots, does it not?"

"Still, just as the Girlingites accreted around a charismatic, visionary leader, might not the Elysians likewise have accreted around Sir Philip Buchanan? Could he be their equivalent of… what was the name of the woman, the Girlingites' leader? Anne Girling?"

"Close. Mary Anne Girling. And there's no telling if Sir Philip Buchanan is anything like her. Not yet. Moreover, these wild flights of fancy are wasteful of our time and mental energies. We should not let our imaginations run away with us. Hard facts are the only sound basis for any theory."

Scadden returned to collect my dishes. "Be that why you gents is gracin' these parts with your presence? Visitin' the Old Place?"

"No," said Holmes. "My companion and I are merely passing through. We are on a walking tour. Our main interest is churches, Pre-Reformation, with a fondness for the Norman above all else. But we also like to pick up titbits of local lore along the way, for our private journals. It is all grist to the mill."

"Well, I'd steer clear o' them folk up there all the same. That be my advice to you. Same advice as I gave to that young lass what wuz 'ere scarcely a week ago. 'Er wuz just passing through too, 'er said."

Holmes pricked up his ears, as did I, although both of us did our best to disguise it.

"A young lass?" my friend said airily.

"Ooh arr," said Scadden with a nod. "Fair-lookin' maid. Right boody, in fact, only don't go tellin' the missus I said so or I'd be knackered. Stayed 'ere just the one night and asked about Charfrome Old Place like you did. 'Er wuz gone on the morrow."

"Do you think she went there?" I said.

"To the Old Place? Can't see as why 'er would 'ave, not after I'd good as warned 'er not to. Women, mind – them be a law unto theirselves, bain't them? Tell 'em to do one thing, them'll do the opposite. Modern women especially, and that maid were as modern as them come. Now, gents, pudding? Mrs Scadden makes an apple cake that'll stick to your ribs like nothin' else."

CHAPTER EIGHT

CHARFROME OLD PLACE BY NIGHT

The stars were out in force that night, filling the sky in their thousands and accompanied by a waning but bright moon. Holmes and I left The Fatted Calf on the pretext of taking a tour about the village churchyard. Scadden bade us farewell, saying he would leave the side door unlocked in case we were not home by the time he and Mrs Scadden turned in. He was a trusting fellow and I felt guilty that we were to some degree abusing his provincial good nature, but then there were higher considerations. Try as I might, I could not get Scadden's talk of human sacrifice out of my head. It must be nonsense… but what if it was not?

Holmes had memorised the maps he had consulted at the Land Registry office, so getting from Waterton Parva to the Charfrome Old Place estate presented little difficulty. Past the church we entered thick woods, and we resorted to dark-lanterns to help us navigate. The susurration of the leaves around us was constant, the sound was punctuated with the rustlings and cries of nocturnal wildlife going about its business in the undergrowth. At one point we surprised a badger with our lights, and the beast greeted us with fangs bared and some deep fierce growls before turning and shambling away, evincing curmudgeonly disdain, as though we were not worthy of its time.

"Friend Brock has put us in our place," Holmes remarked. "By his leave we may proceed."

The woods terminated at a fence. Having straddled this, we extinguished the lanterns and ventured onward by starlight alone. A meadow of rough, hummocky grass gave way to mown lawn, and that was when I spied the first of several outbuildings we would come across during our journey. Perched on a hillock, it was a folly in the Grecian style, a circle of fluted columns supporting a domed cupola. Within I saw an item of marble statuary on a pedestal, something ancient and heroic, a naked male with an arm outstretched and a hip cocked, his modesty preserved by a fig leaf.

"We are on Buchanan's property, then," I said.

"Indubitably," came the reply. "And henceforth we must keep our voices low, Watson, and our movements stealthy. All said and done, we are trespassing, and who knows what lengths the Elysians will go to in order to preserve the sanctity of their realm."

I felt for the Webley in my pocket. The revolver's cold metal was comforting to the touch.

On we went, and shortly passed another folly. This one sat beside a small round pond and was a full-size replica of a Greek temple, complete with porticos and stylobates, architraves and cornices. Close by lay a third structure, built into the slope of a hillside – a theatre in the classical style with raked seating, a semicircular orchestra and a stage backed by a *skene*. It was smaller by some margin than the great theatres of antiquity, capable of accommodating an audience numbering in the dozens, no more than that; but it was still impressive and enchanting.

A winding path took us through a glade of aspens, between whose dappled trunks peeked statues of nymphs, satyrs, and an

Aphrodite in a decorous state of semi-disrobement. Further on we entered an olive grove at the heart of which stood a rather forbidding-looking Zeus. The patriarch of the Greek pantheon was posed with one hand aloft clutching a thunderbolt, as though braced to launch it at some unsuspecting mortal below. His brow was imperiously knotted, his feet widely spaced on the plinth beneath him, every muscle in his physique tensed. All of the statues we had seen so far were well-made, but the sculptor in this instance had executed his craft with singular skill. His Zeus was uncannily lifelike, down to the fine curls of the hair and beard. I had the unnerving sense that at any moment he might loose the thunderbolt at me for having had the temerity to intrude upon his repose.

We were not far past the Zeus when Holmes plucked at my sleeve, indicating I should halt as he just had. For a span of several seconds he canted his head, as though listening. His face was a mask of concentration.

"What is it?" I whispered.

"Perhaps nothing," he replied.

I did not like the sound of that "perhaps". It left room for the possibility of a *something*.

We proceeded at a snail's pace. When I was in Afghanistan a Sepoy in the Bengal Native Infantry, an expert at tracking tigers, taught me how to tread more or less soundlessly by placing down each foot toe first and rolling along the sole to the heel before picking it up. I employed the trick now, all the while casting wary glances about me. What I was looking for, I was not sure. Holmes seemed to suspect that we were not alone. If so, whoever or whatever was stalking us was keeping well concealed. I saw nothing but the undulating moonlit wonderland that was the grounds of Charfrome Old Place. Here was a towering elderly oak beneath the boughs of which a set of stone benches were arranged in concentric circles, as though for a symposium. Here, a narrow finger of manmade lake in whose placid waters tritons and naiads cavorted, their play watched over by Poseidon. There a Hermes in winged cap and matching sandals, clutching his *caduceus* and poised on tiptoe, frozen in the act of running some divine errand. How many tens of thousands of pounds had Buchanan spent? To realise such an elaborate vision must have cost more money, I estimated, than I would ever earn in a lifetime.

Now, ahead, Holmes and I caught our first glimpse of Charfrome Old Place, the house itself. It sat at the head of a horseshoe-shaped valley, in the lee of a ridge of hills, and was a sprawl of projecting casements, towering chimneys and cater-corner pitched roofs. There was so much of it, such a profusion of wings and annexes, that it was nigh impossible to take it all in, even at a distance. The core portion dated, if I had to guess, back to the sixteenth century, but successive owners had added to that over the years, extending what would have been an already grand edifice into something palatial.

Lights burned in several of the windows but not in enough of them to make the house look welcoming. The vast majority of it was dark, suggestive of untenanted rooms, lonely corridors, entire unvisited floors.

Holmes paused again, his head twitching from side to side. This posture of alertness made him look especially birdlike, an impression accentuated by the beaky aquilinity of his nose. I still could not tell if he was merely scanning the area for potential danger or had discerned an actual threat, a foe as yet unseen and unheard by me. As a result of my military service I had developed a fairly reliable intuition about such things. The country around Kabul and the Khyber and Michni passes were rife with lurking Ghazi snipers, and after a while one became attuned to their presence. Some instinct, a prickling of the nape hairs, told one to beware and take precautions. Holmes, however, had powers in that respect which put mine to shame. He had an almost preternatural gift for registering anomalies in his surroundings, as if he could read the very air currents and determine from them whether all was as it should be or not.

In short, if Holmes was perturbed, then I had reason to be too.

Abruptly he caught my elbow and tugged. We moved, quickly but surreptitiously, towards a small copse. Once amongst the shelter of the trees, we withdrew further into this refuge, padding along backwards so that, were anyone pursuing us, we stood a chance of spotting them. I wanted to ask Holmes how certain he was that we were under observation – that our footsteps were being dogged – but knew better than to break silence. Sherlock Holmes did nothing without justification.

The deeper we retreated into the copse, the thicker the canopy of leaves overhead grew, and the darker and danker the atmosphere became. The ground was spongy with moss underfoot. Soon I was straining my eyes in order to see. Holmes was a featureless profile beside me, like a cameo silhouette.

Then I felt a sudden stabbing pain in the small of my back. Startled, I let out an involuntary yelp. Something had prodded me, hard.

I turned to find a man behind me. The hand with which he had prodded me was still reaching for me, fingers stiffly extended. In his other hand he held a weapon, a spear of some sort. And at his side crouched a large dog, jaws agape in a fearsome snarl.

CHAPTER NINE

THE BELLY OF THE WHALE

Terror coursed through me. Every nerve ending in my body jangled. I groped for my pistol. I fumbled it out of my pocket. Cocking the hammer, I began backing away from the stranger and his hound. The moment he moved, I would fire. If he let slip that dog, I would kill it without hesitation or mercy.

The man remained stock-still. The dog likewise was motionless. *It must be perfectly trained*, I thought. It was not even quivering with anticipation or straining at the leash.

I butted up against a hard surface. At my back I felt rough, damp rock. I was cornered. If providence was kind I would pull the trigger before the beast got me.

"Watson..." Holmes hissed.

I barely heard him. My focus was on the man and his canine accomplice. Why was he so static? Why had he not even spoken? His immobility was unnatural. It was almost as though...

My whole body relaxed, like a bowstring slackening after the archer has chosen not to let the arrow fly. I heaved a sigh that was equal parts relief and embarrassment.

The stranger was, of course, a statue, another of the many that dotted the estate. In the pitch darkness of the copse I had mistaken him for a living creature, and what had felt like his hand prodding me was in fact me reversing onto it.

As for the dog, by dint of brushing aside some low-hanging fronds I discovered that it possessed not a single head but rather three; the branches had obscured two of them from view. It was, in other words, a representation of the famous three-headed sentinel of the underworld, Cerberus. That meant that the figure whom it accompanied must be the god Hades, Lord of the Dead. Now that I looked more closely I could see that his spear was in fact a kind of trident, albeit one tipped with a pair of prongs rather than a trio. From the recesses of my memory I dredged up the name for such a weapon, learned during Classics lessons at school: a bident. Hades was often depicted carrying one, his signature armament.

I had an urge to laugh and at the same time to berate myself for my foolishness. In the event, I simply sagged against the rocks. They were part of a large outcrop reaching some twenty feet in height, and just next to where I stood, I perceived an aperture in the sloping wall they formed, a jagged, arched fissure that was tall and broad enough to accommodate a man. It appeared to be the mouth of a cave. Was this supposed to be the entrance to the underworld? Was that why Hades and Cerberus were standing guard outside?

Holmes hissed my name again, bringing me back to my senses. He beckoned to me with a flurried wave of the hand. Pushing myself off the rocky wall, I moved to join him. Just as I did so, I saw two shapes detach themselves from the tree shadows on either side of him.

They were swift, those shapes, like black phantoms, and before I could utter a cry of alarm they converged upon Holmes, pouncing on him.

He reacted speedily, but alas not speedily enough. His

assailants – both large, bulky men – seized his arms and twisted them backwards with vicious force. Holmes struggled, to no avail. He aimed a sideways kick at the fellow to his right, and his instep connected with the man's shin, but he was off-balance and delivered only a glancing blow, not the crippling strike he might have hoped for. The man grunted in pain but did not let go.

In riposte, his colleague drove a foot into the back of Holmes's legs, and my companion collapsed heavily to his knees. His assailants wrenched his arms higher behind him, forcing his head and trunk forward at a more acute angle. Holmes continued to writhe, but now that he was on the ground he had even less leverage against them than before. Nor could he bring his *baritsu* skills to bear on the situation, since the martial art required the free use of all four limbs to be effective.

A third assailant emerged into view, this one clutching a lumpy object of some sort. The subduing of Holmes had taken no more than five seconds, during which time all I could do was stare, dumbfounded. As the third man brandished whatever was in his hand above Holmes's head, however, I collected my wits and galvanised myself. I still had my Webley and it was primed to fire. I raised it, calling out, "You there! Stop this instant or I will shoot!"

I was principally addressing the man with the lumpy object, which I took to be a cudgel or cosh. He was undeterred by my challenge, however. The thing in his hand unfurled, showing itself to be a piece of fabric, roughly rectangular.

"I mean it," I said. "This is your last chance. Move away from my friend – now – or one of you gets a bullet, and I do not much care which one it is."

The man just laughed, as though he knew something I did not. Sure enough, the very next instant I felt something small but hard pressing into my temple, creating a distinct circular impression. I recognised it as the end of a pistol barrel.

"*Who* is getting a bullet?" said a guttural voice right by my ear, mockingly. "I think it may not be one of us after all."

I froze. The gun ground more insistently into the side of my skull.

"In case you don't understand," said the man, "that means hand over the barker. Unless you want your grey stuff all over the ground..."

I thought about spinning round and firing at him, but sensed that he would be quicker on the draw than I. All I could do was let go of my revolver with all but my forefinger and hold it up by the trigger guard. A hand retrieved it from me. Then further hands seized hold of my person. I put up some resistance. My captors, though, outnumbered me, and each was sizeable and remarkably strong. The game of rugby had made me tough, army training tougher still, but even so, in no time I was wrestled to the ground and rendered helpless, with someone's knee in the small of my back.

I heard a rustle of cloth, and a small hessian sack was slipped over my head. Pure blackness enveloped me. My arms were yanked behind my back and a length of cord was lashed around my wrists, fastening them together. Thus securely bound and incapacitated, I was hoisted to my feet.

"Both of them done up good and proper, bluejacket fashion?" said the same guttural voice as before. "All right. Excellent work, lads. Let's go. Hop to it. On the double."

A hand shoved me roughly between the shoulderblades and I staggered. Another hand took my elbow, and its owner, maintaining a vicelike grip, steered me forwards.

So began a lengthy, stumbling march. I trudged along, effectively blind, with the hessian sack pressing against my face, half suffocating me. The smell of the material was pungent, reminiscent of a farmyard. To add to my woes, my shoulder throbbed horribly. My old war wound had flared up, exacerbated by the maltreatment it had just received. The worst I could usually expect from it was a dull rheumatic ache on cold damp days, but now I was experiencing a gruelling agony, as though a drill were boring into my scapula.

"Holmes?" I said at one point, desiring both confirmation that he was still with me and reassurance that he was well.

"Belt up, you!" said the same gruff voice as before. "No talking."

Several times I missed my footing and nearly fell. The hand clamped to my elbow then served as support as well as guide, keeping me perpendicular. It was confoundedly unpleasant, not to mention unmanning, to be forced to walk without being able to see where I was going. The terrain was anything but even, its inclines and declines hard to predict, and we were moving at a brisk lick.

After twenty minutes of this I was thoroughly disorientated and beginning to succumb to despair. I could hardly bear to go another step.

At that moment came a small reprieve. The sound of our footfalls changed, as did the texture of the ground. We were now crunching across gravel, a level pathway of some sort. Echoes suggested we were adjacent to a large structure. Everything indicated that we were approaching the house.

Sure enough, I heard a door open. Another hand attached itself to me, and I was manhandled through the doorway and into an interior space. It was cool and airy. Our footfalls became shuffling and resonant. I registered bare floorboard beneath my soles.

We crossed what I could only assume to be a hall and passed along a creaking corridor. Another door opened.

"Staircase down," said the only one of our captors to have spoken so far. "Mind your step. And your heads."

I descended, half crouching, sidelong, with a man fore and

aft. At the bottom I was pushed to a corner and made to sit on the floor. My wrists were untied but I did not have a chance to massage them or stretch my arms, because almost immediately they were drawn in front of me and retied. This time the cord was wound around my ankles as well, for good measure. I was left bent double, trussed like a Christmas goose.

A brief bout of further activity followed, ending with the clatter of the door closing and a key turning in a lock.

All was quiet.

I took stock. Without doubt I was in a cellar. Even through the sack I could smell mustiness, and a clammy subterranean chill permeated my clothing, most of it radiating from the floor, which felt to be bare earth.

"Holmes?" I ventured in a low tone.

"Here, old fellow."

"Oh, thank goodness. I feared I was alone. How are you faring?"

"As well as can be expected. You?"

"My shoulder hurts like the devil and I can hardly breathe through this damned sack, but all things considered I could be worse. We are inside the house, I take it."

"One must presume so."

"What do you think our captors have in mind for us?"

"I cannot say. The fact that we were taken prisoner and have not been abused too badly, however, bodes well. No punishment has been meted out."

"Not yet," I said. "Perhaps our fate is being decided right now."

"I should not be surprised if it was. As long as we are alive, though, we have hope."

His bravado did little to dispel my gloom. "This is all my fault," I said.

"How do you arrive at that conclusion?"

"When I backed into that statue of Hades, I let out a cry. The noise must have told them where we were."

"They had already narrowed down our position by then. It was only a matter of time before they sprang their ambush. All you did was hasten the inevitable. No, if anyone is to blame for this mess, Watson, it is I. I am the one who took us blundering onto the estate."

"It was not 'blundering'. We were cautious."

"Not cautious enough."

"You were not to know the place would be so well guarded."

"That certainly is true. I anticipated that someone might patrol the grounds after dark, but I thought that it would be a single individual at most, a gamekeeper or a night watchman, not half a dozen former servicemen."

"Former servicemen?"

"Can you not tell? Dear me! The way they closed in on us from several quarters at once, herding us – the organisation of it, the precision – they could not be anything else. These are men well accustomed to working as a unit. Did you not notice, too, how they automatically fell into step while escorting us here?"

"Your presence of mind, under duress, is a marvel. I must confess I was paying more attention to staying upright than to them."

"It is an unconscious habit they will have picked up from hours of drill practice. Nor did any of them once question the authority of the fellow giving the orders – the one who used that distinctly military phrase 'on the double' and also 'bluejacket', army slang for a sailor. There was no debate, no demur. He told them what to do, with officer-class officiousness, and they complied. Respect for the chain of command is ingrained in them, as natural to them as breathing."

"It seems strange – excessive, even – for Buchanan to hire armed soldiers to protect his property."

"I said servicemen, not soldiers. At least one of them used to be in the navy, judging by the knots I am currently exploring with my fingertips. I have identified a bowline, and the other is, I think, a double overhand. They are unmistakably the handiwork of a sailor – our 'bluejacket' – and very well tied they are too. Even if my range of manual movement were not constrained I would find them hard to unpick. As things stand, they are utterly beyond me."

I growled with frustration. "Then we cannot escape?"

"I am afraid not. We are stuck. We are trapped, like two Jonahs, in the belly of the whale."

"How damnable."

"Chin up, Watson. This may still work out to our advantage."

"I do not see how. If only I had managed to get off a shot…"

"It would not have changed a thing. We would have been overpowered regardless, and I suspect we would have suffered a brutal reprisal from our subjugators had you wounded one of their number – a lethal reprisal had you killed him. You being disarmed before you could cause harm was probably a saving grace. We are intact and retain the full use of our wits. What we must do now is exercise patience. Sooner or later someone will return for us, whereupon we shall, God willing, get the chance to turn the tables."

It was undeniably an attractive proposition, the thought that we might yet be able to gain the upper hand and snatch victory from the jaws of defeat; it also seemed highly implausible.

"You are not just saying that to keep my spirits up, are you?" I said.

"Perish the thought. I would prefer it, though, if you did not slip into despondency. I need my Watson in full fighting fettle, ready to leap into the fray should the necessity arise."

I did my utmost to stay positive, but as the night wore on it became harder and harder. I estimate that we were in that cellar for the best part of seven hours, all told, and every minute of those hours ticked by with glacial slowness. As if my shoulder were not torment enough, I was afflicted by a series of muscle cramps owing to the awkward hunched position I was forced to adopt. First my right calf seized up, then my lower lumbar region. I was able to ease the discomfort in both instances through counter-flexion, but not so when the adductors in my thighs went into spasm simultaneously. Straightening my legs was impossible. All I could do was grit my teeth and endure the pain until eventually it subsided of its own accord.

Meanwhile a train of thought repeatedly careered through my brain. People came to Charfrome Old Place and were never seen again, so Scadden had said. If that were true, were Holmes and I about to become the latest additions to the tally of the disappeared? Former servicemen would surely have no qualms about executing us and discreetly disposing of our bodies. Someone only had to give the word, and Sherlock Holmes and Dr John Watson would be summarily eliminated, gone without a trace.

It was, for me, the proverbial dark night of the soul. I knew then how the condemned prisoner must feel as he awaits his appointment with the scaffold or the guillotine. Unlike him, though, I was not facing the just penalty for a heinous crime. Rather, I was due to be the victim of such a crime. I was tempted several times to express my apprehensions aloud, but refrained, not wishing to appear lacking in courage. I took what crumb of comfort I could from Holmes's silent composure. If he could remain stoic in these circumstances, then so could I.

By the time our captors came back for us, I was fully convinced that all was lost. A marrow-deep resignation had set in. I was cold, tired, plagued by pain, abjectly miserable. The likelihood that Holmes and I might reverse our fortunes seemed so remote as to be invisible.

The hessian sack was whipped from my head. I sucked in

my first unimpeded breath in what felt like an age. I blinked, dazzled by the dim light that filtered down into the cellar from the doorway at the top of the stairs. Opposite me, Holmes likewise had just been relieved of his makeshift hood. It was a pleasure to see his face again – those gaunt, ascetic features I knew so well. He flashed me a smile, which, though grim and sardonic, nevertheless kindled a tiny ember of courage in the ashes of my heart. *If I were to die today*, I thought, *at least I would not die alone.* By my side would be the best and the wisest man whom I have ever known. It was some solace.

With us now in the cellar were two men. One was burly and powerfully built, with luxuriant moustaches and a military bearing. A jagged scar traversed the right side of his face, extending from upper cheek to jawline. It had healed in such a way that it permanently pulled down the outer corner of his eye, so that he seemed constantly to be leering in a skewed, somewhat sinister fashion.

This man, in his mid-thirties, was the younger of the two. The other was perhaps three decades his senior and had an altogether more polished, patrician air. His grey hair was receding at the front, sweeping back from a pronounced widow's peak, and a pair of bloodshot but piercingly intelligent eyes looked out from beneath his rounded promontory of a forehead, while a straight, severe nose hung over lips that were thin and curiously bluish, almost to the point of being purple. He was exceptionally tall, several inches over six feet, and slender with it. For someone of his advanced years he appeared to be in excellent physical condition, well-preserved, with few wrinkles and nary a trace of loose skin around the jowls. He was dressed stylishly, too. His suit looked to be Savile Row's finest, cut from an expensive worsted cloth and tailored immaculately. His tie was glossy silk. His tiepin and cufflinks twinkled with inset diamonds.

"Good grief, Hart," said the elder man in refined, mellifluous tones. "Do you realise who we have here?"

"Intruders, sir," said the other. I recognised the voice instantly. It was he, this Hart, who had overseen our waylaying and detention last night. "Caught them, as I told you, sauntering through the grounds, casual as you please, like they owned the place. Reckon they're journalists, by the looks of them."

"Representatives of the yellow press were bound to become interested in our little society sooner or later, scenting a juicy story. These are not they, however. Tell me, do you take *The Strand*?"

"Can't say as I do."

"Well, if you did, you might recognise this distinguished-looking chap here." The well-dressed man pointed at Holmes. "Sidney Paget presents a good likeness of him in his illustrations. And his comrade over there, I'll wager, is the author of the narratives."

"I'm not sure I'm any the wiser, sir."

"Hart, you and your fellow Hoplites have incarcerated none other than Sherlock Holmes, the famous consulting detective, and his bosom friend Dr John Watson." The tall man's expression turned severe. "And I would be much obliged if you would release them immediately, without delay."

CHAPTER TEN

THE LOCAL ECCENTRICS

Holmes and I sat together alone at a large mahogany dining table in a room lit by the slanting rays of the morning sun. On a sideboard nearby was a spread of hard-boiled eggs, barley porridge, raisins, figs, honey, thick-sliced bread and some kind of pancake, of which we were taking advantage, I with alacrity, Holmes only somewhat more circumspectly.

It was a remarkable turnabout. A mere thirty minutes earlier I had been at an absolute nadir, convinced that death was imminent. Now I was enjoying a hearty breakfast and feeling as revived as Lazarus. My shoulder continued to hurt and my wrists were chafed from the cords that had bound them. Sensation was only just returning to feet and hands rendered numb by constricted circulation. But these seemed minor afflictions under the present circumstances. Never had food tasted quite so delicious or the touch of sunlight been so appreciated.

Holmes, for his part, was taking it all in his stride. Glancing across the table at me, he said, "Journalists, eh? I have been insulted before, but that is a new low."

"It is easy to make jokes now, Holmes, but I for one thought that we were goners. Don't tell me it did not once cross your mind that we were destined for a bad end."

"Frankly, no. I anticipated that we would be forcibly evicted come the morning, perhaps sent on our way with a clip round the ear and a boot from behind, but I did not foresee any worse than that. What would have been gained by killing us?"

"Our silence? Dead men tell no tales, after all."

"The living tell none either, if they have not seen anything untoward. All we were guilty of, as far as Hart and his men were concerned, was straying onto Buchanan's land. To kill us for that seems hardly warranted. Besides, any execution, if it were going to occur, would have been carried out under cover of darkness, during the small hours. I was already certain that we were going to survive, and the longer we were left in the cellar, the greater the certainty became."

"You never had even a twinge of doubt?"

"Not one. How much more inconvenient is it to kill two people and cover up the deaths, than it is to give them a bit of a thrashing and toss them out on their ear. These Elysians 'keep theirselves to theirselves', remember." Ever the amateur thespian, Holmes's mimicry of landlord Scadden's West Country inflection was spot-on. "They would not want the police to come sniffing round on the trail of two absent Londoners last seen in the neighbouring village, would they?"

"But Scadden said people go missing here. And what about Hannah Woolfson? Where is she? And, for that matter, Sophia Tompkins?"

"Scadden's claims seem predicated on the flimsiest of evidence. Casual garden labourers are far from credible witnesses. As for the two young women, we still do not have irrefutable proof that either has even been on the premises. I fear you let your imagination run away with you last night, Watson. Is it a propensity of authors, I wonder, always to neglect logic and construe the most catastrophic outcome possible?"

I bristled at the jibe, but would have taken greater affront had I not been distracted by my stomach, which was demanding a second helping of porridge.

As I deposited several liberal dollops from the tureen into my bowl and slathered it with honey, the door opened and in came the tall, refined man.

"I trust you have been well catered for, gentlemen," said he. His manner was both gracious and rueful. "I really cannot apologise enough for the rough handling you have received. Please allow me to introduce myself formally. I am, as you must already have deduced, Sir Philip Buchanan, and not only am I your host but I hope to become your friend, if you can see your way to forgiving this upsetting and regrettable incident. I come from having just delivered a stern dressing-down to my employee Sergeant-Major Malachi Hart. He and his subordinates were overzealous in the extreme, and I would be forever in your debt if were you willing, both of you, to let bygones be bygones."

He extended a hand to each of us in turn, and Holmes and I shook it, as if sealing a compact.

"There is nothing worse," Sir Philip Buchanan continued, "than a grievous misunderstanding – unless it involves one of the prodigies of our era. Then it is a tragedy. You may infer from that, Mr Holmes, that I am an admirer of yours. In fact, I follow your adventures avidly. Every edition of *The Strand* that boasts your name on the front cover, I snap up with an eager hand. And much of that eagerness is down to you, Dr Watson. I devour every word you write, and often I will read your stories twice through in succession, the first time to experience the unravelling of the mystery, the second to see how cunningly you have embedded the clues and, where necessary, hoodwinked the reader. In you, Mr Holmes has found not only a staunch friend but a biographer capable of doing his deeds literary justice."

"Holmes might disagree with you on that last point," I said, "but for myself, Sir Philip, I thank you. Your compliments honour me."

"It is merely a statement of the truth," said Buchanan. "The moment Hart revealed your faces, I felt sick with shame. Sick, I tell you. 'What have I done?' I said to myself. Of course I take full personal responsibility for what befell you. Hart and company had a job to do, they were following instructions, but that is no excuse."

"You called them Hoplites, these men," said Holmes.

"After the heavily armed and armoured infantrymen of Ancient Greece. They are Charfrome's private paladins."

"Indeed. And your instructions are for them to apprehend trespassers and treat them like prisoners of war?"

Buchanan sighed. "Overzealous, as I said. But certainly they are under orders to detain anyone who should not be on my property and present them to me at the earliest convenience. You two, as it happens, are the first to have breached our boundary since I hired Hart last spring and invited him to recruit a small complement of men from a similar background to serve under him. He had no idea what the appropriate etiquette was. I have set him straight. He and his men behaved as their military instincts decreed. They will not be quite so heavy-handed from henceforth."

"For the sake of future interlopers, I am glad to hear it."

"You may be wondering why I have engaged someone like Malachi Hart, previously of the Somerset Light Infantry, to supervise my domestic security."

"It did cross my mind."

"The reason, Mr Holmes, is that I genuinely do foresee the gentlemen of the press turning their jaundiced eye upon us. It is only a matter of time. We try to conduct our affairs discreetly here, but journalists have a habit of making other people's business their business and thence the business of the general public. I would wish to prevent that occurring, to which end I have taken the precaution of installing vigorous defensive measures: our Hoplites. It is not only my privacy I am safeguarding but that of various prominent guests who are adherents to my philosophy."

"Interesting," said Holmes. "And by 'philosophy'—"

Buchanan raised a finger to forestall him. "Before you launch the inevitable salvo of questions – and I will satisfy any and all enquiries you have, I assure you – might I ask you something?"

"Be my guest."

"Why *were* you and Dr Watson here, on my land, at night?"

I looked at my friend, curious to know how he would play his cards.

"A reasonable enough request, I think you would agree," said Buchanan.

"Quite, quite," said Holmes. "I could aver that it was pure error. We lost our way."

"And I would believe that assertion," said Buchanan genially, "were anyone but Sherlock Holmes making it."

Holmes laughed. "The truth is that we are conducting an investigation."

"Of course you are."

"An investigation that has led us to this remote rural back-water."

"To my doorstep, indeed."

"There or thereabouts," said Holmes. "I cannot, in the name of the same discretion that you yourself so prize, Sir Philip, furnish any more detail than that."

"I understand. You have a duty of care toward your client. Confidentiality is paramount."

"A trail of clues has taken me to Waterton Parva, that much I can reveal, and your estate borders the village."

"I see. The implication being that if something untoward happens in Waterton Parva, somehow the people up at Charfrome Old Place must be behind it." A pained and weary expression contorted Buchanan's face. "Yes, that is typical. We are the local eccentrics. We have, to outward appearances, a lifestyle that would seem nonconformist, even outlandish. Naturally, then, accusing fingers will point at us whenever there is a misdeed in the area. Back in March, for example, a number of sheep were taken from a farm not far from here."

I recalled Scadden telling us about the sheep that were "stoled".

"Police came from Dorchester to interrogate us," Buchanan continued. "A constable sat where you are, Mr Holmes, in that very chair, and queried whether I might be behind the theft. Me!" he snorted. "As if, should I have a hankering for mutton stew, I would steal a sheep, rather than order meat from the butcher. As if a man of obvious substance like myself would resort to petty larceny. It was this incident that prompted me to seek out someone to act as my strong right arm, and in Sergeant-Major Hart I found him."

"If you were not the culprit, then who?" said Holmes.

"Gypsies. They were camped, at the time, on common land just to the north. I politely suggested the constable might train his sights on them, and sure enough fresh sheep carcasses were found in their possession. The gypsies maintained that they had bought them fair and square, and unfortunately there was nothing to prove they had not. They had sheared off the fleeces and disposed of them, so that the farmer's dye mark on the wool, which would have identified the flock the sheep belonged to, was nowhere to be found."

"You fell under suspicion first, before gypsies?"

"Seems inconceivable, does it not? But such is the prejudice towards us around these parts. Just for what we are, there is an ever-present underlying animosity."

"And what are you?" said Holmes. "I have heard the word Elysians used in connection with Charfrome Old Place. You talk of 'adherents' and a 'philosophy'. Watson and I last night saw statues and follies betokening a fascination with all things Ancient Greek. The picture I am beginning to form is of some sort of pagan cult. Would I be correct in that surmise?"

Buchanan offered a congratulatory nod. "You would, in essence. And yet I like to think that we are so much more. We Elysians, although we derive our inspiration and iconography from the past, are the future of this nation!"

CHAPTER ELEVEN

THE ELYSIANS IN THEIR NATURAL HABITAT

"Let me expound on that remark," said Sir Philip Buchanan, a lively look brightening those eyes of his with their capillary-webbed whites.

"I would be delighted if you would," said Holmes.

"Better still, let me *show* you. Do you have time?"

"Our current investigation is a pressing matter, but I am sure we can spare an hour or so. Watson? Do you think you can tear yourself away from your repast long enough?"

I gulped down a last mouthful of honeyed porridge. "Ready."

Holmes and I followed Buchanan out into the corridor and thence through the maze of the house to one of its newer wings. There, our guide ushered us into a bright, airy room in which sat a half-dozen men and women on benches in rows. Immediately I was put in mind of a classroom, save that the pupils here were adults not children. They were listening attentively to a man at the front who was addressing them in a foreign language. He, by his appearance, reinforced the impression that a lesson was being taught, for he had a distinctly schoolmasterly air, down to the way one hand clasped the lapel of his tweed jacket while he spoke and the other executed demonstrative flourishes. He also had slightly wild hair and a pair of pendulous, epicene lips.

He broke off mid-flow as we entered. As one, the members of his audience turned to look at us. A signal from Buchanan indicated that our presence should be ignored and everything should continue as before.

The schoolmasterly man resumed his oration. He was reciting, I swiftly determined, a piece of poetry. The lines had a rhythmic, almost singsong quality, reliant for their effect as much on the dance of syllables as the sense of the words. The language itself, I knew beyond a shadow of a doubt, was Ancient Greek. Along with every other schoolboy in the land I had studied it as part of my education. I even recognised a few of the words and phrases the fellow uttered, although I could not for the life of me have translated the sum of them into cogent English. It had been a good quarter of a century since I had last had any proficiency in the tongue, and anyway Greek had never been my scholastic forte. I can still recall the elation I felt immediately after sitting my Senior Examination in the subject, when I was able to throw away the relevant books and primers, safe in the knowledge that I would never need to consult them again.

Buchanan, inviting us to withdraw, closed the door softly behind him. "Dr Archibald Pentecost," he said, "our semi-resident Hellenist. An expert on Aeschylus and Euripides, and at one time the Head of Classics at Eton. Retired from teaching full-time now, but he visits Charfrome on a regular basis to lecture, tutor, and give declamations."

"That was *The Odyssey*, was it not?" said Holmes. "Specifically, the blinding of Polyphemus the Cyclops."

"Was it? Ha! Well spotted, sir. My own Ancient Greek is, sad to say, somewhat deficient. I am more familiar with the culture than the language. Dr Pentecost is the man to go to for the latter. It's why I employ him. As a matter of fact, he knows the entire *Odyssey* by heart, all twenty-four books of it. He can reel off any passage you care to name from the poem, word-perfect. The same goes for *The Iliad*. Quite some feat."

"One rivalled only by Homer, who was himself an exponent of the oral tradition – not to mention as blind as Polyphemus ended up being. The island of the Cyclopes is, I must say, a section of *The Odyssey* that has always made me uncomfortable. Odysseus tricks Polyphemus into believing that his name is Nobody. Then, when he and his crew put out the giant's single eye with a burning stake, Polyphemus cries out to his fellow Cyclopes for help: '*O philoi, Outis me kteinei dolo oude biephin*' – 'My friends, Nobody has killed me by guile and not by force'. That is the line I recognised, which enabled me to identify the passage. I recall it from my school days. The other Cyclopes, none of them being great geniuses, duly ignore Polyphemus's plaint. If nobody has killed him, he must be alive and well, must he not?"

"They turn a blind eye, one might say," I offered.

Both Holmes and Buchanan laughed.

"Well done, Watson," said my friend. "Your pawky sense of humour comes to the fore. Yes, Odysseus utilises an almost criminal cunning as he maims Polyphemus, and one's sympathies are therefore apt to lie with the latter."

"Even though he is an anthropophagous monster?" said Buchanan.

"That is simply his nature. Odysseus embodies a worse kind of nature – human nature, which elevates deceit and cruelty to an art form and considers those attributes praiseworthy."

"How interesting. The great detective feels antipathy towards the hero and sides with the villain."

"In this one instance, perhaps I do, finding Odysseus only

nominally the hero and maybe rather the true villain of the piece. There must have been other ways he could have effected escape from Polyphemus's cave without gleefully inflicting such suffering on the poor, dumb creature and consigning him to permanent darkness. The man who masterminded the sacking of Troy, he whom Homer garlands with epithets such as 'resourceful' and 'wise', exhibits a surprisingly low, vindictive streak."

"An unusual reading of the text," said Buchanan. "But it demonstrates how Homer's works invite all manner of interpretation. The entire Ancient Greek literary canon, for that matter, is an inexhaustible wellspring of cerebral and spiritual nourishment, ever open to reappraisal and fresh analysis. From the never-ending vendettas of the *Oresteia* to the sophisticated satire of Aristophanes's comedies, from the logical intricacies of Plato's dialogues to the dense, sweeping histories of Herodotus, there is always something new to discover in their pages. A culture that flowered two and a half millennia ago continues to have relevance today. By comparison, our contemporary world…"

He trailed off, shaking his head self-mockingly.

"Hark at me. I sound like a priest sermonising from the pulpit. No, more like one of those cranks at Speakers' Corner, haranguing passers-by in their monomaniacal way about vegetarianism or electropathy or what-have-you."

"I assure you, Sir Philip, you do not."

"You are kind, Mr Holmes. I am a passionate man, that I will admit, and sometimes my passion gets the better of me. To continue our tour…"

He led us to another room, which he told us had formerly functioned as a ballroom. Music issued from within, repetitive and rhythmic. We entered to find a quintet perched on a dais. They were plucking, blowing and tapping intently on a range of instruments, none of which belonged in a conventional orchestra.

There was a kind of zither, a box-like guitar and a double-stemmed oboe, alongside a tambourine and a set of pan pipes. A conductor kept time with his baton, eyes dreamily half-closed.

The sound this ensemble created together was strange to my ears, full of quarter-tones and wavering dissonances. The tune's cadences went in unexpected directions, following wayward melodic paths, yet were lilting and plangent for all that.

To the accompaniment of the music, a troupe of dancers circled in stately unison. Their steps had something of the gavotte about them, but their arms described extravagant undulations in the air and they made occasional sudden leaps and prances, interspersing these with pirouettes and curtsies. Each wore a long flowing tunic and laurel wreaths crowned every head. A husky-voiced woman, clearly some sort of *maîtresse de ballet*, stood at the side, offering snippets of advice or instruction.

The performance grew faster and wilder, the music gathering tempo and volume, the dancers swaying more and more frenetically. Everyone involved – musician, dancer and mentor alike – was lost in concentration. Lips were pursed. Perspiration glistened on furrowed brows.

As we withdrew from the room, Buchanan said, "At our previous port of call you saw people honouring Calliope, the muse of epic poetry. Now you have seen the same honour being paid to Euterpe and Terpsichore, muses of music and dance respectively. The instruments are reproductions I commissioned from Signor Raffaela Fiorini, the distinguished Bolognese violinmaker, based upon originals kept in the Victoria and Albert Museum's collection. You will have no doubt identified a lyre, a *kithara* and an *aulos* – the last being that woodwind item whose droning skirl is somewhat reminiscent of the bagpipes. The dance is what was known as a *choreia*, while the music is derived from notation recorded in fragments of scores unearthed by archaeologists.

Usually it is accompanied by singing, but at present the dancers are merely learning the movements. Song will be added later."

"You strive for authenticity, then," said Holmes.

"Quite so. We pride ourselves on that. The Elysian way is to cleave with all possible closeness to the customs of the lost civilisation we so admire. We even eat as the Hellenes used to. Your breakfast bears that out. Our diet revolves around fish, olives, goat's cheese and, when in season, figs. The ingredients are not always easy to come by, but I have various contacts in southern Europe from whom I can order supplies. Moreover, our chef Mr Labropoulos hails from Greece itself and has become well-versed in the culinary practices of his long-ago countrymen." Buchanan lowered his voice confidentially. "Between you and me, he is also regrettably hot-tempered, in common with many of a Mediterranean disposition. And you should hear him moan about the English weather!"

Chuckling, he led us onward.

"Speaking of which," he said, "next on the itinerary is the gymnasium. As I am sure you both know, the Ancient Greeks exercised outdoors, in open-air arenas. Our chilly, rain-prone climate, a far cry from the Mediterranean, hinders us from replicating that experience. Hence our gymnasium is indoors. We do not disport ourselves naked, either, as the Greeks did. Modern decorum does not permit it."

"One can take authenticity only so far," Holmes observed dryly.

A pair of double doors opened onto a huge, sunlight-drenched conservatory that Buchanan said was purpose-built, his sole contribution to the house's rambling layout, designed to his specifications. Here, men and women were engaged in sporting pursuits. Some wrestled in a sand-covered ring, some ran up and down a short track, and others feinted and thrust with wooden swords. The dominant sounds were the patter of bare feet and grunts of effort, and now and then a barked comment from a couple of athletic-looking instructors.

My eye was drawn to a pair of young women who were taking it in turns to throw a small ball at a target on the floor. If the ball missed, the thrower had to give the other a piggyback when retrieving it. To make the task that much more difficult to accomplish, the thrower's eyes were covered by the hands of the girl on her back, who steered her by giving verbal instructions.

"*Ephedrismos*," Buchanan said, seeing where my attention had alighted. "A popular pastime amongst Hellenic youth, depicted in many a terracotta figurine and on many a painted vase. It has value both as physical culture and to reinforce fraternity between the participants – or, as the case may be, sorority."

My focus remained on the two young women, even as Buchanan's gaze roved across the rest of the room. They giggled as they sported together, presenting a very pleasing image of femininity. One of them in particular was as handsome a lass as I had ever laid eyes on. Her face was bewitchingly fetching, the more so for being animated and enlivened from her exertions.

I felt I shared a firmer connection with her, though, than merely being drawn by her looks. She was not just attractive. She was *familiar*.

Then it struck me.

Of course I knew this girl.

I was looking at Hannah Woolfson.

CHAPTER TWELVE

MISS SHIRLEY HOLBROOK

I turned to Sherlock Holmes. He, to judge by the look in his keen grey eyes, had spotted Hannah Woolfson too. I nodded in her direction, as if to ask whether or not we should accost her. He responded with the tiniest of head shakes. I narrowed my eyes enquiringly, but then gave a sign of assent. Whenever I was uncertain how to act during the pursuit of an investigation, I invariably conceded to Holmes and took his lead. Only a fool would do otherwise.

Oblivious to this brief, mute interchange between us, Buchanan had begun expatiating once more on the Elysian philosophy. "The Greeks idolised the perfect bodily specimen, as is amply borne out by their statuary, ceramics and friezes. They founded the Olympic Games to celebrate sporting and martial prowess in all its forms. At Charfrome, likewise, physical culture is an intrinsic component of our routine. Everyone is expected to participate in exercise for at least one hour every day. The schedule operates on a rotational basis. The people you saw listening to a rendition of *The Odyssey* will decamp to this room straight afterwards, and the musicians and dancers will follow in their turn."

"The curriculum seems broad," said Holmes.

"It has many facets," our host concurred. "But that is necessary when you are shaping bodies and minds for the betterment of all."

"The betterment of all? So Elysianism, if I may use that coinage, is not simply about improving oneself?"

"It is, it is. But it has wider ramifications too. Creating individuals who are healthy in every respect leads to the creation of a healthier society as a whole. Correct me if I am wrong, Dr Watson, but disease may occur in the human body as a result of infection by micro-organisms. Is that not so?"

"I have read the German microbiologist Koch's writings on the subject," I said. "His findings support observations made in the past by Moreau de Maupertuis and Pasteur, and would appear to disprove the miasma theory of disease transmission once and for all."

"Something in the body is able to fight these invading micro-organisms and destroy them, something at the cellular level."

"Yes, that is the consensus of opinion."

"And by the same process some people may recover from life-threatening infections. Thucydides, no less, when writing about the Plague of Athens, records that the Athenians who contracted the disease during its first outbreak in 430 BC but did not die of it were immune when it flared up again in 429 and 427. Thanks to their initial exposure, something was propagated inside them, a resistance, which strengthened them against the epidemic's subsequent ravages. The reason I am using this medical metaphor is that I, in a not dissimilar way, am strengthening the British people. Those who undergo our regime – those who embrace Elysianism, to use your word, Mr Holmes – emerge fitter, wiser, signally enhanced both in mind and body. They then take their improved selves out into the world and proceed to contribute to the advancement of country and empire. By their example they raise the levels of aspiration and ambition in the people around them. They boost our nation's immunity to harm from within and without. The corporate entity that is Great Britain benefits as a whole from their presence."

"All through a period of deep immersion in Ancient Greece," said Holmes.

"I detect a note of mild scepticism. Greece was one of the greatest civilisations ever to have existed, Mr Holmes, if not *the* greatest. It lasted nearly a thousand years, beginning with the decline of the Mycenaeans in the eighth century BC and ending with the conquest by the Romans after the battle of Corinth in 146 BC. It encompassed most of what was then the known world, from central Asia to the westernmost tip of the Mediterranean Basin. It gave birth to art, democracy, architecture, science, medicine – those things we esteem so highly today. It balanced conquest and military might with trade and commerce. It understood the importance of naval power and the rule of law. Its nearest modern equivalent is to be found here in these wind-swept isles of ours. Britain is the latter-day Greece, and the one could do well by emulating the other."

"Really? But we are already a prosperous and thriving nation on our own terms. Our empire spans the globe. 'The sun never sets...' et cetera."

"True, but how much more prosperous and thriving might we be with an injection of Hellenistic influence into our bloodstream? How much better equipped to withstand the shocks and storms that the future undoubtedly holds? How much less likely to lapse into decline, decadence and degeneracy, the fate of so many other great civilisations in the past?"

"I daresay it cannot hurt our chances." Holmes shrugged his shoulders. "You are a visionary, Sir Philip, clearly, and I applaud you for it. But it is not axiomatic that one man's vision, however uplifting, can be imparted to others."

"You question how successful I am in inculcating Elysianism in its adherents? Perhaps you would like to find out for yourself. You are welcome to talk to anyone here and canvass their views."

"You have beaten me to the punch. I was about to propose that very thing."

"What about the young lady over there whom your colleague seems unable to tear his eyes from?"

I started. Had I been that obvious? Evidently I had.

"She has only recently joined our ranks," Buchanan continued, "but already she is proving to be the epitome of the Elysian ideal." He clicked his fingers and beckoned to Hannah Woolfson. "Miss Holbrook? May we beg a moment of your time?"

Miss Holbrook? I was momentarily flustered by the unfamiliar surname and wondered whether I had made a mistake. Perhaps the girl was not Hannah Woolfson at all but some lookalike, near identical.

Yet, as she disengaged herself from her partner in the game of *ephedrismos* and strolled over to us, this passing doubt was dispelled. Miss Holbrook was the spitting image of the subject of the photograph Sir Osbert Woolfson had shown us. If the two were not one and the same person, then Hannah Woolfson had a true doppelgänger.

"Sir Philip, how may I help?" said Miss Holbrook who was also Miss Woolfson.

"Shirley, do you know who these gentlemen are?"

"It is rumoured that Sherlock Holmes and Dr Watson are visiting, and I can only assume these are they. Welcome to Charfrome Old Place, both of you."

"Miss Holbrook," said Holmes with a small bow.

"Your servant, madam," I said. I rather meant it, too. Close up, Hannah was even more captivating. I would happily have been her servant, obedient to her every whim.

"Mr Holmes and Dr Watson are curious to learn about the Elysian way," said Buchanan. "In particular they want to know how well my beliefs carry – to what extent I am successful in exporting them to others. I realise you are a neophyte. It has been barely a week since you arrived. All the same, you seem to have taken to the lifestyle."

"Oh yes," said Shirley Holbrook, with wide-eyed enthusiasm. "Like a duck to water."

"Do you feel comfortable here?"

"Never more so. I will admit to a certain initial apprehension. I thought that what you had to offer might be something faddish. My qualms were rapidly dispelled, however. There is a friendliness here and a freedom such as I have seldom before encountered, and a dedication as well. We are all participants in a grand experiment, which Sir Philip is conducting with solicitude and a high degree of personal involvement. We are here to be liberated and, under his gentle tutelage, to grow and evolve as human beings."

She aimed a look at Sir Philip that was full of beatific awe, the look a loyal vassal gives to his lord and master.

"How did you learn of the Elysians' existence?" Holmes enquired.

"Oh, I have long been a seeker after new truths, sir," said she. "I am one of those people who have grown increasingly dissatisfied with the world as we know it. I find modern life tawdry and superficial, bereft of meaning. Since the onset of adulthood I have striven to look beyond the everyday and delve for spiritual sustenance. For a time I felt I might find it in religion. I even contemplated becoming a nun."

"That would have been a pity," I blurted out before I could stop myself. "I mean, that is to say, you seem to have so much to offer, Miss Holbrook, so many admirable qualities, that, that, to shut yourself away, to isolate yourself in a convent… Well…"

She blushed endearingly. "I presume you are complimenting me, Dr Watson."

"Trying to."

"And you are right. As a nun, I *would* have been hiding myself from the world, and that would have been a waste. I am no shrinking violet. I wish to bring change, improve the lot of others, transform those around me as well as myself. Rumours began to reach me of a place where I might learn how to do just that, where I might explore and develop my potential. Charfrome Old Place does not advertise, but within the circuit of likeminded souls to which I belong it is, one might say, an open secret. My footsteps drew me hither. It felt as though this was the natural culmination of a lifelong quest. My path to Sir Philip's door was predestined, and I am so pleased that he consented to take me under his wing."

Buchanan nodded along with a benevolent smile upon his face. He, I could see, was no less beguiled by the girl than I, although his attachment to her seemed paternal whereas mine was of an altogether more quixotic bent.

"To cap it all," the woman who purported to be Shirley Holbrook continued, "he does not charge a penny, not from any of us. All who come to Charfrome stay gratis, for as long as they wish. This enterprise is a charitable one, funded entirely from Sir Philip's pocket. That marks him out, to my mind, as one of the great philanthropists of our times, arguably the equal of George Peabody, John Passmore Edwards and Angela Burdett-Coutts. His goal, like theirs, is social reform, but rather than providing housing or schooling for those who cannot otherwise afford it, his intention is to cultivate an elite, a class of superior, liberated individuals, who will help sustain Britain's global dominance into the twentieth century and beyond."

"A task," said Buchanan, "made that much easier when I have superior material to work with, such as Miss Holbrook. The best pottery is fashioned from the finest clay."

"You are too kind," said Shirley Holbrook. "Charfrome has another attraction for me," she added, addressing Holmes and me again. "The sexes are treated equally. Elysians are not segregated. Women are not regarded as menials or second-class. We stand shoulder to shoulder with the men. It is most refreshing. And now, sirs, with all due respect, I should like to return to my exercise. I trust I have satisfied your curiosity."

"Fully, madam," said Holmes. "We thank you for your trouble."

"Then I shall bid you both a good day."

Shirley Holbrook joined her partner and, without a backward glance, resumed the game of *ephedrismos*.

Buchanan rubbed his hands briskly together. "Thus, our tour ends. I hope it has been educational."

"It has," replied Holmes. "Enlightening, even."

"You flatter me. Shall we?"

He shepherded us out of the gymnasium.

"I have an act of restitution to perform," he said, "and then I am afraid I must take my leave of you, and you of us."

He left us standing alone in an oak-panelled hallway for several minutes, and returned bearing my revolver.

"Still fully loaded," he said, handing the gun to me. "Perhaps the next time you drop by, you will not come armed?" He framed the comment as though it were a light-hearted jest, but I detected a note of reproof.

A moment later, Malachi Hart appeared, along with an accomplice who possessed the shaven head and sturdy, bull-necked build of a circus strongman.

"Sergeant-Major Hart and Mr Quigg will show you to the gate," Buchanan said. "But first, I believe you have something to say to our guests, Sergeant-Major."

Making a stiff bow from the waist, Hart said, "I humbly beg

pardon for the way you were treated last night. Such conduct was uncalled for. It was all a misunderstanding."

"There," said his employer. "Short and to the point. Least said, soonest mended. I want nothing more than to leave you with a good impression of Charfrome and its residents, gentlemen. I pray I have succeeded."

"You have allayed any concerns I might have had, Sir Philip," said Holmes graciously.

We shook hands with him once more, and then we were off down the driveway, flanked by the two Hoplites, Hart and Quigg. They were silent, as were we, until we reached a pair of large iron gates set between pillars that were, perhaps predictably, shaped like Ionic columns.

"Here you go," said Hart, as Quigg opened the gates wide for us. "Your exit. Waterton Parva is thataway. I expect we shan't be seeing either of you again."

The manner in which the gates clanged loudly shut behind us seemed to render his statement less a prediction, more an admonition.

CHAPTER THIRTEEN

AN ENCOUNTER IN THE WOODS

We were halfway back to the village before Holmes, sunk deep in rumination, spoke.

"Miss Shirley Holbrook," he said, rolling his tongue around the name. "Or rather Miss Hannah Woolfson. How did she strike you, Watson? Other than her obvious charms."

"She struck me as a sincere acolyte," I said. "A convert to the faith. Wholly in thrall to Buchanan and his philosophy."

"As ever your opinion scintillates, but I must say I had the very opposite impression."

"Really?"

"Yes. I did not believe one word she said. It was a parade of arrant nonsense. She was telling us only what she knew Buchanan wanted us to hear. All that business about being 'a seeker after new truths'. Pshaw! Nothing we have learned hitherto about Hannah Woolfson would suggest she is anything of the sort."

"She is unconventional, though."

"She is also far too intelligent and wilful to submit so obsequiously to the yoke of authority. What we saw back there was a splendid piece of shamming. Her intended audience was Buchanan, and he lapped it up. Then there is her pseudonym. Why assume a false identity? And why choose that particular name?"

"Perhaps she feels that anonymity is required. Her father is a High Court judge and she fears embarrassing him with her adoption of Elysianism. That or she wishes to be viewed as a person in her own right, not just the daughter of an establishment figure." A further thought occurred to me. "Is it not possible that she is symbolically rejecting her old self? She spoke of once considering entering into holy orders. Nuns are apt to change their names when they take the veil, indicating that they have embarked on a new life in Christ. This is a secular version of that."

"But Watson, my dear fellow – 'Shirley Holbrook'? A name that sounds remarkably akin to 'Sherlock Holmes'? I cannot believe it is mere coincidence. Your books were on the shelves in her room at her home. I know you noticed them too. A smug smile manifested on your face when their spines caught your eye. Hannah has deliberately rechristened herself after me. It is as though she is draping herself in my mantle."

"As a kind of tribute to you?"

"Precisely. Because she is doing some sleuthing," my friend declared. "She is going incognito, playing the part of the starry-eyed ingénue, having settled on a *nom de guerre* that mimics mine, all in order to enable her to infiltrate the Elysian ranks."

"I have to admit I was a tad disappointed to see her simpering at Buchanan like that, eyelashes aflutter."

"Disappointed?" my companion said with a faint hint of a smirk. "Only that?"

"But now that you insist her adoration was feigned, it makes more sense. So her aim, after all, is as we thought – to discover what has become of Sophia Tompkins. Could Sophia be the young lady she was playing that piggyback game with?"

"That I cannot say. The two were of a similar age, so it is possible. Then again, if it *was* Sophia, why has Hannah not been able to coax her away from the Elysians yet?"

"If Sophia has become a fanatical believer of the kind Hannah is only pretending to be, she may require some persuading."

"Were Sophia a fanatical believer, Hannah would not have been able to pass herself off as 'Shirley Holbrook' for an entire week. Sooner or later – and sooner rather than later, I suspect – Sophia would have denounced her to Buchanan as an impostor. As a good, loyal Elysian, she could do no less, even where a friend was concerned. No, the balance of probabilities suggests that Hannah has not yet managed to locate Sophia. That in itself raises disturbing questions. Then there is Charfrome's unofficial police force, headed up by Sergeant-Major Malachi Hart, he of the less than convincing penitence. Is Buchanan genuinely so fearful of journalistic intrusion that he feels the need to surround himself with a band of enforcers drawn from the military? It seems a somewhat disproportionate countermeasure." Holmes shook his head sombrely. "All in all, the home of the Elysians does not seem the paradise intimated at by their name. There is something sinister lurking at its heart, Watson. A serpent in this heathen Eden."

By now we were at the outskirts of Waterton Parva, the weathercock atop its church's crooked spire visible above the treetops. Holmes's foreboding utterance was still hanging in the air between us when, from our left, there came a loud "Hssst!"

We both spun on our heels. At first all I could see was forest. Then, faintly, I made out a figure amongst the leaf-dappled shadows, beckoning with an urgent hand.

"Mr Holmes. Dr Watson. Quick. I do not have much time."

It was Hannah. I darted towards her, climbing the slope of the verge. Holmes, with a glance along the road in either direction, followed suit.

"Miss Holbrook," said he. "Or should I call you Miss Woolfson? Now that we are unaccompanied, it seems safe to do so."

"This way," said Hannah. She was pink-cheeked, short of breath, her hair dishevelled. Evidently she had run full-tilt from Charfrome to catch up with us. "Let us withdraw from sight of the road before we talk any further. I cannot afford to be seen consorting with you."

"Why not? Are we so disagreeable?"

"You know full well why not, Mr Holmes. If you are half as shrewd as the man Dr Watson portrays in his tales, you will have no trouble understanding my reasoning."

Some thirty yards into the woods, Hannah halted. From here the road was scarcely visible through the trunks and low-hanging branches. Hannah adjudged that we could hold a conversation at this spot without fear of discovery.

"I feigned an injury in order to be excused from the gymnasium," she said. "An ankle sprain. I limped out, and once I was alone and the coast was clear I sprinted from the house, taking cover in a rhododendron thicket. As soon as I saw the two of you departing, I raced through the grounds and the woods to the road, hoping to intercept you. I thank God I was able to do so. But we do not have long. I am supposed to be resting in my quarters, keeping my ankle elevated with a cold compress on it. Someone is bound to come to check on me."

"And the consequences if you are not where you are meant to be...?" said Holmes.

"Perhaps there will be none. I do not know yet quite how dangerous life is at Charfrome Old Place. My instinct is that, for those who do not toe the line, it may be very dangerous. For that reason alone, I am grateful to you both for refraining from exposing my true identity to Sir Philip. I could tell you knew who I really am. Your hard stare and agitated eyebrows, Dr Watson, rather gave the game away, as did you, Mr Holmes, from the manner in which you contrived to speak to me out of all the many people in the room. From that I can readily infer why you came to Charfrome. It is at my father's behest, of course."

Holmes nodded. "He is greatly concerned about you."

"I am not surprised, and I feel wretched about leaving home as I did, without notice or explanation. I should have confided in him. But Papa has enough to contend with already, without me adding to his woes. Besides, I know what would have happened. He would have forbidden me to go. Perhaps, if Mama were still alive, he could have been reasoned with. She had ways of mollifying him. I do not, and he has become only more stubborn and intractable since her death, not to mention more protective of me."

"You could have lied – fabricated some plausible pretext for your absence."

"I foresaw being away for a day only, two days at most. Given that Papa has lately fallen into the deplorable habit of drinking far more than he ought and, when he is sober, working all the hours God sends, he might not even have noticed my absence. I did not plan on devoting more than a week to this undertaking, but now that I have embarked upon it I cannot abandon it."

"You have not been able to learn what has become of your friend Sophia Tompkins then?"

Hannah was taken aback. "You *have* been doing your homework, Mr Holmes – although why that should come as a shock, I do not know. Yes, thus far my efforts to track down Sophia have come to naught. When I presented myself at Charfrome the Saturday before last, I expected she would be there."

"And she was not."

"I established as much within the first couple of hours, once I had ingratiated myself with Sir Philip and secured a berth."

"It was not hard for you, I imagine, to convince Buchanan to take you in. If your performance at the gymnasium just now is anything to go by, he would have been putty in your hands."

She smiled drolly. "I am not proud of how easy it is for a young woman with above-average looks and a lively eye to worm her way past a man's defences and bend him to her will, no matter his age or intellect. In this instance, however, neither am I ashamed of it. Needs must. At any rate, with my application readily accepted I set about quizzing various of the Elysians. In a roundabout, casual manner, I would mention Sophia's name, saying that she was a friend and that I had come to Charfrome on her recommendation."

"Was one of your interviewees, by any chance, the young man who lured Miss Tompkins to Charfrome in the first place, Edwin Fairbrother?"

"Your knowledge of the ins and outs of the affair is truly uncanny," Hannah marvelled. "I shall not even ask how you know about Fairbrother. But no, he was not among them. I have not yet encountered him. He is not resident at the house, but I am told he visits from time to time."

"I apologise for interrupting. Do carry on."

"The majority of those whom I spoke to had not heard of Sophia and greeted me with blank looks. One, however, who had been at Charfrome longer than most, told me he recalled a girl matching her description. He had last seen her a month ago, perhaps a month and a half. He said she had moved on. My presumption, then, was that Sophia must have found the situation not to her liking and left. Come the Sunday, I was all set to leave too. It had, I decided, been a wild goose chase. Perhaps Sophia had lost interest in the group, or else found the regime too taxing. She has always been like that – terribly gung-ho in her enthusiasms but then tiring of them quickly, especially if they demand more time and energy than she is willing to spare."

"What happened that made you change your mind?"

Hannah cast a nervous glance over her shoulder. "I really should be getting back. I do not think I was spotted making my way here, but with Malachi Hart and his Hoplites one can never be sure. They are inordinately vigilant. The event that influenced my decision to remain was finding this."

She delved in a pocket and produced a necklace. It consisted of an oval silver locket suspended on a fine silver chain.

"I chanced upon it entirely by accident," she said. "It was lying in long grass not far from the grotto."

"The grotto?" I said. "You mean the cave that is guarded by statues of Hades and Cerberus."

"The very one. You know of it?"

"We were there last night. It is where the Hoplites beset us."

"The necklace, I take it, belongs to Sophia," said Holmes.

"It is hers. I would recognise it anywhere. Her initials are engraved upon the back. See the monogram? 'SJT' for Sophia Jane Tompkins. And look." Hannah turned the locket over and triggered the catch on the side. The lid sprang open to reveal tiny watercolour portraits of a man and a woman. "Henry and Esmerelda Tompkins. Sophia's parents. The locket was their christening gift to her. She wore it all the time. It was already her most treasured possession, but when both her mother and father died while she was still a child – victims of the SS *Princess Alice* disaster back in 'seventy-eight – she cherished it all the more, as her one tangible link to their departed souls. She would not be parted from it for all the world. I remember at school once, she mislaid it. The clasp broke and the locket slipped from round her neck. She searched for it the entire day, ransacking the building from top to bottom. Eventually it turned up, but until she was reunited with it Sophia was inconsolable."

"I see. For her to have been separated from it now does not

bode well. May I trouble you for a closer look?"

Hannah passed Holmes the necklace. He cast an eye over it for a minute before returning it to her.

"The clasp has again broken," he said.

"It has. With a lobster clasp like this, however, it is impossible to tell whether it was snapped forcibly or just fell apart of its own accord, as it did at school."

"I was about to make the very same observation," Holmes said. "The 'thumb' of the clasp has fallen out, which is liable to happen if the spring mechanism becomes faulty but also if the necklace is wrenched hard. Therefore one cannot determine with any degree of certainty how the necklace came to be detached from Sophia's person. It could have been an accident. It could equally have been the result of manhandling."

"What is beyond argument is that Sophia is not at liberty," Hannah said, clutching the item of jewellery to her breast like some religious totem. "Otherwise she would be out looking for the necklace unrelentingly. Which in turn implies that she is still at Charfrome – somewhere on the estate – or else likely to return there in the near future. In either case, I have no choice but to stay put. I must maintain the guise of Shirley Holbrook, while covertly hunting for further traces of Sophia." She looked momentarily sheepish. "By the way, I hope you do not mind, Mr Holmes, that I have appropriated a version of your name for my alias. I am, it goes without saying, an admirer of yours, and I wear 'Shirley Holbrook' as a kind of armour. At the risk of sounding silly, I feel that I am acting as a distaff Sherlock Holmes, and I am doing my best to bring your methods of reasoning and logical analysis to bear on this problem. Not, I might add, that I could dream of being your equal in that sphere."

Holmes made an amenable gesture. "You are free to use the name, Miss Woolfson. That is: Miss Holbrook. I consider it an accolade. I am bound to point out, however, that there is an alternative hypothesis for that necklace to be lacking an owner – a dark and troubling one."

"I am aware of it," Hannah said, choking back emotion. "I refuse to countenance it as yet. Sophia is alive and well. I simply have not yet determined where she is, that is all."

My friend's mouth set in a grim line. "This puts me in a dilemma, Hannah," he said. "I take it I may address you thus, and Watson may too?"

"You may, sir. Both of you. How does it put you in a dilemma?"

"Consider things from my viewpoint. I, like you, am not convinced that the goings-on at Charfrome are as innocuous as they appear. There is a whiff of rottenness about the place. My conscience is telling me that I should not allow you to remain there. The jeopardy is too great."

"I concur," I said.

"At the same time," Holmes continued, "I do not believe for one moment that you will voluntarily abandon your search for Sophia, whatever the potential hazards, until it yields results."

"You would not be wrong there," said Hannah.

"Watson and I could, of course, compel you to return home to your father."

The girl's face hardened, betraying a hint of a sneer. Her fists clenched. "I should like to see you try."

"Tut! I was merely giving vent to an idea. I am not the sort of man to oblige anyone to do something against their will. Neither is Watson."

She unbent somewhat. "Doubtless the pair of you could overpower me, but it would not be without cost to yourselves."

"We are duly warned. What I propose instead is this: an alliance."

"Go on."

"I cannot venture back into Charfrome. Nor can Watson. We have blotted our copybook with Buchanan. We would be *personae non gratae* were we to set foot on his land again."

"I can well imagine."

"We got away unscathed this time. Next time, we might not be so lucky. Buchanan made that clear to us when he directed Hart and Quigg to chaperon us to the gate. It was civilised but it was an eviction nonetheless. You, on the other hand, Hannah, have inveigled yourself into the Elysians' midst very artfully, and so far no suspicion has attached itself to you. Buchanan, indeed, is quite taken with you, to the point where I think he has come to regard you as a protégée. Together we may exploit that."

"What are you suggesting?"

"You become my spy in the Elysian camp. You continue your search for your friend but also broaden the scope of your investigation. You learn everything you can about the Elysians, and report back to me with your findings."

"How?"

"By letter. There is a post office in Waterton Parva. Can you manage, do you think, to steal away from Charfrome on a regular basis to send me a letter from there?"

"I don't see why not. It will not be easy but it will not be impossible either, as I have just proven."

"Good. You know my address, of course. I in return will leave replies for you *poste restante*. They will be waiting for you at the post office, to pick up as and when you visit. I will endeavour to offer you guidance and suggest actions you might take in the light of the content of your reports. Does that sound agreeable?"

Hannah's face was lit up with enthusiasm. "I am to operate as your agent, then?"

"Precisely. My woman on the inside. My Trojan Horse."

"Holmes," I piped up, "I cannot condone this. Able and

accomplished as Miss Woolfson is – excuse me – as Hannah is, you may very well be putting her in harm's way. You and I have far greater experience in these matters and are better equipped to face the perils."

"Your gallantry does you credit, Watson, but she is more than up to the task."

"You took the words out of my mouth, Mr Holmes," Hannah said.

"What I am doing is making the best of adverse circumstances," Holmes said. "You will recall that I did something not dissimilar just this April: the affair at Charlington Hall in Surrey, when Miss Violet Smith was shadowed by a bearded cyclist as she pedalled her own machine to Farnham railway station every Saturday. Then, I miscalculated the severity of the situation and left Miss Smith more or less unprotected."

"Unprotected?" I said. "You despatched me to keep an eye on her."

"A job I should have performed myself, and later did. I mean no disrespect. Even so, Miss Smith impressed me with her fortitude during the unfolding of the case and in its aftermath. She exhibited considerable strength of character, especially in the way she recovered from her molestation by that ruffian Jack Woodley. The young lady before us is cut from the same cloth. I am sure she is capable of fielding whatever slings and arrows come her way. Do we have a deal, Hannah?"

"We most definitely do."

"My one stipulation is that I am allowed to tell your father that I have found you."

"I cannot see that being a problem. You must be careful, though, not to let him know what we have just agreed."

"I shall gauge it so that he knows you are well and your safety is being monitored, and that he is content with that."

"Nor must Papa learn where I am. If he does, it is likely he will come and take me away, before I have a chance to find out what has befallen Sophia. That is the kind of father he is." She spoke with fondness but also a touch of chagrin.

"You can rely on me to handle him appropriately."

"I know that I can. And now I really must be going. I have lingered as long as I dare. Mr Holmes." She shook his hand firmly. "It is an honour to be collaborating with you. I shall not let you down. And Dr Watson?" Her hands, both of them, gently enfolded mine. "Please do not fret. That handsome brow of yours is creased with worry, and while it is appreciated, it is not warranted. I can look after myself. If you will not take my word for it, take your friend's. Mr Holmes is vouching for me. That should suffice."

She turned and loped off into the forest, skipping over exposed tree roots as agilely as any doe.

Holmes and I waited until she was out of sight before wending our way back to the road. Misgiving churned within me. I was deeply unhappy at the arrangement Holmes had reached with Hannah. I hoped he would not live to regret it.

But what also lodged in my mind were the words she had uttered, even as her hands clasped mine, transmitting warmth from her to me.

That handsome brow of yours.

It left me all the more enthralled by her, and all the more ardently solicitous of her welfare.

PART II

CHAPTER FOURTEEN

THE HUGE ONUS OF PARENTHOOD

"Wha-a-at?"

This loud expostulation came from Sir Osbert Woolfson the very next day, in his study in Mayfair. Holmes had just informed him of the arrangement he had reached with Hannah. Woolfson was, to put it mildly, not best pleased.

"Why, sir, you impudent knave," he spluttered, rising from his desk. "I hire you to find my daughter and return her to me, and you stand there and tell me that you have ascertained her whereabouts but will not fulfil the second part of the remit. You have a damned nerve, I must say. Where is she? I demand to know."

My friend remained unflappable. "Sir Osbert, believe me when I insist that I only have Hannah's best interests at heart. She needs to be where she is right now, and she needs to remain there for the foreseeable future. It will serve her ill otherwise."

"Who are you to deem what are and are not her best interests?" said Woolfson, moving out from behind the desk with clear menace. "I am her father. No one is better placed than I to make such judgements. Again I ask you, where is my daughter?"

"I cannot betray that confidence. Rest assured I shall oversee her every move and take full responsibility for her welfare."

"Oh, you will, will you? And I am just supposed to accept that and be content?"

"I am hoping as much."

"And you, Dr Watson." Woolfson rounded on me. "You have no difficulty with this? I imagine a physician understands the meaning of 'duty of care' better than most. You are happy to go along with your friend's point-blank refusal to reveal where Hannah is?"

I shifted my feet uncomfortably. "Sherlock Holmes has never failed a client yet."

"See that?" Woolfson snapped, swinging back towards Holmes. "Even your stalwart Boswell has his qualms. For the third and final time, tell me where Hannah is. Now!"

The last word was more of a roar than anything, and it was delivered from within inches of Holmes's face. Holmes kept up his fixed expression of imperturbability. I myself had often found this rather arrogant behaviour of his aggravating, and it was having the same effect upon Woolfson, if not a worse.

"If all is to be allowed to resolve to its best conclusion," Holmes said, "then I must politely decline to answer."

Woolfson was almost apoplectic. "I should have you horsewhipped, you rogue! Have the truth beaten out of you! In fact…"

No horsewhip was to hand, but a poker lay in the hearth. Woolfson snatched it up and brandished it before Holmes's nose.

"Sir Osbert, a member of the Bench such as yourself must surely realise that to threaten violence is a felony."

"Do I look like I care? Hannah is what matters, and if you will not willingly surrender the information I desire, then it will have to be unwillingly, and to the devil with the consequences."

Holmes's hand flashed out, almost faster than the eye could see, and he wrested the poker from Woolfson's grasp with a single deft flick of the wrist. Then, before the judge's astonished gaze, he bent the iron implement with the power of his arms alone, curving it until its two ends crossed over. He offered the loop of metal back to Woolfson, who took it with a defeated air, his mouth downturned.

The display of main force – Holmes possessed a strength surprising in one so gaunt and wiry – seemed to deprive Woolfson of all momentum. He dropped his hands, the now useless poker dangling from one of them. His anger subsided as quickly as it had swelled; all at once he was close to tears.

"I see it is a hopeless cause," he said. "I detect the hand of my daughter in this. Would I be right? She has constrained you to keep a secret, and you have acquiesced, as all do before her."

Holmes let slip a small, sombre smile. "The arrangement was reached by mutual consent. We shall leave it at that. I swear to you, Sir Osbert, that should I feel even for a moment that the situation warrants revising, I will take the appropriate measures post-haste."

"It appears I have no alternative," Woolfson said, discarding the poker and retreating back to his desk. "You are both of you childless men. You can have no comprehension what it is like to be a parent – especially the sole remaining parent. The onus is huge. However old she is, Hannah is still my little girl. The apple of my eye. Not to know where she is or what she has got herself into…"

At this I very nearly confessed all to Woolfson. My friend seemed to sense that I was on the verge of undermining his decision. A sharp application of the side of his toecap to my shin conveyed his thoughts about that. Not for the first time I found myself chafing under a rebuke from Holmes. In this instance, however, I did not feel that I deserved it, and it rankled me.

Woolfson sat down, planted his elbows on the desk blotter and sank his head into his hands, the picture of dejection.

"Just be true to your word, Mr Holmes, I implore you," he

said softly, not looking up. "Were I to lose Hannah as well as my Margaret, and so soon after, well, I do not know what I would do."

He said no more, and we considered ourselves dismissed. Already I pitied the fellow, but as we exited his study I heard the sound of a drawer of the desk opening and a bottle being taken out and uncorked, and my compassion intensified, as did my resentment of Holmes.

CHAPTER FIFTEEN

PORTRAITS OF HELL

My mood did not lift once Holmes and I were ensconced in Baker Street again. Over the next few days the sun shone brightly on London, but a sullen darkness festered within me. With each delivery of the post I anticipated a letter from Hannah Woolfson, proof positive that she was alive and thriving. I scanned the envelopes after Holmes had slit each open using his jack-knife, the one with which he also fastened unanswered correspondence to the mantelpiece. None bore a Dorset postmark.

For Holmes it was business as usual, which irked me all the more. When he wasn't carrying out noisome experiments at his acid-charred chemistry bench, he was scraping merrily away at his violin or poring over sheaves of newspapers and taking clippings. Once, he even indulged in his regrettable habit of conducting target practice indoors, emptying his revolver into the wall, which brought a barrage of complaint both from Mrs Hudson and from our next-door neighbour, several of whose mural-mounted ornaments were dislodged from their fixtures by the bullet impacts from the other side. If Holmes was worried about Hannah, he did not show it, unless this constant occupation was merely a way of diverting himself.

Clients, as ever, came and went. I would sit there listening to them as they poured their hearts out to Holmes and besought his help, but I felt wholly detached from their various plights.

"It is, Mr Holmes, a family heirloom of some pecuniary worth but even greater sentimental value. Imagine my surprise, therefore, when an artist friend came to visit last weekend, a Fellow of the Royal Academy, and insisted to me that it is a fake, and a clumsy reproduction at that…"

"This would not be the first time the rascal has threatened me, and he spelled out in no uncertain terms what would happen if I did not share with him the secret of what he calls 'the Four Hundred Swords of Fire'. Yet for the life of me I cannot fathom to what that phrase might refer…"

"I was enjoying a perfectly ordinary Sunday luncheon with my friends the Abernettys when the maid came in, ashen-faced and terribly distressed, babbling something about melting butter and a sprig of parsley, although this was merely a foretaste of the horrors to come…"

It was not that I was indifferent to these people, many of whom turned up at our door in a state of high anxiety, zealous for the balm of Sherlock Holmes's attentions. I simply could not get Hannah out of my thoughts. More than once I entertained the notion of travelling to Dorset on my own recognisance and storming the gates of Charfrome Old Place, brooking no obstacle until she was back in London and under her father's roof again. I daresay neither she nor Holmes would have forgiven me if I had followed through on such an action, but I believed I could live with the ignominy.

It was on the fifth day that a letter at last arrived. I happened to be out on my rounds at the time. Although I had sold my

Kensington connection shortly after Holmes's "return from the dead", I retained a select rump of patients both from that practice and from my Paddington days. Without wishing to flatter myself, some of them were adamant that they would be seen by no physician but me. A large proportion of them, furthermore, were happy to pay over the odds for treatment, and frankly I could not afford to turn down the money. I could not live solely off the capital from the sale, nor could I bring myself to have Holmes support me as a dependant.

My last port of call that day, the widow Wyngarde, fell into the lucrative category but was also one of the more tedious entrants on my list. The lady was in the habit of fabricating all manner of ailments in order to get me to her house, whereupon she would unfailingly make amorous advances towards me, pointing out that she was rich and lonely and in want of a husband and I was an accomplished and celebrated professional in want of a wife and that somehow a union between us was meant to be.

When I came home, Holmes gave no indication that the epistolary drought, as it were, was ended. He sat in the window seat smoking his briar pipe, his beady gaze directed upon the traffic and pedestrians clattering by in the street below. The afternoon was infernally hot. It is fair to say that Baker Street was baking, and I mopped my brow as I collapsed into the chair opposite his.

"I see, Watson," said he, "that you have just enjoyed the company of a certain hypochondriac about whom you have complained to me more than once. If your harried demeanour were not sufficient indication, you have a crumb of Madeira cake clinging to your moustache. You are not in the habit of eating said cake except when Mrs Ada Wyngarde plies you with it, and if you had visited another patient subsequently, doubtless the offending addendum would have been brought to your notice and you would have removed it. Really you ought not to indulge the woman. Have some other general practitioner take her on. At the very least do not accept the sweetmeats she tempts you with. It is as though you are a stray dog and she is bribing you with titbits, gradually winning your trust. If you are not careful, you may end up being adopted, with the collar tight around your neck."

"Not funny, Holmes," I said, wiping my moustache.

"Not that she isn't handsome," he went on, regardless. "Your descriptions of her make that abundantly clear."

"Really, that is enough."

"At only a decade your senior, she remains within the bounds of eligibility. Her wealth, of course, is an enhancement and an inducement. Yes, it would be an agreeably comfortable life for you with Mrs Wyngarde as the second Mrs Watson."

"Holmes!" I barked. "Now you have gone too far. You have overstepped the mark."

The vehemence with which I spoke inspired instant contrition. "I do beg your pardon, old friend," he said with sincerity. "I was insensitive. I should have known better."

"Yes, well…"

"Perhaps this will cheer you up."

He handed me a letter that had been tucked into an inner pocket. Before I even unfolded it I knew the sender was Hannah Woolfson. Why else would Holmes have produced it with such a flourish? And why, moreover, would he have deferred its announcement, if not to amplify the drama of unveiling it? For he was perfectly well aware that I was eager for news from Dorset. I had not gone to any trouble to hide the fact.

The handwriting was neat and elegant, an almost perfect copperplate script. Somehow I would not have expected anything less.

The letter itself, which consisted of several sheets of light-blue notepaper, read as follows:

Dear Mr Holmes,

I write in frustration. I have not made anywhere near as much progress as I would have liked or you might have wished. We have been kept fiendishly busy here, our daily regime allowing us scarcely a moment's rest. It is late now, and as I sit here by lamplight my eyelids are heavy. Yet I shall persevere.

Yesterday afternoon I did manage to snatch some time by myself, by dint of claiming I was suffering from a headache. While the others went outdoors to rehearse a performance of *Antigone* – in the original Greek, of course, and supervised by Dr Pentecost – I was excused. I am merely part of the chorus of Theban Elders, and hence disposable.

My goal was to explore the house thoroughly. It is vast and extensive, as you know, and there were whole areas where I had not as yet ventured. I travelled methodically from floor to floor, familiarising myself with the layout. There are numerous attic rooms where furniture moulders beneath dustsheets. There is a servants' wing, and the upper storey of the main part of the building is Sir Philip's private domain. There is an attached outbuilding that was once a barn but now serves as a rather rough-and-ready barracks for the Hoplites.

I don't know what I was hoping to find. I suppose in the back of my mind lay the thought that Sophia might be sequestered against her will in some corner of the property.

Of her, however, there was no sign. I tried the door to every room that seemed disused or abandoned. Had any been locked, I might have taken this as possible evidence of foul play, but all opened to reveal musty, cobwebbed emptiness.

My search was at one stage interrupted by the presence
of one of Hart's Hoplites – Mr Quigg. You have met the
man. He was at some time in his life a prizefighter, as you
yourself no doubt divined. The bent nose, cauliflower ear
and callused knuckles are all testimony to that. As I neared a
staircase I caught sight of him ascending, his bald pate rising
before me. I panicked, fearful of being found by him in a
part of the house where I did not belong. I prepared to turn
and flee. However, there was no immediate refuge for me
within sight, and besides it was too late – Quigg had already
spotted me. So instead I adopted a breezy attitude and, barely
missing a step, continued towards him. He nodded at me as I
sauntered past, and I thought I had managed to brazen it out,
but then he called me from behind.

"It's Miss Holbrook, isn't it?"

My heart was in my mouth, but nonetheless I turned
to face him, putting on a nonchalant air. "You are quite
right – Quigg, is it? How may I help you?"

"This" – he waved a finger, denoting the corridor
we were in – "is pretty far from where you Elysians are
quartered."

"Am I forbidden to be here? Are there parts of the
house where I should not go?" The questions sounded
rhetorical, but were not wholly so.

"No, ma'am," said that hulking ogre.

"Then I have not broken any rules."

"You have not. But I will say this." Quigg took a step
closer to me, and I could smell the sweat of him and beneath
that the carbolic soap with which he had signally failed to
improve his personal hygiene. "You may be a favourite of
Sir Philip's, and that's all very well and fine. But it don't do
to go asking too many questions. Nor, for that matter, to go

wandering about like you own the place. Charfrome plays host to a lot of clever people, but some people can be too clever for their own good, if you catch my drift."

I bent my head in humility. "Were anyone else to have spoken to me like that, I might have taken umbrage. But you, Mr Quigg," I said, looking up from under my eyelashes, "powerful and commanding as you are, have an authority that somehow I have no trouble accepting."

He affected nonchalance, but in those small, piggy eyes of his I saw that I had touched upon that part of male character that loves to dominate others, especially members of the opposite sex.

"You would do well to heed me," Quigg said, and he strutted off, head held high.

Shaken though the encounter left me, it stiffened my sinews at the same time. I had already determined what my next avenue of investigation would be, and if I should bump into Hoplites while pursuing it, I was confident that where I had bamboozled once, I could bamboozle again.

That night I crept out of the house after dark and made for the grotto.

The feat was not as easy to accomplish as it is to write about. I had to wait until everyone else had gone to bed and then a further hour or so, in order to guarantee that all would be asleep. Then I had to tiptoe along hallways and down staircases that creaked like galleons at sea. Each ancient floorboard seemed a booby trap designed to catch me out and flag my progress to anyone within earshot. In the stillness of the house, those wooden complaints under my feet sounded as loud as thunderclaps.

But you must forgive me, Mr Holmes. I am writing in a style not unlike that of Dr Watson, whose propensity for melodrama and incidental detail you so deplore. I will attempt to be more concise from here on – although I should add that I cherish the good doctor's stories precisely because they are not pure reportage but, rather, beautifully structured narratives that display your methodology to its best advantage, as a fine gilt frame shows off the work of an Old Master.

"A-ha," said Holmes. "You have reached the part where Hannah compliments your literary skills. No, don't shake your head in denial. I know that grin."

"And are you not flattered to be likened to an Old Master?"

"I have heard worse comparisons."

The ground-floor entrances at Charfrome are locked at night, and the keys are kept somewhere in the servants' wing. One or other of the domestic staff does the rounds last thing, securing the premises before retiring. The French windows of the gymnasium are the exception; they are fastened by bolts alone. Thus, although it entailed taking a circuitous route through the house, I was able to obtain egress.

My journey to the grotto was uneventful. A waxing crescent moon offered just enough light to see by, at least until I entered the copse that screens the grotto's mouth, whereupon I was submerged in absolute darkness and effectively blind. I had made provision against this, however, in the shape of a box of matches purloined from the kitchen. I struck them one after another and by their faint, guttering illumination found my way to the cave. Why the grotto? Because Sophia's necklace had lain in the grass not far from there, and because it might afford a place of imprisonment, some subterranean dungeon or oubliette.

What began as a narrow tunnel that was barely tall enough to stand upright in gradually broadened and heightened. I had gone perhaps fifty yards through it – some four matches' worth of distance – when I became aware of a change in the quality of my footfalls. They had begun to echo. Not long after that, the match-light revealed an end to the tunnel – and an opening.

This aperture gave access to a roughly cylindrical cavern some thirty feet in diameter and two thirds that span in height. The ceiling was hung with stalactites, but the floor was contrastingly flat and had been made that way by hand, for I perceived there the truncated stumps of stalagmites, dish-like circles that corresponded to the positions of their stalactite counterparts above. The circles were marked with the signs of tool-work, as was the rock surrounding them. Through considerable industry the cavern had been rendered a venue where one might easily move about.

I had heard mention of the grotto from various of the Elysians. Nobody I had spoken to about it, though, owned up to having ventured inside. I would put that down to incuriosity, or perhaps the subtle deterrent effect of the statues of Hades and Cerberus outside. Moreover, the entrance hardly invites exploration. Even in daytime it presents a low, mean aspect, black and seemingly unending. All but the most intrepid troglodyte would think twice before going in.

From what I could now see, however, the cavern formed yet another component of Sir Philip's fascination with Hellenic culture. It was, in point of fact, the antithesis of the Arcadia outside.

For it was Tartarus.

This realisation hit me just as the match between my

fingertips burned out. In the last flickers of its glow I had glimpsed a series of images upon the walls – portraits of hell.

I lit a fresh match and, steeling myself, stared around.

The images were frescoes, painted on lime plaster that had been added in a uniform layer to the rock-face. They depicted the torments of the damned, humiliations meted out upon mythological sinners. Here was Tantalus, up to his neck in water and within arm's reach of a fruit tree but forever denied the relief of either. Here was Sisyphus, repeatedly and futilely rolling a boulder up a mountain. Here was Ixion, tied to a burning wheel. There were others besides, whose punishments were no less degrading but whose identities escaped me. In each image the sky above was grey and foreboding, the background landscape barren save for a few bare, stunted thorn bushes.

The frescoes were skilfully done, the pigments rich. The rendering of the figures was lifelike but exhibited distinct Grecian flourishes, from the slightly elongated anatomy to the stiff, rather formal postures. Theirs was a peculiarly beautiful suffering, as delicate as it was anguished, exquisite in every sense. I could not bear to look, yet I could not bear to look away.

As I scrutinised each vignette in turn, I became aware of a muted hissing sound, similar to the sough of wind through trees. It emanated from close by, yet I could not pinpoint its exact origin. Then I realised what it was: the rush of rapidly moving water.

Somewhere beyond the cavern there must lie an underground stream. I wondered if this aquifer fed the lake and perhaps also supplied the household with fresh water.

I was just returning my attention to the frescoes when I discerned a flash of light at the periphery of my vision. Immediately I shook out the match I was holding.

You can well imagine the thoughts that raced through my brain, Mr Holmes, as I stood frozen to the spot, straining eyes and ears. Then I saw the flash again. It briefly lit up the exit from the tunnel to the cavern.

Someone was coming. Someone with a lantern was making his way along the tunnel towards me.

Fear gripped me, but I refused to give in to it. As with the Quigg incident earlier in the day, there was nowhere I could hide. My only option was to stay calm and behave as though I was not committing any misdemeanour. I told myself that nobody had said I could not be in the grotto. There was no explicit stipulation against being here. Even at night the place was not out of bounds, at least so far as I was aware; and if it was, I could simply plead ignorance.

The light bobbed along, illuminating more and more of the tunnel's rugged interior. Who was carrying it? A Hoplite, I presumed. If so, I hoped it was Quigg, whom I already knew I could manipulate.

In the event the lantern bearer proved to be someone quite unexpected: Dr Archibald Pentecost.

Though he was silhouetted by the lantern glow, I recognised the Classics teacher from his stooped posture and shuffling gait. He, in turn, recognised me, but only after a moment of startlement when the beam of the lantern swung round the cavern and alighted upon my face.

"Good grief!" he exclaimed, clutching his chest. "Miss Holbrook! You scared the life out of me. What the devil are you doing here?"

"I might ask you the same thing, Dr Pentecost," I said.

"It is hardly the hour to go gallivanting through the grounds of the estate, nor to indulge in a spot of speleology."

"Yet here I am, and here you are, speleologists both." He narrowed his eyes. "Your decision to visit this place seems somewhat more impromptu than mine, if you don't mind my saying so. I myself have brought a lantern. I see none in your possession, nor even a candle. All I see is that box of matches in your hand."

"Your implication being that I am here clandestinely."

"Improperly prepared, at the very least. To add to which, you were waiting in the dark when I arrived, as though you feared discovery."

I brazened it out. "It may not be against the rules to enter the grotto, Dr Pentecost, but equally I suspect it is not condoned, certainly not at night."

"That is true," said Dr Pentecost, with a forgiving nod of the head. "It would appear, Miss Holbrook, that we are each as guilty as the other in our nocturnal peregrinations. My excuse is that I do not sleep well. Chronic insomnia. I have had it all my life, even as a lad. A high-functioning brain and a restful night's sleep do not often go hand in hand. I take Kendal Black Drop for it, but sometimes not even that sedative draught works."

"I am sorry to hear that," said I.

"It is no matter," he said with a dismissive wave. "I have accepted it as my lot and try to make the most of each waking moment, whether it be through study, writing, or other forms of intellectual stimulus. This grotto, for instance. It is one of Charfrome's more intriguing attractions." He shone the lantern around. "Such well-executed pieces. They are Sir Philip's own handiwork."

"I did not realise."

"He is an accomplished draughtsman, naturally."

"I suppose, as an architect, he could not be otherwise," I said.

"You are familiar with all the characters on display, I take it."

"Some. Not all. Who is this fellow, for instance? The one imprisoned in a rock, with the table of food outside."

"Him? That is the demigod Phlegyas. A son of Ares, he burned down Apollo's temple at Delphi in a fit of rage. Apollo slew him in revenge, and his reward in the afterlife was to be entombed in a rock with an unattainable feast laid in front of him. See how he peers out through a crevice, his face gaunt. He is starving, but that delicious meal will never be his. Just deserts for one who committed an act of unpardonable hubris."

"And him? The man having his innards pecked out by a pair of vultures? Would that be Prometheus?"

"No. Oh no, my dear. That is Tityos the giant. Admittedly his fate was practically the same as Prometheus's, but the latter was chained by Zeus to a mountainside in the Caucasus, and rather than vultures it was an eagle who came each day to eat his liver, which duly grew back overnight. Prometheus was regarded by the Greeks as a hero for stealing fire from the gods and giving it to mankind, and therefore the victim of a miscarriage of justice, whereas Tityos was an out-and-out scoundrel. He was consigned to Tartarus for, well... I would not wish to be indelicate in front of a lady."

"I am of a robust constitution, Dr Pentecost. Whatever it is, I can take it."

"Let us just say he forced himself upon Leto, daughter of the Titans Coeus and Phoebe."

"In that case, the penalty he received was fully merited."

By now you may be asking yourself, Mr Holmes, why I was quizzing Dr Pentecost so intently about the frescoes. The answer is that if I exhibited a fascination about them to meet his own, my presence in the cavern might seem less incongruous to him, and thus less questionable. Furthermore, by getting him to expound on a topic I knew was close to his heart, I was gaining his confidence, for later exploitation.

I believe, however, that I have furnished you with sufficient detail about that part of the conversation. Dr Pentecost and I then went on to talk more broadly on the subject of punishment, and although I am, as I have said, very tired, I feel the exchange is interesting enough to merit reproducing herewith.

"The Ancient Greeks certainly seemed fond of the idea of harsh retribution being doled out in the next life," I said.

"Yes. Yes," said Dr Pentecost. "Perhaps not quite as much as us Christians. I mean, think of Dante. Think of Hieronymus Bosch. But still, the notion of hell and poetic justice was not alien to them." He leaned closer to the fresco, squinting. "Not alien at all."

"Do Elysians have methods of punishment too?"

"Hmm? What's that?"

"I was just wondering if there are sanctions here for those who transgress."

"Whatever can you mean? Sanctions? Transgress? What makes you ask such a thing?"

"This place. Everything at Charfrome is perfect – paradisal – save for a dank and somewhat sinister cavern adorned with images of torment and suffering, an

Underworld both figurative and literal. What is its purpose? What does it represent?"

"You would have to ask Sir Philip about that," said Dr Pentecost. "I am sure I don't know."

"But if you had to hazard a guess…"

"If I had to hazard a guess, I would say that paradise is meaningless if it has no flaw. The human mind cannot tolerate perfection. There must ever be a hint of contrast, a dash of spice. Picture the loveliest face you know and think how much lovelier it is because it sports some tiny blemish to offset its smoothness and symmetry – a birthmark, a cicatrice, a patch of discolouration in one iris."

For some reason my thoughts drifted to the small mole that adorned Hannah's left cheek, a classic "beauty spot".

"This grotto is undoubtedly that," I said.

"And since the cavern already existed on his land," the erstwhile schoolmaster continued, "what else could Sir Philip have done with it but incorporate it into his scheme in a capacity best suited to its nature? I would have done the same, had I his money and resources."

"You seem quite taken with the whole Elysian ideal."

"It is a project I am proud to be a part of. Whether Sir Philip's stated aim of improving our nation's prospects through an admixture of Hellenism will succeed or not is open to debate. As a lifelong lover of all things Greco-Roman, though, I am hardly likely to object to people receiving greater exposure to the texts and customs of that era, am I? I still get letters from Old Etonians, many of them now in high positions, telling me how much they benefited from my lessons as youngsters – how what they learned under my tutelage has stood them in good stead during adulthood. A mind steeped in Classics is, in my view, broader and nimbler than the average."

"You yourself are living proof of that."

"Why, thank you, my dear girl."

"I enjoy your classes very much."

"Again, thank you." He eyed me shrewdly. "I should point out that these compliments of yours, though welcome, are not liable to have the effect on me that they have on other men."

"I'm not sure I understand."

"Miss Holbrook, you are the kind of young lady who can wrap most males around her finger if she chooses. I have seen how you are with Sir Philip, and how he responds. I am not criticising, merely making an observation. Me, you will find immune. I have never been one to succumb to the feminine allure."

I decided to change tack.

"I wonder if my friend Sophia derived as much pleasure from the Elysian lifestyle as I do."

"Your friend…? Oh yes. Sophia. I remember her. Tompkins was her surname, was it not? I had heard you knew her. She was not here long."

"She has gone?"

"Graduated."

I was somewhat crestfallen. All along, it seemed, I had been chasing a phantasm. Sophia had packed her bags and headed elsewhere. At the same time I was relieved. My concerns for her safety were at least partly allayed. Whatever had become of her, the root cause did not lie at Charfrome Old Place.

Or so I thought, until Dr Pentecost said this: "It

happened while I was absent. I had taken myself off to Turkey for a month to study the ruins at Ephesus, a kind of working holiday. It is a queer thing, though. Without wishing to denigrate your friend in any way, Sophia did not strike me as a viable candidate for graduation. She was neither academically nor athletically gifted, certainly not to the same degree as you. Normally only the best and the brightest Elysians are chosen for graduation. I was more than a little surprised when I learned that her name had come up in the last Delphic Ceremony. But then," he added with a shrug, "the auguries do not lie, do they?"

It was the first time I had heard anyone at Charfrome mention something called the Delphic Ceremony. My expression must have made it plain that I wanted Dr Pentecost to elaborate, but all at once he became maddeningly coy.

"What is the Delphic Ceremony?" said he, voicing my unspoken query. "Ask any of your fellow Elysians who were here at the last full moon or the one before. They will tell you. Except they will not."

"What do you mean?"

"It is a Mystery – the kind spelled with a capital 'M'. And Mysteries are things one is forsworn from revealing. How, otherwise, can they remain Mysteries?" He winked slowly, smiling. "And now, my dear girl, the damp chill in here is rather getting to me." He mimed a shiver. "It may not bother you, but these aged bones of mine are susceptible. 'Fear old age,' Plato warned, 'for it does not come alone.' Shall we wend our way homeward? My lantern will light our path more effectively than those matches of yours. Also, I am familiar with the sequence and timings of the foot-patrols made by Malachi Hart and friends, and am able to evade them."

He was offering me safe passage to the house, and I would have been foolish not to accept. I knew I had been lucky not to run into a Hoplite earlier, but I had not appreciated just how lucky.

Suffice to say that we crossed the grounds without incident. Dr Pentecost used his lantern only while we were in the copse. When we were out in the open he doused it, and moonlight became our sole guide.

"What an adventuresome pair we are, Miss Holbrook," he said once we were indoors. "Quite the rebels."

"I shan't tell if you won't, Dr Pentecost."

He giggled conspiratorially. "Madam, my lips are sealed." And with that, and a tap of the forefinger to the side of the nose, he parted company with me.

So concludes my missive. Would that it were more instructive and illuminating, Mr Holmes. Although I feel I am marginally the wiser about Sophia, nagging questions remain. Was her so-called "graduation" as straightforward an event as it sounds, like the ceremonial conferral of a university degree, or was there more involved? If she is not at Charfrome any more, where is she? I know she and I quarrelled, but if her Elysian sojourn had run its course, why did she not get back in touch to hold out an olive branch, or at least induce me to do so? She cannot surely be nursing a grudge still, now that this particular fever of hers has abated and she has had time to recover.

Please advise me how to proceed. I wish to spend no longer at this place than I must, but I will stay until I receive your response. May it come quickly.

Yours,
"Shirley Holbrook"

CHAPTER SIXTEEN

SHERLOCK HOLMES'S REPLY

"She is incorrect, of course," Holmes said.

"In what regard?"

"There is much that is instructive and illuminating in her report. Would you fetch pen and paper? Then I can compose my reply. Better still, you be my amanuensis, and I will dictate. Your handwriting is superior to my rather cramped scrawl. Newnes at *The Strand* routinely praises the legibility of your fair-copies."

Pen poised, I waited while my friend gathered his thoughts. Then he began to speak and I to transcribe:

My dear Miss Holbrook,

The grotto. Revisit. Use matches again. Guttering of flame suggests flowing air current, therefore possibility of passageway beyond. Perhaps secret door.

Dr Pentecost. Continue to cultivate. Knows more than realises.

Delphic Ceremony. Your attendance at next is

mandatory. Full moon in fortnight's time. What is nature of this event? What connection to famous oracle of same name?

Mysteries mentioned seem to form crucial part of Buchanan's Elysian practices. May be essential to solving the riddle of Sophia's disappearance – a Mystery to clear up a mystery.

Yours,
Sherlock Holmes

"That is it?" I said.

"There is no more to be said. I have raised all the issues that I feel need addressing."

"Yes, but the curtness of it? It reads like a grocery list."

"A not inapt simile."

"Dash it all, Holmes, have you no compassion? You are consigning the girl to another two weeks at that dreadful place, when she is clearly anxious there. The very least you can do is frame it as a polite request, rather than a decree."

"Would you have me sugar-coat my words?"

"I would have you not be so brusque."

"Then redraft the letter, Watson. You have my blessing. Bring your authorial skills to bear upon it and mediate my directives to make them more palatable."

"Very well. I shall."

Holmes refilled his pipe, tamping tobacco into the bowl with more vigour than the action customarily warranted. He was vexed, as was I.

My version of the letter was softer in tone. I added the pronouns and definite and indefinite articles that Holmes had omitted. I ameliorated his repeated use of the imperative mood by inserting phrases such as "Would you kindly…" and "I would be grateful if…". The sentence "Your attendance at next is mandatory" became, after my editorial involvement, "I would strongly suggest that you attend the next", leaving Hannah a small chink of autonomy through which she might escape.

Holmes cast a sceptical eye over my efforts.

"Hum! It is watered down almost to the point of insipidity. Do you want this case cracked or not? Still, Hannah will come through for me. I would wager good money on it. Well-intentioned though your mollycoddling is, she will shrug it off and forge courageously onward. Stick the thing in an envelope and ring for the boy, will you?"

The letter was despatched, and the waiting began anew.

CHAPTER SEVENTEEN

A LOATHSOME LOTHARIO

Seven days elapsed, during which Holmes dealt with two other cases.

One was the affair of Murillo, former president of the Caribbean island of Santa Teresa. This Murillo should not be confused with Murillo of Central American republic San Pedro, that fiendish ex-dictator whose homicidal exploits in London had been brought to light by Holmes three years earlier. Rather, it was another fellow of the same name, by pure coincidence also a one-time holder of high office overseas who had since fetched up on our shores.

The second Murillo had not been deposed like his namesake but simply voted out by the electorate. Nor was he corrupt and tyrannical. By the standards of that region of the world he was, in fact, a shining beacon of integrity. However, certain of his private papers had fallen into the wrong hands, amongst them a dossier cataloguing the venalities and marital infidelities of his political opponents back home, whose party had lately taken power. Murillo, being a man of principle, had refused to exploit this information for his own gain. The thief, whoever he was, might not be so scrupled. The dossier was, potentially, kindling to the fires of insurrection, and Santa Teresa's stability depended on it being recovered before its contents could be made public. Murillo personally hired Holmes to locate and retrieve it.

Holmes achieved the desired result by means of the brilliant impersonation of a Spanish cardinal and the judicious deployment of Wiggins, chief Baker Street Irregular, whose criminal talents had seldom been put to nobler use. As the lad himself said, "If only I'd of knowed before that parlour jumper and screwsman was such 'onest trades! Next time a bluebottle feels my collar, I'll tell 'im it's my burglarising what 'as saved a foreign country from chaos. That's bound to get me off being smugged and hauled before the beak and landed with a stretch in clink."

I will perhaps write up that adventure one day, as I will the shocking affair of the Dutch steamship *Friesland* that occurred during the same eventful week and nearly cost Holmes and me our lives. Cornered by a dozen murderously irate Netherlander sailors armed with boathooks and marlinspikes, we were prepared to fight our way out of our predicament and possibly die in the attempt, but were saved by the timely arrival of Inspector Lestrade with a large contingent of constables. I had never been quite so pleased to see the sallow-faced official as I was that day at the docks at Wapping, and even if he and his small army of policemen turned up somewhat later than Holmes had stipulated by telegram, it was better that than never. Thus was an international ring of tulip bulb smugglers broken. Thus, too, was the strikingly surreal and grisly death of Gilbert Fanthorpe Carswell, importer of rare blooms, avenged.

We returned to Baker Street that evening in high spirits and with a renewed sense of camaraderie. Sometimes it takes a brush with the Reaper to remind one that life is worth living and that friendships and partnerships should be cherished. I found

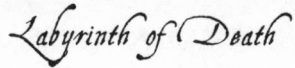

myself able to give Holmes the full benefit of the doubt over his management of the Charfrome case. His intellect being so much more muscular and versatile than mine, he must be correct in his judgement that Hannah was competent to handle whatever the situation threw at her.

Hannah's second missive had come by the last post and, courtesy of Mrs Hudson, was sitting propped up in the letter rack on the table when we got in. Holmes perused it first, passing each page to me as he finished it. The letter was lengthier than the previous one but no less absorbing.

My dear Mr Holmes,

Your reply was eagerly awaited and much appreciated. Would I be right in detecting the influence of a certain amiable physician in its composition? The prose was so similar to that of Dr Watson's narratives, and so unlike what I would have expected of you yourself, that I am forced to conclude you had some assistance from your confederate. It is either that or you have an uncanny knack for literary plagiarism. Please convey my regards to the good doctor, and in the event that he is reading this (I imagine he is) I should like him to know that I am being sensible and taking no inordinate risks. None, at least, that he himself would not be willing to take.

I must confess that I read the paragraph through thrice, relishing being referred to as "amiable" and, indeed, being referred to at all.

Now, to the business at hand.
Free time has again been at a premium. It is almost

as though the regime at Charfrome is designed to militate against leisure. Idleness might leave us Elysians prey to second thoughts, and second thoughts might undermine the efficacy of our indoctrination.

I have done as requested: I went back to Tartarus. Thereby hangs a tale. But first, to set out events in chronological order, I must tell you about Edwin Fairbrother.

Yes, finally I got to meet the fabled Mr Fairbrother in person, and what a perfectly charming fellow he turned out to be.

If you discern a note of acerbity in the foregoing sentence, you would not be wrong. It cannot be denied that Fairbrother is handsome, with flashing blue eyes and an easy, lackadaisical smile that seems to hang on his face more or less permanently. He wears his hair unfashionably long – some might even say effeminately long – yet somehow this only adds to his aesthetic appeal. He dresses well, if his attire that day was typical: a light summer suit with a flower-pattern jacquard-finish waistcoat, topped off with a chrysanthemum buttonhole and a navy-blue silk cravat secured by a diamond pin. In short, he is every inch the dandy, but the kind a woman cannot take her eyes off, the kind she knows is trouble but cannot help being drawn to all the same.

Already I despised this loathsome lothario.

The effect of his arrival on the household was remarkable. Word spread fast. Excitement charged the atmosphere like an electric current. You may recall the young woman with whom I was playing *ephedrismos* the day we met. Her name is Polly Speedwell, and it was she who rushed to my room to bring me the glad tidings.

"You must come, Shirley," she said. "He never stays long, and you will regret missing the chance to see him in the flesh. And such fine flesh it is too!" she added with a leer so lascivious it was almost obscene.

"It sounds too good an opportunity to turn down," I said, and accompanied her to the dining hall.

There, Fairbrother was taking refreshment, and also holding court. A handful of Elysians had gathered around him, and he was engaging them all in conversation. When a comment of his provoked laughter, the laughter was raucous and sycophantic.

Polly elbowed her way to the forefront of his audience, and soon was laughing along with the others. Watching her grovel before him like a dog before its master, I felt a sudden surge of contempt for my own gender. Polly is a pleasant enough creature and has many redeeming qualities. Though of only average looks, and a trifle overweight, there is an admirably feisty streak in her, albeit one that remains well buried beneath her innate reticence. She has strong opinions that she will air only if she knows she is guaranteed a sympathetic hearing. She could, were she but able to overcome her inhibitions, be a great woman.

I should add that she comes from a wealthy background, in which respect she is a fairly typical Elysian, only a few of whom are of humble origin. Charfrome seems not to attract the less affluent, possibly because they have more concrete demands upon their time, such as earning a living. Polly's father runs a chain of millinery shops and does not stint on lavishing money upon his daughter. She always dresses well and in particular she owns a pair of cabochon-cut sapphire earrings, which were a gift to her from him on her twenty-first birthday and which, I regret to say, I rather covet.

And yet here she was, this well-to-do, interesting girl, with so much going for her and so much potential, behaving as though she had no personality at all to speak of, holding up a mirror of admiration to Fairbrother in which he might see his own dazzling beauty reflected. So many women do this, putting themselves second, others first, abasing themselves as though they are unworthy of notice.

Eventually Fairbrother's gaze alighted on me, and straight away he said, "And who is this excellent creature? I do not believe I have had the pleasure."

"You would remember if you had," said I, at which he chortled with amusement, revealing teeth as white and even as sugar cubes.

Polly took it upon herself to make the introductions. "Shirley came to Charfrome of her own accord. She is not one of your finds, Edwin."

"No, not one of mine," he said. "But she would have been, I am sure, had I bumped into her on the social circuit. I can recognise prime material when I see it."

"Prime material?" I said. "You make it sound as though I am a bolt of cloth or a side of beef."

"You are considerably more than either, Miss Holbrook. I say, I don't suppose you would care to take a turn about the grounds with me? I have an appointment to see Sir Philip. Before that, however, I have a few minutes spare, and I should like to get to know you. The weather today is so clement, too."

Naturally I consented. I may even have bobbed a little curtsey to him, to show that I was as beguiled by him as any of the other Elysians present. They, for their part, regarded me with envy and even a touch of resentment, for I was taking their idol away from them. Polly in particular looked hurt, as though by being singled out by Fairbrother I had betrayed her.

Soon enough, he and I were outdoors and perambulating. I shall spare you the verbal overtures he made towards me – they were alternately unctuous and banal, and all delivered with a rakish glint in his eye and a winsome cocking of his head, and sometimes also with a gentle touch on my arm, his hand resting there for several seconds as though both to reassure me and to claim me. On any other woman this treatment would surely have broken down her innermost barriers, and I must say I found it hard to resist. Yet I remained firm of purpose. I was not there to be seduced by Fairbrother. I was there to harvest information from him. I was there to plumb his depths, or rather his shallows, and see what sunken treasure I might dredge up.

Through subtle manipulation of the conversation I turned his focus away from me and onto himself.

Fairbrother, I learned, functions as a kind of roving ambassador for Sir Philip, to whom he is distantly related on his mother's side and whom he addresses as Uncle Philip. A well-connected socialite, he haunts dinner parties, literary salons, gentlemen's clubs and other such sophisticated venues, on the lookout for potential Elysians. He casts his line, hooks a likely candidate, then patiently and painstakingly reels the "fish" in.

The criteria for recruitment are, he told me, broad and ill-defined. Sir Philip has charged him with seeking out those who are of good stock and blessed with prospects, an enquiring mind and a patriotic bent. Fairbrother, however, is entitled to interpret these guidelines as he wishes.

"Often," he said, "it is simply a case of getting a 'feeling' about someone. If a person looks to me as though there is something lacking in his or her life, an emptiness requiring to be filled, then I will act upon that. The Elysian way – well, I am not much of a one for these Classical shenanigans myself. I barely paid attention at school during Greek and Latin, or any other lessons for that matter. Ha ha! But I can nonetheless see that the Elysian way might offer a compass bearing to the lost, to give them heading and direction. Equally, those who already have a clear sense of where they are going will find their voyages accelerated, as though they were becalmed and a fair wind has billowed their sails."

Here was the opening I had been hoping for, and I took it.

"I understand we have a mutual acquaintance," I said. "Sophia Tompkins. Which, in your view, was she? One of the lost, or somebody with a sense of where she was going?"

"Sophia…" For the first time, Fairbrother faltered. There was a ruffle in his smoothness. His expression, just momentarily, lost its blithe self-confidence. "How do you know her?"

"We are friends. It was she who told me about Charfrome. Her endorsement of the place led me here. And I am glad of that."

Now I laid a hand upon *his* arm, as if to imply that but for Sophia I might never have had the honour of the company of the wondrous Edwin Fairbrother.

The gesture served to restore his equilibrium. "Sophia – such a sparky, cheery little thing. Yes, I knew as soon as I clapped eyes on her that she would be an adornment to Charfrome, something to liven up the place. And so she proved."

"I am told she graduated."

"As so many do. On average, a couple of dozen per year. Not all, though. Some adherents leave of their own accord after two or three months. There is a fairly rapid turnover."

"What is strange is that I have had no communication with her in weeks."

"Perhaps she is busy with other things," Fairbrother said. "Those who pass through Charfrome's portals emerge with a renewed zest for life and an eagerness to get on. It so happens that, in the process, they are apt to shed aspects of their past that have come to seem redundant. This, I am afraid, can include friends." He looked at me closely. "Tell me, just how well do you and Sophia know each other?"

"Well enough. Why do you ask?"

"Simply because during my association with her, she never once mentioned your name, Miss Holbrook."

My heart had begun to beat fast, and not in the manner that Fairbrother commonly induced in the opposite sex. "Were you and she intimates?" I said, batting the ball as dexterously as I could back into his court.

"I might not put it like that, but we were certainly on good terms. She did talk of another friend, a Hannah someone-or-other, an old school chum of hers. She and this Hannah had a disagreement. It was around Christmas time. She had reason to curse the woman's name more than once in my presence."

"I am sorry to hear that. I myself am unaware of any Hannah. She sounds a reprehensible sort, if she upset dear sweet Sophia."

You cannot imagine how hard it was to keep my

features impassive at this point. I am not in your league, Mr Holmes, when it comes to acting. I was terrified I might somehow give myself away.

"But enough about her," Fairbrother said. He fixed me with a gaze that was calculated to melt resistance and arouse passion, and doubtless achieved that goal far more often than it did not. "Tell me more about you."

I was desperate to keep Sophia as our topic but, my real name having come up, I felt that I had veered close to a precipice once and narrowly escaped falling in. It would be tempting fate to try again.

Just as I was about to furnish Fairbrother with some entrancing and entirely fictitious details about myself, a voice called out his name.

"Edwin. There you are. I've been looking all over for you."

Bustling towards us from the direction of the house came Sir Philip.

"You are late for our meeting," he added in a tone that, though genial, carried an undercurrent of peremptoriness.

"My apologies, Uncle Philip," said Fairbrother, shooting a glance at me. "I was distracted."

"Yes, well, enough of your dallying. Miss Holbrook, would you excuse us?"

"Of course, Sir Philip. Mr Fairbrother? I have enjoyed our chat. Perhaps we might pick it up again at a later date."

"I cannot think of anything I would desire more, Miss Holbrook. But please, call me Edwin."

"Of course... Edwin."

There the episode might have concluded, but for the fact that Sir Philip took Fairbrother by the elbow and steered him, not back to the house, but further away from it. Neither man looked back, and there was nobody else about. I saw that I had a chance to follow them and eavesdrop upon their colloquy. I could not pass it up.

"Oh dear Lord," I said. "Hannah's foolhardiness knows no bounds. It is as though she is inviting disaster upon herself."

"Yet disaster cannot have struck, otherwise she would not be writing the letter that is now in our hands," said Holmes. "Sometimes, Watson, you are of an altogether too sensitive and illogical disposition. You must compose yourself and think dispassionately."

"Would that I were a reasoning machine like you, Holmes, instead of a mere man. Life would be so much easier."

"Come, come. No need for that. Now, let us read on."

CHAPTER EIGHTEEN

A FASCINATION FOR DARK THINGS

Holmes returned his attention to the letter, continuing to hand across each sheet of paper to me when he was done with it. That, I suppose, is a metaphor for the pair of us: him, ever a page ahead.

The estate, as you know, is surrounded by woodland. I betook myself into the cover of the trees and, as Sir Philip and Fairbrother strode briskly side by side across the lawns, shadowed them. I darted from trunk to trunk, keeping out of view. There was one occasion when Sir Philip happened to glance over his shoulder and I feared I had been spotted. However, he continued onward, unperturbed, and I after a moment's hesitation continued onward too.

My targets – if I may describe them so – ended up at a shrine far to the south of the house and well away from sight of it. The shrine plays host to a statue of Daedalus, who is represented with a pair of compasses in one hand and a feather in the other, the former to symbolise his trade, the latter the loss of his son Icarus. The legendary Grecian inventor and craftsman is, it transpires, a particular hero of Sir Philip's. I have that on the authority of Dr Pentecost, whom I have, as instructed, been cultivating. Dr Pentecost and I, indeed, are now quite thick. More on him anon.

Sir Philip and Fairbrother sat down on a bench beside the pedestal upon which Daedalus is erected, and they began to talk in earnest. It was a still day and their voices carried, but not to the extent that I could hear them with any clarity, at least not while I remained within the woods. I had no alternative but to steal closer to the shrine. There was a small shrubbery some fifteen yards from it and much the same distance from the treeline. I crept low across the grass towards it, the two men so deep in conversation that they seemed oblivious to anything else. Crouching there, I was able to make out distinctly what they were saying. It was apparent that Fairbrother had incurred Sir Philip's wrath, although what his misdemeanour had been was unclear.

"I have sufficient demands upon my time and energy without you adding to them," Sir Philip said testily. "You have one simple task: to find new Elysians for me. I pay you handsomely to do that. Through me, and only through me, do you enjoy the lavish lifestyle you seem to feel is your due. Your father has cut you off without a penny as a wastrel and a rogue. I, at the urging of your mother, for whom I retain a tremendous fondness, agreed to give you gainful employment and have found you a role tailor-made for your talents, such as they are."

"Do not think me ungrateful, Uncle Philip," said Fairbrother.

"And yet I find I must deal, thanks to you, with a most unfortunate set of circumstances."

"It was not my fault," Fairbrother protested.

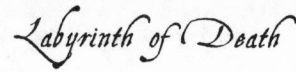

"Not wholly, I will allow."

"Not even half. Much of the responsibility lies with you, if not the greater portion."

"True, I misled others, Edwin. I went against my better judgement, my every instinct. I did so as a favour to you – and not a moment goes by when I do not rue that decision."

"What happened was, yes, unfortunate," said Fairbrother. "But, Uncle Philip, it is not the first time it has happened, is it now? Simms and Kinsella? Remember? It was scarcely a year ago."

"How could I forget?" Sir Philip bowed his head as though all at once it weighed heavily upon his neck. "At least, with those two, my intentions were sincere. That mitigates things to some extent. In this particular instance, by contrast, I made a mistake. I listened to you when I should not have."

"I am not responsible for the choice you made. All I did was proffer a suggestion. You could have said no."

The architect's eyes flashed with anger. "I *should* have said no! But you wheedled, you cajoled…"

"I did no such thing. I merely asked you, as a relative and, I hope, a friend, for help."

"Which I gave."

"Charitably, as is your wont. In that sense, I feel that neither of us has anything to reproach himself for."

"Do you?"

"I do." Fairbrother held Sir Philip's gaze. Even from my vantage point behind the shrubbery, peering through the leaves, I could sense the charisma radiating from him. It was like the rays of the sun. "We are both victims here. We are both reeling from the effects of this misadventure."

"Perhaps so. Yes, perhaps," said Sir Philip, nodding, beginning to be swayed. It was remarkable how Fairbrother was managing to turn the tables on the older man. What had started out as a scolding was becoming, through his careful orchestration, a kind of mutual exculpation.

"Besides, there was another who may be considered at least partially blameworthy."

"You mean Nithercott."

"The very same. Had he but tried harder…"

"But is he not just another victim? Have you forgotten how he ended up?"

"Nithercott was clearly not made of stern enough stuff. At least he took what he knew to the grave with him."

"There is that, I suppose."

"How come all this emotion has been stirred up in you, Uncle?" Fairbrother enquired. "I had thought the matter settled. A line had been drawn under it and we had agreed never to discuss it again."

"You know that we were recently graced with the presence of Sherlock Holmes?"

"I heard. The much-hallowed London specialist."

"That event alone alarmed me, even though it turned out he was drawn to Charfrome tangentially, on a matter unconnected with our activities. Then, however, there is the girl."

"Which girl?"

"You were just with her. Miss Holbrook."

Only by dint of pressing knuckles to mouth was I able to withhold a gasp.

"She," Sir Philip continued, "is a marvellous thing. Her potential is enormous. Her inclusion in our ranks, however, brings complications."

"I am sure that—"

What should occur at that precise moment but a sudden

flurry of activity in the woods directly behind me. There were volleys of loud croaking and chattering and the whir of multiple wings. It seemed that a dispute had broken out between a flock of jackdaws and a lone magpie. The magpie must have strayed onto the jackdaws' territory and they were expelling it with all the vehemence they could muster.

Sir Philip and Fairbrother, startled by the furore, snapped their heads round to look.

It was not until then that I was conscious just how paltry a covering the shrubbery afforded. The countless gaps between the leaves meant it was as penetrable by the eye as any confessional screen. I knelt there on all fours, stock still, scarcely daring to breathe. The slightest movement might give away my presence. I was able to see Sir Philip and Fairbrother; might they just as easily be able to see me?

The avian squabble died down. Sir Philip turned away, but Fairbrother continued to stare fixedly, brow furrowed. Perhaps, being the younger of the two by far, his eyesight was that much keener. He could descry what Sir Philip could not: the interloper skulking behind the trimmed clumps of daphne and camellia.

Eventually he too turned away, and I let out a trembling sigh of relief. I felt I had pushed my luck as far as I dared, and so I beat a hasty retreat back to the woods. The better part of valour, and all that.

"A wise move, Hannah," I said.
"She cannot hear you, you know," said Holmes drolly.
"Would that she could," I muttered under my breath.

My other escapade – the second visit to Tartarus – occurred only last night. I prevailed upon Dr Pentecost to accompany me, largely because of his adroitness in slipping past the Hoplite patrols, but also for moral support. He took some persuading, albeit not much.

"You are an inquisitive sort, my girl," he said. "Whence stems this zeal for re-entering that place of death?"

"If something fascinates me, I cannot resist its call."

"The fascination that cavern exerts is a dark one."

"Are dark things not the most fascinating of all? I chafe against convention. I am drawn towards the grotesque. The cavern presents those unusual and outré features which are as dear to me as I think they are to you."

"She is paraphrasing you, Holmes," I said.

"Or you, Watson," said he.

"I am, I will allow, excited by that which the vast majority shun," Dr Pentecost said. "The mundane depresses me. '*Odi profanum vulgus et arceo*,' to quote Horace. Very well. You have won me over, Miss Holbrook. It is refreshing to come across one as spirited and wayward as yourself. You remind me of me in my younger days. I am pleased you chose to befriend me."

We traversed the grounds, equipped with a pair of lanterns, which Dr Pentecost did not light until we were well inside the grotto. We passed along the tunnel to the frescoed cavern, whereupon I began – according to your suggestion, Mr Holmes – to search for a secret door. I will admit to being sceptical. How could the murals conceal such a thing? More to the point, why? For what reason would it be there? Where might it lead?

I disguised the action as scrutiny. I held my lantern close to each fresco and studied the illustration as intently

as a short-sighted art historian with his nose to a canvas. Dr
Pentecost, ever the teacher, kept up a constant commentary,
furnishing yet further detail about the punishments
depicted and the recipients' crimes.

At last we came to a fresco that showed a number of
young women fetching water from a river.

"They are the Danaides," Dr Pentecost said, "the
daughters of Danaus. There were actually fifty of them,
rather than the dozen or so represented here, and all but
one of them killed their husbands simultaneously on their
wedding night. For that offence they were doomed to spend
eternity carrying ewers of water from a river to a bath,
where they might wash themselves clean of their sins."

"But the ewers look more like sieves."

"Quite. The water would run out through the perfora-
tions before the Danaides ever reached the bath, and they
would have to trudge back to the river to fetch a refill, and
so on *ad infinitum*."

I noticed that the sound of rushing water that I had
discerned on my previous visit was, although audible
throughout the cavern, at its loudest when I stood before
the image of the Danaides. While I continued my study
of the fresco, Dr Pentecost moved on to the subject of
demigods who had journeyed to Hades and returned.

"It is a recurrent motif in Classical myth," he said.
"Odysseus, Aeneas, Heracles, all travel to the realm
of the dead and emerge again alive. It is a mark of their
exceptional status as heroes, as a fusion of god and man –
they symbolically transcend mortality. It is also narratively
satisfying that the descent of each, *katabasis*, is followed
by a concomitant ascent, *anabasis*. It provides a poetic
balance. The *anabasis* is not always wholly successful,

however. Think of Orpheus. Think of Proserpina…"

I pretended to pay attention, while widening my examination of the Danaides fresco to its edges. At last I perceived it: a crack in the cavern wall. It was terribly narrow, the thinness of a hair, but discernible. It ran around the outline of the fresco. Where the artwork terminated and bare lime plaster began, there lay the fissure.

You were right, Mr Holmes. A secret door.

There must, I assumed, be some kind of opening mechanism. I began gently prodding the fresco in order to locate it.

"What on earth are you up to, my dear?" Dr Pentecost said, breaking off from his lecture. "I do not imagine the pictures are meant to be touched. Sometimes with frescoes the paint never fully dries."

The image boasted no embedded catch, no hidden lever or handle. I began inspecting the wall immediately surrounding it. By now my companion was thoroughly bemused and not a little consternated.

"Miss Holbrook, this is altogether irregular. What has got into you?"

I was about to answer him when my fingers fell upon a small rocky protrusion at head height that, when the least pressure was applied upon it, gave. A distinct click was audible, and the next moment the image of the Danaides, landscape and all, swung creakily inward. A roughly square aperture stood revealed, and the sound and fresh scent of rushing water was now strong and clear coming up from below.

Dr Pentecost gaped in astonishment. "Dear Lord," he said fretfully. "What… What *is* this? What did you do? Have you broken something? I told you not to touch the picture. Oh, Sir Philip will not be happy when he finds out."

"Calm yourself, Dr Pentecost. Nothing is broken. Look. Do you not see the hinges? All I have done is uncover that which was latent."

So saying, I leaned into the aperture. I found myself peering down into a lightless vertical shaft, cylindrical in shape and some four feet in diameter. How far the shaft sank or what lay at the bottom, I could not make out with the unaided eye. I struck a match and dropped it in. It tumbled through the blackness until it was a faint distant star, which all of a sudden winked out. I estimated it had fallen perhaps fifteen yards. I dropped another match, and in its last instant of life saw its flame briefly reflected as a myriad of sparkles, scattered and fragmented, in a moving surface. This confirmed what I had deduced, that the underground aquifer lay directly at the foot of the shaft, racing along in a turbid torrent. Both times the waters had doused the matches and whisked them away.

I invited Dr Pentecost to lean in and look for himself. He shone his lamp around, its conical beam limning the shaft's rough-hewn sides but not powerful enough to reach all the way to the aquifer.

"I fail to understand," he said. "What is this shaft for? What purpose can it serve?"

"I do not know."

"I can only assume it was sunk relatively recently."

"What makes you say that?"

"Well, the picture of the Danaides is a late addition to the gallery of frescoes. I remember Sir Philip asking me – late last summer, I believe it was – if I could think of a further Tartarean punishment to add to the existing ones. The Danaides were not included at the time, so I suggested them. I simply thought he had a space on the walls and wished to fill it. It appears there was more to it than that."

"He installed this door and painted the Danaides over it as camouflage," I said.

"That can only be the case."

"Yet there is no ladder, nor a hook for a rope. No means of descending the shaft. And even if there were, nothing lies at the bottom except for a channel of fast-moving water. It is not a well. It is not a vent or a flue. I cannot for the life of me fathom its purpose."

"Nor I, unless it is simply to connect this Hades with its very own river Styx. We should ask Sir Philip about it."

"Ask Sir Philip? Oh no. I don't think so."

"Why ever not, dear girl?" said Dr Pentecost. "He is a personable fellow and I count him a friend. I do not believe he would be averse to me enquiring."

I felt otherwise. I was sure it would be an imprudent move. The conversation I had overheard between Sir Philip and Edwin Fairbrother had dispelled any last lingering doubts in my mind that there were sinister doings afoot at Charfrome. Both those men were complicit in some heinous misdeed, and I could not help but think this hidden shaft was not unrelated to that, although I could not – and still cannot – guess how.

"In answer, he will say that it is simply some innocent piece of engineering," Dr Pentecost continued. "To facilitate the plumbing at the house, perhaps."

"And the shaft is intended to provide access. The door is concealed behind a fresco solely in order to allow it to blend in with its surroundings."

"Quite so. Sir Philip is fond of such stratagems. I have told you how he admires the mighty Daedalus. Him above all the other noted figures of the Hellenic period does he exalt. In every one of his constructions, be it building, bridge or tunnel, he acknowledges Daedalus somehow."

"Really?"

"Oh yes. It is his 'signature', so to speak, on his work. Often on a façade or a keystone an architect will mount a carved emblem – a lion, an urn, a garland of flowers – something that has some private significance to him. In Sir Philip's case it is sometimes an image of Daedalus's head, but more commonly it is a triangular compasses-and-feather symbol. The head resembles others of its ilk, a bearded, high-browed visage that could belong to just about any sage of antiquity. No one observing it would realise whom it represented, not without prior knowledge. The same goes for the compasses-and-feather symbol. If anyone thought anything about it at all, they might infer that it has some link with Freemasonry."

"And because Sir Philip venerates Daedalus," I said, "he would make a door like this one."

"Daedalus was famously cunning. His name has become a byword for ingenuity and craftiness. One thinks of the Labyrinth he built at Knossos, naturally, and of the wings of wax and feather he fashioned for himself and son Icarus to escape imprisonment by King Minos. But one thinks, too, of the puzzle with which Minos attempted to ensnare him after he found refuge on Sicily and the method by which he solved it."

I could have requested further detail about this puzzle, but did not need to, for Dr Pentecost was, as I am sure I have made clear by now, an educator through and through. He couldn't help himself. Whatever the circumstances – even in a dingy cavern with but a single "pupil" in attendance –

he was only too keen to impart knowledge.

"Daedalus at the time was the guest of Sicily's King Cocalus, who had offered him sanctuary after he fled from Crete. Minos was searching for him; he did not wish him to share the secrets of the Labyrinth with anyone. His plan was to lure him out of hiding by travelling from city to city, publicly announcing a puzzle that was so difficult, only Daedalus himself could solve it. Daedalus was unable to resist the bait and, with Cocalus urging him on from the sidelines, accepted the challenge."

"What was this puzzle?"

"How to thread a piece of string through a spiral seashell. Daedalus's solution was to attach the string to an ant and entice the insect through the seashell by placing a drop of honey at the other end. Minos knew then that he had found his quarry, but luckily for Daedalus – and not so luckily for Minos – Cocalus's daughters killed him. Playing the hospitable hosts, they drew him a bath and then poured boiling water over him. A ghastly demise, but not undeserved."

"Minos was no saint, as I recall."

"A despot and a murderer," said Dr Pentecost, nodding. "His death at least proved Thales's dictum that the strangest sight of all is a *geronta tyrannon*."

"An… aged tyrant?"

"Correct! But back to Daedalus. Aside from the things he is best known for – the Labyrinth, the wings – he was an unparalleled innovator. Pliny the Elder credits him with the invention of carpentry, no less. He is alleged to have devised the saw, the drill, glue, isinglass, as well as the pair of compasses. He also came up with the notion of masts and prows for ships. He was a superb sculptor, by all accounts.

He built a sprung dancing ground for Minos's daughter Ariadne. Perhaps most notoriously, he devised a way for Minos's wife Pasiphaë to – how shall I put this delicately? – conjoin with a bull for which she had developed an unnatural passion."

"Bless me, sir!" I exclaimed, pressing the back of one hand to my forehead and fanning myself with the other hand. "I feel near overcome with a fit of the vapours."

Dr Pentecost was amused. "It involved a hollow wooden cow-shaped armature covered in the hide of a real cow. The rest I can leave to your imagination. The offspring of this aberrant union was, of course, the Minotaur. All in all, Daedalus was a master of the technical marvel, an artist of artifice. Why, then, would Sir Philip not seek to emulate his idol by creating a door that does not appear to be a door? He has, after all, been paying tribute to him throughout the course of his professional career."

I digested this intelligence, then restated my opinion that our discovery of the door remain between the two of us. "We cannot have been meant to find it," I said. "No one can."

"But we did so by accident. That exonerates us from blame. Does it not? Unless... *Was* it an accident?" Dr Pentecost arched a sly eyebrow. "Miss Holbrook, I do believe you knew all along this door existed. That is why we came here tonight, so that you might disclose it."

"No, I..."

"You had at least an inkling it was there."

"Really, Dr Pentecost, I..."

"There is something you are keeping from me."

"No. No."

"Come, my dear. I may be old but I am not senile. Just as I am good at keeping secrets, I am good at sniffing them out. You have been an efficient dissembler up until now, but the mask has slipped. Confess."

I saw no alternative. I feared that otherwise Dr Pentecost would go straight to Sir Philip and tell all. And then what? At best, Sir Philip might feel moved to eject me from Charfrome, which would bring our investigation to a grinding halt. At worst? Well, let me tell you, as I stood in that cavern beside that doorway, I had a feeling – a presentiment, if you will – of grave consequences. The shaft loomed, a sheer drop into frigid unseen waters that churned through the bowels of the earth from nowhere to nowhere.

I revealed to Dr Pentecost that I was in alliance with you, Mr Holmes; that my name was not really Shirley Holbrook; that I was in the throes of investigating Sophia's disappearance; that as Shirley Holbrook I was writing letters to you, keeping you abreast of my doings; everything.

"I see," said he slowly, when I had finished unburdening myself. "Sherlock Holmes, you say? I have some small, tenuous connection to him, not one I am particularly proud of. A former student of mine, a certain John Clay, met his comeuppance at the great detective's hands."

"Wasn't Clay behind an audacious bank robbery that Mr Holmes foiled?"

"The very man. He hoodwinked a red-headed pawnbroker called – what was he called? Something Biblical."

Familiar as I am with your exploits, Mr Holmes, and with Dr Watson's oeuvre, the name was at my fingertips. "Jabez Wilson."

"That's it. Took a job as his assistant and duped him into working elsewhere so that he might burrow through from the cellar at Wilson's premises into the City and Suburban Bank behind. Always a scoundrel, even as a boy, was Clay. I once had cause to send him to the Lower Master for a caning. That was after I had given him three rips – the term at Eton for a black mark – for handing in profoundly substandard work. He vowed revenge, and took it by secreting a dead hare under the floorboards in my rooms, the presence of which I became aware of only when it began to announce itself aromatically. It was never proved beyond doubt that Clay was the guilty party, but I knew, and he knew I knew. He was a braggart, too, forever going on about his royal blood. Despite that, or because of it, amongst his peers he was highly regarded. He was not only a member of Pop but a kind of magnet for similarly roguish young toffs. He would lead a gang of them into Windsor and carouse at pubs and get into scrapes with the townies and the constabulary. It is a wonder he was never rusticated for such behaviour, let alone expelled, but what with his father being a lord, one imagines that that protected him against all repercussions. Remind me, I have forgotten – why am I talking about him?"

"Clay fell foul of Mr Holmes."

"So he did. So he did. A bad sort, and I cheered when I read in the newspaper that he had been gaoled, and I cheered again a year on when I read Dr Watson's account of the events surrounding his arrest. Such is my one glancing association with Sherlock Holmes. And you, Miss Holbrook, are collaborating with him? You rise further in my estimation."

"I would not call it a collaboration. I am more his proxy."

"He must rate you nonetheless, to have conferred that role upon you."

"Circumstances played a part. It was *force majeure*. Yet

I like to think he would not have enlisted my aid were I just anyone."

"Quite. Quite. Now then, are you certain your friend Sophia has been the victim of malfeasance?"

"Increasingly, ineluctably, I am drawn to that conclusion."

"And Sir Philip is somehow involved?"

"Again, yes, it seems so."

Dr Pentecost deliberated for some while.

"Doctor?" I prompted.

"Hmmm?"

"You are silent, and I fear you are troubled. Speak your mind."

"You must appreciate that you have placed me in something of a quandary, my dear girl. I owe a debt of loyalty to Sir Philip. You are at Charfrome under false pretences. I must inform him."

"I beg you not to."

"I have not finished," he said with pedagogical severity. "From all you have just told me, allied with the evidence of the singular door and shaft before us, it would seem that your and Mr Holmes's suspicions are not wholly baseless. There are forces at work in this place that even I, a regular visitor, have been blissfully ignorant of. For that reason I am willing to keep mum and not expose you."

"Thank you."

"In a strange way I feel I have sensed all along that Charfrome was too good to be true. Call me cynical, but why would Sir Philip have created so seemingly beneficent an establishment if he did not have some hidden agenda? Nobody is that civic-minded; even the greatest philanthro-pists operate out of self-interest, however tiny and deeply embedded. A time-worn phrase of Virgil's springs to mind: '*timeo Danaos et dona ferentes*.'"

"Beware of Greeks bearing gifts," I said, "or Englishmen bearing the gift of Greekness."

"Neatly put. A chiasmus, too."

"All this Classicism is rubbing off on me."

Dr Pentecost smiled wanly. "Perhaps we should call it a night. You can close that door, can't you? We must not leave it ajar."

"I presume so. No doubt the same method by which it is opened…" I groped for the rocky protrusion and depressed it. "Yes. The catch engages as well as releases." The door swung shut into its close-fitting frame, becoming once again just a fresco amongst frescoes.

On the way back to the house we had a close shave. A pair of Hoplites were loitering at the edge of the copse. We might well have blundered straight into them had they not been smoking cigarettes and we not been downwind. The smell of burning tobacco gave us fair warning, however, and the glow of the cigarettes betrayed the two men's exact position. Dr Pentecost closed the vents of his lantern in time and we crouched amidst the trees, breath bated, until the Hoplites resumed patrolling.

"Well, really," my companion whispered. "If you cannot rely on ex-servicemen to keep to a schedule…"

"We ought to report them to Sergeant-Major Hart."

"Agreed. Hart should be told. It is our duty as good Elysians."

It felt good to indulge in silly banter like this. It was a distraction from our fast-beating hearts.

Once I was back in my room and abed, sleep did not come easily. My mind was racing. I wondered if it had been unwise to take Dr Pentecost fully into my confidence. Perhaps he may have second thoughts about throwing in his lot with me. Perhaps he will decide he should put his longstanding friend and paymaster Sir Philip ahead of some girl he has known only a handful of weeks. I hope not. I hope you, Mr Holmes, will judge that I have gambled sensibly, the odds stacked in my favour.

It was as I finally began to drift off into slumber that a nagging thought occurred. Said thought kept me awake a further half-hour and has been itching away in my head ever since.

I was musing on Sir Philip's fascination with Daedalus and on the symbol with which he is wont to "sign" his work – the compasses and feather. It struck me that I had seen that symbol sometime during the foregoing few days. I do not mean at the shrine in the grounds, where the statue of the great inventor holds both items, but rather somewhere in or around the house.

Racking my brains, I could not recall where. I still, twenty-four hours later, cannot, and am resolved to search for the symbol at the earliest opportunity. I would have done so today had final rehearsals for *Antigone* not filled our timetable from morning to evening.

With that, I conclude this prolix epistle. Midnight is long past and I can scarcely keep my eyes open. Tomorrow, around noon, I have a rare lull between Elysian commitments and shall use it to steal away to the village and the post office. Notwithstanding your reply, I know that I must bide my time and wait for the full moon and the Delphic Ceremony a week hence. Rest assured that I am of good cheer and that my commitment to seeing this task through is undiminished. I am in fact feeling emboldened,

perhaps because, just as you have a confederate whom
you can call upon in time of need, so now do I. Sherlock
Holmes has his Dr Watson and Shirley Holbrook has her
Dr Pentecost. We are both of us reinforced and made
braver by virtue of that.

Cordially yours,

S.H.

CHAPTER NINETEEN

A SUICIDAL SOLICITOR

Holmes, as before, dictated a reply. I, as before, redrafted and modified it so that it became less the Ten Commandments, more the Sermon on the Mount.

The gist of it was that Hannah had made good progress and must persevere. She should search, if she could, for some evidence of the people mentioned by Sir Philip and Fairbrother, Simms and Kinsella, and also Nithercott. All three were, on the balance of probabilities, former Elysians. She should not, however, make open enquiries in that connection. It would, Holmes averred, be unwise to seem too inquisitive. It was enough that she had been asking people about Sophia Tompkins. Add a further three names to that list, and suspicions would mount.

She should, also, look for the compasses-and-feather symbol, as she herself proposed. Were it appended to a door in some obscure corner of the house, somewhere it seemed either portentous or incongruous, so much the better.

"What if there is no such symbol?" I said.

"Hannah is observant. If she thinks she saw it, then in all likelihood she did. And if the impression I am starting to form of this affair is accurate, then the symbol's situation will be highly pertinent."

"Holmes, you know something, don't you?"

"I know nothing, as of this moment. But I am beginning to grasp the shape of something. A sketch is forming in my mind's eye of Sir Philip Buchanan's mentality and the lengths he will go to in order to realise his vision. Hannah, through her continued diligence, should be able to help me fill in the details."

"Do you think those two whose names Fairbrother brought up – Simms and Kinsella, was it? Do you think they are germane to the affair?"

"Whether they are or not, it certainly bears looking into."

"And the third one – Nithercott. Might he be considered a useful lead too?"

"An unusual surname, Nithercott," Holmes said musingly. "Do you recall that a fellow answering to that name killed himself a month ago? It was in the papers. Pass me down the most recent scrapbook, would you? I believe I took a clipping." He leafed through page after page adorned with rectangles of pasted-in newsprint. "Ah yes, here it is. From *The Telegraph*. 'Mr Tobias Nithercott, aged 35, of Bolton Gardens, Chelsea, was found in his drawing-room yesterday, dead by his own hand. Neighbours reported hearing a gunshot circa four AM, whereupon the alarm was raised and a collective decision was made to break into the house, in order to furnish any assistance necessary. The body was discovered within, gun in hand. Mr Nithercott, a solicitor and a bachelor, had lately returned from a sabbatical and was said to have been in depressed spirits since resuming his London life, prompting concern for his wellbeing. Police have confirmed that there are no suspicious circumstances and they are not looking for anyone else in connection with the incident.'" He closed the scrapbook. "Well, what do you make of that?"

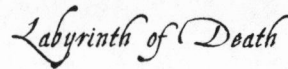

"Seems like a clear-cut case of suicide."

"Really? Nothing odd about it at all?"

"I would say no, but you obviously felt it of sufficient intrigue to be worth clipping out of the paper."

"Who, Watson, comes back from a sabbatical 'in depressed spirits'? A sabbatical traditionally refreshes mind and body and leaves one better equipped to face the rigours of daily life again."

"Does it not depend, though, on the individual's frame of mind *prior to* the sabbatical? Could Tobias Nithercott not have been in an even worse state beforehand, which a leave of absence did something to mitigate, albeit not enough?"

"Well, at any rate, I was happy to abide by Scotland Yard's judgement that there was nothing worth investigating. Had any significant anomaly cropped up relating to the suicide, doubtless Lestrade or Gregson or another of their ilk would have come knocking."

"But now, of course, we have Sir Philip and Fairbrother alluding to Nithercott."

"Alluding to *a* Nithercott. Not necessarily Tobias Nithercott."

"It is a suggestive coincidence all the same."

"Yes," said Holmes, "and according to Fairbrother, Nithercott 'took what he knew to the grave with him'. If, as seems more than possible, it is the same Nithercott and his so-called sabbatical was in fact a sojourn as an Elysian at Charfrome Old Place, something may have occurred there which weighed heavily upon his conscience – so heavily that it became unbearable and he took his own life. We must also not ignore Fairbrother's comment to Sir Philip that 'it is not the first time it has happened, is it now?'"

"Other Elysians have committed suicide? Simms and Kinsella perchance?"

"Not necessarily. I need more data, Watson. Until then, I cannot arrive at a firm conclusion. I can only hazard guesses. More data!"

CHAPTER TWENTY

DEPTHS OF DECEPTION

During the next few days Holmes's career experienced one of its periodic lulls. After the roaring tempests of the previous week he found himself in the doldrums. No clients called. No telegram came from Scotland Yard requesting urgent consultation. This ebb and flow of cases – feast followed by famine – was typical, but the discrepancy between the one and the other was seldom so marked as then.

London simmered in the midsummer heat and Holmes quietly stewed in our rooms, falling into that lassitude of body and spirit that habitually plagued him when his brain was not occupied. He smoked incessantly and indulged in his cocaine habit, pipe alternating with syringe. He scarcely moved from his armchair and ate only the bare minimum to stave off starvation. The nearest he got to any form of activity was gazing out of the window with a wistful, almost forlorn air, as though willing some passer-by or cab to halt at the front door.

I, meanwhile, was on tenterhooks. I busied myself with my rounds, such as they were. I listened as attentively as I could to my patients' litanies of woe and ministered to their needs with all the skill that was mine to summon. Yet my mind was always at least partly elsewhere, down in the bosky folds of Dorset, imagining what Hannah Woolfson was up to and wishing I could be there to look after her. She might have found an ally in Dr Pentecost, but he could never be as steadfast a champion as I would have been, nor as willing a one.

Each evening I came home hoping for a new missive from Hannah. I would enter an apartment so fogged with tobacco smoke that it seemed a London particular had taken up exclusive residence in our rooms. I would attempt to rouse Holmes from his torpor, fail, and console myself that if Hannah's letter had come during my absence he would surely be more enlivened than he was. Then I would change into evening dress and venture forth alone in search of diversion, to a West End theatre or else to a gaming club where faro and hazard were played.

Such was the pattern of my existence for four days, broken on the fifth by the arrival of the much-anticipated letter. It came by first post, and I demanded that Holmes unseal the envelope even before he and I had embarked upon breakfast. With an insouciant smile, he obliged.

My dear Mr Holmes, and of course Dr Watson,

First of all, I must tell you that I was followed on my journey from Charfrome to Waterton Parva and back when going to pick up your previous letter from the post office. I am certain of it. Almost certain. I had not even a glimpse of a pursuer but one knows when one is not alone. Both ways through the woods I had the distinct impression of stealthy footfalls behind me. Or was I imagining it? Conceivably I was. The mind can play tricks, not least when it is in a constant state of heightened tension. I am doing my best to remain calm and collected, but it is not easy when an awareness of peril dogs my every waking moment. There may well have been no pursuer, only a phantom projection of my own anxiety. And yet…

Our *Antigone*, for what it is worth, went off without a hitch. Everyone thoroughly enjoyed taking part – except me. It was a riot of masks and masquerade and exaggerated acting, but all I could think throughout was that Charfrome itself was a stage where performances were being given and where certain people were pretending to be that which they were not. (I include myself among them.) We players paraded back and forth across the amphitheatre's proscenium beneath a balmy evening sky, intoning Sophocles's doom-laden verse about death and burial and suicide, and to me it was both a hollow experience and one all too fraught with connotation. Antigone is prepared to defy royal edict and give her brother Polynices, slain on the battlefield, a proper funeral. For that she suffers the punishment of being interred alive in a tomb. Might a similar dark fate lie in store for me if I persist in my efforts to delve into Sophia's disappearance? Must doing what feels right inevitably incur a penalty?

Our audience was sparse – just Sir Philip, Fairbrother, Dr Pentecost and various of our other tutors and instructors. They all lapped up the play and applauded lustily enough at the end that it felt as though the auditorium was packed. Again, though, as we thespians took our bows, there seemed a falseness to it all. On both sides, dissimulation. Behind Sir Philip's ready grin and bonhomie lies, I am sure, depths of deception. Behind Fairbrother's too. And who else's amongst the staff at Charfrome? Who else is privy to the secrets this place hides?

Could one of those audience members have been my unseen stalker in the woods? Assuming that stalker ever existed. For heaven's sake, nothing is certain any more…

"Good Lord, Holmes!" I exclaimed, looking up from the letter. "The girl is becoming half unhinged from the strain. Her every word proclaims it. Even her handwriting is erratic. I really must insist that we intervene. We should pull her out of there right away. Her sanity is at risk."

"She is merely undergoing a crisis," replied Holmes. "It is to be expected."

"Merely!? I have seen how crises like this can damage even the hardiest constitution, sometimes irreparably."

"Have faith. Hannah will endure. Look. The very next page of the letter finds her in more sanguine mood. The handwriting neatens again, too."

As to Simms, Kinsella and Nithercott, I regret to say I have drawn a blank. There is, as far as I can gather, no paper record of Elysians' comings and goings, no ledger, no visitors' book, at least none known to me or generally available. Sir Philip himself may log the names of Charfrome residents past and present, but if so, it is not in any documentation to which I have access. And since I am denied the recourse of asking other Elysians or members of staff about the three, it leaves me with little option. I am sorry.

On the other hand, with regard to the compasses-and-feather symbol, you will be glad to know that I have had greater success. I have, in fact, found it. After a comprehensive hunt through every nook and cranny of the house, I at last hit upon its location. You suggested that the symbol might seem either portentous or incongruous in its placement, and I would aver that it is both, for it adorns a door adjacent to the scullery. It is carved into the panelling, which to my mind implies that the door – though otherwise ordinary and unremarkable – is an addition of Sir Philip's to the house. Why, though, has he inserted it in the servants' wing, where only domestic drudgery is carried out?

Naturally I tried the handle. Naturally the door was locked. I put my ear to the wood but heard nothing through it. I had had the vague notion that the room beyond might be a prison, with some miserable wretch – Sophia, perchance – confined within.

All I can say about that room is that it is small. By poking my nose into the scullery on the left and into the laundry whose entrance lies on the right-hand side of the door, and seeing the internal dimensions of both, I can estimate that the space between them cannot be wider than about five or six feet, while the depth of the room presumably matches theirs. In other words, it is not dissimilar in size to a pantry. But the house already has a pantry elsewhere. So what is this room used for?

Charfrome's irascible Grecian chef, Labropoulos, happened to pass by as I was surveying the door. He came bustling purposefully along the corridor, clutching an object in both arms: a large glass jar with a tea towel draped over it. No sooner had he laid eyes on me than he challenged me in a fairly aggressive manner, asking what I was doing there. The reason for this upbraiding, it seemed, was broadly territorial. The kitchen parts of the house were his domain. I did not belong.

There was alcohol on the man's breath, which doubtless contributed to the lowering of his inhibitions and the heightening of his temper. It contributed also to my eagerness in apologising to him and absenting myself from his vicinity. As I made to take my leave, however, my eye was caught by movement within the jar. The vessel was, it seemed, host to something alive. A number of living things, in fact. Beneath the lower edge of the tea towel I glimpsed several small creatures moving about, crawling over one another. Insects of some sort, each an inch long, predominantly brown, with long rear legs and waving antennae.

"What are those?" I said. "They look like crickets."

"Is not your business," Labropoulos replied curtly.

"Where are you taking them?"

"Never you mind. Is not for you to know. Now go."

He flapped a hand at me a fraction of an inch from my face, much as though he was miming a backhand slap. I felt the waft of its passage.

I took the hint and stepped back to let him proceed on his way. In the event, Labropoulos stood his ground and waited for *me* to depart. Once I started moving, he refused to take his eyes off me until I gained the end of the corridor. I imagine he continued to stare long after I was out of sight.

I can only speculate what that jar of crickets was for. Labropoulos is a chef, so could it perhaps be food? But, if so, food for whom? I am not sure I want to know the answer. I have a feeling crickets were an Ancient Greek delicacy. I hope we Elysians will not be expected to eat them too.

"Ugh," I said with a shudder. "I hope not either. Makes me feel queasy even at the thought of it."

It is now only three days until the full moon. Finally people are beginning to murmur about the Delphic Ceremony. It remains a taboo subject, but here and there it is mentioned in hushed tones, Elysian affirming to Elysian its imminence, a wry look often accompanying the remark. Those who already know what the event entails stay tight-lipped, making those who don't all the more curious to find out for themselves.

I have pressed Dr Pentecost on the subject more than once, but even he, my newfound confidant, is less than forthcoming.

"It is just a ritual, my dear," he said to me yesterday when I engaged him after a Greek language lesson. I waited until all my fellow pupils had filed out of the classroom and we two were alone. "Bizarre to a degree, gruesome too, but oddly affecting, and essentially harmless."

"Bizarre? Gruesome?"

"Trust me, it is nothing you need concern yourself over."

"You might at least give me some hint as to the ceremony's nature. It is connected with graduation, yes?"

"It is a winnowing process," Dr Pentecost said. "It assists Sir Philip in choosing from those who have excelled themselves as Elysians. Three evenings hence, we staff members are getting together, as we do each month the night before the full moon, to consult together and draw up a shortlist of potential candidates. We discuss various names, but Sir Philip has final say. A half-dozen are selected, and the Delphic Ceremony then, a day later, singles out two of them as graduates. A bit of mummery, a bit of mumbo-jumbo, a few Hellenic flourishes, and that is that."

"What becomes of the lucky two?"

"They may stay on at Charfrome if they wish, but the great majority of them leave, as is expected of them. The outside world beckons. They take the skills they have acquired here, and the cultural lessons they have learned, and apply them in their daily lives. Spreading the Elysian gospel, as it were, amongst the great unwashed."

More than that I could not prevail upon him to reveal. It so happened, anyway, that we were interrupted by Polly Speedwell, who knocked tentatively on the classroom door.

"Dr Pentecost," she said. "Sorry to trouble you. May I have a word?"

"Of course you may, my dear."

"On a private matter."

"Absolutely. Miss Holbrook was just leaving. Weren't you, Miss Holbrook?"

"I was," I said, somewhat puzzled. I had not been aware that Polly had any sort of relationship with Dr Pentecost beyond that of student and teacher.

Polly must have registered my mild bafflement. "Dr Pentecost is such a good listener," she said confidingly as I passed her by. "I feel as though I can talk to him about anything."

"And it shall never go further than me," the man himself chimed in. "You can guarantee that."

He added, for my benefit, a surreptitious wink, implying that the secrets that I had shared with him were perfectly safe.

I left the classroom feeling obscurely jealous. I had believed my friendship with Dr Pentecost was an exclusive one, special. It seemed, however, that Polly shared a closeness with him which rivalled if not surpassed mine. Perhaps it was because he is just that kind of person, one who engenders trust, especially in women.

In that respect, his opposite is Edwin Fairbrother, who only *seems* trustworthy and is in truth anything but.

Regardless, in my quest to glean information about the Delphic Ceremony I tried my hand with him – and met with no more success than with Dr Pentecost. Fairbrother, incidentally, has spent the entire past week at the house. This is unusual for him, as I understand it, and I believe, without immodesty, that I am the reason. He does his best to engage me at every available opportunity, intercepting me between lessons and pouncing on me whenever I am alone. How I managed to evade him long enough to conduct my house-wide search for the symbol, I shall never know. It was some kind of miracle.

At any rate, Fairbrother is persistent in his attentions, and I am under no illusion as to what he wants from me. Beneath that suave exterior lurks a savage. I can no longer bear to feign interest and so I brush him off at every turn, but this serves only to make him the more ardent, and the more irksome.

I affected to find him fascinating again briefly, just for the purpose of probing him about the Ceremony. I invited him to take a walk with me through the knot garden, which lies to the west of the house, not far from the servants' wing. You may have seen it: a maze of knee-high privet hedge that covers perhaps half the acreage of a football pitch, with gravelled pathways and a peculiar octagonal building at its centre, made of brick and windowless, accessible only by a low iron door – some sort of storage place, I imagine, for gardening tools. I chose the knot garden as a venue for the assignation because it is exposed to view on all sides, and therefore Fairbrother might be deterred from any attempt at physical impropriety, for fear of eyewitnesses.

I was at my coquettish best. After acting as though his siege was beginning to wear down my fortifications, I subtly drew the conversation around to the ceremony.

To no avail. Fairbrother, like everyone else, would not be drawn on the subject. He made it plain that he *would* tell me something about the ceremony in exchange for a kiss. I rejected the offer, thinking the price too high. Maybe you will chide me for that, Mr Holmes, but one must have standards.

"Frosty, eh?" he said after I had turned him down. "Well, I have known a fair few like you, Miss Holbrook. Known 'em and thawed 'em. Your friend Sophia for one."

I can barely describe the hideousness of the smirk that smeared itself over his face as he said this. The temptation to strike him was so strong, I had to spin on my heel and flee, lest I give in to it.

"I wish you had," I said.

Holmes refrained from comment. He had ceased to find it strange how invested I was in Hannah's welfare.

I hastened out of the knot garden, with Fairbrother's mocking laughter ringing in my ears. As I neared the house, I ran into the Hoplite called Quigg. I say "ran into" because that is practically what happened. In my hot-tempered indignation, my blind eagerness to put distance between me and Fairbrother, I was not looking where I was going. The large, bald hulk of a man loomed suddenly before me, as though out of nowhere, and I had to halt sharply in my tracks to avoid a collision.

"Miss Holbrook—" said he.

"Excuse me," I said, and made to bypass him.

"Wait. I would have words."

"And I would rather not."

A hand flashed out and seized my wrist. His grip was painfully strong.

"Unhand me, sir," I demanded, squirming. "This instant."

"No, you just listen, missy," Quigg growled. "You need to mind what you are doing. I cannot put it any plainer than that. I heard from Labropoulos that you were down by the kitchens yesterday, for no good reason."

"So?"

"A girl snooping around the place, a girl poking her nose where it doesn't belong – that kind of girl can come a cropper if she's not careful. Same goes for a girl who is not fussy about the company she keeps."

"I have no fondness for the company I am keeping right this instant," I said. "Again, sir, unhand me, or I shall scream."

"I am warning you."

"And *I* am warning *you*," I said. "I shall have no hesitation in alerting the entire household to the fact that you are molesting me, unless you let me go immediately."

Before Quigg could reply, I heard Fairbrother yell, "Hallo! What is the matter? What is going on there?"

At that, the Hoplite relinquished his hold on me. He shot me a severe, menacing look, his jaw jutting. Then he donned a servile attitude as Fairbrother came hurrying over to us.

"The young lady stumbled, Mr Fairbrother," he said in a mild voice. "I was helping her up."

"Stumbled, eh?" said Fairbrother. "Is that what happened, Miss Holbrook?"

I glanced from one man to the other, unsure what to do. If I told Fairbrother the truth, he would doubtless feel moved to castigate Quigg on my behalf and I would then be in his debt. On the other hand, if I colluded in Quigg's falsehood, I would be condoning his loutish behaviour. Talk about the devil and the deep blue sea.

All said and done, the latter alternative seemed the lesser of two evils. Quigg is a plain brute, whereas Fairbrother is a scheming, manipulative brute and I would rather not be beholden to him for anything. Quigg, besides, appeared to have been advising me to steer clear of Fairbrother – as if I needed such a recommendation! – and so, of the two of them, I was narrowly inclined to feel a greater kinship with him.

"My heel caught in the hem of my skirt," I said. "I apologise, Mr Quigg, for discommoding you."

"It was no trouble," Quigg said stiffly.

"Then all is well," said Fairbrother. "Perhaps, Miss Holbrook, you would be willing to resume our little tête-à-tête…?"

"Kind of you, Mr Fairbrother, but no. I think I shall just go to my room."

He tipped his hat, and I absented myself from his company and Quigg's as swiftly as I could.

Nothing remains for me to add except that I feel no nearer a resolution to this affair than when I last communicated. I seem to be going round in circles. The continuing hot weather enervates me. The rural isolation of Charfrome Old Place oppresses me. Tomorrow night the Delphic Ceremony is held. I will write again once I have witnessed it. At least then I may have something to report that is of practical use to you.

I will stay the course.

S.H.

CHAPTER TWENTY-ONE

CERTAINTIES, CERTAINTIES, CERTAINTIES

Holmes regarded me evenly across the breakfast china as I finished the letter.

"Well?" he said.

"Well what?"

"Are you not going to harangue me about fetching Hannah home? Am I not due for another patented Watsonian bleat about the girl's safety?"

"I have observed that my protestations fall on deaf ears," I replied somewhat tartly.

"In my view, she is acquitting herself admirably. Her nerve has wavered but she has held it nonetheless. I cannot ask for more than that from her. And no, I forbid it."

"Forbid…?"

"I saw your gaze rove to the bookshelf. I saw which book it alighted upon. *Bradshaw's*. You are contemplating taking a train down to Dorset. Please do not. Not yet."

"I am wondering how you would stop me."

"By force if I must, but I would prefer by argument. Consider this. You turn up at Charfrome, service revolver in hand, chest puffed up with chivalry and indignation. Say that you are somehow able to get past Malachi Hart and his fellow Hoplites without taking a bullet for your pains. Say, too, that you reach Hannah and succeed in convincing her to leave with you. Those are both improbable scenarios, given the Hoplites' strategic superiority and the tenacity that Hannah has amply displayed, but let us proceed with the assumption that they both come to pass. What then? Our case is at an end. Our best chance of finding out what has become of Sophia Tompkins is gone. No longer do we have our woman on the inside, our spy in the enemy's camp. No longer do we have the advantage that nobody at Charfrome, save for Dr Pentecost, realises that Sherlock Holmes is investigating. All you will have achieved is to trample over the crop we have been so patiently and carefully nurturing."

"I could—"

"No." Holmes held up a bony forefinger. "Again, I can read you. Your eyes darted to our 'client chair', the very place where Sir Osbert sat and smoked while waiting for us. You are thinking of contacting him, knowing that his position and influence will furnish you with an army of policemen to serve as reinforcements. With them by your side, mounting a siege on Charfrome would be an easy matter. The Hoplites would concede. The fair damsel would be yours to rescue. But still we would be in the same bind. We do not yet have sufficient evidence of a crime. We have no way of proving that Sophia is dead or, if alive, being held against her will."

"Someone is covering up something at Charfrome," I insisted. I felt resentful, as I always did when Holmes intuited my thoughts and brought them into the light as deftly as a heron plucking fish from the water. It was as though I had no privacy from him, even inside my own head.

"Indubitably," said he. "But which someone? What something?

We are in a realm of nebulousness. All we can see are vague silhouettes, ghosts in the gloom. We need certainties, Watson." He banged the table with a fist, making crockery jump and cutlery shiver. "Certainties. Certainties. Without them, we flail and then we fail. If you surrender to the impulses you are presently feeling, noble and laudable though they are, you tip our hand, and our opponent, whoever he is, wins."

"What must we do, then?" I said dispiritedly.

"Like Hannah, stay the course."

"Are we to write back to her?"

"Not until she has written again to us. Her attendance at the Delphic Ceremony tomorrow night should yield further intelligence. Cheer up, old friend. This will end well."

I grumbled but acquiesced.

If nothing else, Hannah's letter pulled Holmes some way out of his funk. The very next day, he was able to shake it off altogether, for just as he was lamenting how "from the point of view of the criminal expert" London had become uninteresting since the death of Professor Moriarty, a visitor arrived at Baker Street in the flustered shape of John Hector McFarlane.

The name will be familiar to those who have read my recently published chronicle "The Adventure of the Norwood Builder" and I shall not re-state the facts of the case in these pages. It is pertinent to note, however, that Holmes spent the whole of that day and much of the next clearing McFarlane from suspicion of having murdered said builder, Mr Jonas Oldacre.

Ebullient after this triumph, Holmes proposed that he and I go out for the evening. I was not in the mood and said I would rather stay home and make notes on the Norwood case while the events were still fresh in my memory.

Thus it was that I was alone at Baker Street when Hannah's fourth letter arrived.

I should not have opened it, for it was not addressed to me. Technically it was Holmes's private correspondence.

But had I not been mentioned in the greeting at the start of her two previous letters? Even if the envelope did not have my name on it, the pages within must do.

With this justification established, I slit open the envelope.

The handwriting was shaky but unmistakably Hannah's. The letter appeared to have been written in a state of profound emotional turmoil.

Dear Mr Holmes and Dr Watson,

Everything is clear now. I have been mistaken, indeed foolish. There is nothing amiss at Charfrome Old Place. Any fears I may have had are unfounded. You need be concerned for me no more.

I am grateful for the assistance and reassurance you have provided. Please tell my father that all is well. I am being looked after and want for naught.

As Plutarch says, quoting Caesar: "ἀνερρίφθω κύβος". The die is cast.

Yours sincerely,
Hannah

An image flashed into my head: the odious Edwin Fairbrother bending over Hannah, dictating to her while bandying about dire threats – what he would do to her if she did not comply. That snatch of Ancient Greek at the end was his attempt to make the letter sound even more as though it came from an Elysian, a flourish he no doubt thought clever; yet I saw through it.

Rage coursed through me like lightning. The villain!

I knew I should wait for Holmes to return home. I knew I should consult with him before taking action.

But I had a very clear idea what he would say. He would say what he had been saying repeatedly for three weeks now. We should be patient. Everything was under control. Hannah would be fine.

She would *not* be fine. I knew it with every fibre of my being. Not unless I went to her, post haste.

A quick consultation of *Bradshaw's* showed me there was a late train to Dorchester, and I had time to catch it if I hurried.

I grabbed my trusty Webley and a box of Eley's No. 2 cartridges and ran into the street to hail a cab.

CHAPTER TWENTY-TWO

TRAVEL TRAVAILS

How long that journey from Paddington to Dorchester took! The train dawdled through the gathering dusk, westward into the sunset, stopping at every station and halt along the way and spending what felt like an eternity at each until finally the guard blew his whistle and the engine lurched into motion again.

Once at Dorchester I had the devil of a task securing onward transportation to Waterton Parva. The hour was nearing midnight and the town was all but dead. Eventually, having enquired at a string of inns and taverns, I found an elderly provincial, a carpenter by trade, who was willing to drive me. He proposed an extortionate fare, which I, seeing no alternative, agreed to.

We had to walk to his house, somewhere on the town's outskirts, and then the carpenter had to harness his horse to his trap. This procedure, like the train journey, seemed to take an absurdly long time, and all the while anguish was eating at me within. I kept picturing Hannah at Edwin Fairbrother's mercy. The thought of it made my blood boil.

At last we were on our way, clip-clopping through the dark.

The carpenter seemed content to travel at a snail's pace, and no matter how often I told him it was a matter of urgency and we should speed up, he would not comply. At best he would give the horse's flank a desultory tap of the whip, which the beast hardly registered. I was aware that he was fairly drunk. He had been when I first encountered him, but I had been prepared to overlook this. Beggars cannot be choosers. However, I had expected that he would sober up, and in the event, he did not. Then all at once his head drooped and he was snoring.

With a cluck of disgust, I deposited him in the back of the trap and occupied the driving seat myself. Now at least I was able to inject some velocity into the journey. The only problem was that I had no clear idea where I was going. Fingerposts there were aplenty, but none bore the magic words 'Waterton Parva'.

I forged on regardless. We cantered through slumbering hamlets, up hill and down dale. The trap's lanterns illuminated just a few feet of the road ahead, and dimly, so that my eyes soon ached from straining to see. The ring of the horse's hooves became monotonous, as did the stertorous breathing of the carpenter in the back. A downpour added further to my discomfort. Yet nothing could quench my determination to rescue Hannah from Fairbrother's clutches. I would get to her come hell or high water.

Suddenly, to my surprise, we entered a smallish town whose sign announced it was Waterton Magna. The name had not featured on any fingerpost I had passed lately, at least not to my knowledge. I had stumbled upon the place more or less by happenstance.

I felt jubilant. Providence had smiled on me. As if to confirm the change on my fortunes, the rain eased off. The sky cleared, stars appeared, and lo and behold, the way to Waterton Parva was plainly designated.

Within half an hour I was outside the entrance to Charfrome Old Place. I tethered the horse to a fence and tossed a few coins at my supposed driver, still fast asleep in the back. I gave him every shilling he had asked for. The carpenter might not have kept his end of the bargain, but I am someone who always does and I wanted to prove a point.

Drawing my revolver, I nudged open the gates and stepped through.

Into the lions' den.

CHAPTER TWENTY-THREE

FORTUNE FAVOURS THE BOLD

After the delays I had experienced getting this far, I had no reason to believe that the final leg of the journey would be plain sailing. Far from it. Between me and the house stood half a mile of parkland and an uncertain number of Hoplites. I knew full well that at least one of them went armed. Possibly they all did.

I kept to the grass at the edge of the gravelled driveway, to muffle my footfalls. I was weary and travel-sore. My clothes were sodden. I was at a low ebb, but a core of nervous energy kept me alert. The Webley brought its own reassurance. It had seen me out of numerous tight spots, both in Afghanistan and, subsequently, in the company of Sherlock Holmes. I felt an affinity for that gun as I might for a close comrade. Never once had it failed me. Its two pounds of British steel were as valuable to me as ten times that weight in gold.

I had gone no more than a couple of hundred yards when there was a flicker of movement at the periphery of my vision. Without thinking twice I swivelled round, pistol raised.

"Who goes there?" I challenged. "Show yourself or I fire."

There was no answer. I could see only a thin line of trees, a salient of the woodland that bounded the estate.

"I know someone is there," I said, although I was not so sure. "You have to the count of three. One. Two."

"Wait. Wait," said a panicked voice.

A figure emerged from the tree shadows, hands aloft.

"Do not shoot," this man said. "I am a friend. Don't you recognise me?"

"Dr Pentecost," I said, lowering the gun.

"One and the same," said the classicist. "And you are Dr John Watson. We have not been formally introduced but I remember your face from a fortnight or so back, when you and your famous colleague looked in on one of my lessons. I have been waiting for you to come. Praying for it." He glanced past me hopefully. "Mr Holmes is not with you?"

"I am alone."

Dr Pentecost was silent for a moment, before saying, "Well, one is better than none, I suppose. I appreciate you being here, Doctor. Miss Holbrook – Miss Woolfson, as you know her – is in terrible danger, and I cannot rectify that by myself. I am not suited, physically or temperamentally, for the job."

"Where is she?" I demanded. "Where is Hannah? You must take me to her."

"But of course. We will have to follow a roundabout route, though. You know just as I do that these grounds are well guarded. This way."

He trotted off towards the woods, and I set off eagerly in his wake. It was good finally to be taking direct action, having been forced to play the passive spectator for so long. I did not care what might become of the Sophia Tompkins investigation now; I cared only about Hannah. It seemed probable that by saving the latter I would be resolving the entire case anyway, for doubtless she had got herself into the same predicament as her friend. The scoundrel behind Sophia's disappearance was the scoundrel also menacing Hannah.

"It is Fairbrother, is it not?" I said to Dr Pentecost as we passed amongst the trees.

"Hmm? What's that you say?"

"Edwin Fairbrother has abducted Miss Holbrook with a view to having his wicked way with her."

"Absolutely. Just so."

"I knew it!" I ejaculated. "She could not fend him off indefinitely. An unprincipled rogue like him never gives up and will go so far as to take by compulsion what is not given by consent. Fairbrother made her write that last letter she sent. It was meant to sound like a valediction, to put us off, but anyone with eyes to see could tell it was a cry for help."

"How astute. You came to that conclusion by yourself?"

"I did. Holmes was not around when I read the letter, but I flatter myself to think that I have picked up a bit of his analytical prowess during our many years together. The overall tone of the letter, I thought, was 'off'. But what clinched it for me – what told me that the writing of it had been coerced – was the signature. Hannah put down her real name. Fairbrother would not have known all her previous letters were signed 'Shirley Holbrook' or 'S.H.' One can only assume that he had already got her to admit to being an impostor. Consequently her use of 'Hannah' would not seem anomalous to him, but it did to me. Hannah was counting on being able to slip that past him and use it as a way of flagging up that she was in trouble, a coded distress signal."

"Clever girl."

"The more so because she was under pressure. Her presence of mind, in the circumstances, was truly commendable. I only hope that I am not too late. Fairbrother must have had her in his possession for at least twenty-four hours. I dread to think—"

"Shhh!"

Dr Pentecost seized me by the shoulder and pulled me down. On our knees we hid behind the ivy-wreathed trunk of a fallen elm.

"What is it?" I whispered. "Hoplites?"

"Three of them. They have deviated from their customary patrol routes. How frightful."

I peeked above the tree trunk. "I don't see anyone."

"Keep your head down. They are only a dozen or so yards away. They are coming straight towards us."

I steadied my breathing and pricked my ears. There was no sound detectable save the susurration of leaves overhead, but I knew from bitter experience how stealthy the Hoplites could be. I tightened my grip on the Webley. If I had to shoot my way out of this situation, if that was what it would take to clear a path to Hannah, I would do it.

I was aware of Dr Pentecost shifting position slightly beside me.

"*Audentes fortuna iuvat,*" I heard him murmur.

"Come again?" I said.

"'Fortune favours the bold.' Forgive me, Doctor. I have never done this before. I trust I shall gauge it right."

He had a short, stout branch in his hand.

It whisked through the air.

I felt a stunning impact on the back of my head and went sprawling. I tried to recover, but a second impact followed in swift succession, harder than the first. A burst of white light exploded in my vision, and after that there was only a profound, all-engulfing blackness.

CHAPTER TWENTY-FOUR

ANTECHAMBER

In the popular imagination it is a simple matter to recover from being knocked unconscious. The square-jawed heroes of adventure fiction, having received a wallop to the head that renders them insensible, awaken in the next chapter feeling no ill effects whatsoever. They brush off the injury, leap to their feet and re-enter the fray as though nothing has happened. Perhaps the author may grant them a bruise, usually "egg-sized" or at least "egg-shaped", which they touch gingerly at the cost of a manly wince or two, but beyond this they do not suffer.

Let me tell you, as a medical man and someone, moreover, who has personally been the recipient of just such a blow, it is not like that at all.

Firstly, one does not snap back into consciousness. It is a slow, incremental process. Then there is the attendant disorientation. Memories of events leading up to the concussion have to be pieced together. One cannot readily recall what brought on the sudden oblivion, nor fathom where one is now.

Pain comes next – the feeling that the skull is in fragments, shards of it piercing the brain – and with that, nausea. There is also a blurring of the vision, which can take some time to pass.

In short, it is a profoundly unpleasant experience, and it was mine to endure as, some unknown length of time later, I came to. For several minutes all I could do was lie where I was, flat on my face, cold flagstone beneath my cheek. The floor seemed to be pitching and yawing like the deck of a ship wallowing in heavy seas, and I fought to keep my gorge down.

Once this sensation faded I attempted to rise from my prone position. My muscles, however, mutinied. I felt as weak as a new-born calf.

That was when I heard someone speak. It was a voice I had despaired of hearing ever again, and it cut sweetly through the pain and the enfeeblement, like a melody amid dissonance.

"Dr Watson," said Hannah Woolfson. "You poor thing. Take care. Do not exert yourself."

I managed to turn my head and, with some effort, focus my gaze. Hannah's lovely face was looking down on me, full of solicitude. Her features were haloed by the light of a Tilley lamp that hung from a hook on the wall, its flame turned low.

It embarrasses me to admit that I made some comment about being in heaven and seeing an angel. In my defence, my thoughts were scattered, disorderly. It was creditable that I could frame any sentence at all, let alone a flirtatious compliment.

Hannah had the good grace to smile at my gaucherie. Yet the smile was troubled and hollow.

"You have fallen prey to Dr Pentecost's chicanery," she said, "just as I did."

"It would appear so."

"I was wholly taken in by him. I thought him a friend."

"Do not berate yourself." I made a second stab at getting up. I succeeded in elevating myself onto all fours. With gritted teeth and a lot of groaning I translated this posture into a seated one, after which feat I had to wait some while until my head stopped whirling and another bout of biliousness had abated.

"Where are we?" I said.

"Beneath the house," came the reply. "Behind the door."

"Which door?"

"The one with the symbol on it. Sir Philip's door."

Blearily I took stock. We occupied a narrow corridor-like space with a cold, clammy atmosphere. At one end, steps led up to a door – that to which Hannah had referred, for she had gestured towards it. It was firmly shut. At the other end lay a second door, its threshold level with the floor we were sitting upon. This door, also shut, was made of steel and set within a frame of stone – solid granite, it looked like. Into the lintel was carved the triangular compasses-and-feather symbol that was the trademark of Sir Philip Buchanan. The feather formed the triangle's base, the compasses its two other sides, their hinge its topmost vertex.

"This is some sort of antechamber," I said. "But to what? What lies beyond?"

"I wish I knew," said Hannah. "How come you are alone, Doctor? Not that I am not pleased to see you, but I must say I was hoping Mr Holmes too would have answered my call."

"I shall choose not to feel slighted, Hannah."

"No offence was meant."

"None was taken. The truth is, I acted independently, without conferring with Holmes first. Rashness, perhaps, on my part. But I felt I could not delay a moment longer. I had visions of you… Well, I would rather not say."

"Me in dire straits?"

"It was abundantly clear that you did not write your last letter willingly. You were prevailed upon to pretend all was well."

"I meant to subvert that by signing it 'Hannah'. Dr Pentecost ought to have been none the wiser. I forgot that I had told him I wrote to Mr Holmes as Shirley Holbrook."

"If it had been Fairbrother, as I first supposed, you might have got away with it."

"You thought Edwin Fairbrother was behind the letter?" She sounded mildly incredulous.

"I know better now."

"Fairbrother may possess a low cunning but he is far from shrewd. Dr Pentecost on the other hand… Still, with that signature, I hoped to deceive him."

"But you did not succeed."

"No. Rather, I was the one deceived. As were you."

"That is, sadly, all too true," I said, exploring the occipital region of my cranium with careful fingers. There were a brace of contusions, one larger than the other but both equally tender when palpated. They felt spherical rather than ovoid. So much for "egg-shaped".

"The only conclusion one can draw is that he did not prevent me signing the letter 'Hannah' because he was well aware what I was doing. He knew that I was surreptitiously trying to alert you that I was in difficulties, and did not mind because he was not intending to deter you with the letter. The opposite. He was laying a trap, and I was the unwitting agent of it."

"Confound it all. Yes. What an idiot I have been!"

"It may not be a comfort, but you are not the only idiot here," Hannah said. "Dr Pentecost duped me as though I was a mere child. Now I must face the consequences of my naivety and gullibility."

"Are we prisoners?" I asked.

"Both doors are locked. The door above is guarded, too. I would say that is the definition of imprisonment."

"Who guards it?"

"Malachi Hart. I heard Dr Pentecost giving him orders that

no one may enter for any reason whatever. Furthermore, if either of us makes too much noise, Hart is to come down and – a direct quotation – 'address the matter'."

"Shouting for help is out of the question, then."

"Not that anyone would hear, at this time of the night, in this section of the house."

"Hart is loyal to Dr Pentecost, I take it."

"He was the one who bore your unconscious body down here. Dr Pentecost himself could not have done that. Dr Pentecost has some hold over Hart. I am not sure what it is, although I can hazard a guess. Whatever its nature, it appears sufficient to ensure his full compliance."

"You doubt, then, that Hart could be persuaded to let us out."

"I do. Very much."

"A pity." I patted my jacket pocket. The box of Eley's was still there, although of my gun there was no sign. "Bullets," I sighed, "but no revolver."

"Dr Pentecost was carrying a revolver when you were brought in," Hannah said. "Yours, presumably. Never have I seen a man look less adept at wielding such a weapon. He appeared not to know one end from the other."

I laughed, for all that it made my head throb sickeningly. "Maybe he will do us a favour and shoot himself by accident."

Hannah laughed too, albeit in a sombre manner. "I would certainly consider volunteering to pull the trigger, now that I know who he is. What he is. What he has done."

"It sounds as though there is a tale to tell."

"There is," she said grimly.

I shrugged my shoulders. "We appear not to be going anywhere for the time being. Regale me."

CHAPTER TWENTY-FIVE

THE TRIPOD AND THE LAUREL SMOKE

Things were uneventful, Hannah said, until the night of the Delphic Ceremony.

The ceremony itself was just as Dr Pentecost had foretold: bizarre, gruesome, yet oddly affecting. It commenced with a torch-lit procession that meandered through the grounds of the house to the temple, the largest of the follies on the estate. Leading the way was Buchanan, decked out in the garb of an Ancient Greek priest – an embroidered purple cloak and a golden headband. The rest of the Elysians had donned Hellenic clothing too, every man in a *chiton*, every woman in a *peplos*, both genders with a long flowing *himation* draped over the shoulders and sandals upon the feet. These were the outfits they had worn for the performance of *Antigone*, adopted now for a stranger, more sacred purpose.

At the temple, everyone gathered in a semicircle around Buchanan, who began reciting a pagan liturgy, each section in Greek first then English. He opened by declaring that all unclean persons must remove themselves from the premises. Then he made the attendees vow never to talk about the Mysteries they observed tonight, not to friends, not to relatives, not to loved ones, not even to one another."

"But Hannah," I interjected, "are you not breaking that vow at this very moment by detailing the proceedings of the Delphic Ceremony to me?"

"I could not care less," said Hannah, with some rancour.

Once the oath had been sworn, Buchanan started to intone a series of ritualistic prayers and incantations. He beseeched the gods to look upon tonight's events with favour from their lofty vantage point on Mount Olympus. He invoked the entire pantheon from All-Father Zeus downward. He asked for divine guidance, begging to become the conduit through which the gods' will would be done. As he made these imprecations he time and again raised both arms to the skies, a pious supplicant.

So far, the atmosphere at the occasion remained festive and buoyant. Buchanan was taking the role of hierophant very seriously, but amongst the Elysians there was a certain level of gaiety. Those who did not know what was coming, like Hannah, were all smiles and quizzical frowns. Those who did were gleefully braced for the reaction from the uninitiated. Quite a lot of wine had been imbibed at supper beforehand, which helped elevate the general mood. Edwin Fairbrother was, in Hannah's estimation, one of the drunkest present. Glassy-eyed and crapulous, he had surrounded himself with a coterie of young females, amongst them Polly Speedwell. His every boorish remark evoked peals of girlish giggles, with Polly contributing loudly and feigning shock at his more outrageous pronouncements. Of all the women around him, Fairbrother seemed to pay her the least attention, which somehow spurred her to seek it all the more. Now and then he would aim a look at Hannah, as though by gathering a bevy of admirers around himself he was advertising to her his desirability.

A large, bowl-shaped brazier was brought out by members of

Charfrome staff acting as officiants. Hot coals glowed within. The brazier was placed before Buchanan and a three-legged iron stool positioned over it. Buchanan seated himself athwart this tripod, and laurel branches were thrown onto the coals. As they burned, smoke curled up around him and he inhaled deeply.

Thereupon, in short order, he fell into a dramatic trance state. His head toppled backward, his eyes rolled upwards in their sockets, and his whole body began to quiver and convulse. Hannah averred that under any other circumstances these antics might have been disturbing or comical, but the effect they produced on her and those around her was, instead, mesmerising. If Buchanan was play-acting, he was doing so sincerely, with every fibre of his being. The twitches and wrenches he put himself through looked effortful and painful. It was no mean feat to contort one's limbs thus, to bend one's wrists almost double, to wind one's torso sinuously in circles like a snake about to strike...

"I wonder," I said, "whether the fumes from the laurel branches might be at least partly responsible. The plant is notoriously poisonous. The reaction you are describing could well be caused by the release of noxious chemicals contained in the leaves. Prussic acid and benzaldehyde, to be precise."

"Your medical expertise comes to the fore," Hannah said.

"It is in the toxicology textbooks. But also, I know about laurel because I once had to tend to a family who, as one, came down with acute gastric distress after the cook mistakenly put laurel leaves in a stew rather than bay leaves. Using a charcoal purgative I was able to treat all of them successfully apart from the youngest child, a boy of five, who I regret to say succumbed to internal haemorrhaging and died."

"How awful."

"It is strange that one always remembers one's professional failures more vividly than any of the triumphs, especially when there are youngsters involved," I mused. "As for Buchanan, when first meeting him I was struck by how blue his lips were and how bloodshot his eyes. Exposure to the chemicals in the laurel smoke would result in mild hypoxia, which if reiterated on a monthly basis would lead to someone presenting symptoms of central cyanosis chronically, while the smoke itself would cause recurrent irritation and inflammation of the sclera."

Buchanan continued to writhe strenuously within that rising column of smoke, to the extent that all the veins upon his neck and forehead stood proud, the sinews likewise upon his arms. Then, of a sudden, he fell still. His eyes were wide, staring into space. His jaw was slack. A froth of spittle glistened at the corner of his mouth.

A hush descended over the assembled Elysians. The only sounds to be heard were the snap of the coals in the brazier and the torch flames crackling.

"These are the nominees," Buchanan said. "These are the chosen twain."

He spoke in a voice not his own. The words boomed out of him, seeming to echo up from some vast cathedral-like hollow deep within. There was a hoarseness to them, and a sonorousness, that was utterly inhuman. It was as though Buchanan had vanished and something else now inhabited his frame, something not of this earth.

Hannah admitted that she felt silly saying this to me. "In hindsight it sounds absurd. At the time, though, that was exactly the impression I got. Sir Philip had become a vessel for something 'other'. In the same way that psychic mediums get possessed by spirits, he had been taken over by some supernatural entity. Some *supernal* entity, even."

"But psychic mediums are, to a man, charlatans."

"And who is to say that Sir Philip is not too? All I can tell you,

Dr Watson, is that if it was charlatanism, he gave a very convincing performance – so much so that the hairs on the back of my neck stood up and I thought, if only for a few fleeting moments, that I was witnessing a genuine paranormal phenomenon. The veil between planes of existence had been pierced, and all that."

Buchanan continued to deliver pronouncements in that eerie, otherworldly voice.

"I speak for the gods," said he. "I am their instrument. Through me they state their bidding. Two among you have shown themselves to be worthy of divine benediction this night. Two surpass the rest and deserve recognition for that. Two must be exalted."

He paused, and the air was pregnant with anticipation. Something momentous was coming. Every Elysian present, Hannah included, bent forward in eagerness. Who were the two? Who would earn the promised accolade?

"They are," said Buchanan, "Cedric Strickland… and William Dorr-Timperley."

Sporadic gasps greeted the announcement. Then, as though a dam had burst, there was an eruption of cheers and applause.

At a gesture from Buchanan, the named pair stepped forward from the semicircle. Both, Hannah told me, were men of standing within the Charfrome community. Strickland, an insurance clerk from Greenwich, had played the part of King Creon in *Antigone*, a pivotal role, with aplomb. He had also excelled as a wrestler and come first in a long-distance run around the estate. He was a forceful personality. Dorr-Timperley, a curate's son from somewhere near Northampton, was altogether milder-mannered. He had learned how to play the *kithara* from scratch, attaining a high degree of proficiency with the instrument, and had memorised the whole of Hesiod's *Works and Days*, all eight hundred lines of the poem, in the original Greek. Whatever the definition of an Elysian was, each man might be reckoned to be it.

"These two," Buchanan said, "shall have bestowed upon them the mark of divine approval, so that they remember henceforth and for all time the values they have learned as Elysians and the transformation this education has wrought upon their lives."

With these words, Buchanan arose from the tripod and drew from beneath his cloak a dagger. It was a beautiful thing of silver and jewels, its blade a good ten inches long. Briefly Hannah thought that the "mark" he had just mentioned was one he himself was going to inflict upon Strickland and Dorr-Timperley with that knife. If so, neither of the chosen ones appeared particularly apprehensive about such a wounding.

This was because both, having been at Charfrome for a while, were no strangers to the Delphic Ceremony. They knew what awaited them now.

Labropoulos the chef appeared from the rear of the temple, bringing with him a young billy goat, which he led by a rope. The creature nickered nervously, flicking its ears. Possibly it was unsettled by the crowd of people and the torches everywhere, but Hannah wondered whether it was aware of the fate in store for it. Animals could sense the proximity of death, couldn't they?

"To you, oh gods," said Buchanan, "we offer this sacrifice." His voice had returned to normal, as had his demeanour, although there was still a tangible differentness about him. He remained weirdly disassociated, subtly altered, not quite the person he had been prior to his immersion in the laurel smoke. His movements were stiff and hesitant, as though he had to think hard before executing each.

"The lingering effects of narcosis," I said.

Labropoulos grasped the billy goat by the horns, steadying its body between his knees and raising its head to expose its throat. Then Buchanan, with a swift sideways slash of the dagger, sliced open its neck. The beast kicked its hind legs even as its lifeblood gushed out over the temple floor. The Grecian chef kept a tight grip upon the goat as it vainly resisted succumbing to the inevitable. Seconds later the creature slumped, hot blood still pumping from the gash, steaming in the cool night air. Its eyes dulled. Its tongue lolled. Its chest ceased heaving and it lay still.

Hannah said that she had been appalled by the slaughter of the goat but not as much as she might have expected. Somehow the deed seemed appropriate, a natural climax to the ritual. Looking at the Elysians around her she saw disgust on many a face but it was coupled invariably with a strange, beatific approval. The bloodletting had touched something deep and dormant within them, all of them, some inborn instinct. Even the coppery smell that reached Hannah's nostrils, though rank and repugnant, carried a sort of primal message. It reminded her that she was alive, and what a fragile, cherishable thing that was.

"We were warned, Holmes and I, that animal sacrifices were conducted here," I said. "The landlord of the inn at Waterton Parva, Scadden, said so. We pooh-poohed the idea. How wrong we were."

"I would not have believed it either," Hannah said.

Buchanan raised the dripping dagger, ran a thumb along the flat of the blade to gather up some of the goat's blood, and applied the thumb to the faces of Strickland and Dorr-Timperley in turn. He smeared the blood down their cheeks and daubed it in a line across their foreheads.

"Death grants you a new lease of life," he told them. "It is in death's shadow that we discover how precious our lives are. Chilled by the draught from the beating of its wings, we realise we must make the most of the time available to us. You, Cedric, and you, William, must – and will – prosper as our anointed representatives. The future awaits you!"

So the ceremony concluded, and the Elysians traipsed back to the house in dribs and drabs, chattering excitedly, while

Labropoulos stayed behind to clean up the remains of the goat. Strickland and Dorr-Timperley received more than a few pats on the back and congratulatory embraces from well-wishers. As Hannah understood it, the two men's tenure at Charfrome was over. This was their graduation. They were fully fledged Elysians, and from now on they would live in the world, to all intents and purposes as normal Englishmen, while subtly doing their bit to make an already great nation greater still.

Dr Pentecost fell in step beside Hannah. "Do you know what, Miss Holbrook? After all that bloodletting and hullabaloo, I rather fancy a nightcap. How about you? I have a more than passable bottle of tawny port in my room, a Colheita. Matured fifty years, somewhat nutty, very tasty. Would you care to join me?"

"Some would consider a lone woman going to a gentleman's room unaccompanied to be unacceptable, Doctor, especially after dark."

"My study is, I would think, public enough not be considered private quarters. In addition, I shall leave the door to the corridor wide open. Surely then no hint of impropriety can attach itself to the assignation."

Hannah pondered the invitation. At that stage she still deemed Dr Pentecost an ally and trusted him. Moreover, were it to come to it, there was little that a man of his advanced years and indolent bearing could attempt that a young, physically capable woman could not successfully counter.

All the same, she said no. Dr Pentecost was phlegmatic about the refusal, saying that if she changed her mind, she would still be welcome.

Half an hour later, Hannah did change her mind – one little drink with a friend, what harm could it do? – and with that decision, her fate was sealed. And, by extension, so was mine.

CHAPTER TWENTY-SIX

BLACK DROP

As Hannah neared Dr Pentecost's study, she heard sobbing coming from within. It was the sound of a woman in bitter distress. The door was slightly ajar, but as she raised a hand to knock, someone flung it fully open from the other side. It was Polly Speedwell. Polly's eyes were red and swollen, her cheeks streaked with tears. She took one look at Hannah and wailed, "He is a monster, I tell you. A monster!" Then she thrust past her, shouldering her aside, and hastened off down the corridor, still wracked with sobs.

Hannah entered the study to find Dr Pentecost standing with his head bent and his hands folded, the picture of solicitous concern.

"Whatever has happened?" she enquired. "What is the matter with Polly?"

"Poor girl," said Dr Pentecost. "She has had an… upset."

"Who is this monster she spoke of?"

"Who do you think?"

Hannah uttered the first name that sprang to mind. "Edwin Fairbrother."

Dr Pentecost acknowledged it with a small bow. "None other."

"He has used her cruelly."

"So it would seem. Polly came to me to complain about him. I have been a shoulder for her to cry on."

"I must say I had no inkling that she and Mr Fairbrother were even intimates. Having said that, I saw them together at the ceremony just now. Well, not together as such, but in close company. He looked to be ignoring her. Now that I think about it, he may have been cutting her, even as she fawned upon him. Oh, poor girl!"

"Evidently she has been keeping from you what she has not from me." Dr Pentecost motioned towards an armchair. "Why don't you sit down and I shall tell you all I know."

"I think you better had," said Hannah, seating herself. She was bristling with indignation on Polly's behalf. "I should like very much to learn what that shameless rogue has done. Then I shall confront him. I shall report him to Sir Philip too."

"Spoken like the fine, redoubtable lass you are. How about some of that port first? Since that is why you originally came, doubtless having rethought my offer."

Without waiting for a reply, Dr Pentecost went to a side-table and busied himself pouring out two glasses of the Colheita from a decanter. His back was to Hannah, and she let her gaze rove around the room, taking in the densely populated bookshelves, filled with volumes of Tacitus, Catullus, Virgil, Sophocles, Plutarch and of course Homer, and the series of framed mezzotints depicting scenes from Classical myth. Her eye alighted upon a pair of earrings that lay on the desk blotter. She marked briefly this incongruity without querying it, then resumed her survey, which travelled as far as a second door that led, she assumed, to a bedroom.

Dr Pentecost handed her a glass of topaz-coloured liquid and invited her to join him in a toast. "To our new graduates, Cedric and William. And to you and me, my dear, and a sound friendship."

Hannah took a deep sip of the port and found it as flavoursome as advertised, although it carried an aftertaste that she found a touch disagreeable. With a couple more sips, she became accustomed to it.

"Well," said Dr Pentecost, "now that you have seen the Delphic Ceremony for yourself, the apotheosis of Sir Philip's project, what do you make of it?"

"It was hard to take seriously, yet hard not to feel moved by."

"My sentiments exactly. You know, I shouldn't really tell you this, but yours was one of the names that came up during our staff consultation meeting yesterday. You were on the shortlist."

"Me? Already? But I have been here barely a month."

"A mark of how impressed we all are with you. The gods inspired Sir Philip to select Cedric Strickland and William Dorr-Timperley from the list, but one of the nominees could quite easily have been Shirley Holbrook."

"The gods?" Hannah said with a dash of cynicism.

"The Delphic Ceremony takes its cue from the ritual at the original oracle at Delphi," the classicist said. "Sir Philip assumes a role similar to that of the Pythia, the priestess whose prophecies had the force of law. The Pythia communed with Apollo and delivered his verdicts in response to queries from petitioners, which more often than not were precisely the verdicts they wanted to hear. Did the god really speak to her, though? Or did she, having entered into a frenzied state of spiritual ecstasy, simply listen to her subconscious mind, the inner voice we all possess, and believe it to be Apollo?"

"Or maybe it was all just a pretence, a grand charade."

Dr Pentecost shrugged. "Maybe it makes no difference. As long as the petitioners went away happy with the outcome, their endeavours given a divine seal of approval, the Pythia had discharged her responsibility."

"A rubber-stamp from on high."

"Ha ha! Quite. Some scholars, by the way, argue that it was not laurel branches that were burnt at Delphi but must rather have been oleander branches. Oleander is known to have a psychoactive effect, whereas laurel does not."

"So if Sir Philip is using laurel branches…"

"His trance could therefore be bogus, or at any rate self-induced." Again, Dr Pentecost shrugged.

They discussed the ceremony a little further, then, as Dr Pentecost was recharging her glass, Hannah brought the subject back round to Polly.

"So, what has Fairbrother done?"

"What many a young man has done to many a young woman over the course of history," replied Dr Pentecost. "He has toyed with her emotions, encouraged her to believe his feelings were greater than they are, strung her along, then spurned her."

"Is that all?"

"Is it not enough?"

"I thought, from the anguish she exhibited just now, that it was something far worse. To reject someone's affections is hardly the act of a 'monster'. Insensitive perhaps, if done unsympathetically, but not monstrous."

"Polly is a somewhat dramatic girl," said the classicist with a sigh. "She has led a cosseted, sheltered life. This may well be her first experience of heartbreak."

"I should go to her," Hannah said. "I can comfort her."

"Believe me, I have done all I can on that front, and you saw for yourself how successful I was. It may be some time before Polly is receptive to consolation. Ah, I see your glass is empty again. Another refill?"

As Dr Pentecost returned to the side-table, Hannah glanced back at the desk blotter and the pair of earrings on top. It had struck her as odd that an item of women's jewellery should be in a man's room. Now, perhaps belatedly, she thought to ask herself why Dr Pentecost of all people would have such a thing.

That was when she recognised them. They were not just any earrings but a particular pair of cabochon-cut sapphire earrings.

"Those are Polly's," she said.

"Hmmm?" Dr Pentecost followed her gaze. "Oh yes."

"She left them behind. Why?"

"Carelessness, I suppose."

"They are one of her most treasured possessions. She would not discard them willy-nilly."

"Possibly not."

"Has she given them to you for some reason?"

"And what reason would that be?" Dr Pentecost handed her the refreshed glass.

"I… I cannot think."

It was no mere figure of speech. All at once Hannah was finding that she could, indeed, not think. Her mind was occluded, as though clouds were piling up around it on every side, dimming its light. Her vision swam. Her entire body felt weak, subsumed by drowsiness.

"You look somewhat peaky, if I may say so," said Dr Pentecost.

"I am not… I am not sure what has come over me," Hannah stammered. Her words sounded thick and muddled, even to her own ears.

The third glass of port slipped from her fingers, but Dr Pentecost had a hand cupped beneath it, ready, and caught it neatly without spilling a drop.

"Perhaps you have had too much to drink," he said, going to the doorway. He checked the corridor, then gently closed the door.

"I have not drunk much…"

"Even so."

Hannah knew she must leave. Every instinct told her to. She tried to rise, but a wave of dizziness swept over her, leaving her unsteady on her feet. She crumpled back into her chair.

"Dear me," said Dr Pentecost. "You really are in a bad way. Well, there is always my bed. Let me help you to it."

"No, I... I could not possibly... It is..."

"Tush! You can barely keep your eyes open. You will never make it back to your room. You are quite safe here. You have nothing to fear from me."

Hannah felt as though she were deep underwater. As Dr Pentecost assisted her across the study and through the door to the bedroom, her feet dragged and her limbs were sluggish, held down by invisible weights. It was how she imagined trudging over the sea floor in a diving suit must feel.

"There you go," the classicist said as Hannah stretched herself out on the bed. His voice seemed to be emanating from further and further away. "Let me pull the counterpane up over you. Nice and snug."

All at once, Hannah plunged into a bottomless black pit.

Her sleep was dreamless except for interludes of waking, which felt like dreams.

In one of them she was writing a letter. A pen was in her hand, moving across the page, and the words it inscribed came from her but also from elsewhere. From Dr Pentecost, who told her what she must say.

She knew she should not be writing the letter but somehow she was powerless to do otherwise. Her will was not her own. And Dr Pentecost was her friend, was he not? If he wished her to inform Sherlock Holmes that everything was fine, then everything must be fine, yes?

Dr Pentecost coaxed and cajoled, and soon the letter was drafted. All that remained was to sign it. Hannah wanted to show that it was not purely her own creation. Somehow she must communicate to Mr Holmes that she had mixed feelings about the letter. It was not quite right.

So she signed her real name, to signify that the letter was false.

Having made her address the envelope, Dr Pentecost said, "I shall take this to the village to post myself. Save you the inconvenience of trekking thither and back through the woods."

"I can… I can do it," Hannah said. Her tongue was numb. Her brain seemed swaddled in cotton wool. Simply to frame a coherent sentence required every ounce of concentration she could muster.

"Post the letter?"

"Yes." She had a vague inkling that, once at the post office, she might be able to amend the letter's content; at the very least she could make it more explicitly clear that she was not its sole author. This struck her as important, although she didn't know quite why.

"But my dear, you are so tired, aren't you?"

"I am," she admitted. "Really, really tired."

"There is only one thing you should do, and that is go back to bed. Sleep is the remedy, my girl."

The next time Hannah awoke, Dr Pentecost was at her bedside with a teaspoon in one hand and a small brown bottle in the other.

"Here you go," he said. "Take this."

She didn't want to drink the brown liquid in the spoon. It smelled pungent, both spicy and vinegary, very much like the aftertaste she had detected in the Colheita. Dr Pentecost insisted it would make her feel better, however, and she did desperately want to feel better, more like herself again. She coughed down three spoonfuls of the stuff. She assumed it was medicine.

She slept again.

And slept some more.

Dawn, then midmorning, then afternoon, then evening. An entire day stuttered past. Outside the window, beyond the closed curtains, the sun progressed along its usual arc in flickering stages, like images on a zoetrope. Dr Pentecost was ever-present in the room, always on hand to supply her with another dose of the medicine.

At one point she caught a glimpse of the label on the bottle. "Kendal Black Drop," it said. The name was known to her, but she couldn't immediately recall where or when she had last heard it.

Night fell.

"It is time," said Dr Pentecost. He was standing over Hannah, beckoning her to rise. "We have places to be."

"Where?"

"You will see."

Lamp in hand, he led her through dark, silent corridors and hallways to the door with the symbol. He produced a key to unlock it. He ushered her down the steps, into the antechamber. Hannah went, unresisting. Her thoughts were a complete fuddle, a tangled ball of string, impossible to unpick. Something inside her was crying out in protest, a tiny voice insisting that she should not be going along with Dr Pentecost so meekly. She kept thinking, for some reason, of the goat at the Delphic Ceremony. In the end it seemed easier not to think at all, just let her mind continue to hover and bob, balloon-like, within the haze that engulfed it.

Later, there was a muffled conversation nearby. Hannah opened her eyes to see Dr Pentecost and Malachi Hart leaning together, talking softly.

Dr Pentecost and Malachi Hart?

Her name was mentioned. Hart was receiving instructions from Dr Pentecost. He was to look after her. Check on her at regular intervals.

"She will be coming out of her stupor soon," Dr Pentecost said. "Lucidity will be returning. Make sure she does not kick up a fuss."

"As you wish, Doctor," said Hart. The scar that zigzagged

down one side of his face shone palely in the lamplight, like the ghost of a lightning bolt. "And when this is all over, my obligation to you is discharged. Do I have that right? We are done, you and me."

"After this favour, you will owe me nothing and I will ask nothing more of you."

"Good," said Hart gruffly. "I have no wish to be beholden to you ever again."

"You shall not be. You have my word on that."

Later still, Dr Pentecost was back in the antechamber. He was squatting beside Hannah, patting her face none-too-gently.

"Miss Holbrook?" he said. "Miss Holbrook?"

Hannah blinked up at him.

"There you are," he said. "How are you feeling?"

"Wretched."

"But clearer-headed? It has been a while since your last dose. The fog should be lifting."

It was. Hannah's brain had slowly begun to stir back into life. There was still an undertow of grogginess, but her thoughts were sharpening, coming into focus.

"You have been drugging me," she said. "First you spiked the port with Black Drop. Then you just gave me the preparation neat."

"I am afraid so. It was the prudent course of action, but also the only one. I needed you… co-operative for twenty-four hours."

"Paralysed, you mean. Under your thumb."

"Precisely. To explain your absence I have been telling everyone that you suffered an attack of brain-fever. The onset occurred while you were in my study and I have been nursing you there since then."

"Brain-fever?"

"Brought on by delayed shock from seeing the goat slaughtered at the ceremony. Sir Philip asked to see you, to check on your condition, but I dissuaded him. I told him that your recuperation would be swifter if you were left alone."

"While you continued to feed me your soporific draught, to keep me sedated."

"Black Drop's opiate content has another effect, useful in this case. It makes the person who takes it extremely malleable. Even someone as strong-willed as you."

"Which was how you were able to make me write that letter."

"You remember that?"

"To Mr Holmes. You want him to stay away. So that you can carry on doing what you are doing unimpeded."

"That is one way of looking at it."

"And what you are doing," Hannah said, "is blackmail."

Dr Pentecost's eyebrows rose, and a small, wry smile insinuated itself across his face. "However did you work that out, my dear?"

"Polly's earrings," she said. "I see it now. It is the only explanation that makes sense. Why would she have left them in your study? She was wearing them during the Delphic Ceremony. Hence she would have been wearing them when she went to see you in your study. She must have removed them while she was there, with you. Why would she have done that? I could not fathom a reason. Now I can. They are payment."

"Generous payment," said Dr Pentecost.

"And the 'monster' she referred to as she left? It was not Edwin Fairbrother at all. Rather, it was you."

"That story about Fairbrother spurning her was something I fabricated on the spot, once you mentioned his name. It sounded plausible. You certainly fell for it."

"What do you have over her?" Hannah asked.

"Polly, in an unguarded moment, told me about her father. He is not faithful to his wife, a hopeless philanderer. Polly found out about this only recently. That was, indeed, the impetus which drove her to leave home and find succour in the bosom of Elysianism."

"And when she was unwise enough to admit it to you…"

"I was ruthless enough to threaten to share the fact with the newspapers unless she made it worth my while not to. Can you imagine how the Speedwell millinery chain might suffer if such a scandal came to light publicly? Can you imagine the ignominy? In return for preserving her father's business and reputation, those earrings were a small price to pay."

"She is not the first, is she? You have blackmailed other Elysians."

Dr Pentecost shook his head ruefully, in such a way that he seemed both to be admitting to the accusation and at the same time denying responsibility.

"It was not something I set out to do when I accepted Sir Philip's offer of employment. It just… evolved. You know as well as anyone that I am an approachable fellow, to women especially. To young women even more so, who see me as a father figure. I am old enough to pose no threat. I am sympathetic. I engage people's trust. Then all it takes is a careless aside, an injudicious comment, and I am privy to that which I would not normally be and perhaps should not be."

"Many of us end up in that position. Not all of us decide to use such snippets of information for personal gain. Most of us give a promise of discretion to the other and abide by it."

"The first couple of times it happened, I felt the same way," said Dr Pentecost. "Soon, however, it became a repeated pattern and I began to see that it might be turned to my advantage. Elysians are, as a rule, a biddable lot. They come here looking for purpose, looking for something more in their lives. There is something missing in them, some absence needing to be filled. Many of them lack self-esteem. Sir Philip knows this and believes he gives it to them. He believes that people are elevated by exposure to the regime at Charfrome, freed by his philosophy from the mental chains that hold them back. Perhaps they are, after a while. Until then, they remain lost sheep."

"Sheep whom you may fleece."

"They have money, most of them, or some precious knick-knack. I never ask for much, certainly for nothing the person cannot afford to do without. I supplement my income and augment my pension. It is, I would say, a fairly harmless occupation."

"Was Sophia one of your victims?"

"Why do you ask that?"

"I am wondering why you have gone to all this trouble to drug me, take me captive and have me write that letter to Mr Holmes," Hannah said. "Why would you do that if you were not concerned by my efforts to unearth the truth about Sophia? That leads me to deduce that you have some connection with her disappearance."

"'Deduce,'" Dr Pentecost echoed. "Isn't Mr Holmes rather fond of that word? His influence is rubbing off on you."

"I am right, though, am I not? Where is she? What have you done to her?" Hannah found she was dreading the answers to these questions.

The classicist heaved a deep sigh. "You realise, my dear girl, that if I am to tell you everything, I shall have to dispose of you."

"As you did Sophia?"

"Perhaps. Perhaps not."

"I feel you have already made up your mind to dispose of me anyway. Hence hauling me off to this place, wherever it is. There is no point pretending I am going to come out of this unscathed." It was a struggle for Hannah to control her voice, which trembled with emotion. "You may as well make a clean breast of it, Doctor. Confession is good for the soul, they say."

The classicist laughed mirthlessly. "And you are the priest who is going to grant me absolution for my sins?"

"No," said Hannah, "I am the woman who is going to make you pay for them, if they are as terrible as I fear they are."

"An empty threat." Dr Pentecost deliberated, then said, "Perhaps you have a right to know the truth. And now is as good a time as any to give it to you. '*Veritas odit moras*', as Seneca the Younger once said. 'Truth hates delay.'"

CHAPTER TWENTY-SEVEN

SOPHIA'S FIRST MISFORTUNE

"Sophia Tompkins was a victim of misfortune twice over," Dr Pentecost said to Hannah. "The first misfortune was to fall under the spell of Edwin Fairbrother. She is not alone in that, of course. Who can say how many females have melted before that young man's incandescent charms? Even he has probably lost count of the full tally. But where Sophia went wrong was thinking he was sincere about her, as sincere as she was about him. She got into her head the notion that he loved her."

"Edwin Fairbrother does not love anybody but himself," Hannah said. "One would be a fool not to see that."

"Sophia was that fool. She would have given the boy everything – everything she owned, everything she was – in order to keep his favour. I watched it all unfurl over the course of several weeks, from her initial exploratory forays here to her decision to give up her position as a governess and commit full-time to being an Elysian. I say 'decision', but she didn't even think twice. Fairbrother wished it, so she wished it. Sir Philip got another new recruit while Fairbrother had a fresh conquest. It has happened before, over the years. Fairbrother installs a girl at Charfrome, and there she is, pinned in position like a mounted butterfly, his to dust off and pore over whenever the fancy takes him."

"While he, between times, entertains other women elsewhere."

"No doubt about it. For Fairbrother, a girl at Charfrome is there in case of need, an understudy he can reliably call up if there is no one else available to fill the starring role."

"How sordid."

"It was this situation, by the way, that I drew upon when spinning my yarn about Polly Speedwell and Fairbrother. A lie is more convincing when it is rooted in reality. I have seen Polly making cow eyes at him but she has not, to my knowledge, been one of his paramours. Too plain. When it comes to the opposite sex Fairbrother is, if nothing else, consistent. He likes a shapely, good-looking girl. At any rate, it took Sophia some time to grasp that she was not the epicentre of Fairbrother's life as she supposed. She tried her best to be a good Elysian, in the hope that this would somehow endear her to him, but he did not care one whit whether she danced well or improved her conversational Greek or memorised the entire genealogy of the Hellenic pantheon. His sole concern was her being available to him at his convenience, as and when required. Gradually it dawned on her that Fairbrother was not going to sweep her off her feet and bear her away to a happily-ever-after. The realisation crushed her, poor lamb."

"You could at least try to sound sympathetic."

"Do not get me wrong. I felt sorry for Sophia. But the trials and tribulations of young people in love do provide a certain amusement for old stagers like me who are long past that sort of brouhaha. I became Sophia's confidant during her period of growing disenchantment with Fairbrother. She and I struck up a companionable relationship when I chanced upon her by the lake one afternoon. She was all alone, sobbing her heart out. A few gentle entreaties from me, and soon I had the whole story. Not that I didn't know most of it already. It was 'Edwin this' and 'Edwin that'. She was angry, ashamed, rueful, resentful, self-recriminating, self-pitying, dejected, a dozen things at once. Not to mention suicidal."

"No!"

"Oh, the girl was seriously contemplating throwing herself into the lake. 'I would rather end it all, Dr Pentecost,' she said, 'than live with this agony.'"

"But Sophia is terrified of water," said Hannah. "I am astonished that she was anywhere near the lakeside. She has long had the fear – irrational but unshakable – that she is destined to die by drowning. It has plagued her ever since the deaths of her parents, who were on the SS *Princess Alice* when it collided with the collier *Bywell Castle* on the Thames near Gravesend. Six hundred and fifty 'Moonlight Trippers' aboard that paddle steamer perished in the disaster, Sophia's mother and father among them. Now she can hardly bear to look at a body of water, let alone approach one."

"So she told me. She also told me that she cannot swim. She never learned the skill as a child, and the tragedy of her parents, rather than persuading her of its necessity, somehow only convinced her of its inutility. All in all, it would seem she went to the lake intending to fulfil that destiny she so dreaded."

"A mark of how truly disordered her state of mind was," said Hannah. "One presumes you talked her out of it. One hopes so, at least."

"I did. The main plank of my argument was that the lake, being manmade and purely ornamental, is not conducive to drowning. Nowhere is the water any deeper than three feet. 'With determination,' I told Sophia, 'you might be able to accomplish the deed, but more likely you will just wind up cold and wet and looking rather asinine.' She laughed at that, through her bitter tears. 'Come,' I said, offering her the crook of my elbow. 'Wouldn't you prefer to take a stroll with me? I will be your audience, and you may curse and rail against feckless Edwin Fairbrother and call him all manner of dreadful names, and with luck exorcise him from your soul.' Thus did Sophia and I form a bond."

Hannah eyed him coolly. "You affected not to know her that well. When we first discussed her in Tartarus, you had trouble recalling her surname. Deceit, it seems, is second nature to you."

"Miss Holbrook, of course I was not going to admit to you that I had been well-acquainted with Sophia. Given the dark and tragic turn that acquaintanceship would take, the very mention of her name by you put me on my mettle. I knew I must proceed with caution. Hence the dissembling."

"I believed you."

"I am very believable. But in this respect I am being honest: I grew fond of Sophia and would not have wished any harm to befall her. Not at first. That would change."

"How? Why?"

"I am coming to that. It is necessary to relate events in order. It is easier to keep track of them that way. For perhaps a fortnight I provided Sophia with succour and comfort. I was a vessel into which she poured out her troubles. Increasingly her distress drained away, and what remained was bitterness. When Fairbrother next put in an appearance at Charfrome, Sophia was no longer the submissive little dormouse he knew. She had become vengeful, a proper Fury. She arranged with him that he should come to her room at midnight, as was their custom during his visits. He duly turned up at the appointed hour for the tryst, full of his usual inflated self-opinion."

Dr Pentecost shook his head, chuckling at the reminiscence.

"Imagine his surprise," he said, "upon entering the bedchamber to find the occupant not Sophia but a plump, unprepossessing middle-aged lady, a Mrs Philomena Caversham, whom Sophia had prevailed upon to swap rooms with her. There was a tremendous hue and cry. The doughty Mrs Caversham gave vent to all the indignation one would expect from a respectable married woman who discovers a strange man in her boudoir in the middle of the night. By all accounts she was like a man-o'-war in full sail, belabouring Fairbrother with slaps and kicks as he stumbled out into the corridor. He in turn did his best to fend her off, flustered and flummoxed and mumbling apology."

In spite of the situation, Hannah felt a small smile form upon her face. "Serves him right," she said. "A solid humiliation. Good for you, Sophia."

"Sophia capitalised on it the next morning, snubbing Fairbrother at breakfast and airily going about her business as though nothing was amiss. Philomena Caversham, by contrast, was in a state of high dudgeon. Sir Philip tried to smooth things over, but nevertheless she packed her bags and quit Charfrome that same day. For the other Elysians it was a humorous interlude, a break from routine. Fairbrother had had one of those unfortunate mishaps that come to all rakes at some time or other during their progress. Men like him tend to get forgiven for all but their most egregious transgressions. All the same, he knew he had been made to look an ass. Sophia had turned the tables on him, and she had done it in a manner expressly designed to puncture his masculine pride."

"I would wager he seethed about it."

"Very much so. Sophia continued to ignore him, compounding her victory, and Fairbrother grew more and more aggravated. Not only had she weaned herself off him, now she was rubbing his nose in it. As far as he was concerned, that could not stand."

"Was that the second of Sophia's two misfortunes?" Hannah asked. "She provoked Fairbrother's ire, and there were unforeseen and devastating consequences?"

"Not exactly. We have already established that I, not Fairbrother, am responsible for what happened to Sophia. You really must try to keep up, Miss Holbrook. What would your patron think of such a sloppy lack of attention? Were he here, Sherlock Holmes would surely have some harsh words for you."

"Harsher words for *you*, I fancy. But yes, he is not here, and I am not he, more's the pity. My assumption was that you and Fairbrother conspired together in some sort of plot against Sophia. In retrospect that does seem unlikely. I am confused, however, as to how her embarrassing him might lead to you perpetrating some foul misdeed upon her."

"The two are connected," said Dr Pentecost. "Sophia's second misfortune, generally speaking, was getting close to me. Specifically, it was a visit she paid to my study two full moons ago, straight after she was selected for graduation at a Delphic Ceremony."

"You told me you were not at Charfrome when Sophia graduated," Hannah said. "You said you were holidaying in Turkey. Unless it was just another lie."

"I am full of them, am I not? Again, I was deflecting suspicion from myself, distancing myself from direct association with Sophia. It worked, didn't it? Sherlock Holmes might not have taken my statement at face value. He might have sought to substantiate it. Shirley Holbrook, however, was happy to accept it as gospel."

"Shirley Holbrook is kicking herself about that," Hannah said, with sincere feeling. "Hannah Woolfson the more so."

"Of course, if you had made the appropriate enquiries and discovered that I was not telling the truth, I would simply have claimed I had erred. You would have fallen for it, I am certain. 'Daft old Dr Pentecost,' you would have said to yourself. 'Cannot keep his dates straight. Head too stuffed with Classical allusions.' But, in the event, it was not necessary. Mr Holmes's agent at Charfrome proved less thorough than she ought to have been. I am inclined to wonder why he placed so much faith in you."

Feeling an up-swelling of defiance, Hannah said, "Should I disappear as Sophia did, you can be certain Mr Holmes will get wind of it and will not rest until the mystery is resolved. He will sniff out the culprit, Dr Pentecost. You will pay the price."

"I have made provision against that, my dear," said the classicist, unruffled. He took out his fob watch. "Indeed, Mr Holmes may be here sooner than you think, with trusty Dr Watson in tow. So allow me to finish my tale, if I may, since time is short."

CHAPTER TWENTY-EIGHT

SOPHIA'S SECOND MISFORTUNE

"Sophia's selection for graduation came as a surprise to many," said Dr Pentecost. "Certainly hers was not among the names offered at the staff meeting the day before. We put forward several viable candidates to Sir Philip. However, the gods spoke at the ceremony, and one of the two nominees was Sophia."

"The gods, it would seem, are capricious," said Hannah.

"Their human mouthpiece is, at least. I can only assume that another voice had whispered in Sir Philip's ear beforehand, suggesting Sophia's candidacy, and he chose to heed it in preference to any divine voice."

"The other voice being Fairbrother's. That is my thinking."

"That is my thinking too."

"Fairbrother twisted his arm somehow."

"Sir Philip would never admit it in my presence, but it is the only explanation that fits."

Hannah's mind went back to the conversation she had eavesdropped on, out by the shrine to Daedalus. She recalled how Buchanan and Fairbrother had argued, each heaping blame onto the other for some calamity.

"Just the other day I overheard Sir Philip complain to Fairbrother that he had been cajoled into helping him, against his better judgement," she said. "The two of them had schemed together and it had backfired in some way. Fairbrother had played upon their consanguinity, forcing Sir Philip into some moral compromise he now regretted. Fairbrother himself did not appear to be regretful, but then I do not think he has ever been too troubled by a conscience."

"I do not think he possesses one at all," said Dr Pentecost. "Your evidence does seem to support my theory. I take back what I said just now. You are not a wholly incompetent sleuth."

"You are too kind, Doctor," Hannah said with heavy drollery. "I suppose Fairbrother stood to gain from Sophia's graduation. She would be expected to leave Charfrome, for one thing, in which case, he would be shot of her."

"There is more to it, however. Graduation is not the pleasantest of experiences."

"The goat sacrifice. Sir Philip's speaking in tongues."

"That is the Delphic Ceremony. I mean the actual graduation."

"I do not understand. There is a further level of ritual?"

"A deeper one," said Dr Pentecost. "A Mystery beyond the Mystery. Answer me this. What must all those who aspire to graduate from any course of learning face?"

"An examination."

"Correct. A final test of knowledge and aptitude. Proof that they have absorbed everything they have been taught and that they are ready to move on to whatever awaits them next. Sir Philip has manufactured just such a test – an intricate, ingenious trial of wit and fortitude, one that Daedalus himself would have been proud to have devised. It is a baptism by fire from which the participating Elysian emerges toughened, exhilarated and suffused with self-confidence. It is, if you will, a hero's journey of the kind I spoke about in Tartarus. *Katabasis* followed by *anabasis*, descending to arise."

Although his tone was triumphal, Hannah felt a vague, inexplicable chill.

"I cannot help but think," said Dr Pentecost, "that Fairbrother made Sir Philip choose Sophia for graduation specifically because he wanted her to undergo the difficulties and indignities it involves."

"As a punishment."

Dr Pentecost nodded. "Getting his own back on her for the Philomena Caversham incident. You do not make a laughing stock of Edwin Fairbrother and expect to avoid retaliation. Only, as it happened, the retaliation was severer than he bargained for."

The classicist paused, collecting himself.

"Sophia called by at my study as soon as the ceremony concluded. She was in a rush, eager to share the glad tidings. As it happened, I was not there at the time. Nor had I attended the ceremony. I was suffering from a digestive complaint."

"Perhaps a physical manifestation of guilt," Hannah said drolly.

Dr Pentecost waved a dismissive hand. "Merely a case of mild dyspepsia, that is all, but I felt that seeing a goat slaughtered – not to mention smelling the spilled blood – would not be beneficial to me in any way, in that condition. I had gone downstairs to the kitchen to brew myself some chamomile tea, to settle my stomach. I lost track of time and did not realise that the ceremony had finished. When I returned to my study, there was Sophia. Streaks of drying goat blood caked her brow and cheeks. She had a book in her hands."

"A book?"

"Mine. A notebook. I had left it out upon my desk. This is it."

From his pocket Dr Pentecost drew a small clothbound notebook, which he showed to Hannah. Upon the cover were written the words *Veritas Vitarum*.

"*The Truth of Lives*," Hannah said.

"It is where I keep a record of others' indiscretions."

She opened the notebook and glanced through. At the top of each page, in the same hand that had written the title upon the cover, was a name, with several lines of Latin below. Hannah knew the language well enough to get the gist of each entry. The word *peccatum* – "sin" or "crime" – recurred, as did *adulterium*, which was easily enough translated, and *peculatus*, which bore a close resemblance to a legal term her father would often use for embezzlement, peculation.

"This is your blackmail journal," she said.

"At my age, when the memory is not what it used to be, it is prudent to write things down," said Dr Pentecost. "The Homeric texts I learned by heart in my youth remain indelibly with me, but more recently apprehended facts have a tendency to slip away unless somehow preserved for posterity. Who knows? One of my blackmailees might make a belated attempt to call my bluff, and where would I be if I could not recall what misdeed I was dangling, like the sword of Damocles, over that individual's head?"

He took the notebook from Hannah and tucked it back into his pocket.

"I had been completing a new entry," he said, "and neglected to put the book away in a drawer, out of sight, when I left my study. Upon such small lapses do great tragedies hinge. Sophia picked it up out of curiosity and started flicking through."

"She realised what the notebook was."

"It was writ large upon her face as I walked in. Beneath the goat's blood, her expression was appalled. She threw all manner of swingeing rebuke at me. She was near hysterical."

"How readily do men accuse women of hysteria," said Hannah, "when it is simply righteous anger."

Dr Pentecost disregarded the interjection. "I withstood her

castigation for as long as I could bear, then when she paused for breath I asked her, as challengingly as I dared, what she proposed to do. Her answer was to go to Sir Philip and tell all. Her mind was quite made up."

"Sir Philip, I imagine, would take a very dim view of your behaviour."

"Sir Philip comes across as a moral, upstanding fellow, but he is not as saintly as you might think. I said as much to Sophia, telling her she would be lucky to find much satisfaction with him. To that, she retorted that if she had no joy there, she would go to the police instead. Scotland Yard, she said, would do what had to be done."

"Good for her."

"She seemed determined to make good on the threat, what's more," Dr Pentecost said. "I stood to lose everything. It would be the ruin of me. The notebook was sufficient evidence to send me to gaol for a long time."

"Did you…" Hannah found the words hard to voice. "Did you kill her?"

"It would perhaps have been the simplest solution to my predicament. I keep a paper knife upon the desk, you may have seen. I could have snatched it up and used it. But, although the idea flitted through my mind, I rejected it. Stab the girl? I lacked the wherewithal. I am not that sort of man. Moreover, it would have created complications. How to dispose of the body? How to clean up the blood?"

"Yes, how inconvenient for you, such 'complications.'"

"Sarcasm ill suits you, my girl."

"Yet strangely, under the circumstances, I find it a comfortable fit."

Dr Pentecost leaned closer to her. His genial façade remained in place, but his eyes were cold and hard, as was his voice. "I did not do lightly what I ended up doing. You should be under no illusion about that. It was an agonising choice. It haunts me to this day. I did it only because I had to, because there was no acceptable alternative."

"Your future over Sophia's."

"Precisely. Precisely! I made that calculation. One flighty little girl with not much brain and nothing of great value to offer the world, versus me, a noted academic, a scholar, an educator..."

"A jumped-up schoolmaster."

"You cannot provoke me, Miss Holbrook. I know the weight of my talents, and it exceeds Sophia's by far."

"So you ever so decently refrained from killing her straight away. What did you do?"

"First, I obtained an assurance from her that she would not do anything about the notebook until the following morning."

"How did you manage that?"

"By pleading, mostly. I begged her to get a good night's sleep first. I suggested that tomorrow, when we were calmer, we could perhaps discuss the matter again. In essence, I was throwing myself on her mercy, or seeming to. Sophia had power over me, and I was inviting her to wield it with the same cool restraint with which she had got her own back on Edwin Fairbrother. '*Festina lente*,' I told her. 'Hasten slowly.' It was Octavian's favourite adage, according to Suetonius. The emperor despised rashness in anyone but especially in a leader or a military commander."

"I'm sure Sophia responded well to another contribution from your inexhaustible fund of Classical quotations," Hannah said.

"Sophia responded well to my importuning as a whole. She agreed to postpone any action until the morrow. She left the room with a gracious, rather regal air, my notebook firmly in her possession. I retrieved it later, of course, after..."

"After you did whatever frightful thing you did to her."

"I needed it back and, once Sophia was out of the picture, I had very little trouble stealing into her room and locating it. Her efforts at hiding the notebook were pathetic. She had stowed it under her pillow, like some schoolgirl with a keepsake of her lover, as if it were not the incendiary document it was. Under her pillow! Even though she must have realised that, while she had it, my fate was firmly in her hands."

"Whereas in fact hers lay in yours."

"And," said Dr Pentecost, with sinister detachment, "there was not a smidgeon of doubt in my mind what that fate would be."

CHAPTER TWENTY-NINE

EVIL, OR BLIND NECESSITY

As Hannah reached this point in her narrative, I felt moved to air an opinion of the man.

"I have known some blackguards in my time," I declared. "Jonathan Small. Colonel Sebastian Moran. Dr Grimesby Roylott. Not forgetting Professor James Moriarty. Dr Archibald Pentecost unquestionably belongs in their ranks. Give me a common, knife-wielding street-ruffian any day. Somehow villainy is all the more reprehensible when it adopts a smiling countenance and a veneer of sophistication."

Hannah concurred. "Somebody as intelligent as Dr Pentecost," said she, "could surely have thought up a less drastic solution than he did. It is not as if he was in the grip of a raging homicidal passion. His actions were cerebral and premeditated."

"How did he kill her?"

"That is the truly fiendish part. He did not. Not as such. As I understand it, he engineered things so that Sophia brought about her own demise."

"He coaxed her into killing herself? She was suicidal once,

when he found her in tears by the lake. Did he resurrect those turbulent emotions in her again? Prey upon them until they overwhelmed her?"

"I confess I do not know the full details," Hannah said. "I know that he manipulated her in some way. 'I did nothing to Sophia directly,' he said to me. 'Her blood is not on my hands.' More than that, however, he did not divulge, for he had run out of time and our conversation was at an end. He had a rendezvous to keep, he said. That was over two hours ago. I did not see him again until he returned with Hart, and you in Hart's arms, out cold."

"I was the rendezvous."

"One must presume so. He anticipated that you would be arriving – you and, he hoped, Mr Holmes – and went out to head you off."

"What would he have done if it had been the two of us rather than just me?" I mused, touching my bruised skull. "He would never have been able to knock both out."

"He had reinforcements. Hart must have been lurking nearby."

"You think so?"

"It stands to reason. Hart was there to scoop you up and carry you to the house."

"I am surprised Hart himself did not carry out the assault."

"You would have been on your guard if Hart had met you at the gates. Dr Pentecost, on the other hand, was above suspicion as far as you were concerned. He lulled you into a false sense of security."

"That is true. I never saw the attack coming. Hannah, if I have not made this plain already, I am an absolute halfwit. I raced here impetuously, with every intent of making things better, and have succeeded only in making things worse."

"Worse?" said she. "For yourself, perhaps."

"And for you. I have added to your woes by engendering feelings of guilt in you."

"What ought I to feel guilty about?"

"That my death is on your conscience, for I am quite certain Dr Pentecost means to despatch the two of us in some way or other. Please do not chide yourself for one moment, though. I came willingly, and I assure you I would do so again, a hundred times, without hesitation, even knowing what I do now."

"Oh, Dr Watson," Hannah said, mock-sternly. "How can I feel guilty when all I feel is grateful? If we are shortly to meet our maker, I cannot think of anyone in whose company I would rather be. Any woman, even one as generally unimpressed by the male species as I, could not fail to be affected by such a display of selfless bravery."

These words were like a charge of electricity to my heart, filling me with tingling vigour.

"But," she went on, "let us not be quite so ready to abandon all hope just yet. You seem more or less recovered now from your injury."

"I am much improved, although I would not say at my peak."

"Between us, nonetheless, we might launch a coup against our gaolers. You said you have bullets in your pocket."

"A couple of dozen."

"And up there hangs a Tilley lamp. I am no explosives expert, but if we were to introduce the gunpowder of the one to the flame of the other…"

"It would create a very loud bang, a bright flash, plenty of smoke, but not much else."

"It would also create a momentary distraction, startling to someone entering. It would dazzle and disorientate him sufficiently that we could leap upon him and attempt to disable him. With the element of surprise, we might just succeed."

"Good heavens!" I said. "Hannah Woolfson, what a capital idea."

"One not without its pitfalls. The timing would be crucial. We would need to ignite the small heap of gunpowder at precisely the right moment, somewhere by the door. I am not sure how we would arrange that. Nor am I sure how easy it is to dismantle a bullet cartridge in order to extract the charge."

"To remove the bullet itself from the casing, unaided by tools, takes some doing. A pair of pliers would help, but I appear to have left mine in my other trousers."

"How curious. I, too, neglected to bring a pair of pliers with me. I am appalled by my own lack of foresight."

"I have, however, seen soldiers do it with their teeth. I just hope these old gnashers of mine are up to the task."

As I reached into my pocket for the Eley's box, sounds of activity came from the other side of the door leading to the rest of the house. A key turned and the door opened.

I was crestfallen. Just when Hannah and I had hit upon a course of action, we had been pre-empted. My spirits sank further still as I saw Malachi Hart appear at the top of the staircase. He looked tense and alert, and I knew that even at my best I would not have been able to beat him in a straight fight. The man was tigerishly dangerous, that scar on his face testament to his indomitability. He would make mincemeat out of me.

Dr Pentecost was visible just past him, and I spied my Webley clutched in his hand. Hannah was correct in suggesting that he wielded it with no obvious expertise or familiarity. His forefinger was nowhere near the trigger, for one thing, but that was probably just as well, since he held the gun canted at such an angle that the barrel was pointing almost directly at his face. Still, it galled me that he had the revolver and not I. To have one's own sidearm arrayed against one feels deeply wrong.

"In you go," Dr Pentecost said, addressing a third individual as yet out of my line of sight. He gestured with the Webley in a way that made me think of a diner at a restaurant summoning the waiter over.

Who was this unseen party? Buchanan, perhaps? Fairbrother? Was Dr Pentecost tying up some loose ends? Did either of those men know too much and need to be eliminated alongside Hannah and myself?

"Ah, Watson."

In stepped a person I was not expecting to see and had indeed despaired of ever seeing again.

"Holmes!" I cried.

PART III

CHAPTER THIRTY

A PENCHANT FOR ALL THINGS DAEDALIAN

Sherlock Holmes sidestepped around Hart and descended the staircase. He looked arch and slightly abashed, much as though he were arriving late for a soirée and anticipating censure from the hostess and his fellow guests.

"And Miss Woolfson, of course," said he. "We can dispense with the 'Shirley Holbrook' pseudonym in this company, can we not, Hannah? How delightful it is to be reunited with you both. I only wish it were under more auspicious conditions."

"But how are you here?" I said.

"If by 'how' you mean 'through what method of conveyance', the answer is prosaic enough: the West Country post train. It leaves Paddington at midnight and performs the most tedious and monotonous journey known to mankind, stopping a hundred times along the way, or so it seems. Someone who is not an employee of the rail company or the Royal Mail may obtain a berth for himself on said train as a passenger, provided that that someone befriends the guard. The guard, in this instance, was not known personally to me beforehand but happened to be an old ally of yours. It was he who brought Victor Hatherley to your house some years ago, the hydraulic engineer who lost a thumb in most singular circumstances. I, through our mutual association with you, was able to present a good argument for travelling on his train, namely that I needed to get to Dorchester as swiftly as possible in order to deliver you from harm. He declared that you had done him a fair few favours in the past, and regulations be damned. He even cooked me tea and crumpets on the stove in his van. Excellent fellow. Thereafter, I hitched a ride to Waterton Parva on a milk cart."

"That is all very well," I said, "but—"

Before I could finish, Dr Pentecost said, "You two may catch up at your leisure. You will have a few minutes to do so while I make preparations. Miss Woolfson? It seems your Shirley Holbrook alter ego is surplus to requirements now, so I shall call you that instead. I would appreciate it if you would join me up here."

Hannah rose stiffly to her feet, shooting me a worried glance.

"Dr Pentecost," I said, "and you too, Sergeant-Major Hart. I have no idea what you propose to do with Holmes and me. Frankly, I do not want to know. But let me tell you this. That young lady is no danger to you. She deserves to go free, unmolested. Promise me you will honour this request. Give me your word as gentlemen."

The classicist emitted a rattle of hollow laughter. "If I were you I should be more concerned about myself than Miss Woolfson, Doctor."

"Then you are obviously not me."

"At any event, I need the girl where I can keep an eye on her. Mr Holmes's not entirely unexpected appearance has forced me to alter my plans somewhat, but not to their detriment. Rather, to their benefit. In Miss Woolfson I have, now, not bait but a hostage. Concern for her welfare will ensure your acquiescence – yours and your colleague's – during that which lies ahead."

Hannah gave me one last plaintive look as she climbed the steps to join Dr Pentecost. I reciprocated with a gaze that I trusted was steady and nerveless, to impart reassurance. If only I had felt as optimistic as I tried to appear.

"There we are, my dear," said Dr Pentecost condescendingly, yoking an arm around her shoulders. "Just continue to behave with the meekness traditionally associated with your sex, and all shall be well."

She shrugged the arm off, but he replaced it, more emphatically. This time she took the hint and let it remain.

Then they were gone, Dr Pentecost, Hannah and Hart. The door was shut and locked, and Holmes and I were left to our own devices in the gloomily lit antechamber.

"Well, old friend," said he, "here we are again."

"Yes. Captives in a room below ground at Charfrome Old Place."

"That and side-by-side once more, facing what I fear will be a daunting and possibly life-threatening test of our mettle. But tell me. I saw the look Hannah gave you just now, and the one you gave her in return. She seems to be reciprocating the attraction you have to her. Is that so?"

I declined to reply, not sure myself what the answer was.

"It was only a matter of time, I suppose," Holmes continued. "Your charms, bluff and hearty as they are, do seem to tell in the end when it comes to the ladies. Naturally your concern for her wellbeing overrode your caution when you read that last letter from her. Hence your hasty departure from Baker Street, without waiting to consult me."

"I knew it was a trap."

"That is something."

"I did not know the true originator of the trap, however," I added sheepishly. "I thought it Fairbrother."

Holmes clapped his hands in incredulity. "Fairbrother? With a quotation from Plutarch appended to the letter? In Greek script, moreover?"

"Why not? Would he not think it an appropriately Elysian touch?"

"Fairbrother is patently a dunderhead. I highly doubt he could conceive of such a ploy, not least as he told Hannah that he barely paid attention during his Classics lessons at school. I might understand if you had thought Sir Philip Buchanan the instigator of the letter, but not Fairbrother. Never him."

"Sir Philip!" I declared. "I must say, the idea had not occurred to me, but now that you mention it…"

"But it was not him either. I imagine he is blissfully ignorant of all that is going on under his own roof right now."

"Then he has no part in this affair?"

"As far as our immediate predicament goes, no. Sir Philip is, in fact, just as unlikely as Fairbrother to have been the one who made Hannah write the letter. He told us himself that his Ancient Greek was 'somewhat deficient' and that he was more familiar with the culture than the language. No, the only really credible perpetrator was the man who cannot help but make Classical allusions, the man whose daily discourse is littered with the things."

"I was not thinking clearly," I said.

"Or indeed at all. Your heart overpowered your head."

"I refuse to be ashamed of that."

"Just as I refuse to be ashamed for racing after you through the night, sure in the knowledge that you would become a victim of Dr Pentecost's machinations."

"You do me an injustice. It was by no means a given that I would wind up his captive."

"But it was predictable. And, when all is said and done, that is precisely what happened, is it not? Now then…"

Holmes began pacing the length of the antechamber, back and forth. To some this might have appeared the restless prowling of a caged animal, but I could tell that he was appraising our place of confinement, gauging its dimensions and purpose. I hoped he was also evaluating its strengths and weaknesses with a view to fathoming a way out.

Finally he halted beside the steel door. He rapped upon it with a knuckle a few times. It rang like a gong.

"Yes," he said to himself. "Yes." Then, jerking a thumb at the door, he said, "You do realise what lies beyond, don't you?"

"I have not a clue."

"Yet clues there have been aplenty. Hannah's correspondence was as burdened with them as an apple tree in season. The position of this antechamber we are in, for instance."

"What of it?"

"We are in the servants' wing, and the antechamber points towards the exterior of the house. This door therefore leads to an area outlying the footprint of the house. And what is to be found in the grounds immediately adjacent to the servants' wing?"

"I cannot readily recall at this moment."

"The knot garden," said Holmes, "the maze of low privet hedge where Hannah attempted to interrogate Edwin Fairbrother about the Delphic Ceremony and then had a sobering encounter with the Hoplite Quigg."

"I see. The door connects to the knot garden."

"To something that lurks below the knot garden. Something whose nature is reflected in what lies above."

"Another kind of garden?"

"Sometimes I wonder if you are wilfully dense, Watson, out of a kind of misplaced charity, so that I may appear all the cleverer."

"Holmes, I really do not understand what you are trying to describe."

"I even used the word 'maze,'" Holmes said with exasperation, "as did Hannah in her letter. Think, man!"

"I *am* thinking," I protested, although in truth I was thinking predominantly about Hannah and about what I would do to Dr Pentecost and Hart if they so much as laid a finger on her.

"Then let me make it easier for you. Whom does Sir Philip Buchanan admire most? Who is his inspiration?"

Here was a query I could answer. "Daedalus."

"At last. Progress. And what is Daedalus most renowned for?"

"Making wings from wax and feathers that allowed him and Icarus to fly free from imprisonment."

"Aside from that."

"Building the Labyrinth at Knossos."

"The great subterranean maze that housed the Minotaur," said Holmes, nodding. "The one that Theseus penetrated in order to slay that monster and rescue the young Athenians who were due to be sacrificed to it."

"You mean on the other side of that door there is a replica of that Labyrinth?"

"Of some sort, yes. Buchanan has constructed it in tribute to his hero. I inferred as much from the evidence Hannah provided. Of particular value in this deduction was the small windowless octagonal structure she mentioned that sits at the centre of the knot garden. It seemed to me an odd horticultural addition, entirely out of keeping with its surroundings and of no obvious purpose, until I hit upon the notion that it might not be for storage or even for ornament, but rather for access."

"Access to beneath the ground."

Holmes nodded. "That was when I began to extrapolate the existence of this underground labyrinth of Buchanan's. Further, I descried that it might have some exotic function, something beyond being simply another manifestation of his penchant for all things Daedalian. But what, I asked myself, might that function be?"

"I believe I can help you in that regard," I said. "Dr Pentecost told Hannah about a trial that graduating Elysians must undergo."

"I had already imagined as much myself," Holmes said. "It was Dr Pentecost's anecdote about the seashell and the ant that set my thoughts straying in that direction. It struck me that a man like Buchanan, so in thrall to Hellenic myth and tradition, would wish to put his Elysians through a similar sort of trial. That, in conjunction with a labyrinth – well, the two suppositions mesh together like watch parts."

"So you realised that the Delphic Ceremony is not the be-all and end-all of an Elysian's tenure at Charfrome?"

"From its name alone I fancied it an occasion of prophecy and mysticism."

"One of animal sacrifice as well."

"Proving that the rumours shared by landlord Scadden were not as absurd as we thought after all. Buchanan, of course, assumes the role of vatic priest, inhaling laurel smoke."

"You deduced that too?"

"The eyes. The lips. I am surprised you did not diagnose the symptoms accurately yourself."

"I did," I said, adding, "belatedly."

"Yet, given that I had divined the existence of a labyrinth on the estate, it seemed to me that the ceremony alone must be mere preamble. What would be the point of such an installation if it were not to be used? And what might it be used for but as a proving ground for those selected in the ceremony?"

"Holmes, I must say it is marvellous that you have been able to put so many diverse and seemingly opaque facts together and come up with these answers. I can corroborate them with intelligence I have received lately from Hannah in person. You are correct in practically every detail. The only thing I cannot vouch for is the labyrinth, but your postulation makes sense, especially in the light of other snippets of information I have learned during this past hour."

"What a relief it is to hear that."

"It does beg a question, however."

"Let me have it."

"Did you know all along that Dr Pentecost was not the harmless, amiable old duffer he purported to be?"

"Ah. There, I must confess, I was wrong-footed. With only the content of Hannah's letters to go on – her limited and very subjective viewpoint – I had no cause to believe that he was to be feared. It is something I regret deeply and will rebuke myself over to my dying day. You must remember, Watson, that I am not infallible, *pace* the impression people have of me, promulgated somewhat by your published chronicles. It was only when I saw the Greek phrase in that last, inordinately suspect letter from Hannah that the light dawned and I apprehended what a monumental blunder I had made. You should have seen me, old fellow. I literally hit myself. I am surprised there is not a bruise upon my forehead to show for it."

Somewhere, well embedded in this speech of Holmes's, lay an apology. I could hear it, although a less experienced ear might not. He was admitting that he had been wrong to have left Hannah to fend for herself at Charfrome, and I had been right to be concerned for her.

"To be met by Dr Pentecost at the gates of the estate, brandishing a gun..." he went on, "that, I will say, put the seal on it. The man was quite insouciant. He asked what had kept me and averred how rare it was, indeed unheard-of, for Dr Watson to blaze the trail while Sherlock Holmes tagged along in his wake. This while aiming at me a weapon I instantly recognised as yours. I was tempted to try to disarm him. It would not have been too difficult."

"Why did you not?"

"Because I had no way of knowing your and Hannah's situation. Were you alive? Dead? In either case, where? It seemed sensible to play safe and allow Dr Pentecost to lead me to you. Besides, while I have seen toddlers wielding spoons with greater dexterity than he did your Webley, there was always the remote chance that he might loose off a shot, and that I might be in the bullet's path. The better part of valour won the day."

"Now at least you know what sort of a man he is," I said.

"Desperate. Cunning. And, I would submit, some sort of confidence trickster."

"A blackmailer."

"Ah, indeed."

Briefly I imparted the new intelligence about Dr Pentecost that Hannah had supplied while she and I were alone together in the antechamber.

"Yes," said Holmes, shaking his head. "Again, curse me, I should have spotted it. The willingness to befriend others. The constant mention of how good he is at keeping secrets. Dr Pentecost is an inveigler, a spider who entices flies into his web before pouncing and sucking them dry. We have encountered his like before and shall doubtless encounter his like again. I have not given this affair my fullest attention, Watson, as I should have. I have been too distracted by other cases or too sunk in self-absorption. It is not too late, however, to remedy the oversight."

"Is it?" I said. "Even now that we are both at Dr Pentecost's mercy?"

"I am of the view that we are, in fact, about to be at the mercy of Sir Philip Buchanan's ingenuity," said Holmes. "And it is an ingenuity which, although motivated by the best of intentions, has claimed lives."

CHAPTER THIRTY-ONE

INTO THE LABYRINTH

I was about to ask Holmes to qualify that remark. Then, however, the steel door abruptly began to move. It slid sideways with a low grinding noise, exposing a darkened passage that was walled and flagged with smooth stone. There was no one behind the door. Some automated mechanism had opened it.

A moment later, a voice spoke. It reverberated from the passage, an echoing, weirdly attenuated version of Dr Pentecost's.

"Gentlemen. Before you lies a challenge of your skill, your intellect, your endurance and your resilience. Enter and excel. Never before has Sir Philip's labyrinth played host to quite so illustrious a pair. I trust you will find it sufficiently engaging and improving. There is an old Greek saying, '*pathemata mathemata*': 'sufferings are teachings'. The labyrinth purifies people through hardship, just as metallic ore is purified through smelting and water through boiling."

I spied a small dome-shaped device suspended from the ceiling just past the door, a cage of fine metal mesh. Out of this was the voice emanating. The sound must, I assumed, be conveyed from elsewhere by a system not unlike the speaking tubes used to communicate between decks on a ship.

"Step forward now," Dr Pentecost said. "Take the lamp to illuminate your way. Prove yourselves worthy of survival. And remember: do not even think of deviating or defaulting. Sergeant-Major Hart has Miss Woolfson firmly in hand, if you get my meaning. For her sake, do exactly as is required of you, no more, no less."

Holmes plucked the Tilley lamp from the wall, as bidden. He worked the pump with his thumb to pressurise the gas generator, the burner flared, and rapidly the mantle became more incandescent, shedding a corona of illumination several feet in all directions. He padded forward, through the doorway, into the passage.

"Well, Watson? Are you with me?"

"Yes," I sighed. There seemed no alternative. There *was* none. As so many times before, I was obliged to follow Holmes into the teeth of danger.

No sooner did I join him in the passage than the door rumbled shut behind us. Holmes proceeded towards a narrow doorway that afforded access to a chamber that was somewhat broader than the passage but still narrow. It was long, too, so long that the far end was lost in darkness, beyond the reach of the lamplight. The moment we entered, a door slid across the opening at our backs, cutting off egress that way, sealing us in.

"The first test," said Dr Pentecost. His voice now came from within the chamber, via another speaking-tube dome overhead. "A riddle that challenged the wit of Oedipus. Advance!"

The light from the Tilley lamp revealed, directly in front of us, a sheer-sided pit that straddled the width of the chamber. It was a distance of some seven or eight yards across to the patch of floor beyond, and as for the pit's depth, Holmes determined – by dint of lowering the lamp into it to the full reach of his arm – that it

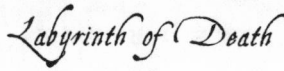

was sunk at least twenty feet into the earth. The bottom was hard-packed soil.

Bridging this obstacle was a set of sturdy-looking oak beams, four in all, several inches thick. Each was embedded into the wall of the pit at both ends, just below floor-level, and the four were evenly spaced apart, the gaps between them no wider than three feet.

"Seems straightforward enough," I said. "We are to cross the pit by means of the beams. It is merely a question of balance. The only drawback is that, should one topple, and fail to catch oneself, one is liable to break one's neck."

"I believe there is more to it, old fellow," Holmes declared. He held the lamp out over the pit, inclining his whole body forward. Now I could make out a second pit that lay beyond this one, and past that, faintly, a third. Both of these pits looked identical to the first, right down to the number and situation of their beams.

"So we must do it three times in succession," I said. "Perhaps the further two pits are even deeper, so as to increase the peril to life and limb."

"Perhaps," said Holmes. "But you should note, too, Watson, the carvings that adorn the chamber wall to our left."

He swung the lamp in that direction, and by its light I discerned a design engraved into the stonework immediately adjacent the pit.

"A clue?" I wondered aloud. "Does it mean something?"

"Of course it means something," Holmes snapped. "The question is what."

"Could it be suggesting that we leap the pit rather than use the beams to cross? The arc of the semicircle could be said to describe the arc of a jump."

"Even with the short run-up available to us, I cannot leap such a distance. Neither can you, I daresay. Moreover, your interpretation of the symbol is rendered debatable by the symbol that adorns the wall next to the second pit."

The lamp's glow made this second design just visible:

"I would be very surprised," my companion continued, "were there not a corresponding third symbol beside the third pit, although the gloom prevents us from seeing it at present. I would be very surprised, too, if the second symbol were inviting us to leap, as you surmise about the first. Unless, that is, the use of a full circle implies that one is to perform a somersault while doing so."

"All right, Holmes. I take the point. I am wrong about the leaping. What do *you* think the symbols stand for?"

"They provide a hint as to the solution to the test," said he. "Of that there is no doubt. Dr Pentecost's remark, as we entered this chamber, is also some sort of hint: 'A riddle that challenged the wit of Oedipus'. The trouble is, my Classical knowledge is not as extensive as it might be."

"You sounded authoritative enough when discussing Polyphemus the Cyclops with Buchanan."

"It is one of the few morsels of Hellenic myth that piqued my interest at school," Holmes said, "for the reasons I gave Buchanan

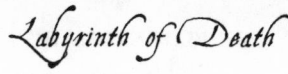

at the time: it was an instance of unjust deserts. As for the rest of that portion of my education, I have forgotten much, and what I have not forgotten I remember dimly at best. Did I not tell you, in the earliest days of our acquaintance, that the brain is like a little empty attic that a man must stock with such furniture as he chooses? Useless facts must not elbow out the useful ones, and a working knowledge of ancient literature, to someone in my profession, could not be ranked amongst the latter."

"Until now," I said, "when it might have been of help."

Holmes quirked his mouth to show that he appreciated the irony, even if he did not relish it. "Well," he said, "since I am as yet incapable of fathoming this conundrum through recourse to literary data, there remains the alternative of fathoming it by more practical methods – to wit, deduction. Lying before us are four wooden beams spanning a pit. They are clearly intended to be trodden upon. But observe how their ends are not firmly secured in place with, say, right-angle braces or cement pilings. Rather, they disappear into niches that are much larger than they need to be, with inches of clearance around them in every direction. Hence it is feasible that the beams' ends are not in fact secured at all. They are at liberty to wobble, or rotate on their axis, or possibly retract. The trick is to establish beyond doubt what form of deceit they practise, without oneself coming to harm."

Having passed the lamp to me, Holmes went from the leftmost of the four beams to the rightmost, placing one foot tentatively down on each and gradually adding more and more of his weight. In every instance, no sooner was significant pressure put on the beam than it began to display unsteadiness, twisting clockwise or anticlockwise.

"Yes, all are mounted at either end on unseen gimbals," he concluded. "Each works along a single axis, the roll axis."

"Then, surely, more than ever a keen sense of balance is called for," I said.

"I would say that even a tightrope walker would not be able to thread his way across these beams. Their precariousness is too great. A tightrope at least allows for a certain amount of instability. It has elasticity and it can sway, which the acrobat may exploit to his advantage, to compensate for any instability of his own, whereas these beams will pitch over and decant their occupant off them at the least wavering. This entire contraption has one express purpose: to prevent safe passage across."

"But that is ridiculous. An impossible test."

"Quite. Nevertheless there must be a solution, for why else would…?"

Holmes's voice trailed off and a sudden gleam of inspiration entered his eyes.

"Of course!" he ejaculated. "I remember now. The riddle Oedipus was confronted with. The riddle of the Sphinx."

"The Sphinx? Is that not an Ancient Egyptian beast? As in the giant effigy made of stone next to the Pyramids at Giza? Yet Oedipus is from Hellenic myth: the lame-footed tragic hero who inadvertently killed his father and married his mother. How are the two associated?"

"The Greeks had a Sphinx of their own, Watson. Like the Egyptians' Sphinx this one was a composite beast, a human head on a lion's body, but differed in so far as it was female and had the wings of a bird as well. It was in the habit of bearding unwary travellers on the outskirts of the city of Thebes and posing them a riddle. Should they fail to answer correctly, the Sphinx would strangle and devour them. The most famous of its riddles, and the one Oedipus successfully solved, runs as follows: 'What is the creature that goes on four legs in the morning, two legs in the daytime and three legs in the evening?'"

"The answer being…?"

"Man," said Holmes. "As infants, in the morning of our lives, we crawl on all fours. Thereafter we walk on two legs, until with old age, in our twilight days, we require the help of a walking stick to get around – a third, artificial leg. When Oedipus unravelled the riddle, the Sphinx, infuriated, hurled itself off a cliff."

"I see." Now that he had mentioned it, I did recall the riddle. It surfaced from the dark recesses of memory, where it had been lodged alongside heaps of other childhood trivia. "And you are convinced it applies here?"

"The symbols on the wall at least confirm that I am on the right track. The first can be taken to depict the rising sun showing itself over the horizon in the east. The second, the sun at midday, at its zenith. If I am right, the third symbol will be a reflection of the first, with the semicircle at the opposite end of the line, denoting sunset."

"But does that tell us how to traverse each set of beams?"

"It must do."

"Should we crawl across these ones here like babes, then?"

"That cannot be so. Whether we go upright or on all fours, the beams are no less apt to tip over. No, it will be something else. Something more cunning than that." Holmes ruminated for several moments. "Hum! Yes. Elysians graduate in pairs, is that not the case? Hannah mentioned as much in her last letter. Two of them are singled out each time. And here are you and I, likewise a pair. It cannot be irrelevant. What if, on the contrary, it is crucial?"

After a further moment of contemplation, he turned to me.

"Watson, I believe I have it."

CHAPTER THIRTY-TWO

CROSSING THE BEAMS

"It is elegantly simple," said Holmes. "We cross the beams together, using all four of them, one foot upon each."

"How will that help? They will still be unsteady."

"I reckon not. I reckon they are constructed so that pressure on all four will deactivate the gimbals. Here my knowledge of safe-cracking and lock-picking, which is extensive if not comprehensive, comes into play. I envisage the gimbals as being perched atop notched wheels like the tumblers in a safe. Individually the wheels may move freely, rotating on spindles when weight is placed upon the gimbals above, which are joined to them by drive cams. When all the beams are depressed at once, however, the wheel notches align, allowing a 'fence' – a kind of cylindrical bar mounted on springs – to rise up and lock the gimbals in place with pins. In other words, when sufficient downward force is applied to the beams simultaneously, it triggers an immobilising mechanism that prevents them from rolling."

"That is only your theory."

"Yet it is a sound theory, I feel, and one worth putting to the assay."

"And if you are wrong?"

"I am not. Trust me."

I did trust him. I always had and always would.

That said, it was not without trepidation that I lined myself up before the right-hand two beams while Holmes did likewise before the left-hand two.

"Carefully now," he said. "The moment of truth. We must each place both of our feet simultaneously on adjacent beams. A small, artfully executed jump. Are you ready?"

I steeled myself. The pit seemed, at that moment, preternaturally deep. It yawned below me like a bottomless crevasse.

"On my cue," said Holmes. "Three. Two. One. Go."

We leapt, landing in concert, and all at once there was a set of loud, significant clicks from within the beams' mountings, at either edge of the pit. Through my boot soles I felt both beams beneath me give a tiny shudder, then become fixed and stable.

"What now?" I said, damping down a sigh of relief.

"We shuffle," said Holmes. "We may not walk as normal, since any variance in our cumulative weight might release the immobilising mechanism and free up the gimbals once more. Slide your feet forwards. But slowly, slowly... And, it goes without saying, do not lose your footing. Should you do so, we could both be unseated."

Like a cross-country skier I shunted my feet alternately along the beams, keeping pace with Holmes. After perhaps twenty seconds – although it felt infinitely longer – we arrived at the other end. With my companion verbally choreographing our movements as before, we jumped off the beams in unison.

"Admirably done, Watson," said he. "Two more crossings remain."

"I presume the second and third pits are to be traversed in much the same fashion."

"Much the same, yet different. Remember, man 'goes on two legs' at the midday of his life. So logic dictates that for the second pit we may avail ourselves of only two of the beams in total. The system of notched wheels will be rigged so that the gimbals will not lock otherwise."

"I see. So we are to share two beams at once?"

"Which makes life somewhat harder. I shall go first. You must alight directly behind me. The beams will not achieve stability until the weight of two people is brought to bear on them."

"Which pair of adjacent beams are we to cross?" I asked.

"I suspect it does not make any difference," came the reply. "If there were a choice to be made but no clue to indicate as much, that would not be fair, and if nothing else I think Sir Philip likes to play fair with those graduating. Shall we try the central pair?"

Holmes, with the utmost delicacy, positioned himself atop the two centremost beams. He extended both arms sideways, his legs shaking slightly as he strove to counteract the beams' treacherous tendency to revolve. With brow furrowed in concentration, he inched forwards until there was room for me to accompany him.

"Hurry, old friend," he said. "Maintaining my balance like this is trickier than it looks."

No sooner was I aboard the beams too than, as Holmes had forecast, they locked themselves in place under our combined weight. Thereupon, like a couple of dancers in a chorus line, my friend and I moved in procession over the gulf of the pit. All the while I kept the Tilley lamp aloft in one hand, feeling the heat from its burner bathing the side of my face.

At the other end of the beams, Holmes cautioned me to keep still. "Once I dismount, the gimbals will unlock. Simply stand firm. I will help you over the threshold."

He stepped lightly onto the next patch of floor, and at the selfsame moment the beams suddenly became shivering, unsettled things beneath me, like skittish animals.

"Pass over the lamp."

I handed it to him, and he set it down and reached for me with both arms.

"Give me your hands."

The beams' uncertainty intensified; that or I was losing my poise. Either way, my legs were trembling, and no amount of frantic swaying back and forth or windmilling of the arms was remedying the situation. I knew I was going to fall. I could feel it happening and was helpless to prevent it.

Both beams rolled over at once, in towards each other. My feet slipped off. My legs shot together. I plummeted.

I stopped plummeting. Two exceptionally powerful hands had clamped themselves about my wrists, arresting my descent. For a brief moment Holmes was supporting my entire weight with just the strength of his body alone, a remarkable feat of physicality. His teeth were clenched, his neck a writhe of sinews.

My feet scrabbled for purchase on the pit's side. My toecaps found no hold on the stonework. However, by flattening my soles against the masonry I was able to gain a bit of traction and relieve Holmes of at least some of the burden of my bulk. He hauled upwards with all his might. I assisted by "walking" up the side of the pit. Together – although he did most of the work – we contrived to get me onto solid ground. Thereafter, I sank to my knees, panting hard, heart racing.

"A near thing," Holmes observed.

"Too near," I said, mopping my forehead. "Shall we endeavour not to let that happen again?"

"We can do our best, old man, but there is still one pit left."

The lamp's radiance picked out a third carved symbol on the wall beside the final pit. In accordance with Holmes's earlier postulation it was indeed an inversion of the first:

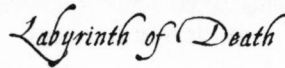

"Sunset," he said. "Three legs."

"How on earth do we manage a crossing on three legs? Do we tie one of my ankles to yours, as in a three-legged race?"

"I think it is a little more straightforward than that. We go in procession like last time, but across three beams rather than two. Where my right foot goes, your left foot does as well. Do you concur?"

I could not gainsay the proposition. Holmes had been proven correct twice so far. He would surely be correct a third time.

And so it transpired. We started each with his outside foot upon a beam, Holmes's left upon the first beam in the row, my right upon the third. Then each added his inside foot to the middle beam between the other two. Accordingly all three beams stabilised, and off we went. Both of us gained the other side without incident, springing off synchronously onto the furthermost section of floor.

There, another steel door awaited, closed.

"My congratulations," said Dr Pentecost. "You struggled there briefly, but redeemed yourselves."

"Ah, the godlike voice from on high," said Holmes. "He speaks again."

"He does," said the classicist.

"And can hear us, it seems. The speaking-tubes work both ways, carrying sound to and from whatever eyrie you are nesting in, Doctor."

"Naturally."

"You are able to see us, too."

"How astute."

"I caught sight of a glint of glass within each of the cage-like structures. Would I be right in thinking that a network of mirrors runs concurrently with the speaking tubes? Thus, in the manner of someone using a periscope, you are able to monitor our activities by eye."

"The images are small and blurry, but nonetheless give me a fair idea of your progress," said Dr Pentecost.

"How else would you know when to operate the doors and how Watson and I fared when crossing the pits?"

"How else indeed?"

"What perplexes me, Doctor, is why you are putting us through this whole ordeal. If it were Sir Philip co-ordinating things from above, instead of you, I could understand that he might wish to see how Sherlock Holmes measures up against his own brilliance. Without wishing to flatter myself, I am perhaps more adroit at this kind of puzzle-solving than the average Elysian. If he can outwit me, it would reflect well upon him. What, however, do you stand to gain from it?"

"Maybe it is what *you* stand to gain, Mr Holmes. Namely the life of Miss Woolfson."

"That is undoubtedly a prize," said Holmes, "but you must surely know, Doctor, that when we come through the labyrinth safe and sound, as we surely shall, you yourself will suffer for it. We shall be at liberty to expose your crimes and hold you to account for them."

"It is a gamble I am willing to take."

"No, you are no gambler, sir," said Holmes darkly.

"Perhaps not," Dr Pentecost rejoined. "That is enough badinage for now, at any rate. You have passed the first test. It is also the easiest test. They get progressively more arduous. Onward you go."

The door slid open, and Holmes went through, as did I, having elected myself lamp-bearer once again. Another narrow passage beckoned, this one executing a couple of right-angle turns before it deposited us at the next door.

That portal led to a chamber considerably bigger than the previous. Seen from above, it was in the shape of an isosceles trapezoid, like a triangle with its apex shorn off. The end where Holmes and I stood – the base of this blunted triangle – was broad, with the two walls on either side of us converging so that the far end was considerably narrower. The ceiling and all four walls were blank, uniform brick, while the floor was paved with two kinds of tile: large hexagons and small triangles, all of glazed white ceramic. These were arranged in a tessellated pattern:

The pattern covered the entirety of the chamber floor. The sole exception, as far as I could see, was a strip of rectangular tiles a couple of feet wide, the same dimensions as a hallway runner, which lay beneath my and Holmes's feet.

Presiding over everything was a huge and hideous sculpted head that leered across at us from the far wall. It consisted of a woman's face, crone-like, with wide, hollowed-out eyes and a snarling mouth from which projected a forked tongue. Framing this grotesque visage were numerous snakes, like a serpentine mane of hair. Each of the reptiles was rendered in a coiled, aggressive posture, fangs bared, as though poised on the verge of delivering a deadly strike.

Dr Pentecost's voice insinuated itself down from above. "Gentlemen, you may recognise the Gorgon Medusa there, she whose gaze would turn a man to stone. The challenge itself is called the Perseus Stratagem. That is all I am going to tell you. The rest you must work out for yourselves."

With that, the door closed, trapping us in the chamber with that vile, gaping head.

CHAPTER THIRTY-THREE

THE GORGON'S GAZE

"Well, Holmes?" I said. "Any thoughts?"

"At present, nothing springs to mind," said my companion, "save that it is apparent that we must cross the floor, for a second door lies ahead, to one side of Medusa's head, and can only be our exit."

"I see it. I would not be so foolish, however, as to assume that we may simply stroll over there and, as if by magic, it will open for us."

"Your sagacity does you credit. There is also a matter of singular interest that you have no doubt already registered."

"Perhaps you can spare me the effort of floundering around in ignorance and just tell me straight out what has caught your attention and eluded mine."

"You ruin my fun. Very well, then. Look at the wall behind us. See how it is scarred and pitted?"

The brickwork was covered in pockmarks. None occurred above head height or below ankle height. It gave the wall the appearance of being diseased, like skin afflicted by the aftermath of smallpox.

"The rest of the wall is perfectly smooth," I said, "as are all the other walls. What can have caused blemishes of such a sort, and why only in the one area?"

"The answer to that might well give us insight into the nature of the threat this room poses," said Holmes, tapping his lips, which were pursed in a small, pensive smile.

"Holmes," I said, "something tells me you are rather enjoying yourself."

"I cannot deny, Watson, that I am finding these puzzles not a little invigorating. Sir Philip Buchanan possesses a great brain, and I am intrigued to learn how my own measures up against it."

"Even though we risk injury, and perhaps death, if you fail to meet the mark?"

"No, we shall survive this gauntlet, I assure you. Countless Elysians have, so why not us? Although, admittedly, not every Elysian who has entered the labyrinth has emerged unscathed, or for that matter alive. That is the dark truth behind Charfrome Old Place. Sir Philip's altruism has led to unfortunate consequences that, I am afraid to say, he has not sought to rectify or ameliorate but instead somehow countenances as justifiable."

"You think some dire fate has befallen Elysians in the labyrinth?"

"A fall from one of the beams in the previous chamber might well prove fatal. The drop is sufficient to break a man's neck. And if, as Dr Pentecost has intimated, the tests become progressively harder, they may also become concomitantly more dangerous."

"Might that be what happened to Simms and Kinsella, for instance? They became the labyrinth's victims?"

"Really, Mr Holmes, Dr Watson," said the disembodied voice of Dr Pentecost, sounding impatient. "We don't have all night. Would you kindly do me the honour of getting on with it?"

"Duty calls," said Holmes. "Now then. The distribution of the pitting on the wall is certainly suggestive. Hold the lamp a little closer, would you? That's it. The marks appear chiselled. Or... No. The result of impacts. Each is roughly conical, like a tiny crater, as though some small, pointed object has struck the wall with force, repeatedly. A hail of such objects, perhaps."

He turned to look across at Medusa.

"Her gaze turns a man to stone, eh?" he mused. "Or does it, in the event, inflict damage upon stone? Those eyes of hers are suspiciously hollow. More like gun barrels than eyes. Would you not say so?"

I had stared into a gun barrel on more occasions than I cared to recollect. "There is a resemblance, I agree."

"At this distance one cannot confirm that they are anything other than empty sockets. Yet I am convinced they are not. Within their interstices they hide a secret."

"The marks on the wall are bullet holes?"

"They are far too diminutive for that. It is, by my estimate, twenty yards from here to that head. Even bullets of the smallest calibre would inflict deeper gouges than these, especially if fired from so close a range. No, we must consider other forms of projectile, minuscule ones, such as nails or pellets. We must likewise consider what causes those projectiles to be launched. That, I feel, is the nub of it. Medusa is passive right now. She must somehow be incited to attack."

"Her field of fire seems extensive," I said, eyeing the pock-marked wall. "She can enfilade the entire breadth of the chamber."

"Which accounts for its trapezoidal design," said Holmes. "There are no places where shots from her eyes cannot reach, no safe refuges for us. Wherever we go, we are exposed, until such time as we can gain entrance through the other door. All of this is conjecture, of course, but the evidence supports it and seems incontrovertible."

"And the name the Perseus Stratagem. How does that fit in to this?"

"It was the demigod Perseus who slew Medusa, was it not? Beheaded her, as I recall."

"So we, then, must somehow 'slay' that representation of her."

"Figuratively speaking, yes." Holmes fixed his attention upon the floor. "I am inclined to think that those ceramic tiles are no mere decoration. They look innocuous enough, but scrutiny reveals a notable absence of grout surrounding each hexagon. The triangles do have grout between them where they adjoin one another, but not where their edges meet those of the hexagons."

He dropped into a crouch and gently explored the nearest hexagonal tile with his fingertips.

"Yes, it betrays the tiniest amount of give under my touch. The hexagons are detached, independent. They rest loosely in slots rather than being affixed to planking below. A certain springiness suggests that this one, and all its cohorts, are actually triggers."

"And there you have your provocation," I said. "Treading upon a hexagonal tile will launch one of those hypothetical projectiles from Medusa's eyes."

"Hypothecation must invariably yield action," Holmes said.

"Spoken decisively. You are going to attempt to get her to open fire on us."

"At me. We must know what we are dealing with, and this is the best – the only – way to find out. It is reasonable to infer – at least as an opening gambit – that when Medusa shoots from her eyes, she does so in the direction of the tile that has been pressed. At what height the projectile emerges is less easy to determine. Her salvoes seem subject to some variability. The pockmarks are spread wide and evenly across the wall, with a rare few instances of clustering. The projectiles are therefore likely to be lightweight and, as a consequence, easily deflected during the course of their flight. They do not necessarily travel straight and true. All the same, they retain some degree of accuracy, enough to guarantee striking a target the size of a human body."

"Then how will you avoid becoming just such a target?"

"By ducking down, like so, and bending to one side, so that only my arm lies within the line of fire."

"You may still be hit."

"As may you, for there is no telling where precisely the projectile may go. For that reason, I would advise you to crouch as low as you can."

I did as bidden, hunching to present as little of my bodily surface area as possible.

"You have every right to look concerned, Watson," my companion said. "I have minimised the risk as far as possible. I can do no more. And should the worst happen, either or both of us shall at least satisfy his curiosity as to what it feels like to be turned to stone."

"Dr Pentecost was speaking in metaphors, surely," I said. "That carved head over there cannot literally petrify one with its gaze."

"Who knows? Perhaps it can."

With these words, Sherlock Holmes stretched out his arm to its fullest extent, so that his hand just reached the chosen tile. His features were impassive, but I thought I detected a flicker of anxiety in his eyes. Even he was not immune to twinges of self-doubt.

He tapped the tile, and instantly there was a loud, sharp hiss from the far end of the chamber. This was matched by a loud, sharp hiss from me as something embedded itself in the meat of my thigh – something that stung horribly for a second, before the pain ebbed and was replaced by a spreading icy numbness.

I looked down and beheld the feathered butt-end of some kind of dart protruding from my trouser-leg. I groped for it, but Holmes's hand was swifter. In a single deft motion he plucked the inch-long missile out.

At much the same moment, my leg gave way under me. All

sensation had left it, and all strength. The muscles went as slack as blancmange.

As I sagged to the floor, my knee landed heavily on another of the hexagonal tiles. Again there was that hiss from the end of the chamber where the Gorgon glowered. A second dart whisked across the room, this one thudding into the wall behind us, mere inches above Holmes's head. It ricocheted away, having added yet another pockmark to the multitude.

Holmes wrestled me fully onto the strip of rectangular tiles. "Here is the safety zone, Watson. Do not let any of your limbs stray off it."

"My leg," I gasped. "I cannot feel my leg. I cannot move it."

Holmes held up the dart he had pulled out of me, studying its bloodied point. He took a sniff. Then he retrieved the one that had narrowly missed him and sniffed its point too. He followed that action by touching the tip of his tongue to it very briefly, before spitting out a gobbet of saliva straight away.

"Curare," he said.

"My God!" I cried. "Are you certain?"

"I am. A fairly dilute dose, but potent enough. Contrary to popular opinion, curare has no smell. It is one of the few poisons to lack a distinctive aroma. It does have an extraordinarily bitter taste, though, and oral contact with it leaves the tongue tingling, as mine is right now. To confirm my analysis, there is the effect it has had upon you. You know as well as I do that curare acts as a muscle relaxant."

"Of course. For which reason it has been used to treat lockjaw and polio, and also as an antidote to strychnine poisoning. In excess, however…"

"It may lead to full bodily paralysis and, potentially, cardiac arrest." Holmes turned to look at the Medusa's head. "So she can, after all, turn a man to stone – or at least render him as stiff as a statue. Bravo, Sir Philip."

"What are we to do?" I said. "I am incapable of walking."

"The effects of the curare should pass relatively soon. But we definitely cannot risk you being pierced by further darts. I estimate it would take only two or three more doses to leave you stricken to the point of helplessness."

"Or worse."

"Hush a moment, Watson, while I think."

Holmes studied the tessellations once more, then Medusa, then the pockmarks. I could almost hear the cells in that magnificent grey matter of his fizzing industriously.

"Pneumatic firing mechanism," he muttered to himself, "akin to that of an air-gun. Endlessly replenishable. Supply of darts limited, no doubt, but sufficiently copious. Direction of fire, variable. Randomised? No. There must be a pattern. These traps are meant to be solvable. But touching of *this* tile… Whereas touching of *that* tile…" He swivelled his head from side to side, at the same time sketching imaginary vectors in the air with a forefinger. "It is a case of angles. Of geometry. Yes. That's it. With a dash of Newtonian physics thrown in. 'For every action…'"

Meanwhile, feeling was returning to my leg, albeit incrementally and not without discomfort. My quadriceps muscles were twitching and leaping as though galvanised.

"Watson," Holmes said. "I have worked it out. It is really quite elementary."

"Elucidate."

"We may regard this trap as the opposite of the previous, in so far as here the presence of two people in the chamber works against them, whereas before, back there, it worked in their favour. Nonetheless co-operation is required."

"I regret, I am still none the wiser."

"The Perseus Stratagem. How did Perseus defeat the Medusa? How did he avoid being turned to stone by her stare?"

"I am drawing a blank."

"It does not matter. All that matters is that you are able to stand. Can you?"

I struggled upright, gripping the pockmarked wall for support. I shifted my curare-deadened leg around, flexing the joints. I put weight on it.

"My leg functions well enough," I said.

"You do not have to be at your most agile," Holmes said. "Rudimentary locomotion will suffice. Just stay behind me."

"That I can manage, and gladly, if it means you are my bulwark against further perforation by poison darts."

"Neither of us should have to worry about that, not if I have truly divined the secret of the Gorgon's gaze."

Together, we went to one end of the "runner" of rectangular tiles, on the same side of the chamber as the door next to Medusa.

"Now we go on tiptoes, I suppose," I said. "We tread only on the triangles, avoiding the hexagons."

"It would be impossible to guarantee success by that means. The sections of triangle are narrow. The least carelessness, the slightest misstep, will inevitably result in a hexagon being pressed."

"What, then?"

My friend, without another word, ventured boldly and brazenly onto the floor, inviting me to follow suit at his rear. Over the tiles we went, hexagon and triangle alike, and with practically every step he or I took, a dart was disgorged from one or other of Medusa's eyes. Yet the darts came nowhere near us. On the contrary, they pinged one after another into the rear wall at the side furthest from us. I flinched at each crisp, pneumatic puff of air, at each silvery glimmer of dart in flight, but not once during the journey across the chamber did the Gorgon's gaze directly threaten us with injury.

In next to no time we presented ourselves at the door. We were on another rectangular-tiled "safety zone", the barrage of darts having ceased now that no more hexagons were being pressed.

"Dr Pentecost," Holmes announced primly. "If you would not mind…"

The door duly opened.

"Do you not see now, Watson?" said my friend. "The rationale behind the puzzle? Perseus approached Medusa walking backwards, employing a polished shield as a mirror so that he did not have to look her straight in the eye. He also wore a Cap of Invisibility, a gift from Hades, so was able to sneak up on her unseen and behead her. But the shield mirror is the pertinent factor, for our purposes."

"Reflection."

"Precisely! It is all about reflection. Mirroring. Medusa here shoots, not in the direction of the tile that is trodden upon, but at a point symmetrically opposite. I apprehended as much by inference. I pressed a tile; you were hit. You pressed another by accident; I was nearly hit. Devious, but once one determines the relationship between cause and effect, beatable. Accordingly, we both took a path along the wall on this side, and Medusa's shots ranged exclusively along the wall on the other side. Had we not done so, had we attempted to reach the door two abreast rather than in single file, or else each along one of the side walls, the outcome may well have been very different."

"Two tests down," Dr Pentecost announced. "Three to go."

"Five in all?" I exclaimed in dismay. "Then we are not even halfway there yet."

"Five is not such a great number, Doctor," said Dr Pentecost. "Hercules faced Twelve Labours. Theseus faced six challenges on the road from Troezen to Athens. Five is reasonable by comparison."

"Look at it another way, Watson," said Holmes. "We have had a one hundred per cent success rate so far. That bodes well."

"If you say so," I murmured.

"Onward to the next test, gentlemen," said Dr Pentecost. "Orion's Nemesis."

Holmes ducked through the doorway. I, limping a little still, followed in his wake. Uppermost in my thoughts was Hannah. I pictured her in the clutches of that brute Malachi Hart, and I seethed. For her alone I was willing to see this ordeal through to its conclusion – for the chance to be reunited with her and look upon her face again.

It had occurred to me, however, that Dr Pentecost could surely not wish Holmes and me to navigate all the way to the end of the labyrinth and come out the other side free and clear. That would be entirely antithetical to his own interests.

Rather, he would do everything in his power to ensure we failed.

Failed fatally.

CHAPTER THIRTY-FOUR

THE OSTOMACHION

A few twists and turns of passageway, another sliding door, and we were in the third chamber.

This one was compact indeed, a six-foot cube. Holmes had to stoop slightly in order to keep the crown of his head from scraping the ceiling.

Set into the wall facing us was another door. Adjacent to it was a shallow recess containing a two-foot-square shelf mounted at a steep inward angle. A raised edge surrounded the shelf, making it seem like some sort of empty picture frame.

Resting on the floor at our feet were a number of terracotta tiles – a mixture of polygons, predominantly triangles. These had been laid out adjacent to one another so that together they formed a shape. It looked like a queer geometrical letter J lying on its side. The curved stroke of the J hooked over one end of the main bar, reaching a third of the way along, while at the other end two triangles were arranged pointing outwards in a V-formation like a pair of flamboyant serifs.

Holmes drew my notice to a series of vertical trapdoors

positioned equidistantly along both of the side walls at wainscot height, seven a side. Each was not much larger than a man's handkerchief.

"You have doubtless spotted a correspondence between the trapdoors and the tiles," he said.

It took me a moment to grasp what he was driving at. "There are the same number of both."

"Excellent. Yes. Fourteen of each. That cannot be irrelevant. The tiles, moreover, are inset snugly into moulded trays. Given Buchanan's patent fondness for hidden trigger mechanisms, it would therefore be reasonable to deduce that any action upon one of them may cause a trapdoor to activate."

"Releasing… what?"

"Some kind of animal, I'll be bound," Holmes said. "A small one, to judge by the size of the trapdoors and also by the scuff marks in the dust in the corner there, which betray the passage of dainty feet."

"A mouse? I cannot say the thought of mice scampering about the chamber is an unduly alarming one. It does not fill me with the urge to hitch up my skirts and shriek."

"No, I do not think it is mice."

"Rats? Again, hardly the most terrifying prospect. Some may detest them but I find them inoffensive. A boy at my school, Percy Phelps – remember him? – kept a couple as pets. They were amiable and rather intelligent things."

"No, the scuff marks do not resemble those such as any rodent might leave. They are not paw-prints at all. I have an inkling they belong to something not mammalian, something altogether colder-blooded and less agreeable. This outline on the floor before us is, itself, a pointer towards its identity. Think of it as a crude side-elevation silhouette. I believe, too, that the particular fauna in question may well account for Labropoulos the chef's jar of crickets. Those were not some exotic human foodstuff after all, as Miss Woolfson supposed. They were intended as prey for the animals we are shortly to be exposed to. Labropoulos's duties, it would seem, include feeding livestock as well as Elysians."

"Please, Holmes. Do not keep me in suspense. I am keen to know what awaits behind those trapdoors." I was not so keen, however, to meet whatever it was in the flesh. Holmes's face had taken on a grim aspect, and I could only assume that to mean we were in for some considerable unpleasantness.

Instead of answering me, my companion bent a knee and surveyed the arrangement of terracotta tiles.

"This test is called Orion's Nemesis," I said. "Orion was a hunter, I know that much. As the victim of what creature did he meet his demise?"

"The Ostomachion," said Holmes, ignoring my question.

"I beg your pardon?" I said.

"These tiles comprise a dissection puzzle known as the Ostomachion, set down by Archimedes in a mathematical treatise called the *Archimedes Palimpsest*. It is both a game and an arithmetical proof. The fourteen shapes may be put together to form a square, or they may be laid out in various configurations crudely representing such items as a tree, a ship, an elephant, a dog, and so forth. The arithmetical element has to do with surface areas. The square represents a twelve-by-twelve grid, its surface area totalling 144 units. The ratio of the surface area of each polygon to the overall surface area of the square they cumulatively create is always an integer, and each integer is a multiple of one forty-eighth of the entire square. I am sure the late Professor Moriarty, with his expertise in mathematics, could have explained it more fully."

"Thank God he is not here to do so," I said. "Things are bad enough as they are."

"We are being called upon, in this test, to remove the pieces from the floor and insert them into that recessed frame by the door. Once the square is complete, the collective weight of the pieces will cause the frame to bear down upon a switch. The switch requires precisely that much weight to function, doubtless by means of a carefully calibrated counterweight against which it is suspended. This will in turn unlock the door. We will then be permitted to leave the cramped confines of this chamber." Holmes hesitated. "Unfortunately, the Ostomachion has at least five hundred possible solutions, if I recall rightly. And as we pick up each piece, so a trapdoor opens, unleashing something rather loathsome upon us.

"The logical approach is not to go about this bullishly – not to dive straight in and hope for the best. It is, rather, to solve the puzzle in theory first, before assembling it in practice. That would result in the shortest possible amount of time spent in the company of hazardous arthropods, whose presence might unsettle and lead to panicked, inaccurate thinking."

"Hazardous arthropods?" I echoed.

"Once again, Watson, I pray you be silent while I direct all my mental energies onto the problem at hand."

I loitered by the entry door while Holmes stared intently at the terracotta tiles. Occasionally he flicked a glance to the frame, before returning his gaze back to the floor. Into how many permutations must he have been organising those fourteen shapes, in his mind's eye? I imagined him aligning and realigning them, flipping them over, translating them in space, fitting them one next to the other, subjecting various potential formations to trial and error, all without touching them, using his remarkable brain alone.

About five minutes passed, during which time I became aware of a faint scratching sound that originated from behind the trapdoor nearest my feet. I crouched to get closer, bracing myself with a hand on the floor because my leg was still not yet working as it ought.

Putting my ear to the trapdoor – a mere thin sheet of metal – I heard a frantic scuffling and clicking on the other side. It was multifarious, this noise, as of dozens of tiny feet moving, dozens of hard bodies scraping against one another.

Hazardous arthropods. But of what species? Spiders? Not long since, Holmes and I had had a brush with a pair of monstrous *Galeodes* spiders in Deptford, brought over from the jungles of Cuba by the notorious canary-trainer Wilson. I prayed we were not about to be confronted by further similar specimens of venomous arachnid.

"Yes…" Holmes said softly. "That should do the trick."

"You have hit upon the solution?"

"One of the five-hundred-odd. But listen to me, Watson. Once I commence setting the tiles into the frame, we are going to be surrounded very quickly by stinging insects. I will work as swiftly as I can, but I am relying on you to do your bit and safeguard me from harm in the meantime."

"I am your man, Holmes."

"Spoken like the true hero you are. Then without further ado…"

Holmes snatched up one of the largest tiles, a long irregular pentagon shaped not unlike a tall, skew-roofed townhouse. No sooner had he done so than the trapdoor midway along the left-hand wall snapped open.

Out from the aperture in the wall crawled first one, then several multiple-legged creatures. They were of various hues – yellow, black, reddish-brown – and ranged in size from the length of a thumb to the breadth of a handspan. Their carapaces glistened dully in the light from the Tilley lamp, as did, more brightly, the several pairs of pinhead-sized eyes perched atop the front of their bodies. Each of them wielded a pair of pincers and a long, segmented tail that bore a bulbous, wickedly pointed tip.

They were scorpions, and like felons newly escaped from gaol they scattered in all directions across the floor, exploring the bounds of the chamber and drawn inexorably, so it seemed, towards the two human occupants.

CHAPTER THIRTY-FIVE

ORION'S NEMESIS, IN DROVES

A wave of horripilation swept over my body as the scorpions rushed out of their place of confinement. Although several of them made straight for Holmes and me, there did not seem any malicious intent in the action. Perhaps our scent attracted them, or the heat of our bodies. I do not know. I am no entomologist. All the same, for a few terrible, stunned seconds the only thing I could do was stare, dumbfounded, almost giddy with revulsion and fear, as the creatures approached.

"Watson!"

Holmes's barked cry brought me back to my senses. He had placed the first piece of the Ostomachion in the frame and was retrieving another. Immediately after a second piece was in his hand, a second trapdoor sprung open, affording the ingress of a further dozen scorpions into the room.

"Our bargain?" he prompted.

"Y-yes," I stammered. "Yes, of course."

A scorpion so big that one might have mistaken it for a langoustine was scuttling directly towards my friend's feet. I raised my foot and stamped hard on the wretched beast. The crunch of its destruction beneath my boot-heel was loud, wet and sickening but also supremely satisfying. A smaller scorpion hurried over to the mess of chitinous fragments and oozing flesh and began picking at it, shovelling morsels with its pincers into its mouth. I stamped on that one too, more because its carrion cannibalism disgusted me than because it posed a threat to Holmes.

I spotted a third scorpion stalking towards my companion with its pincers aloft and agape, like a soldier marching onto the battlefield with weapons at the ready. It was matte black, dark as ebony, save for the teardrop-shaped bulb at the end of its tail, which was orange. I brought my foot down on it, but it was crafty, this one, and managed to dodge my assault. In retaliation it charged straight at me, tail arched, moving almost more quickly than the eye could follow. It seemed undaunted by the fact that I was an opponent a hundred times larger. It must have fancied itself a David, fearless in the face of Goliath.

Yet Goliath, in contravention of the Biblical tale, was the victor in this bout. I kicked the scorpion so that it flew against the wall, and while it was busy righting itself, I pulverised it under my sole.

Holmes by now had four tiles in place in the frame and was gathering a fifth. To do so he first had to swat aside a couple of scorpions that had taken up residence on the very tile he needed. One of the creatures managed to grab hold of his shirt-cuff and clung grimly on as he picked up the tile. Only by dint of vigorous arm-shaking was he able to dislodge it.

I went about the chamber, squashing scorpions underfoot as methodically as possible. Try as I might, though, my actions were anything but precise and cool-headed. I wanted those diminutive monsters dead, every last one. I could feel how my lip was curled in revulsion. I could hear myself growling curses in the back of my throat.

Yet the scorpions' numbers were growing faster than I was able to exterminate them. With each newly opened trapdoor fresh reinforcements appeared, adding to the scurrying, rustling horde about us. The corpses of the ones I killed did at least provide a distraction to some of the new arrivals, who stopped to snack on them, while a few of the living entered into combat with one another, motivated by rivalry or enmity or I cannot say what; but the vast majority seemed interested in Holmes and me above all else and had no qualms about besieging us.

I heard Holmes give vent to a loud expletive, and saw that he had been stung on the hand while collecting the latest tile.

"Holmes, I should take a look at that."

"No time, no time. I can continue."

"Some people react badly to scorpion stings." I had had experience of this in Afghanistan, when my friend Colonel Hayter disturbed a scorpion that had crawled into his bedroll. Stung on the wrist, his forearm swelled up with severe anaphylaxis, and for a while amputation looked to be on the cards, in order that the inflammation might be prevented from spreading further and closing his windpipe or imperilling his cardiovascular system. Under my care, however, he made a full recovery and to this day Hayter credits me with saving his life, while I ascribe his survival to his stout constitution.

"Then let us hope I am not one of them," Holmes said, applying himself to his task once more.

The frame was almost filled with tiles. The chamber, likewise, was almost filled with scorpions. The floor was bedecked with the sticky, ichorous residue of those I had massacred. Not only the soles but the uppers of my boots were encrusted with pieces of arthropod.

I spied several of the creatures clambering up Holmes's trouser-legs. He was aware of their presence but refused to be put off by it. Briskly, efficiently, he slotted the final few tiles into position. Together, they formed an ensemble thus:

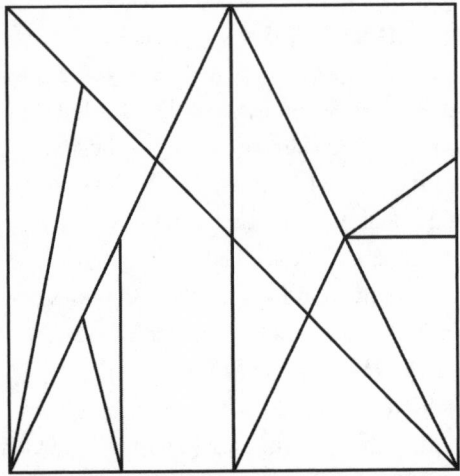

As Holmes had anticipated, the combined mass of the fourteen tiles pressed the frame downward. A latch clicked. The door opened. Holmes lunged out into the corridor beyond, I hard on his heels. The door then rolled shut, causing the deaths of three more scorpions in the process as they, making a bid for freedom, were swept sideways by it and crushed against its jamb.

In gingerly fashion Holmes detached the scorpions still adhering to his person. He ground them to paste underfoot, all save one, which he held up by the tail for close examination. One of the more modest-sized specimens, its carapace as yellow as pus, the scorpion writhed this way and that in his grasp, legs and pincers flailing.

"I count the scorpion amongst the Creator's most perfect handiworks," he said, evincing fascination. "A predator that can withstand both the searing heat of the desert day and the freezing cold of the desert night and that has no objective save to kill, eat and reproduce. The palaeontological record shows that it has survived on Earth since the Silurian era. It lives without fear, acts without hesitation…"

"And should be obliterated without mercy," I added.

"Give me a moment at least to admire it as the Platonic ideal of pure, conscienceless purpose. Biologists say that the scorpion's venom liquefies the internal organs of its victims, making them easier for it to ingest and digest. Essentially it is a stomach on legs."

"Really, Holmes. That is enough. Get rid of it and be done."

With a show of regret – mostly but not wholly feigned – my companion dropped the scorpion to the floor and despatched it.

Then he said, "Stay very still, Watson."

I knew better than to disobey the command. Holmes's face had gone abruptly rigid, his voice icy.

"Where is it?" I said. "Where is the damned thing?"

"There," he said, pointing. "Making for your ear."

Swivelling my eyes as far to one side as they would go, while not turning my head, I glimpsed a rust-coloured scorpion perched upon my shoulder, mere inches from my face. It was close enough that I could distinguish the fine bristles that sprouted all over it, and its eyes in their paired rows. I could also make out its mouth parts, an agglomeration of glistening, interlocking mandibles. These splayed and clenched with what looked to me like sheer greed, the lip-smacking relish of a glutton about to tuck into a gourmet meal.

"Oh God," I murmured. "Get it off me, Holmes. Get it *off*."

With painstaking slowness Holmes reached for the beast. The scorpion, meanwhile, began to probe my cheek with its pincers. I then felt its legs touch my jaw, my sideburns, my earlobe…

Nothing can compare with the horror of feeling those insectile feet prickling my skin. Even as I write these words, eight years on, the sensation recurs, vividly. It is as though that same scorpion is seated upon my shoulder at this very moment. I am squirming inside, now, just as I was squirming inside, then.

Holmes pounced, brushing the scorpion off me with a swift sideways swipe of his hand. No sooner did it hit the floor than he crushed it. Even with its abdomen a pulpy ruin, its legs continued to writhe for nearly a full minute until, with one last spasmodic twitch, they fell still.

It took my pulse rate some time to return to normal. Nausea roiled in my belly.

"I think," I said, "that my phobias about dogs and snakes have been surpassed by a new one. If I never see another scorpion again, it will be too soon."

"A sentiment I am sure the demigod Orion would have shared in his dying moments," said Dr Pentecost, "as the venom of the giant scorpion sent by Artemis to slay him coursed through his veins and stopped his heart. Gentlemen, once again you have acquitted yourself impressively. Pray carry on through the labyrinth. The fourth test awaits."

CHAPTER THIRTY-SIX

MOTIONLESS

"Gracious me, Holmes," I said as we arrived at the door to the next chamber. "That hand of yours…"

The base of his thumb was twice the size it ought to be, and the distension was of an angry red hue.

"Pay it no heed, Watson. I am paying it none myself."

"Let me know should you experience any of these symptoms: dizziness, shortness of breath, blurred vision."

"Do not mollycoddle me. The pain is disagreeable, I cannot deny, but no worse than a severe bee sting. If I do not die from this, then if nothing else I will know that I need not alter my plans to pursue apiary in my retirement."

It was a feeble quip, we both knew it, yet I chortled as though it were the funniest thing I had heard in a long time. In many ways it was.

"Enter now," said Dr Pentecost. "You will find this test the most challenging of all and, by the same token, the least."

"Dr Pentecost," I said hotly, "when we get out of this, you will pay for what you have put us through. You will pay for the abuses you inflicted upon Hannah. You will pay, above all, for whatever you did to ensure that Sophia Tompkins did not escape the labyrinth alive."

"Brave talk, Doctor, but you should really concentrate on escaping it yourself. Anything else is otiose."

The chamber was cylindrical, like a large, squat barrel. Positioned around its circumference at regular intervals were what appeared to be alcoves. The exit door stood ahead, opposite. Holmes and I trod forward, tense and wary, braced for the inevitable hazard to present itself. The very absence of an obvious trap led me to think that it was only a matter of time before we sprang one. What would be the menace this time? A ravenous tiger perhaps? Jets of flame? Some form of poison gas?

In the event, as we gained the centre of the chamber, the floor gave an abrupt lurch beneath us. The unexpected movement caught us off-guard, causing us to stagger.

Then, from all around, came sounds of ratcheting and whirring. As one, the alcoves became apertures. The backs of them opened like curtains parting, and from the holes thus revealed, crossbows emerged. The weapons thrust outward on armatures, the mechanism that caused this also drawing their strings at the same time by means of a complex system of cams and pulleys.

Suddenly Holmes and I were surrounded by a bristling array of steel-tipped crossbow bolts, all trained straight at us and primed to fly.

"Stay perfectly still," Holmes warned.

"You do not have to tell me twice," I replied, although my every instinct, my every nerve-ending, was screaming at me to run and take cover.

"The floor is unstable now. Can you feel it? It teeters as though poised atop a fulcrum. Whatever was securing it in place has been detached, and now one can only imagine that the least imbalance, the tiniest deviation of the floor from horizontal, will prompt all the crossbows to unleash their bolts. Not all of them will find their mark, but only one need do so to finish one of us off."

"How do we beat this?"

"I am thinking."

We stood still as statues for minute after long minute. When I shifted my weight even fractionally, the entire floor trembled underfoot. A bead of sweat trickled from my hairline, down my brow. I longed to wipe it away but dared not raise a hand. The droplet rolled into my eye, stinging. I was scared to blink, lest so minuscule an action had disproportionately huge consequences. Breathing itself took on momentous significance. Was I inhaling and exhaling too hard? Was my ribcage rising and falling too expansively?

Soon I had begun to feel lightheaded with the effort of remaining motionless. The Tilley lamp was growing heavy in my grasp. I did not know how much longer I could continue. My muscles seemed eager to disobey my wishes, to act of their own accord.

Then Holmes said, "I see."

"What do you see?"

"This test is, as Dr Pentecost told us, both the most challenging of them all and the least."

"I have no idea what that means, other than that it is a paradox. How can the test be both?"

"Precisely, Watson. That is the key to the puzzle. You have cracked it."

"I have?"

"Well, no. Not as such. But you have hit upon the operative word: paradox. One has to remember that everything Buchanan has presented us with so far in the labyrinth has an Hellenic theme. At first I could not for the life of me see how Hellenism applied here. Then I recalled the Greek philosopher Zeno of Elea. He it was who devised various thought experiments to challenge the human perception of time, motion and change. They are set out in Aristotle's *Physics*, and I studied them briefly while at university in the hope that they might help sharpen my powers of logical analysis. I gave it up quickly, once I realised the thought experiments were designed merely to provoke debate rather than yield solutions through deduction. They were of no use to me."

"And what is the pertinence of this Zeno fellow to our current situation?"

"You may be unfamiliar with his name but you will surely have heard of at least one of his famous paradoxes. The best known is that of Achilles and the tortoise. The two are in a foot race, and Achilles sportingly gives the tortoise a hundred-yard head start. Who wins?"

"Achilles, obviously. A man is faster than any tortoise."

"Wrong. Achilles never catches up with his competitor. By the time he has run the one hundred yards to the tortoise's starting point, the tortoise has itself gone, let us say, ten yards. By the time Achilles has covered those ten, the tortoise has travelled a further one yard. And so on *ad infinitum*. Achilles can never overtake the tortoise."

"That does not stand to reason."

"And yet, paradoxically, it is true," said Holmes. "Hence my dislike of mental exercises of that ilk. The only answers they provide are equivocal. Whereas I, by every inclination, prefer to deal in empirical absolutes."

"All of this is very interesting, Holmes, but…"

"There is another paradox of Zeno's," said my companion. "It involves an arrow and is sometimes known as the fletcher's paradox. Zeno claims that for motion to occur, an object must change position."

"That goes without saying."

"However, Zeno argues that an arrow in flight, at any given

instant, is static. It is moving neither to where it is nor to where it is not. Since time is composed of instants, it may be asserted that for the duration of its flight – which, however brief, is nonetheless a series of instants – the arrow is perpetually motionless."

"Holmes, I am woozy and on the verge of toppling over. Your filling my brain with mind-boggling conundrums is only making my head spin even more. Come to the point, please."

"My inference is that this trap is nothing but a glorious bluff. The floor gives the illusion that it is a trigger for the crossbows – and why would we not assume as much, given the nature of the traps we have hitherto encountered? But in actuality, we have nothing to fear. We may cross the rest of the way to the exit with impunity."

"You are sure of this?"

"Were I not, would I say so?"

He smiled, as aware as I was that the statement was no less of a paradox than anything Zeno might have dreamed up.

"Very well then," said I, masking my uncertainty.

Holmes set off with a determined stride.

Immediately, from the walls around us, there came the massed *twang* of a score of taut crossbow strings being released.

CHAPTER THIRTY-SEVEN

A LABYRINTH OF DEATH

I threw myself headlong at Holmes, bringing both of us crashing to the floor. I arranged it so that I was on top, my body covering his. I did not think about this consciously. It was a deep-seated impulse, that was all. The world needed Sherlock Holmes more than it needed another general practitioner. I envisaged myself quilled with the bolts, like a porcupine. I wondered whether death would be instantaneous or a slow, agonising process, consciousness ebbing as the blood leaked out of me.

"Watson?"

"Yes, Holmes?"

"Would you be so good as to clamber off? There's a good fellow. Your bulk is uncomfortable and I am finding it hard to breathe."

I slithered off Holmes, onto all fours. The floor no longer teetered, having become as solid and stable as when we had entered.

I peered around. The Tilley lamp, which I had dropped in my eagerness to be Holmes's human shield, had by some miracle landed upright and continued to burn. Its light revealed all the crossbow bolts still in place in their flight grooves but now at the front of those channels rather than the rear. The strings likewise had returned to their resting position, slack between the crossbows' limbs.

Holmes picked himself up and went to inspect one of the weapons. "The bolts are fixed to tracks embedded in the grooves. They are not free agents. The crossbows, in short, are like some conjuror's stage paraphernalia, rigged to appear dangerous when they are in fact harmless. Here is Zeno's paradox made flesh: an arrow that flies but does not fly."

"A cruel jest all the same," I said, "to have the crossbows seem to fire when they do not."

"The labyrinth is a test of mettle as much as of brain," Dr Pentecost chimed in. "Sir Philip believes intellect is nothing if not based on a foundation of courage."

"Damn you, you madman!" I exclaimed, shaking my fist in the direction of the periscope mirror. "Every time I hear your smug voice, my wish to throttle the life out of you grows ever stronger."

"Temper, temper, Dr Watson. That is not a very Hippocratic sentiment, is it?"

"Do not forget that I have performed military service as well as medical. The instincts of the one may well yield to the instincts of the other."

"Inveigh all you like. Your words cannot hurt me."

The truth of that was inescapable. I was, for the time being, impotent. I could threaten and fulminate, but it altered nothing.

Holmes echoed these thoughts of mine. "Save your energies, Watson, for the task at hand. We shall have plenty of opportunity afterward to deal with Dr Pentecost. Just one last test stands between us and him. Once we have successfully completed it, you may inflict such retribution upon him as you feel he deserves. I would suggest that, when the moment comes, what you will find is a man begging for mercy, and you will no longer deem him worthy of vengeance, only of contempt."

"Mr Holmes, you wound me," said the classicist, mock-affronted. "Let me assure you that, in the event you pass the final hurdle, I shall concede defeat gracefully, with dignity."

"I will believe it when I see it, Doctor."

As Holmes and I progressed through the labyrinth to the next chamber, I said to him, *sotto voce*, "Dr Pentecost is exhibiting a remarkable confidence, do you not think? Here we are, four tests under our belts, one more to go. Given such a track record, the odds are strongly in our favour that we shall survive the fifth. Yet he remains imperturbable, phlegmatic. It is almost as if—"

"As if he does not expect us to come through the ordeal alive?" said Holmes in similarly low tones. "As if our deaths have been foreordained from the outset?"

"Well, yes."

"I agree."

"You agree?"

"Dr Pentecost would never have sent us into the labyrinth in the first place if he were not sure, beyond doubt, that it would be the end of us."

"You have known that all along? Then how come you have said nothing? How come you have meekly subjected yourself, and me, to test after test, as though we were just like any pair of Elysians undergoing graduation?"

"An element of pride came into it. As I said earlier, my wits versus Sir Philip's. But also, what alternative was there? Our antagonist has Hannah as his insurance policy, for one thing. More to the point, while we are in the labyrinth we are alive, and while we are alive there exists the possibility of a favourable outcome, however remote. Not to go through the labyrinth to the bitter end would be not to court that possibility. It would be an abrogation of all hope."

"But if Dr Pentecost is hell-bent on killing us and has a guaranteed means…"

"Death shall not claim us tonight, Watson. Not if I have any say in the matter."

The fifth and final chamber loomed. This one had the customary sliding door, but beyond that lay a second door, altogether smaller and sturdier. Rivets studded its edge and also its frame, while a locking wheel occupied its centre. It put me in mind of a bulkhead door on an ironclad ship, one capable of being closed so firmly that it formed a watertight seal.

The locking wheel turned, seemingly of its own accord, and the door swung inward to reveal an oblong space that had the approximate proportions of a train compartment, albeit half as tall again. Walls, ceiling and floor, as we discovered upon ducking through the doorway and stepping inside, were composed entirely of steel plates, the joins between them solidly welded.

Above us there were a half-dozen circular holes some three inches in diameter, arranged in two rows of three. Below, inset into the centre of the floor, was some kind of vent, covered with a mesh grille. Another such vent was situated at the top of the far wall, where it met the ceiling. Each was the size of a chessboard.

Also on the ceiling was a locking wheel identical to that on the door, yet unattached to any door of its own. The short shaft ascending from its hub simply disappeared up into the ceiling.

There was no speaking-tube outlet in this chamber. Dr Pentecost's voice emanated from the small vestibule outside.

"Gentlemen," he said, "you have penetrated to the labyrinth's heart, and come to its most rigorous and definitive test. It is called the Wrath of Poseidon. You will shortly learn why. I have to congratulate you on the adroitness with which you have got yourselves this far. Sir Philip, were he here, would no doubt dearly be wishing he could claim you as his own. You would, if you had submitted to the Elysian regime beforehand, be perfect exemplars of his ideals. However…"

"Somehow I knew there would be a 'however,'" I murmured.

"You are not Elysians. You are, on the contrary, a threat to this entire enterprise. More to the point you are a threat to me. To that end, you cannot be allowed to live. Consequently, not without regret, but not without relief either, I consign you to this final trap. You will find it 'final' in every respect."

No sooner had he said this than the door began to close. I leapt for it, clamping my hands around its edge in order to arrest its progress. It was being operated by a powerful screw-driven torsion spring, however, the strength of which exceeded mine. The door swung inexorably towards its frame, and try as I might, digging my heels in and heaving backwards, I could not retard it. In the end, with the door a mere inch from shutting, I had to admit defeat and let go. It was that or have my fingers crushed flat.

"Dash it all!" I swore, as a series of clanks from the other side of the door suggested it was being fastened tight. I could see no opening mechanism on this side of it, nor even any handle. We were sealed within that chamber as securely as though within a bank vault.

I looked round at Holmes. "What now? Dr Pentecost seems to think he has doomed us. Tell me he has not."

My companion's face was pinched and, I thought, apprehensive.

"Come along," I cajoled. "All is not lost, surely."

"Unless I miss my guess, Watson," Holmes said, "it was in this very chamber that Sophia Tompkins met her end."

His words chilled me to my core.

CHAPTER THIRTY-EIGHT

THE WRATH OF POSEIDON

I felt a sudden shortness of breath. The chamber all at once seemed smaller than I had first reckoned. It was not the size of a train compartment; more the size of a larder. No, still smaller than that. The very walls of it were shrinking, closing in on us. I thought of the engineer Victor Hatherley and the hydraulic press in which he had nearly been squashed to death. Was this chamber something similar? Were Holmes and I to be flattened to a pulp?

"Watson, get a grip on yourself," Holmes said. "I can see you panicking. This is no time for losing one's head."

I gathered my wits. The chamber's proportions remained as they had been before. It was not, after all, shrinking. That had been my mind playing tricks, making my worst imaginings seem real.

"My apologies, Holmes," I said. "A touch of claustrophobia."

"Understood and forgiven. But we do not have the luxury of giving in to fear. At any moment the chamber is going reveal why it is named the Wrath of Poseidon, and we must do all we can beforehand to prepare for that. Firstly, you observe the hook up on the wall there?"

"I had not noticed it until now."

"If it is not to suspend the Tilley lamp from, then I cannot see what other purpose it might serve. We should use it."

"But the hook is too high to reach."

"Make a step of your hands."

Having passed Holmes the lamp, I interlaced my fingers. He hoisted himself up on me and, at full stretch, was able to hang the lamp from the hook by its wire handle.

"There," he said. "Now we have both hands free. Next, we must consider the locking wheel overhead. It is the matching counterpart of that on the outside of the door. Therefore one can only conclude that it fulfils the same function."

"A secondary opening mechanism. But again, it is too high to reach."

"*Ephedrismos*, my dear Watson."

"Excuse me?"

"The game we saw Hannah playing with the other girl, Polly Speedwell, at the gymnasium, whereby the one perched upon the other's shoulders."

"Ah. Yes."

"In our case you, with your stout rugby player's physique, are best suited to be the carrier. I – being the lighter of us and, at the risk of sounding immodest, possessed of a greater gripping strength – should be the carried."

"Say no more." I bent down, ready to have Holmes straddle me.

Then came a rattling, rumbling sound above our heads, and a deep churning gurgle, and all of a sudden water began pouring from the six holes in the ceiling. It sluiced down fast as though from a fire-engine hose and spattered hard onto the floor. Within seconds our boots and trouser-legs were soaked.

"That is it," Holmes said, as though the deluging water confirmed his suspicions. "Poseidon, god of the oceans. Drowner of men. That is how Dr Pentecost did it. He knew of Sophia Tompkins's crippling dread of water. He knew how she believed she was destined to die by drowning, as her parents had. He knew she could not swim. He could have forewarned her about this trap, giving her a chance to decline to take part in graduation, but he chose not to. He could also have forewarned Buchanan, who might then have re-thought his decision to select Miss Tompkins and excused her from entering the labyrinth. Instead Dr Pentecost deliberately, by omission, left her to face a test that he knew full well would reduce her to a gibbering, terrified wreck. He must have realised the odds were overwhelmingly against her surviving it."

"She would have had a partner with her at the time," I said. "Elysians always face the labyrinth in pairs. Did that other person survive, or drown too?"

"That other person was, I believe, Tobias Nithercott, the Chelsea solicitor who subsequently shot himself. The timing suggests it, for his 'sabbatical' came to an end, as did his life, not long after his and Sophia's graduation."

"He saved himself but not Sophia."

"And could not live with the guilt. But that is something we can establish with more certitude at a later date. I believe that our own survival is a far more pressing concern."

The water was already up to our ankles. It was shockingly cold – as cold as ice.

"Now brace yourself," my friend said. "Hup!"

I stood erect, with Holmes hoisted upon my shoulders. I parted my legs somewhat to alleviate the strain and be better balanced. Holmes grasped the rim of the wheel, which lay just within arm's length. I felt his thighs tighten around my neck as he hauled upon the wheel.

"Well?" I said.

"It is stiff. Very stiff." He grunted as he spoke, still grappling with the wheel. "I cannot seem to budge it at all."

"Keep trying."

"Sound advice. Whatever would I do without you?"

The water was about my shins and continuing to cascade from above without let-up.

"It is imperative," Holmes said, still giving it his all with the wheel, "that the door be opened before the water level gets too high. Once the water reaches the door, it will begin to exert pressure against it and the door will resist opening, the more so the higher the water rises. By the time the door is submerged completely, it will be impossible to open. Although…"

"Although…?"

"I am beginning to suspect that this locking wheel is not going to turn at all. It has been disabled."

"By Dr Pentecost?"

"Who else? He controls the locking wheel on the outside of the door. Logically, he must control this one too. It has been fastened so that no human force can move it. Let me down, would you?"

I crouched down and Holmes climbed off. His face was twisted with chagrin.

"Dr Pentecost has seen to it that we cannot solve the trap as anyone else might," said he. "He has deprived us of all possibility of escape."

"Dear Lord!"

"Or so he believes." Holmes scanned the chamber from end to end. The water level, meanwhile, crept remorselessly upward, heading now for our hips. The iciness of it was both painful and numbing. I had lost almost all sensation below the knees, and the upper portions of my legs were going the same way.

"Below us," Holmes said, "lies a drain. It is blocked now, stoppered like the plug-hole in a bath. Only Dr Pentecost can unblock it, presumably by pulling a lever that opens a sluice. There is, however, that second drain near the ceiling. It must act as an overflow, and as a safety precaution. Thanks to it, the chamber can never be entirely filled. There will always remain a gap at the top, a few inches of air, so that even if one fails the test one may nonetheless stay afloat, treading water, with one's face above the surface, for such time as is necessary. Sir Philip, in short, has built in a margin for error. Let us say that the two Elysians in the chamber have not managed to open the door. After a predetermined period has elapsed, the decision is made to activate the drain. The water starts to run out. The Elysians need only keep swimming until their feet touch the floor again. Then they need only wait until the water has emptied out altogether and the door is opened for them remotely. That is what happens in the normal course of events. Sir Philip has no wish for anyone to die in here, not if it can be prevented."

"Although Sophia did."

"Hence the crisis of conscience Sir Philip exhibited during his conversation with Fairbrother. Her death preyed heavily upon his conscience, albeit less so upon Fairbrother's."

"It preyed, too, upon the conscience of Tobias Nithercott."

"Quite. One assumes Nithercott was in the invidious position either of treading water and watching helplessly as Sophia drowned, or doing his best to save her but failing."

"That was the secret he took to his grave. Sophia's death."

Holmes nodded. "Dr Pentecost, of course, has no intention of obliging us by draining the chamber. The water will continue to come in, and we will be left to swim for as long as we are able to until exhaustion gets the better of us."

"Hypothermia will play its part as well," I said. My teeth had started to chatter. Holmes and I were now immersed up to the navel. "Well before our limbs tire, the sheer frigidity of this water will render us enfeebled and drowsy. I would estimate we have ten minutes at most before we pass out."

"Then we must not stand idle but use the time profitably. There is a reason why the water is so cold, and why the supply of it seems inexhaustible."

"And that is…?"

"It can only be drawn from the underground aquifer, the existence of which Hannah informed us about. These pipes overhead are fed directly from that source. Would you not say, then, that both drains must likewise feed back into it?"

"I do not know, Holmes. They might."

"They could, by that reckoning, provide us with an impromptu way out. Or at any rate, the overflow could, since unlike its counterpart in the floor it will not have the facility to be blocked."

He waded over to the drain in question and peered up at it.

"The mesh grille is held in place by eight screws. I do not have a screwdriver on me, and neither do you, so removing them the conventional way is not an option."

"Please, Holmes," I said. "Can we hurry this up?" I could feel the chill of the water increasing its insidious hold. I was shivering and my breathing had become rapid. Holmes was not immune to its effects either. He was shivering too, and his complexion had taken on a greyish pallor that I knew was reflected in mine.

"Even with a pocket-knife," Holmes continued, "which I do have, turning the screws will not be easy. Certainly I could not undo them all in the time available, and anyway my dexterity will be compromised because at some point I will be swimming as well as unscrewing, in addition to my swollen thumb. There is, however, the alternative of brute force."

"You mean tug the grille off? Kick it out?"

"I have something more impressive, more explosive, in mind. Would I be right in thinking that you have a box of cartridges on your person? A rhetorical question. No need to answer. I noticed the bulk of it earlier, making your jacket pocket bulge. The shape is distinctive. It could not be anything else."

"By Jove, yes, I do." I retrieved the Eley's box and held it out to Holmes. The cardboard was sodden but still maintained integrity, for now.

"These, in conjunction with the Tilley lamp, may well do the trick."

I recalled how Hannah and I, while in the antechamber to the labyrinth, had come up with an escape plan involving the lamp and the cartridges, although we had not been given the opportunity to put it into action.

"What are you proposing?" I asked. "If it entails decanting the gunpowder from the cartridges, then I should have you know it is no easy procedure."

"Who said anything about decanting the gunpowder? We have neither the time nor the means, even if plain gunpowder were capable of generating the potency of explosion we require to dislodge the grille. No, what I wish to do is altogether more basic." Holmes outlined his idea. "There is only one drawback that I can see," he concluded.

"What is it?"

"It is as apt to kill us as save us."

CHAPTER THIRTY-NINE

A POTENTIALLY LETHAL LIFELINE

The chamber would kill us, come what may.

What Holmes was proposing was potentially lethal, but it still offered a lifeline. Given that caveat, we both agreed that the risk was acceptable. Better a slim, hazardous chance of survival than none at all.

The deluging water had reached our necks, and we allowed natural buoyancy to take effect. Floating, arms and legs pumping, we trod water. In order to put Holmes's idea into practice we would have to wait until the Tilley lamp was readily accessible to us. Holmes estimated that would be in a little over two minutes, if the rate at which the chamber was filling remained consistent. Our main concern in the interim was keeping the cartridges as dry as possible, to which end Holmes was supporting the box out of the water with one hand. If the gunpowder became saturated, it would not fire and all would be for naught.

"Now, Watson," Holmes said. "Fetch down the lamp."

I swam over and unhooked it.

"Keep it aloft, at all costs," he urged, "and avoid the gouts of water. The flame must not go out. We have no way of reigniting it."

Executing an ungainly, one-armed doggy-paddle I made it to the other end of the chamber with the lamp. I bent the top of the wire handle over, creating a makeshift hook, which I fed into the mesh of the grille. Thus the lamp hung directly in front of the overflow.

Holmes uncapped the lamp and opened the lid of the Eley's box.

"When I pour the cartridges in," he said, "the heat from the burner will cause them to detonate. There is no telling how quickly it will occur. Our only recourse is to be as far away as possible when it does, as the bullets will fire wildly in all directions."

I was already making for the door end of the chamber as Holmes tipped several cartridges into the globe of the lamp. He hastened across to join me even as the ammunition's damp casings sizzled in the lamp's flame.

"What lies beyond the overflow?" I asked. The words came out slurred and clumsy. I was finding it hard to move my lips.

"Salvation," said Holmes. "Or a cold, miserable demise," he added grimly. "It all depends."

"On…?"

Before he could reply, one of the cartridges detonated with an ear-splitting *crack*. The bullet whined as it ricocheted around the chamber.

Holmes yelled, "Under, Watson!"

We both dived below the water.

At the same instant all the other cartridges went off. The crackle of their reports, though muffled by the water, was loud.

The lamplight went out.

Holmes tapped me on the back and we re-surfaced. All was darkness and pouring water.

We swam towards the overflow, groping along the chamber wall to maintain direction.

Holmes, by touch alone, found the grille.

"A hole," he said. "The bullets have caused damage, enough that I have something to grip on. Now all I have to do is pull."

I heard him gasping with effort. There was a metallic grating sound, a shrill wrenching. I pictured the sheet of wire mesh being pried loose from its mounting, Holmes hauling with all his might, leaning back with feet braced against the wall.

At last there was a dramatic, conclusive screech.

"That's it. That's it! The grille has come free. Now, Watson, I shall go in first. I can just about fit through the gap, as can you. Stay right behind me."

I was starting to feel disorientated, numb in mind as well as body. Hypothermia was well and truly setting in. My movements were becoming uncoordinated, my thoughts sluggish, even as my breathing rate increased to the point where I was in danger of hyperventilating. I could not tell if Holmes had entered the overflow aperture yet. All I knew was the pitch-blackness around me and the cataracts of water plummeting relentlessly from the pipes. Together these formed an unending, nightmarish continuum, an infinity of roaring void. I was blind and deafened at once. Would it not be a blessed relief simply to sink beneath the water and succumb to its gelid embrace? The overflow did not promise anything, certainly not release, whereas death did.

In the midst of these despairing thoughts, all at once I beheld an image of Hannah. It was as though she were summoning me, a lighthouse in a storm. I knew I must not give up.

I seized the sides of the overflow and pulled myself in. Next thing I knew, I was sliding head-first down a narrow chute. Then I had plunged underwater and was being whisked along at speed through some kind of subterranean channel.

CHAPTER FORTY

COMING BACK TO LIFE

I was tumbled, twirled, tossed about and thrown around. I lost all sense of which way was up, which down. Time after time I collided with something hard – it felt like rock – and rebounded. Water was all around me, and spun me mercilessly in all directions, like a cat toying with a mouse. I could see nothing; I could hear nothing save a thunderous liquid burble in my ears. I was human flotsam, a twig caught in a raging current, being dragged helplessly along.

I needed air. I had had no opportunity to fill my lungs before entering the torrent. The breathing reflex was building within me and I could feel spasms at the back of my throat, urgent precursors to inhalation. The whole of my chest cavity seemed afire. I knew that a breaking point would come soon.

All at once a clawing hand seized me by the collar. I was yanked upward. My head emerged from the water and I sucked in air with desperate gratitude.

Sherlock Holmes's voice came down from above.

"I cannot hold you for long, old friend. The current is pulling you from my grasp. You must climb out of the water."

"I – I don't seem to…" I stammered, "d-don't s-seem to have mastery of… m-my limbs."

"Hush now. Just climb out. I know you can do it."

His sureness instilled me with confidence. I reached up with hands that I could scarcely feel, like two chunks of marble on the ends of my arms. My fingers slithered across cold, wet rock. I groped until I found a couple of projections that could serve as handholds. With Holmes assisting by hauling upon my collar, I pulled myself clear of the torrent.

"Use your legs," Holmes advised. "We are in a narrow vertical shaft. Wedge yourself athwart, as I have. There we go. Not so hard, eh?"

"I just… need a moment… to catch my breath."

"I would suggest that you do not. Holding this position takes effort. Our best tactic is to keep moving, utilising what strength remains to us while we still have it. Upward is the way to go."

I could not see a thing. Utter blackness engulfed us. However, I was aware of Holmes above me, exerting himself. He was shuffling up the shaft, his soles scraping on the rock.

I did the same. Keeping my back braced against one side of the shaft, I used my feet and hands to propel me upward, like some sort of bizarre tortoise. It was a slow, painstaking process, a series of vertical shunts each of which gained me just a few inches of ground. The industry it required did at least get my circulation going again and generate some warmth in my body to stave off the lingering effects of the hypothermia. Indeed, it wasn't long before I started sweating.

"How much further?" I asked Holmes.

"Not much," came the reply.

"Good. I am not sure I can keep this up for long."

My muscles had begun trembling. Then my foot slipped, and for one dreadful moment I thought I was going to slide back down the shaft all the way to the aquifer. If I re-entered that flood of water I would be swept away, and this time there was precious little likelihood of rescue.

I managed to maintain my grip, and as I pushed myself upward another few inches, my head bumped against Holmes's leg.

"You have stopped."

"We are at the top. I am presently working on… Ah yes. One last manipulation. That should do it."

There was a sudden loud *creak* above me, and I perceived a lozenge of faint light that widened until it was a square.

A doorway!

Holmes eased himself into it, and I followed. To complete that climb and squirm through the doorway drained the last dregs of my stamina. I flopped onto the floor on the other side in a panting, rubbery-limbed heap.

"I take it you know where we are," said Holmes. The dimmest of illumination limned his features. He was a paler shadow amongst shadows. Around us I glimpsed walls adorned with painted images, barely definable.

My mind was too disordered to formulate a response, and Holmes answered his own question.

"Tartarus, of course."

"Of course," I said, thinking he was joking. "Myself, I was rather hoping I would end up in the other place, but clearly I did not lead a virtuous enough life."

"No, Watson," Holmes said pedantically. "Charfrome's Tartarus. I calculated that this was where the aquifer would lead to. Recalling the existence of the shaft that Hannah uncovered, I reckoned we could avail ourselves of it to escape the water. As the aquifer bore me along, I endeavoured to keep one hand in contact with the roof of the tunnel at all times. Thus when a gap appeared I knew I had reached the foot of the shaft, and I seized hold of one edge of it and arrested my progress. I sprang up out, lodged myself in the shaft and dangled an arm back into the water like a trawlerman's line so that I might catch you coming past."

"What if you had missed the shaft's opening? What if you had failed to grab me?"

"Then one or both of us would have been consigned to a watery grave. The aquifer would have carried us further on into the depths of the earth, where our drowned corpses would remain forever interred with no headstone to mark their location and no funeral service to commemorate our passing. We would, however, provide Sophia Tompkins with company for all eternity. There is that."

"How so?"

"Her mortal remains were dumped down the shaft. Don't you see? This is where Sir Philip disposed of her and would do likewise for any other Elysian who died in his labyrinth. Tartarus is a burial ground."

"My God. Hence Sophia's necklace being found not far from the entrance to the grotto."

"Indeed. It must have fallen off her neck as the body was being brought to this place. The person or people carrying her didn't notice."

"Given that the installation of the door pre-dates her death by almost a year…"

"Then it stands to reason that she was not the first to perish during graduation," said Holmes with a nod. "That, in turn, confirms the impression we received from the conversation between Sir Philip and Fairbrother. Sir Philip must have had prior experience of the rigours of the labyrinth proving fatal."

"Simms and Kinsella."

"Indeed, and in expectation of that contingency arising again, he chose to add the secret door to Tartarus and sink the shaft down to the aquifer. A handy method for getting rid of the evidence without trace."

"The man is a scoundrel," I declared. "Tossing the dead away as though they were so much household detritus."

"A scoundrel he may be, but at heart a pragmatic man. He had a problem and he devised what to him seemed an expedient solution. Now, my friend, are you sufficiently recovered from your ordeal that you feel capable of walking? For the night is not yet over and neither are our labours. Principally, we must wrest Hannah from Malachi Hart's clutches."

Those last words of Holmes's were as effective on me as any tonic. I launched myself to my feet.

"I'll have at the blackguard," I growled. "You see if I don't."

Holmes guided us out of Tartarus and along the tunnel towards the mouth of the grotto. We had the merest glimmer of light to navigate by – the glow of the outside world seeping in. It resolved itself into the silvery gleam of pre-dawn as we emerged from the grotto's entrance. Here was the copse, and the statues of Hades and Cerberus, and a spectral ground-mist coiling through the undergrowth, and the first tentative chirrups of waking birds as night receded. The earth was coming back to life, and I felt much as though I was too.

CHAPTER FORTY-ONE

AN UNEXPECTED SAVIOUR

Across the dewy grass we went, at a fair lick. I had thought our destination would be the main body of the house, but in the event we skirted it and made for the servants' wing.

"Why are we going this way?" I asked Holmes. "To find a back entrance?"

"No," came the reply. "We must locate Dr Pentecost before we do anything else."

"Dr Pentecost? But I thought you said we must rescue Hannah."

"Subduing Dr Pentecost is our priority. He has no idea that we are alive and at large. He is under the impression that we are breathing our last in the Wrath of Poseidon chamber, if not fully expired by now. He will be waiting, biding his time until he is sure we must be dead before he drains the chamber, opens the door and checks for our corpses via the periscope situated just outside. The fact that we are no longer in the labyrinth is our main advantage. It gives us the element of surprise."

"Then your mention of Hannah's name back in Tartarus was

merely a ruse," I said, "a goad to get me up and going."

My friend shot me a crooked grin. "It worked, did it not?"

I scowled at him in return.

"Think about it this way, Watson. We do not know where precisely Hannah is. Hart could be holding her anywhere on the premises. It is a big house and we are a search party of but two. In the time it takes us to find her, Dr Pentecost could well discover that we have cheated death and raise the alarm. On the other hand, if we grab Dr Pentecost first, then to coax him into surrendering up her whereabouts should not be difficult. I imagine you would be happy to do the coaxing yourself, would you not?"

"It might be fun," I allowed, mentally picturing myself brandishing a fist in front of the classicist's alarmed and frantic face. "But then, we do not know exactly where Dr Pentecost is either."

"I believe I do."

"Where?"

"Consider that the knot garden overlies the labyrinth."

"It does."

"And that Dr Pentecost is ensconced in some kind of hub from which he can oversee and govern all that occurs within the labyrinth. There has, therefore, to be a control room of some nature. It cannot lie in the house itself, since it must be in close enough proximity to the labyrinth that the periscopes and speaking tubes may function."

"The octagonal building," I said. "The one that lies in the centre of the knot garden. Is that what you are referring to?"

"If it is not the control room itself, it must afford access to one."

We rounded the far end of the servants' wing, whereupon the knot garden itself and the small building in question came into view. No sooner had we taken a few steps in that direction, however, than a cry from within the house reached our ears. I recognised the voice instantly. It was Hannah's.

Without hesitation I deviated towards the source of the cry.

The next instant, an external door in the servants' wing was flung open and Hannah came rushing out. She threw her arms around me, seeming to care little about my sodden, dishevelled state.

"Oh, Dr Watson!" she exclaimed. "I despaired of ever seeing you again. I could hardly believe it when I caught sight of you and Mr Holmes rushing by outside. Hence my rather indecorous shriek."

I, overcome with relief and joy, was incapable of speech. That was until I spied a hulking figure sidling from the house in Hannah's wake.

It was Quigg.

I cast Hannah to one side, somewhat more roughly than I might have liked, and squared up to the bald, cauliflower-eared Hoplite.

"Halt right there, sir!" I said, closing on him. "You shall not have her back, unless it is over my dead body."

"Dr Watson, no," Hannah said, but I scarcely heard her. My blood was up. So were my fists.

I aimed a punch at Quigg. He, surprisingly light on his feet for one so large, ducked out of the way. I put up my guard, for fear of retaliation, but none came.

Puzzled, but not one to look a gift horse in the mouth, certainly not during a fight, I pivoted round and swung at him again. Quigg swatted my fist aside with a meaty forearm like W.G. Grace flicking the ball past the slips. The ease with which he deflected my blow is, in hindsight, not a little embarrassing.

It was then that I recalled that Quigg was a former prizefighter, and I felt a queasy sensation in the pit of my stomach. I had bitten off more than I could chew. Quigg was humouring me. He could lay me out flat whenever he wished, with those fists of his and the walnut-like calluses on their knuckles.

Nevertheless, I gamely drew back my fist for a third punch.

A hand caught hold of my wrist. Hannah, gripping my arm, interpolated herself between me and the Hoplite.

"Stop it," she said. "You have got the wrong end of the stick. Mr Quigg means me no harm."

"But he was chasing you."

"No, Dr Watson, he was not. It may have looked that way, but nothing can be further from the truth. He was merely accompanying me. Mr Quigg is on our side. I might even go so far as to call him my saviour."

I eyed the Hoplite, who nodded as if to confirm the veracity of Hannah's statement.

"Were it not for him," Hannah continued, "I would still be Malachi Hart's captive. Whereas now, instead, I am free and Hart is the captive."

"Tied him up good and proper, I did, with a length of window sash cord," Quigg said. "Sailor's knots to secure it. Same ones as I used on you and Mr Holmes a month back. He won't get out of 'em. That's assuming he comes round any time soon to try."

"Well, that is good to know," said Holmes briskly, "but, delightful though this reunion is, time is wasting. We must get on."

"Hannah is safe, Holmes," I said. "The urgency of apprehending Dr Pentecost is somewhat diminished."

"True, but we must also consider the fact that, standing out here like this, one of the other Hoplites might remark upon us and be moved to intervene."

"I am sure, in that event, Mr Quigg will be able to deal with it," said Hannah.

Holmes looked exasperated but could see that we were not to be deterred. "Very well. From this position, we do at least have a clear view of our quarry's lair." He pointed in the direction of the octagonal building. "Should he emerge, we shall see him."

"Dr Pentecost is still down in the panopticon?" said Quigg.

"If that is the name for the labyrinth's control room, then yes. If he is elsewhere, I should be very surprised. Let us keep watch on that door and be prepared to move with all haste."

Addressing Quigg, I said, "So you are Hannah's saviour, eh?" I did not know whether to be pleased or envious. "Then why have you been acting so aggressively towards her?"

"Oh, that is not what he has been doing at all, Watson," said Holmes. "Is it, Able Seaman Quigg? On the contrary, you have been watching out for her. You have been repeatedly expressing concern for her, although she has misconstrued your intentions. I see it now. Where you meant to caution her against enquiring into Sophia Tompkins's disappearance, she took you to be trying to intimidate her."

"Yes," said Hannah. "Mr Quigg has just explained as much to me, and I deeply regret my past behaviour towards him."

"I was only trying to help," said Quigg. "I had to be subtle about it, but I wanted Miss Holbrook to realise that she was playing a dangerous game."

"I have told you, Mr Quigg. It is 'Miss Woolfson.'"

"Oh yes. Pardon me, miss." He turned back to Holmes. "It is simply that Miss Woolfson's behaviour had aroused my concern. If she wasn't careful, I thought, she might wind up the same way as Miss Tompkins. I couldn't come right out and say so. In this place you never can tell who might be listening, and I had my position to think about. I only hoped that, by acting a bit menacing, muttering vague but dire warnings, I might get her to take the hint and leave. It would have been better for her if she had."

"You even followed her to Waterton Parva one day, did you not?" said Holmes. "She told us about sensing the presence of an unseen pursuer. It was you."

"I was curious to know what she was up to. I could not follow her all the way to the village; she would have spotted me then for sure. Already, in the woods, she seemed wary, forever casting looks over her shoulder. Out on the road I would have had almost no cover. I knew, at least, that she was going to Waterton Parva and that she did not stay there long. My hunch was that she was reporting to someone."

"You are not far off the mark."

"I thought this ill-advised of her. Just as I thought her consorting with Edwin Fairbrother" – Quigg winced with distaste as he spoke the name – "was also ill-advised. He is a malign influence, that lad. Rotten to the core. I have no proof, but I am sure he talked Sir Philip into setting Miss Tompkins up for graduation, something she was hardly fit for."

"He did," said Holmes. "Out of pique more than anything. He did not mean for her to perish the way she did. He simply wished to teach her a lesson."

"That was my reading of it too. And who was to say he might not arrange something similar for the young lady here, were she to cross him?" Quigg nodded at Hannah. "The more I have seen of this place, the less comfortable I have become with its practices. What happened to Miss Tompkins took me to the tipping point. She was the third."

"The third to die during graduation."

"Yes, in that weird labyrinth of Sir Philip's. Hart and I lugged her body across the grounds under cover of darkness into the cave over yonder – the one outside which we ambushed you and Dr Watson that night. Sir Philip had a kind of shaft built in the cave last year. We tipped the body down that hole into an underground river like it was a bag of old laundry. The two previous ones…"

"Simms and Kinsella," said Holmes.

"Yes, I believe those were their names. Them we simply buried in the grounds, far from the house. Sir Philip must have been keen not to repeat that practice, for a grave, however well dug, may always be discovered. Hence the shaft. I shudder to recall how the two fellows looked as we shovelled earth over them. Their lips purple, tongues protruding, their faces so white..."

"It sounds as though they asphyxiated," I said.

"Medusa got them, both at once, in the labyrinth's second chamber," said Quigg. "By all accounts they got into a right pickle. Couldn't fathom the solution to the puzzle, and when the darts started flying they panicked. Both ended up riddled."

"Such a high dose of curare would have brought on respiratory paralysis. Their lungs would have stopped working within a couple of minutes."

"Sir Philip saw what was happening and disengaged the workings of the chamber, but it was too late. When Hart and I went in to retrieve them, they were stone cold dead." There was a distinct tremor in Quigg's voice, all the more notable coming from so large and loutish-looking a man. "Sir Philip was all casual-like about it, at least after we had put them six feet under. They were both quiet types, no friends or family to speak of. He said he doubted anyone would come looking for them."

"And no one did."

"No one did. He was the same with the girl, Miss Tompkins. An orphan, with hardly a friend in the world – she would not be missed. The impression I got was that, to him, people perishing in the labyrinth was something that could not be avoided, just bumps on the road to success. Hart did not have any difficulty with it either, but then he is made of flint. I, on the other hand, did. I still do. I'm no angel, and Lord knows I have done some bad things in the past, but even I have my limits. If those three deaths are not murder, they are as near as, and I, heaven preserve me, have helped cover them up."

The man looked genuinely contrite, his face contorted with guilt.

Holmes laid a hand upon Quigg's shoulder. "You have redeemed yourself, sir. You have made amends."

"I have tried, sir. When Miss Woolfson supposedly fell ill, that was when I truly began to worry for her. It was so sudden, and Dr Pentecost claimed he was looking after her and it was a touch of brain-fever, but I had my doubts. She never struck me as the sort. Then, tonight, Sergeant-Major Hart was absent from patrol, without explanation. My instinct was that Dr Pentecost and he were up to something. I went to investigate, but had all but given up hope of finding her when I heard a commotion on an upper floor. I found Miss Woolfson struggling with Hart in an attic room."

"He was keeping me prisoner there," said Hannah. "I had just broken free from him and was attempting to run, but he caught me again."

"She was battling him gamely but there could be only one outcome. Hart was in a fury and his hand was bleeding."

"I had bitten him as he attempted to muffle my cries for help."

"And he had raised the other and was about to strike her."

I gasped.

"That was it, for me," said Quigg. "The final straw. I manhandled Miss Woolfson a few days earlier, but the intent behind it had been noble. Hart's was anything but. I demanded that he let her go. Told him it was a disgrace. He responded that it was none of my business. But I made it my business. Hart is no weakling, and for a time it was touch-and-go which of us would win out. My experience told, though. I had him on the ropes and was about to finish him off, when…"

"When I intervened," said Hannah.

"A lovely hit, it was. She had picked up a chamber pot, of all things."

"Hart had brought it to the room for my convenience. And convenient it proved to be."

"Nice, heavy piece of solid porcelain, it was. Miss Woolfson approached Hart from behind while he was busy with me. *Wham!* – to the back of his noggin. Knocked him cold."

If I hadn't already been besotted with Hannah, I would have adored her right then.

"Much though I'd have liked to put him on the deck myself," Quigg said, "I could not begrudge her that. Hart deserved what he got. And here we all are." He spread out his arms. "Miss Woolfson has told me everything, her real name, what she has been doing here. Not to mention why you two came and how Pentecost sent you into the labyrinth. We were coming to help when we spied you from a window."

I extended a hand. "Mr Quigg, it would seem I owe you an apology, and a debt of gratitude."

His grip, as his hand enfolded mine, was painfully crushing, and I could tell he was exercising only a small fraction of his full strength.

"If the apology is for attacking me, Dr Watson, then none is necessary. I did not feel I was in any danger."

I bridled at that, and felt somewhat less magnanimous towards him than before.

Turning to my friend, Quigg said, "Mr Holmes, I am aware that I have done criminal acts. I am prepared to face the consequences. I can only beg that you will vouch in court that I have done what I can to atone."

"I will go one better," said Holmes. "Help us apprehend Dr Pentecost, and I will argue strenuously for clemency for you from the authorities, and even exoneration, if possible."

"You are a true gent," said Quigg. "I am your servant."

As Holmes and Quigg moved off towards the knot garden and the octagonal building, I turned to Hannah.

"Are you going to insist I stay behind, Dr Watson," said she, correctly interpreting my expression, "while the men do manly things?"

"I was," I replied. "But seeing the look on your face, not any more."

"Good."

She trotted off after the other two, and I, with a bemused shake of the head, took the rear.

CHAPTER FORTY-TWO

THE ULTIMATE SACRIFICE

The labyrinth's control room – the so-called panopticon – reminded me somewhat of the cab of a locomotive. There were levers, dials, pipes, gauges and valve handles, all of brass or steel. These fringed the walls in a fantastic, prolific array, along with horn-shaped mouthpieces for the speaking-tube system and bulbous lenses that magnified the images relayed by the periscope mirrors.

To reach the room, we entered the octagonal building via its low door, which gave onto a spiral staircase. As we descended the stairs single file, with Holmes leading the way, my friend commented that Dr Pentecost in all likelihood still had my revolver.

"We must therefore proceed with caution," said he. "He may not be adroit with the use of guns, nor any kind of marksman, but a bullet is a bullet and has the same effect on its target whether fired clumsily or with skill."

Some ten feet underground, there was Dr Archibald Pentecost. He had heard our footfalls on the stairs and knew we were coming, but where could he go? There was only one way in or out. He was cornered like a fox run to earth. His demeanour was crestfallen and wistful.

"Mr Holmes. Dr Watson. Ah, Quigg. And Miss Woolfson. Your presence, my dear, tells its own story. Malachi has been bested. I trust he has not come to permanent harm?"

"That would depend," said Hannah, "on the thickness of his skull."

"The game is well and truly up. *Eheu*, as the Greeks might say. Alas."

"Very much so, Doctor," said Holmes, "and in that spirit I would advise you to come quietly. Do not do anything rash. Watson's revolver is in your pocket. The outline of it is plain. You should either leave it there or hand it over."

"Or perhaps I shall do neither."

Dr Pentecost's hand flashed to his pocket. Holmes darted towards him, swift as a striking snake, but not quite swiftly enough. Out came the gun.

"You will forgive me if I do not wish to make it easy for you," Dr Pentecost said, thumbing back the hammer.

Holmes froze on the spot, as did the rest of us.

"Since last we met, Sergeant-Major Hart has given me some instruction on the use of this weapon," the classicist continued. "I am now more adept than I was. Besides, at such close quarters, one does not have to be a terribly good shot."

It was true. In the confined space of the panopticon, the classicist could hit any of us and barely need to take aim.

"You may be ruthless but you are no assassin, Dr Pentecost," said Holmes. "I have met a fair few of those in my time, and I know the type. You do not have it in you. I do not see it in your eyes."

"Try me," said Dr Pentecost. "I am a desperate man. Perhaps, *in extremis*, I will find it in me to go down fighting."

"Nonetheless, direct bloodshed is not your way. If it were, you would have had Hart kill the three of us – Watson, Hannah and me – when you had us at your mercy. That or you would have done the deed yourself. Since you could manage neither, one may reasonably infer that you lack the requisite barbarous streak."

"Hart refused to be a party to killing you, when I put the proposition to him. He said he would assist me in detaining you but would go no further."

"Your sway over him was insufficient to persuade him otherwise."

"He is compromised," said Dr Pentecost. "Compromised in the same way that Mr Quigg there is. Disposing of dead bodies. I am not sure if it is a capital offence, but it certainly must carry a stiff gaol sentence. One night last year, when he was in his cups, Hart admitted to me what he and Quigg had done the previous summer – carting two bodies into a distant corner of the estate and interring them there. Covering up Sir Philip's sins."

"You knew, if you ever needed Hart's assistance in any endeavour, that that was something you might use against him."

"I called in my marker last night. Hart was disgruntled, to be sure, and muttered that if he were to go down, he would take Sir Philip with him and all of Charfrome, but I could see this was a patent bluff. Hart knows when he is onto a good thing, and his job as a Hoplite is just that. He will do anything to protect it, and Sir Philip's integrity, as he has already amply demonstrated."

"Getting rid of Dr Watson and me, then, was something which he was content to leave to you."

"And which I, in turn, was content to leave to the labyrinth. The labyrinth would accomplish for me what I could not. All I had to do was disable the locking wheel in the ceiling of the final chamber. I had no doubt that you would get that far."

"It was to be murder, but at one remove," said Holmes. "Just as with Sophia Tompkins."

"All to keep your hands clean," Hannah chimed in. Her lip was curled in a bitter sneer.

Dr Pentecost nodded. "I was surprised, not that Sophia died, but that I was able to get away with it. If Greek tragedy teaches us anything, it is that fate always catches up with murderers. Violence begets violence, in an endless cycle. Yet days went by after Sophia's death, and nothing came of it."

"Not nothing," said Holmes. "Tobias Nithercott, her fellow graduate, could not live with himself for failing to save her. He, at least, had a conscience, and it led him to blame himself for her drowning and ultimately take his own life. That poor, innocent man's death is as much your responsibility as Sophia's."

"And our deaths too, nearly," I said, "for what that's worth."

"Yet here you are, alive and well," said Dr Pentecost, then snapped, "Oh no, Mr Holmes!" He levelled the revolver at my friend. "I saw you inching towards me. While you had me busy talking, you were hoping to pounce. I think not!"

Holmes smiled grimly. "I invite you once more, Doctor, to put the gun down. You are only making things worse for yourself. We outnumber you four to one. You will manage to get off a single shot at most. Whosoever your target may be, the rest of us will have no difficulty bringing you down and disarming you."

"Are any of you willing to die, simply to guarantee that I shall be apprehended and made to pay for my crimes? Are you, Mr Holmes?"

"I am," said Holmes resolutely, and I am quite certain he meant it. "I have nearly given my life several times so that justice may be served. Do not think that I am not prepared to make the ultimate sacrifice."

For a moment, just a moment, Dr Pentecost's defiance wavered.

I spied my chance. The classicist's attention was wholly on

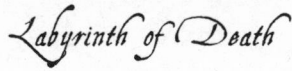

Holmes. He stood just a short leap away from me. If I moved fast, I could jerk his gun arm up to the ceiling, then lay him low with a swift right hook to the jaw.

I tensed, all set to leap.

Dr Pentecost must have caught sight of this from the corner of his eye. He swung towards me.

"Ah-ah, Doctor!" The revolver waved like a wagging finger. "Don't even think about it."

"You fool," I said. "The pistol is not even loaded. I can see it from here. There are no cartridges in the chambers."

"There are. As I said, Hart has taken it upon himself to teach me the basics of how to use the thing. You cannot bamboozle me like that, Doctor."

"It would seem that Hart has emptied the cylinder without your knowing," I said, "precisely so that you would not hurt yourself, or by accident him."

That got him. Briefly, ever so briefly, Dr Pentecost hesitated. His gaze flicked down to the Webley.

I sprang.

Perhaps I was a fraction too slow. Perhaps some reflex reaction caused his trigger finger to tighten.

The gun went off. The report was almost inconceivably loud in that cramped room.

I struck him bodily, in a rugby tackle, and together we crashed against one bank of levers. I imagined that I had been shot. I was practically on top of him when the gun fired. I felt no impact, but in the thick of the moment, when the fire is in his belly, a man is not wholly aware of everything that is happening.

It was only when a shrill scream came from behind me that I appreciated that someone other than me had been hurt.

Hannah.

I heaved myself off Dr Pentecost and whirled round. Hannah

was staggering backwards, one hand clutched to the front of her blouse. Blood was spilling out between her fingers.

I was by her side in a trice. She collapsed in my arms and I helped her to the floor. The bullet had entered her shoulder, just below the collarbone. The blood was coming fast and I feared the subclavian artery had been breached. I tore off my jacket, bundled it up and pressed it to the wound.

"Hannah," I said, "you are not going to die. I swear it. Just lie still and be calm. I will stop the bleeding. You are not going to die."

She, dear creature, looked up at me trustingly. I am sure she believed me. I only wished that I believed myself.

"Dr Watson…" she said.

There was a commotion elsewhere in the room. I glanced round to see Holmes grappling with Dr Pentecost. Another gunshot sounded. The round went wild, ricocheting harmlessly off a wall.

I caught only glimpses of the rest of the contest between Holmes and Dr Pentecost, for my attention was directed mainly upon Hannah. I believe – and Holmes has affirmed it – that it was less a struggle, more the unfolding of the inevitable. The gun lay between the two of them, a bone of contention. There was no way that the classicist could have overcome my friend. Physically he was outmatched, by some considerable degree.

That was when he canted the barrel of the pistol up towards his own chin.

Holmes, I daresay, could have wrested the gun off him. That he chose not to, and instead let events take their course, suggests to me that he knew as well as Dr Pentecost did what lay in the classicist's future. At the end of a long path stood, inexorably, the gallows. Holmes was simply allowing an abbreviation of the journey.

The gun went off a third and final time. I heard, but did not

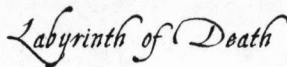

see, Dr Pentecost's brains spattering the wall and ceiling of the panopticon. Thereafter I devoted myself exclusively to Hannah, whom I would keep alive, whom I refused to lose, whom death would not steal today, not if I could prevent it.

CHAPTER FORTY-THREE

THE AFTERMATH

Events in the immediate aftermath of Hannah's shooting are muddled in my recollection. I have, with Holmes's help, been able to piece them together. I shall rehearse them as succinctly as I can, but readers should bear in mind that I was not a direct participant in them. My focus was only on Hannah.

Charfrome Old Place awoke that morning to a bustle of untoward activity that shortly escalated to become pandemonium. Sherlock Holmes despatched Quigg to Waterton Parva, whence he sent for the police in Dorchester. In the meantime Holmes himself went to confront Sir Philip Buchanan. He set out before the architect, who was still in pyjamas and dressing-gown, a list of his crimes: his culpability in the deaths of the Elysians called Simms and Kinsella, and of Sophia Tompkins and, by extension, Tobias Nithercott. Buchanan did not attempt to deny any of it. It was as though, Holmes told me, he was relieved to have it all out in the open at last. "I suppose," Buchanan said, "that I have been anticipating this moment for a while – ever since you first showed your face, in fact, Mr Holmes. It was inevitable, given your famed propensity for unearthing the truth. I can only say that what I have done, I have done for my country. For the benefit of all. I hope that that is enough."

You may remember, if you followed the trial, that Buchanan's defence rested largely upon that argument: he wanted to improve Great Britain and prolong the tenure of the Empire indefinitely, and some people may have died in the realisation of that dream, and he regretted it, but, if he had his time over again, he would do nothing differently. The families of Sophia Tompkins and Tobias Nithercott, of course, vehemently disagreed, as did those of Jerome Simms and Dennis Kinsella, something that the lawyers representing all four made quite plain both to the jury and to the journalists outside the Old Bailey.

Quigg gave evidence on the stand that helped secure Buchanan's conviction. It also earned the former sailor just a short spell in Pentonville, a matter of months. His willingness to comply with the law, and a signed affidavit from Holmes that attested to his usefulness in foiling Dr Pentecost's machinations, won him leniency from the judge.

Buchanan did not get the noose, as many expected and predicted. His death sentence was commuted on appeal to ten years' penal servitude, with the possibility of time off for good behaviour. Was Buchanan's knighthood a factor in that decision? Did his status as a pre-eminent member of the establishment incline the establishment to go easy on him? It is not for me to say. As for Sergeant-Major Hart, a mere commoner, his punishment was twenty years' hard labour without chance of parole.

Edwin Fairbrother, slippery to the last, managed to escape justice, at least the justice of the courtroom. He had fled from Charfrome while the household was in uproar. Some animal instinct had warned him that trouble was brewing and that he might bear some of the brunt of it, so he had raced off into the

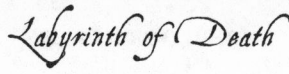

countryside with nothing but the clothes on his back. I do not know with any surety what has become of him since, but Holmes did draw to my notice a short article in the international column of *The Times* a year or so later. A young Englishman matching Fairbrother's description had been fatally stabbed in a fight at a bar in Buenos Aires. His name was unknown to the Argentine police, but the cause of the fracas was a young *señorita*, and the killer was her father, a local cattle rancher of high standing.

"If it was Fairbrother," Holmes opined, "then the circumstances of his death hardly give one pause. Ever the libertine, what he did not count on was the hot-blooded Latin temperament. Where in his homeland one may bring about a woman's downfall more or less with impunity, in South America one is apt to reap violent rewards."

Charfrome Old Place presently stands untenanted and is, so I am told, lapsing into ruin. Its Hellenic outbuildings are overgrown with weeds and ivy. Its labyrinth, that marvel of misapplied genius, gathers mildew and rust. A huge, elaborate monument to one man's folly, it moulders like the broken statue in Shelley's "Ozymandias".

And what of Hannah Woolfson?

For three days she languished in a Dorchester hospital, hovering close to death. Not once did I leave her bedside. Finally, after three days of vigil, my reward was to be there when Hannah opened her eyes. Mine was the first face she saw and the first she, albeit feebly, smiled at.

Dealing with her father was no easy task. Sir Osbert Woolfson took amiss – understandably – the fact that his daughter had been shot, which he learned about via telegram from Holmes. The day after the incident he came down to Dorchester in a paroxysm of bilious outrage, which the sight of Hannah lying pale and unconscious in bed did little to allay. He threatened me with a lawsuit; Holmes too. "If she dies, sir," he thundered, "I will see to it that you and your friend are held to account at the highest levels. You will never practise medicine again, and Sherlock Holmes will be run out of London on a rail. I swear this on my wife's grave." He left barely consoled by my reassurances that I would not rest until Hannah was whole and well and restored to him.

I am delighted to report that a week later Hannah was out of danger and within the month she was back home, safe under her father's roof, with a nurse to tend to her in her convalescence. I visited her a couple of times and was received by Woolfson with an animus that his daughter's imprecations on my behalf just barely kept in check. I will confess that I took the opportunity to make love during the moments Hannah and I spent alone in the drawing-room, but it soon dawned on me that the bond we two had so tentatively formed at Charfrome had been damaged, seemingly to the point of irreparability. My overtures were rebuffed with all sweetness and civility, in such a way that I was not made to feel foolish for making them.

"You saved my life, Dr Watson," Hannah said, "and for that I am eternally in your debt. As is my father, if only the silly old goat would bring himself to admit it. You have my gratitude and my respect. I will continue to enjoy your writings, of course, but..."

There was much packed into that last monosyllable, a freight of sorrow and apology. It was a conjunction that was also a separator.

"I have had an experience of your and Mr Holmes's world first-hand," she resumed after a pause, "and it is a place of misery, death and pain. I do not envy you it. I admire that you stick with it, day after day. I find, though, that I would rather read about it than participate in it, and I fear that were you and I to become affianced, participating is indeed what I would end up doing. Not only that but I would live in constant dread that a man dear to me was facing foes who would not hesitate to do him harm. Am I a terrible coward for not wanting that? Do you hate me for it?"

"Hate you?" I said, aghast. "My dear Hannah, I could never hate you for anything. Your decision is courageous and I can do naught but honour it."

"You are not going to try to make me change my mind?"

"Do you wish me to?"

For a moment it seemed as though she might say yes. Then, with sadness, she shook her head. "I have my fight to fight," said she. "The fight for women. You have yours. The fight for justice. I shall watch you from afar, cheering you on. May I hope that you might do the same for me?"

"On that, Hannah," I said, my voice thickening somewhat, "you have my solemn vow."

AFTERWORD

As promised in the Foreword, this chronicle is not just an account of a case investigated and solved by Mr Sherlock Holmes. It brings into relief an aspect of my own life.

Even now, reflecting across a span of some eight years to the events I have been describing, I think of Hannah Woolfson with nothing but fondness and a tinge of regret. One cannot change what has been, but one is entitled to wish it had developed otherwise.

I have had a wife, Mary. For the few years that we were married, she was my companion and helpmeet and the most supportive and decorous spouse a man could hope for. I will never cease to mourn her.

I had hoped, briefly and in the event vainly, that Hannah might take her place by my side. It was not to be. I draw some cold consolation from the fact that the lady remains to this day unwed. She uses her time profitably to carry on prosecuting her causes, campaigning for the emancipation of women and their right to vote. She has even helped Emmeline Pankhurst with the setting up of the Women's Social and Political Union. No doubt this makes her father grind his teeth with frustration, and if so, long may it continue.

There may yet be, for me, the prospect of another wife on the horizon, a second Mrs Watson. Until then, I shall cherish the memory of Hannah and keep it dear in my heart. She embodies a lost ideal, a missed opportunity, and the surrender of personal happiness to duty. In that regard, as Irene Adler is to Sherlock Holmes, Hannah Woolfson will always be, to me, the woman.

J.H.W.

ABOUT THE AUTHOR

James Lovegrove is the *New York Times* best-selling author of *The Age of Odin,* the third novel in his critically acclaimed *Pantheon* military SF series. He was short-listed for the Arthur C. Clarke Award in 1998 for his novel *Days* and for the John W. Campbell Memorial Award in 2004 for his novel *Untied Kingdom.* He also reviews fiction for the *Financial Times.* He has written *Sherlock Holmes: The Stuff of Nightmares*, *Sherlock Holmes: Gods of War* and *Sherlock Holmes: The Thinking Engine* for Titan Books; his new series, *The Cthulhu Casebooks*, launched in 2016 with *Sherlock Holmes and the Shadwell Shadows.*

SHERLOCK HOLMES
THE STUFF OF NIGHTMARES
James Lovegrove

A spate of bombings has hit London, causing untold damage and loss of life. Meanwhile a strangely garbed figure has been spied haunting the rooftops and grimy back alleys of the capital. Sherlock Holmes believes this strange masked man may hold the key to the attacks. He moves with the extraordinary agility of a latter-day Spring-Heeled Jack. He possesses weaponry and armour of unprecedented sophistication. He is known only by the name Baron Cauchemar, and he appears to be a scourge of crime and villainy. But is he all that he seems? Holmes and his faithful companion Dr Watson are about to embark on one of their strangest and most exhilarating adventures yet.

"[A] tremendously accomplished thriller which leaves the reader in no doubt that they are in the hands of a confident and skilful craftsman." *Starburst*

"Dramatic, gripping, exciting and respectful to its source material, I thoroughly enjoyed every surprise and twist as the story unfolded." **Fantasy Book Review**

"This is delicious stuff, marrying the standard notions of Holmesiana with the kind of imagination we expect from Lovegrove." **Crimetime**

TITANBOOKS.COM